"How do I stop them from finding Noah?" Marin asked.

"I won't let anything happen to Noah, understand?"

She shook her head. "I can't lose him."

"I know." And because he truly understood her concern and fear, Lucky reached out and slid his arm around her.

Marin stiffened, but she didn't push him away. Then she looked up at him, and he felt the hard punch of attraction. A punch he'd been trying to ward off since the first time he'd watched Marin and considered her simply part of his case. But she was more than that now.

Lucky couldn't lose focus. A knock at the door interrupted anything stupid he was about to say. Or do. Like kiss her blind just to prove the attraction that was way too obvious.

HIS 7-DAY FIANCÉE

He shouldn't touch her.

He was pushing the limits, testing his already strained self-control. For hours he'd been watching her smile and talk, worry and frown. He'd memorised the provocative way her lips quirked and her forehead creased, how her hair shimmered over her back. And all night long he'd been holding her, inhaling her feminine scent as he played the part of her fiancé.

It had been four hours of exquisite torture.

And if he didn't get away from her now, he was going to break. "It's late. You'd better go inside."

"I know." Her voice came out breathless. She stayed rooted in place.

He shifted closer, drawn to the heat in her eyes, the lure of her lush, sultry lips. He stroked his hands up her arms, his blood pumping hard. Hunger built in his veins.

To hell with self-control.

All the characters in this book have no existence outside the imagination of the author, and have no relation whatsoever to anyone bearing the same name or names. They are not even distantly inspired by any individual known or unknown to the author, and all the incidents are pure invention.

First published in Great Britain 2010
Harlequin Mills & Boon Limited,
Eton House, 18-24 Paradise Road, Richmond, Surrey TW9 1SR

Security Blanket © Delores Fossen 2008
His 7-Day Fiancée © Harlequin Books S.A. 2009

Special thanks and acknowledgements are given to Gail Barrett for her contribution to the LOVE IN 60 SECONDS mini-series.

ISBN: 978 0 263 88190 5

46-0110

Harlequin Mills & Boon policy is to use papers that are natural, renewable and recyclable products and made from wood grown in sustainable forests. The logging and manufacturing processes conform to the legal environmental regulations of the country of origin.

Printed and bound in Spain
by Litografia Rosés S.A., Barcelona

SECURITY BLANKET
BY
DELORES FOSSEN

HIS 7-DAY FIANCÉE
BY
GAIL BARRETT

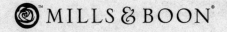

SECURITY BLANKET

BY
DELORES FOSSEN

Imagine a family tree that includes Texas cowboys, Choctaw and Cherokee Indians, a Louisiana pirate and a Scottish rebel who battled side by side with William Wallace. With ancestors like that, it's easy to understand why Texas author and former Air Force captain **Delores Fossen** feels as if she was genetically predisposed to writing romances. Along the way to fulfilling her DNA destiny, Delores married an Air Force Top Gun who just happens to be of Viking descent. With all those romantic bases covered, she doesn't have to look too far for inspiration.

To the Magnolia State Romance Writers.
Thanks for everything.

Chapter One

The man was watching her.

Marin Sheppard was sure of it.

He wasn't staring, exactly. In fact, he hadn't even looked at her, though he'd been seated directly across from her in the lounge car of the train for the past fifteen minutes. He seemed to focus his attention on the wintry Texas landscape that zipped past the window. But several times Marin had met his gaze in the reflection of the glass.

Yes, he was watching her.

That kicked up her heart rate a couple of notches. A too-familiar nauseating tightness started to knot Marin's stomach.

Was it starting all over again?

Was he watching her, hoping that she'd lead him to her brother, Dexter? Or was this yet another attempt by her parents to insinuate themselves into her life?

It'd been over eight months since the last time this happened. A former "business associate" of her brother who was riled that he'd paid for a "product" that Dexter hadn't delivered. The man had followed her around Fort Worth for days. He hadn't been subtle about it, either, and that had made him seem all the more menacing. And she hadn't given birth to Noah yet then.

The stakes were so much higher now.

Marin hugged her sleeping son closer to her chest. He smelled like baby shampoo and the rice cereal he'd had for lunch. She brushed a kiss on his forehead and rocked gently. Not so much for him—Noah was sound asleep and might stay that way for the remaining hour of the trip to San Antonio. No, the rocking, the kiss and the snug embrace were more for her benefit, to help steady her nerves.

And it worked.

"Cute kid," she heard someone say. The man across from her. Who else? There were no other travelers in this particular section of the lounge car.

Marin lifted her gaze. Met his again. But this time it wasn't through the buffer of the glass, and she clearly saw his eyes, a blend of silver and smoke, framed with indecently long, dark eyelashes.

She studied him a moment, trying to decide if she knew him. He was on the lanky side. Midnight-colored hair. High cheekbones. A classically chiseled male jaw.

The only thing that saved him from being a total pretty boy was the one-inch scar angled across his right eyebrow, thin but noticeable. Not a precise surgeon's cut, a jagged, angry mark left from an old injury. It conjured images of barroom brawls, tattooed bikers and bashed beer bottles. Not that Marin had firsthand knowledge of such things.

But she would bet that he did.

He wore jeans that fit as if they'd been tailor-made for him, a dark blue pullover shirt that hugged his chest and a black leather bomber jacket. And snakeskin boots—specifically diamondback rattlesnake. Pricey and conspicuous footwear.

No, she didn't know him. Marin was certain she would have remembered him—a realization that bothered her because he was hot, and she was sorry she'd noticed.

He tipped his head toward Noah. "I meant your baby," he clarified. "Cute kid."

"Thank you." She looked away from the man, hoping it was the end of their brief conversation.

It wasn't.

"He's what…seven, eight months old?"

"Eight," she provided.

"He reminds me a little of my nephew," the man continued. "It must be hard, traveling alone with a baby."

That brought Marin's attention racing across the car. What had provoked that remark? She searched his face and his eyes almost frantically, trying to figure out if it was some sort of veiled threat.

He held up his hands, and a nervous laugh sounded from deep within his chest. "Sorry. Didn't mean to alarm you. It's just I noticed you're wearing a medical alert bracelet."

Marin glanced down at her left wrist. The almond-shaped metal disc was peeking out from the cuff of her sleeve. With its classic caduceus symbol engraved in crimson, it was like his boots—impossible to miss.

"I'm epileptic," she said.

"Oh." Concern dripped from the word.

"Don't worry," she countered. "I keep my seizures under control with meds. I haven't had one in over five years."

She immediately wondered why in the name of heaven she'd volunteered that personal information. Her medical history wasn't any of his business; it was a sore spot she didn't want to discuss.

"Is your epilepsy the reason you took the train?" he asked. "I mean, instead of driving?"

Marin frowned at him. "I thought the train would make the trip easier for my son."

He nodded, apparently satisfied with her answer to his intrusive question. When his attention strayed back in the general direction of her bracelet, Marin followed his gaze. Down to her hand. All the way to her bare ring finger.

Even though her former fiancé, Randall Davidson, had asked her to marry him, he'd never given her an engagement ring. It'd been an empty, bare gesture. A thought that riled her even now. Randall's betrayal had cut her to the bone.

Shifting Noah into the crook of her arm, she reached down to collect her diaper bag. "I think I'll go for a little walk and stretch my legs."

And change seats, she silently added.

Judging from the passengers she'd seen get on and off, the train wasn't crowded, so moving into coach seating shouldn't be a problem. In fact, she should have done it sooner.

"I'm sorry," he said. "I made you uncomfortable with my questions."

His words stopped her because they were sincere. Or at least he sounded that way. Of course, she'd been wrong before. It would take another lifetime or two for her to trust her instincts.

And that was the reason she reached for the bag again.

"Stay, *please*," he insisted. "It'll be easier for me to move." He got up, headed for the exit and then stopped, turning back around to face her. "I was hitting on you."

Marin blinked. "You…what?"

"Hitting on you," he clarified.

Oh.

That took her a few moments to process.

"Really?" Marin asked, sounding far more surprised than she wanted.

He chuckled, something low, husky and male. Something that trickled through her like expensive warm whiskey. "Really." But then, the lightheartedness faded from his eyes, and his jaw muscles started to stir. "I shouldn't have done it. Sorry."

Again, he seemed sincere. So maybe he wasn't watching her after all. Well, not for surveillance any way. Maybe he was watching her because she was a woman. Odd, that she'd forgotten all about basic human attraction and lust.

"You don't have to leave," Marin let him know. Because she suddenly didn't know what to do with her fidgety hands, she ran her fingers through Noah's dark blond curls. "Besides, it won't be long before we're in San Antonio."

He nodded, and it had an air of thankfulness to it. "I'm Quinn Bacelli. Most people though just call me Lucky."

She almost gave him a fake name. Old habits. But it was the truth that came out of her mouth. "Marin Sheppard."

He smiled. It was no doubt a lethal weapon in his arsenal of ways to get women to fall at his feet. Or into his bed. It bothered Marin to realize that she wasn't immune to it.

Good grief. Hadn't her time with Randall taught her anything?

"Well, Marin Sheppard," he said, taking his seat again. "No more hitting on you. Promise."

Good. She mentally repeated that several times, and then wondered why she felt mildly disappointed.

Noah stirred, sucked at a nonexistent bottle and then gave a pouty whimper when he realized it wasn't there. His eyelids fluttered open, and he blinked, focused and looked up at Marin with accusing blue-green eyes that were identical to her own. He made another whimper, probably to let her know that he wasn't pleased about having his nap interrupted.

Her son shifted and wriggled until he was in a sitting position in her lap, and the new surroundings immediately caught his attention. What was left of his whimpering expression evaporated. He examined his puppy socks, the window, the floor, the ceiling and the ruby-red exit sign. Even her garnet heart necklace. Then, his attention landed on the man seated across from him.

Noah grinned at him.

The man grinned back. "Did you have a good nap, buddy?"

Noah babbled a cordial response, something the two males must have understood, because they shared another smile.

Marin looked at Quinn "Lucky" Bacelli. Then, at her son. Their smiles seemed to freeze in place.

There was no warning.

A deafening blast ripped through the car.

One moment Marin was sitting on the seat with her son cradled in her arms, and the next she was flying across the narrow space right at Lucky.

Everything moved fast. So fast. And yet it happened in slow motion, too. It seemed part of some nightmarish dream where everything was tearing apart at the seams.

Debris spewed through the air. The diaper bag, the magazine she'd been reading, the very walls themselves. All of it, along with Noah and her.

Something slammed into her back and the left side of her head. It knocked the breath from her. The pain was instant—searing—and it sliced right through her, blurring her vision.

She and Noah landed in Lucky's arms, propelled against him. But he softened the fall. He turned, immediately, pushing them down against the seat and crawling over them so he could shelter them with his body. Still, the debris pelted her legs and her head. She felt the sting of the cuts on her skin and reached out for something, anything, to use as protection. Her fingers found the diaper bag, and she used it to block the shards so they wouldn't hit Noah.

The train's brakes screamed. Metal scraped against metal. The crackle and scorched smell of sparks flying, shouts of terror, smoke and dust filled the air.

Amid all the chaos, she heard her baby cry.

Noah was terrified, and his shrill piercing wail was a plea for help.

Marin tried to move him so she could see his face, so she could make sure he was all right, but her peripheral vision blurred. It closed in, like thick fog, nearly blinding her.

"Help my son," she begged. She couldn't bear his cries. They echoed in her head. Like razor-sharp daggers. Cutting right through her.

Sweet heaven, was he hurt?

There was some movement, and she felt Lucky maneuver his hand between them. "He's okay, I think."

His qualifier nearly caused Marin to scream right along with her son. "Please, help him."

Because she had no choice, because the pain was unbearable, Marin dropped her head against the seat. The grayness got darker. Thicker. The pain just kept building. Throbbing. Consuming her.

And her son continued to cry.

That was the worst pain of all—her son crying.

Somehow she had to help him.

She tried to move again, to see his face, but her body no longer responded to what she was begging it to do. It was as if she were spiraling downward into a bottomless dark pit. Her breath was thin, her heartbeat barely a whisper in her ears. And her mouth was filled with the metallic taste of her own blood.

God, was she dying?

The thought broke her heart. She wasn't scared to die. But her death would leave her son vulnerable. Unprotected.

That couldn't happen.

"You can't let them take Noah," she heard herself whisper. She was desperate now, past desperate, and if necessary she would resort to begging.

"Who can't take him?" Lucky asked. He sounded so far away, but the warmth of his weight was still on her. She could feel his frantic breath gusting against her face.

"My parents." Marin wanted to explain that they were toxic people, that she didn't want them anywhere near her precious son. But there seemed so little breath left in her body, and she needed to tell him something far more important. "If I don't make it…"

"You will," he insisted.

Marin wasn't sure she believed that. "If I don't make it, get Noah out of here." She had to take a breath before she could continue. "Protect him." She coughed as she pulled the smoke and ash into her lungs. "Call Lizette Raines in Fort Worth. She'll know what to do."

Marin listened for a promise that he would do just that. And maybe Lucky Bacelli made that promise. Maybe he spoke to her, or maybe it was just her imagination when the softly murmured words filtered through the unbearable pain rifling in her head.

I swear, I'll protect him.

She wanted to see her son's face. She wanted to give him one last kiss.

But that didn't happen.

The grayness overtook her, and Marin felt her world fade to nothing.

Chapter Two

Working frantically, Lucky slung off the debris that was covering Marin Sheppard and her son.

No easy feat.

There was a lot of it, including some shards of glass and splintered metal, and he had to dig them out while trying to keep a firm grip on Noah. Not only was the baby screaming his head off, he wriggled and squirmed, obviously trying to get away from the nightmare.

Unfortunately, they were trapped right in the middle of it.

"You're okay, buddy," Lucky said to the baby. He hoped that was true.

Lucky quickly checked, but didn't see any obvious injuries. Heck, not even a scratch, which almost certainly qualified as a miracle.

As he'd seen Marin do, Lucky brushed a kiss on the boy's cheek to reassure him. Though it wasn't much help. Noah might have only been eight months old, but he no doubt knew something was horribly wrong.

This was no simple train derailment. An explosion.

An accident, maybe. Perhaps some faulty electrical component caused it. Or an act of terrorism.

The thought sickened him.

Whatever the cause, the explosion had caused a lot of damage. And a fire. Lucky could feel the flames and the heat eating their way toward them. There wasn't much time. A couple of minutes, maybe less.

And even then, getting out wasn't guaranteed.

They couldn't go through the window. There were jagged, thick chunks of glass still locked in place in the metal frame. It wouldn't be easy to kick out the remaining glass, and it'd cut them to shreds if he tried to go through it with Noah and Marin, especially since she was unconscious. Still, he might have to risk it. Lucky had no idea what he was going to face once he left the car and went into the hall toward the exit.

Maybe there was no exit left.

Maybe there was no other way out.

"Open your eyes, Marin," he said when he finally made it through the debris to her.

Oh, man.

There wasn't a drop of color in her face. And the blood. There was way too much of it, and it all seemed to be coming from a wound on the left side of her head. The blood had already seeped into her dark blond hair, staining one side of it crimson red.

"Look at me, Marin!" Lucky demanded.

She didn't respond.

Lucky shoved his fingers to her neck. It took him several snail-crawling moments to find her pulse. Weak but steady.

Thank God, she was alive.

For now.

But he didn't like the look of that gash on her head. Since she was breathing, there was no reason for him to do CPR, but he tried to revive her by gently tapping her face. It didn't work, and he knew he couldn't waste any more time.

Soon, very soon, the train would be engulfed in flames, and their chances of escape would be slim to none. They could be burned alive. He wasn't about to let that happen to her or the precious cargo in his arms. He'd made a promise to protect Noah, and that was a promise he intended to keep.

Moving Marin could make her injuries worse, but it was a risk he had to take. Placing Noah on her chest and stomach, he scooped them both up in his arms and hugged them tightly against him so that Noah wouldn't fall. Noah obviously wasn't pleased about that arrangement because he screamed even louder.

Lucky kicked aside a chunk of the displaced wall, and hurrying, he went through what was left of the doorway that divided the lounge car from the rest of the train. A blast of thick smoke shot right at him. He ducked his head down, held his breath and started running.

The hall through coach seating was an obstacle course. There was wreckage, smoke and at least a dozen other passengers also trying to escape. It was a stampede, and he was caught in the middle with Noah and Marin.

The crowd fought and shoved, all battering against

each other. All fighting to get toward the end of the car. And they finally made it. Lucky broke through the emergency exit and launched himself into the fresh air.

Landing hard and probably twisting his ankle in the process, he didn't stop. He knew all too well that there could be a secondary explosion, one even worse than the first, so he carried Noah and Marin to a clear patch about thirty yards from the train.

The November wind was bitter cold, but his lungs were burning from the exertion. So were the muscles in his arms and legs. He had to fight to hold on to his breath. The air held the sickening smell of things that were never meant to be burned.

He lay Marin and Noah down on the dried winter grass beside him, but Noah obviously intended to be with Lucky. He clamped his chubby little arms around Lucky's neck and held on, gripping him in a vise.

"You're okay," Lucky murmured. And because he didn't know what else to say, he repeated it.

To protect Noah from the wind and cold, Lucky tucked him inside his leather jacket and zipped it up as far as he could. Noah didn't protest. But he did look up at him, questioning him with tear-filled eyes. That look, those tears broke Lucky's heart. It was a look that would haunt him for the rest of his life.

"Your mom's going to be all right," Lucky whispered.

He prayed that was true.

Lucky pulled Marin closer so his body heat would keep her warm, and used his hand and shirt sleeve as a compress. He applied some gentle pressure against her injured head, hoping it would slow the bleeding. She didn't move when he touched her, not even a twitch.

He heard the first wail of ambulance sirens. Already close. Thankfully, they were just on the outskirts of Austin so the response time would be quick. The firefighters wouldn't be far behind. Lucky knew the drill. They'd set up a triage system, and the passengers with the most severe, but treatable injuries would be seen first. That meant Marin. She'd get the medical attention she needed.

"You're going to stay alive, Marin," Lucky ordered. "You hear me? Stay alive. The medics are on the way. Listen to the sirens. Listen! They're getting closer. They'll be here in just a few minutes."

Noah volleyed uncertain glances between Lucky and his mother. He stuck out his quivering bottom lip. For a moment Lucky thought the little boy might burst into tears again, but he didn't. Maybe the shock and adrenaline caught up with him, because even though his eyes watered, he stuck his thumb in his mouth and snuggled against Lucky.

It wasn't a sensation Lucky had counted on.

But it was a damn powerful one.

What was left of his breath vanished, and feelings went through him that he'd never experienced. Feelings he couldn't even identify except for the fact that they brought out every protective instinct in his body.

"What are your injuries?" Lucky heard someone shout. He looked up and saw a pair of medics racing toward him. They weren't alone. More were running toward some of the other passengers.

"We're not hurt. But she is," Lucky said pulling back his hand from Marin's injured head.

The younger of the two, a dark-haired woman, didn't take Lucky's word about not being injured. She began to examine Noah and him. Noah whined and tried to bat her hands away when she checked his pupils. The other medic, a fortysomething Hispanic man, went to work on Marin.

"She's Code Yellow," the medic barked to his partner. "Head trauma."

That started a flurry of activity, and the woman yelled for a stretcher.

Code Yellow. Marin's condition was urgent, but she was likely to survive.

"I need your name," the female medic insisted, forcing his attention back to her. "And the child's."

Lucky's stomach clenched.

It was a simple request. And it was standard operating procedure for triage processing. But Lucky knew it was only the beginning of lots of questions. If he answered some of those questions, especially the part about Noah being a near stranger, they'd take the little boy right out of his arms, and the authorities would hold on to him until they could contact the next of kin.

The very thing that Marin didn't want to happen.

Because her parents and her brother, Dexter, were Noah's next of kin.

Some choice.

As if he understood what was going on, Noah looked up at him with those big blue-green eyes. There were no questions. No doubts. Not even a whimper.

But there was trust. Complete, unconditional trust.

Noah's eyelids fluttered down, his thumb went back in his mouth, and he rested his cheek against Lucky's heart.

Oh, man.

It seemed like some symbolic gesture, but it probably had more to do with the kid's sheer exhaustion than anything else. Still, Lucky couldn't push it aside. Nor could he push aside what Marin had asked of him when they'd been trying to stay alive.

If I don't make it, get Noah out of here. Protect him.

And in that crazy life-or-death moment, Lucky had promised her that he would do just that.

It was a promise he'd keep.

"Sir," the medic prompted. "I need you to tell me the child's name."

It took Lucky a moment to say anything. "I'm Randall Davidson. This is my son, Noah," he lied. He tipped his head toward Marin. "And she's my fiancé, Marin Sheppard."

In order to protect the frightened little boy in his arms, Lucky figured he'd have to continue that particular lie for an hour or two until Marin regained consciousness or until he could call her friend in Fort Worth. Not long at all, considering his promise.

He owed Noah and Marin that much.

And he might owe them a hell of a lot more.

Chapter Three

Marin heard someone say her name.

It was a stranger's voice.

She wondered if it was real or all part of the relent-less nightmare she'd been having. A nightmare of explosions and trains. At least, she thought it might be a train. The only clear image that kept going through her mind was of a pair of snakeskin boots. Everything else was a chaotic blur of sounds and smells and pain. Mostly pain. There were times when it was unbearable.

"Marin?" she heard the strange voice say again.

It was a woman. She sounded real, and Marin thought she might have felt someone gently touch her cheek.

She tried to open her eyes and failed the first time, but then tried again. She was instantly sorry that she'd succeeded. The bright overhead lights stabbed right into her eyes and made her wince.

Marin groaned.

Just like that, with a soft click, the lights went away. "Better?" the woman asked.

Marin managed a nod that hurt, as well.

The dimmed lighting helped, but her head was still throbbing, and it seemed as if she had way too many nerves in that particular part of her body. The pain was also affecting her vision. Everything was out of focus.

"Where am I?" Marin asked.

Since her words had no sound, she repeated them. It took her four tries to come up with a simple audible three-word question. Quite an accomplishment though, considering her throat was as dry as west Texas dust.

"St. Mary's," the woman provided.

Marin stared at her, her gaze moving from the woman's pinned-up auburn hair to her perky cotton-candy-pink uniform. Her name tag said she was Betty Garcia, RN. That realization caused Marin to glance around the room.

"I'm in a hospital?" Marin licked her lips. They were dry and chapped.

"Yes. You don't remember being brought here?"

Marin opened her mouth to answer, only to realize that she didn't have an answer. Until a few seconds ago, she'd thought she was having a nightmare. She definitely didn't remember being admitted to a hospital.

"Are you real?" Marin asked, just to make sure she wasn't trapped in the dream.

The woman smiled. "I'm going to assume that's not some sort of philosophical question. Yes, I'm real. And so are you." She checked the machine next to the bed. "How do you feel?"

Marin made a quick assessment. "I feel like someone bashed me in the head."

The woman made a sound of agreement. "Not someone. *Something*. But you're better now. You don't remember the train accident?"

"The accident," Marin repeated, trying to sort through the images in her head.

"It's still under investigation," the nurse continued. She touched Marin's arm. "But the authorities think there was some kind of electrical malfunction that caused the explosion."

An explosion. She remembered that.

Didn't she?

"Thankfully, no one was killed," the woman went on. She picked up Marin's wrist and took her pulse. "But over a dozen people were hurt, including you."

It was the word *hurt* that made the memories all come flooding back. The call from her grandmother, telling Marin that she was sick and begging her to come home. The train trip from Fort Worth to San Antonio.

The explosion.

God, the explosion.

"Noah!" Marin shouted. "Where's my son?"

Marin jackknifed to a sitting position, and she would have launched herself out of the bed if Nurse Garcia and the blinding pain hadn't stopped her.

"Easy now," the nurse murmured. She released her grip on Marin's wrist and caught on to her shoulders instead, easing her down onto the mattress.

Marin cooperated, but only because she had no choice. "My son—"

"Is fine. He wasn't hurt. He didn't even get a scratch."

The relief was as overwhelming as the pain. Noah

was all right. The explosion that had catapulted them through the air had obviously hurt her enough that she needed to be hospitalized, but her son had escaped unharmed.

Marin considered that a moment.

How had he escaped?

A clear image of Lucky Bacelli came into her head.

The man she'd been certain was following her. He'd promised to get Noah out, and apparently he had.

"I want to see Noah," Marin insisted. "Could you bring him to me now?"

Nurse Garcia stared at her, and the calm serenity that had been in her coffee-colored eyes quickly faded to concern. "Your son's not here."

Marin was sure there was some concern in her own eyes, as well. "But—"

"Do you have any idea how long you've been in the hospital?" the nurse interrupted.

Marin opened her mouth, closed it and considered the question. She finally shook her head. "How long?"

"Nearly two days."

"Days?" Not hours. Marin was sure it'd only been a few hours. Or maybe she was simply hoping it had been. "So where is he? Who's had my baby all this time?" But the moment she asked, the fear shot through her. "Not my parents. Please don't tell me he's with them."

A very unnerving silence followed, and Nurse Garcia's forehead bunched up.

That did it.

Marin pushed aside the nurse's attempts to restrain

her and tried to get out of the bed. It wasn't easy, nowhere close, but she fought through the pain and wooziness and forced herself to stand up.

She didn't stay vertical long.

Marin's legs turned boneless, and she had no choice but to slouch back down on the bed.

"There isn't any reason for you to worry," the nurse assured her. "Your son is okay."

Marin gasped for breath so she could speak. "Yes, so you've said. But who has him?"

"Your fiancé, of course. His father."

What breath she'd managed to regain, Marin instantly lost. "His...father?"

Nurse Garcia nodded, smiling. The bunched up forehead was history.

Marin experienced no such calmness. Adrenaline and fear hit her like a heavyweight's punch.

Noah's father was dead. He was killed in a boating accident nearly eight months before Noah was even born. There was no way he could be here.

"Your fiancé should be arriving any minute," the nurse cheerfully added.

Nothing could have kept Marin in the bed. Ignoring the nurse's protest and the weak muscles in her legs, Marin got up and went in search of her clothes. But even if she had to leave the hospital in her gown, she intended to get out of there and see what was going on.

Nurse Garcia caught on to her arm. Her expression changed, softened. "Everything's okay. There's no need for you to panic."

Oh, yes, there was. Either Randall had returned from the grave or something was terribly wrong. Noah had no father, and she had no fiancé.

There was a knock at the door. One soft rap before it opened. The jeans, the black leather jacket. The boots.

Lucky Bacelli.

Not Randall.

"Where's Noah?" she demanded.

Lucky ignored her question and strolled closer. "You gave me quite a scare, you know that? I'm glad you're finally awake." And with that totally irrelevant observation, he smiled. A secretive little smile that only he and Mona Lisa could have pulled off.

"I want to see Noah," Marin snapped. "And I want to see him now."

Another smile caused a dimple to wink in his left cheek. He reached out, touched her right arm and rubbed softly. A gesture no doubt meant to soothe her. It didn't work. For one thing, it was too intimate. Boy, was it. For another, nothing would soothe her except for holding her son and making sure he was okay.

"The doctor wants to examine you before he allows any other visitors so Noah's waiting at the nurses' station," Lucky explained, his voice a slow, easy drawl. The sound and ease of Texas practically danced off the words. "And I'm sure they're spoiling him rotten."

Marin disregarded the last half of his comment. Her son was at the nurses' station. That's all she needed to know. She ducked around Lucky and headed toward the door. Marin had no idea where the nurses' station was, but she'd find it.

Lucky stepped in front of her, blocking her path. "Where are you going, darling?"

That stopped her in her tracks.

Darling?

He said it as if he had a right to.

That was well past being intimate. Then he slid his arm around her waist and leaned in close. Too close. It violated her personal space and then some. Marin slapped her palm on his chest to stop him from violating it further.

"Is there a problem?" Nurse Garcia asked.

"You bet there is," Marin informed her.

And she would have voiced exactly what that problem was if she'd had the chance.

She hadn't.

Because in that same moment, Lucky Bacelli curved his hand around her waist and gently pulled her closer to him. He put his mouth right against her ear. "This was the only way," he whispered.

Marin tried to move away, but he held on. "The only way for what?" she demanded.

"To keep you and Noah safe." He kept his voice low, practically a murmur.

Even with the pain and fog in her head and his barely audible voice, she understood what he meant. Lucky had needed to protect Noah from her parents, just as she'd asked him to do. He'd pretended to be Randall Davidson, a dead man. Marin couldn't remember how Lucky had known Randall's name. Had she mentioned it? She must have. Thankfully, her parents had never met Randall and knew almost nothing about him. They certainly didn't know he was dead. She'd kept that from them because if she'd explained his death, she would have also had to endure countless questions about their life together.

Marin stopped struggling to get away from him and wearily dropped her head on his shoulder. He'd lied, but he'd done it all for Noah's sake. "My parents tried to take him?"

Lucky nodded. "They tried and failed. But I'm pretty sure they'll be back soon for round two."

That wasn't a surprise. With her in a hospital bed, her parents had probably thought they could take over her life before she even regained consciousness. It'd been a miracle that Lucky had been able to stop them, and if he'd had to do that with lies, then it was a small price to pay for her to be able to keep her son from them.

"Thank you," Marin mouthed.

"Don't thank me." Lucky moved back enough to allow their gazes to connect. The gray in his eyes turned stormy. "I don't think that train accident was really an accident," he whispered.

Stunned, Marin shook her head. "What do you mean?"

It seemed as if he changed his mind a dozen times about what to say. "Marin, Noah and you were nearly killed because of me."

Chapter Four

Lucky braced himself for the worst. A slap to the face. A shouted accusation. But Marin just stepped back and stared at him.

"What did you say?" she asked. Lucky wasn't sure how she managed to speak. The air swooshed out of her body, and the muscles in her jaw turned to steel.

Lucky didn't repeat his bombshell. Nor did he explain. He glanced over at the nurse. "Could you please give me a few minutes alone with my fiancée?"

Nurse Garcia nodded. "But only if Ms. Sheppard gets back in bed."

"Of course." Lucky caught on to Marin to lead her in that direction, but he encountered some resistance. Their eyes met, and in the depth of all that blue and green, he saw the debate going on. He also saw the moment she surrendered.

He knew she expected her cooperation to get her some fast answers. Unfortunately, Lucky didn't have any answers that she was going to like.

"You have five minutes. I don't want Ms. Sheppard

getting too tired," the nurse informed them. "I'll see if I can figure out a way to get Noah in here so you can have a quick kiss and cuddle."

"Thank you," Marin told the woman without taking her gaze from Lucky. She didn't say another word until the nurse was out of the room.

"Start talking," Marin insisted, her voice low and laced with a warning. "What do you mean you're responsible for nearly getting us killed? The nurse said it was an accident. Caused by an electrical malfunction."

That warning was the only thing lethal looking about her. She was pale and trembling. Lucky got her moving toward the bed. He also gave her gown an adjustment so that it actually covered her bare backside. Then, he got on with his explanation.

"The police first believed the explosion was caused by something electrical," Lucky explained. "But there are significant rumblings that when the Texas Rangers came in, they found an incendiary device."

But that was more than just rumblings. The sheriff had confirmed it.

Which brought him back to Marin's question.

"I'm a PI. And a former cop," he told her. With just those few crumbs of info, he had to pause and figure out how to say the rest. Best not to give Marin too much too soon. She was still weak. But he owed her at least part of the truth. "I've been working on a case that involves some criminals in hiding."

Well, one criminal in particular. That was a detail he'd keep to himself for now.

"I think someone associated with the case I'm investigating might have set that explosive," Lucky explained. "I believe there are people who don't want me to learn the truth about a woman who was murdered."

He waited for her reaction.

Marin paused, taking a deep breath. "I see."

Those two little words said a lot. They weren't an accusation. More like reluctant acceptance. He supposed that was good. It meant she might not slap him for endangering her son. Too bad. Lucky might have felt better if she *had* slapped him.

"The authorities know the explosion might be connected to you?" she asked.

"They know. The train was going through LaMesa Springs when the explosives went off. The sheriff there, Beck Tanner, is spearheading the initial investigation. He's already questioned me, and I told him about the case I was working on."

Sheriff Tanner would likely question Marin, too. Before that, Lucky would have to tell her the whole truth about why he was really on that train.

And the whole truth was guaranteed to make her slap him.

Or worse.

Marin looked down at her hands and brushed her fingers over her scraped knuckles. "The explosion wasn't your fault," she concluded. "You were just doing your job. And I put you in awkward position by asking you to protect Noah." She lifted her head. "I don't regret that. I can't."

Lucky pulled the chair next to her bed closer and sat down so they were at eye level. But they were still a safe distance from each other. Touching her was out. Her weakness and vulnerability clouded his mind.

And touching her would cloud his body.

He didn't need either.

"Yeah. After I met your parents, I totally understood why you asked me to take care of your little guy," Lucky continued. "Though at the time I thought I'd only have to keep that promise for an hour or two."

She nodded. "And then I didn't regain consciousness right away."

That was just the first of several complications.

"Like you asked, I tried getting in touch with your friend, Lizette Raines, in Fort Worth. She didn't answer her home phone, so I finally called someone I knew in the area and asked him to check on her. According to the neighbors, she's on a short trip to Mexico with her boyfriend."

Marin groaned softly. "Yes. She met him about two months ago, and I knew things were getting more serious, but she didn't mention anything about a trip."

She ran her fingers through the side of her shoulder-length hair and winced when she encountered the injury that had caused her concussion and the coma. In addition to the bandage that covered several stitches, her left temple was bruised—and the purplish stain bled all the way down to her cheekbone. It sickened him to see that on her face, to know what she'd been through.

And to know that it wasn't over.

This—whatever this was—was just beginning, and Lucky didn't care much for the bad turn it'd taken on that train.

"I wonder why Lizette didn't call me," Marin said. "She has my cell number."

"Your phone was lost in the explosion so even if she'd tried that number, she wouldn't have gotten you. Don't worry. Your friend's trip sounded legit, and none of your neighbors are concerned."

Before Lucky could continue, the door flew open, and a couple walked in. Not the nurse with Noah, but two people that Lucky had already met. And they were two people he had quickly learned to detest.

Marin's parents, Lois and Howard Sheppard.

The unexpected visit brought both him and Marin to their feet. It wasn't a fluid movement for Marin. She wobbled a bit when she got out of bed, and he slid his arm around her waist so she could keep her balance.

Lucky so wished he'd had time to prepare Marin for this. Of course, there was no preparation for the kind of backstabbing she was about to encounter.

"Mother," Marin said. Because she was pressed right against him, Lucky felt her muscles tense. She pulled in a long, tight breath.

No frills. That was the short physical description for the petite woman who strolled toward them. A simple maroon dress. Matching heels. Matching purse. Heck, even her lipstick matched. There wasn't a strand of her graying blond hair out of place. Lois Sheppard looked like the perfect TV mom.

She hurried toward Marin and practically elbowed Lucky out of the way so she could hug her daughter. When Lois pulled back, her eyes were shiny with tears.

"It's so good to see you, sweetheart," Lois said, her voice weepy and soft.

Marin stepped back out of her mother's embrace.

The simple gesture improved Lois's posture. "Marin, that's no way to act. Honestly, you'd think you have no manners. Aren't you even going to say hello to your father?"

"Hello," Marin echoed.

And judging from Marin's near growling tone, she didn't like her dad any better than Lucky did. Unlike Lois, Howard had a slick oily veneer that reminded Lucky of con artists and dishonest used car salesmen. Of course, his opinion probably had something to do with this whole backstabbing mission.

"Mother, why are you and Dad here?"

Lois shrugged as if the answer were obvious. "Because we love you. Because we're concerned about you. You're coming back to the ranch with us so you can have time to recuperate from your injuries. You know you're not well enough or strong enough to be on your own. You never have been. Clearly, leaving home was a mistake."

Lucky pulled Marin tighter into the crook of his arm.

"I'm not going with you," she informed her mother.

Lucky wanted to cheer her backbone, but he already knew the outcome of this little encounter.

There'd be no cheering today.

"Yes, you are," Lois disagreed. "I'm sorry, but I can't give you a choice about that. You and Noah are too important to us. And because we love you both so much, we've filed papers."

Lucky felt Marin's muscles stiffen even more. "What kind of papers?" Marin enunciated each syllable.

Lucky didn't wait for Lois Sheppard to provide the explanation. "Your folks are trying to use your hospital stay and your epilepsy to get custody of Noah." He turned his attention to Lois and made sure he smirked. "Guess what—not gonna happen."

The woman's maroon-red mouth tightened into a temporary bud. "I don't think you'll have much of a say in that, Randall."

"Lucky," he corrected. Because by damn he might have to play the part of Marin's slimeball ex, but Lucky refused to use the man's name. It'd been a godsend that neither of Marin's parents had ever met said slimeball. If they had, the charade of Lucky pretending to be him would have been over before it even started.

"I don't care what you call yourself," Howard interceded. "You're an unfit father. You weren't even there for the birth of your own son. You left Marin alone to fend for herself."

Lucky shoved his thumb to his chest. "Well, I'm here now."

"Are you?" Howard challenged.

"What the hell does that mean?" Lucky challenged right back.

Howard didn't answer right away, and the silence intensified with his glare. "It means I don't think you love my daughter. I think this so-called relationship between you two is a sham to convince Lois and me that we don't need to intervene in Marin's life."

Since that was the truth, Lucky knew it was time for

some damage control. Later, he'd figure out if Howard really knew something or if this was a bluff.

Lucky pulled Marin closer to him. Body against body. Marin must have felt the same need for damage control because she came up on her toes and kissed him, a familiar peck of reassurance. Something a real couple would have shared.

That brief lip-lock speared through him, causing Lucky to remind himself that this really was a sham.

"What papers have they filed?" Marin asked him.

Lucky didn't take his gaze from Howard. "Your parents convinced a judge to review your competency as a parent. A crooked judge is my guess, because we have to go to your parents' ranch for an interview with a psychologist."

Lucky expected Marin to lose it then and there. Maybe a tirade or some profanity. He wouldn't have blamed her if she had. But her reaction was almost completely void of emotion.

"Mother, Dad, you're leaving now," Marin said. And she stepped out of Lucky's arms and sat back down on the bed. A moment passed before she looked at her mother again. "I'm tired. I need my rest. Nurse's orders."

Lois took a step closer, and even though she wasn't smiling, there was a certain victory shout in her stance. "If you don't return to the ranch and do this interview with the psychologist, the judge will intervene. Noah will be taken from you and placed in our custody."

And with that threat, Lois and Howard finally did what Marin had asked. They turned and walked out the door.

All that cool and calmness that Marin had displayed went south in a hurry. She began to shake, and for a moment Lucky thought she might be going into shock or on the verge of having a seizure.

Instead, she wrapped her arms around herself. "What do I have to do to make this go away?"

Since there was no easy way to put it, Lucky just laid it out there for her. "We'll have to go to the ranch because as your legal next of kin, your parents managed to get an emergency hearing in front of a judge who's also their friend. They persuaded this judge that you need to be medically monitored—by them, under their roof. And the judge signed a temporary order. Once we're at the ranch, we'll have the interview where we'll need to convince a psychologist that we're a happy couple fit to raise Noah. If we do that, the psychologist will pass that on to the judge, and there won't be another hearing. The temporary order will expire, and you'll keep sole custody of Noah."

Marin slowly lifted her eyes and looked at him. She didn't exactly voice a question, but there were plenty of nonverbal ones.

"The interview could be as early as tomorrow afternoon," Lucky added. "If the doctor releases you from the hospital today. That means we wouldn't have to keep up the charade for long. Then, after visiting with your grandmother, you can go home."

Well, maybe.

That was one of those gray areas that Lucky hadn't quite figured out. Marin might never be able go home. It might not be safe.

"And what happens if we come clean and tell everyone that you're not Noah's father?" she asked. But Marin immediately waved that off. "Then my parents will use that against me. They might even want a paternity test. They'll brand us as liars. And if the judge knows we lied about that, he'll assume we're lying about my ability to be a good parent."

The Sheppards might even try to file criminal charges against him for preventing them from taking Noah. The couple certainly had a lot of misplaced love, and they were aiming all of it at Marin and Noah.

"I'll fight it," Marin said, sounding not nearly as strong as her words. "I'll hire a lawyer and fight it."

"I've already talked to one," he assured her. "I called a friend of a friend, and she says to cooperate for now. Your mother and Howard might have this judge firmly in their pockets, and he's the one who arranged for the interview with the psychologist. I've requested a change of venue, and he denied it. The only way we could have gotten a delay is if you hadn't come out of the coma."

"Great. Just great." She paused a moment. "So you're saying we should go to the ranch and do as my parents say?"

"I don't think we have a choice."

Her chin came up. "Yes, I do. There's no reason to drag you into this. And you shouldn't have to be subjected to staying with my parents. You have no idea the emotional hell they'll put you through, especially since they believe we're a couple. A couple they want to see driven apart."

Lucky didn't doubt that. But there was another

problem. "Marin, your parents aren't going to just give up. It took some fast talking for me to stop an immediate transfer of custody. Your mother was here early yesterday morning. She came prepared to take Noah then and there."

Marin groaned and buried her face in her hands. "Oh, God."

Lucky groaned right along with her. There were a lot of things wrong with their plan. For one thing, it wasn't legal. But what Marin's parents were trying to do wasn't right, either. So maybe two wrongs did make a right.

That still didn't mean this would be easy.

For two days, he'd have to pretend to be Noah's father and Marin's loving fiancé. The first was a piece of cake. It was that second one that was giving him the most trouble.

Lucky blamed it on the blazing attraction between them.

Before he'd held Marin in his arms, before that brief kiss, he'd only lusted after her in his heart. Now, he was lusting after her in all kinds of ways. And he couldn't do anything about it.

Because Marin might become a critical witness when he busted his investigation wide open. She might be the key to finally getting justice. He couldn't compromise that—it was the most important thing in his life.

He couldn't get involved with Marin. He could only live a temporary lie.

"Okay," Marin mumbled. She cleared her throat. "So, you have to do the interview, whenever that'll be, but you don't have to stay at the ranch in Willow Ridge. You can drop Noah and me off and then say you have an urgent business appointment or something, that you'll return in time for the interview."

Lucky just stared at her, wondering how she was going to handle what he had to say.

"You're already having second thoughts?" Marin concluded.

"No. That interview has to happen. You have to keep custody of Noah."

Now it was Marin's turn to stay silent for several moments. "And you'd do this for me?" Marin asked. Her gaze met his again, and there was no cowering look in her eyes. Just some steel and attitude. "Why?"

She wasn't requesting information. She was demanding it.

This would have been a good time to tell another half truth. Especially since—much to his disgust—he was getting good at them.

But another lie would stick in his throat.

"I'm looking for your brother, Dexter," he confessed.

Her eyes immediately darkened, and he saw the pulse pound on her throat. "You followed me on the train?"

Lucky nodded. "I followed you."

"Why?" she repeated, though this one had even more steel than the original one.

"Because I thought you might lead me to him."

She tipped her eyes to the ceiling and groaned. "I was right about you. You're one of those men. The ones who've followed me and tried to scare me."

He reached out to her, but Marin batted his hands away. "Scaring you was never my intention. I just need to find your brother."

"What do you want from Dexter?" she snapped.

Lucky was betting this answer wasn't so obvious. "The truth?"

She sliced at him with a scalpel-sharp glare. "That would be nice for a change."

He debated if Marin was strong enough to hear this. Probably not. But there was no turning back now. He toyed with how he should say it. But there was only one way to deliver news like this. Quick and dirty.

He'd tell her the truth even if it made Marin hate him.

Chapter Five

Marin stared at Lucky, holding her breath.

Even though she'd only known him for a short period of time, she was already familiar with his body language.

Whatever he had to say wouldn't be good.

"What do you want from my brother?" she repeated.

Lucky stood and looked down at her. He met her gaze head-on. "I want him dead."

Everything inside her stilled. It wasn't difficult to process that frightening remark since she'd been through this before. For the past year, she'd had to deal with other men who had wanted to find Dexter, too. And like Lucky they probably had wanted him dead, as well. But this cut even deeper to the bone because Lucky had saved her son. He'd saved her.

And she trusted him.

Correction, she *had* trusted him. Right now, she just felt betrayed.

Marin tried to keep her voice and body calm, which was hard to do with her emotions in shreds. She silently cursed the pain that pounded through her head and made it hard to think. "Then, you already have what you want. Dexter *is* dead."

Lucky lifted his left shoulder. "I'm not so sure about that."

The other men hadn't been sure, either. But then neither had her own family. "If Dexter were alive, he would have contacted me by now. He wouldn't have let me believe he was dead."

At least she hoped that was true. But Marin couldn't be certain, especially considering the dangerous circumstances surrounding his disappearance.

"Let's just say that I know a different side of your brother," Lucky insisted. "The man I know would do anything—and I mean anything—to save himself. And in this case, making everyone think he's dead is about the only thing that could save him from the investors who poured millions of dollars into research that didn't pay off for them because Dexter didn't deliver what he promised he would."

She couldn't disagree with that. Marin had examined and reexamined every detail she could find about the night Dexter had disappeared.

Lucky had no doubt done the same.

"What do you know about the night my brother died?" she asked.

His eyes said "too much." "Your brother was a chemical engineer working on a privately funded project. He was supposed to be testing antidotes for chemical agents, specifically a hybrid nerve agent that might be used in a combat situation against ground troops. The investors believed they could sell this antidote to the Department of Defense for a large sum of money. But something went wrong. The Justice Department got some info that Dexter was selling secrets, and they were about to launch a full-scale investigation."

Yes, she knew all of that—after the fact. Before that night, however, Marin hadn't known exactly what Dexter's research project entailed. Even now, she doubted that she knew the entire truth. Maybe no one did. But something had indeed gone wrong with the project, and the Justice Department investigation hadn't happened as planned because there had been an explosion in the research facility.

There was also evidence of some kind of attack that night, and a security guard who was actually an undercover Justice Department agent had been killed. The body had been found in the rubble of the facility.

Unlike Dexter's.

No one had been able to locate his body or those of the two women who'd been in the facility that night. But Marin believed Dexter had indeed been killed in the attack, which might have been orchestrated by someone who wanted to get their hands on her brother's research project.

Since the project was missing, as well, Marin was convinced that the culprit had succeeded.

"Your brother is a criminal," Lucky informed her.

Even though she was in pain and exhausted, Lucky's words gave her a boost of anger and adrenaline that she needed. But then, defending her brother had always been a strong knee-jerk reaction.

"There were never any charges brought against Dexter," Marin reminded him.

"Because the authorities think he's dead."

"No. Because there's no evidence to indicate he's done anything wrong."

"There's evidence," Lucky insisted. "I just haven't found it. Yet. But before his disappearance, Dexter was working on more than a chemical antidote. A chemical weapon. He was playing both sides of the fence, and three days ago a key component of that weapon surfaced for sale on the black market."

Now, that she didn't know. But perhaps her parents did. According to the phone conversations she'd had with her grandmother, the federal authorities had kept her parents informed about the investigation, and they'd visited the ranch often.

"That's still not proof Dexter's alive," Marin insisted, certain that her voice no longer sounded so convinced of Dexter's innocence.

Lucky lifted his hands, palms up. "Who else would be trying to sell that component?"

"The person who stole it."

He didn't toss his hands in the air again, but he looked as if he wanted to do just that. "Other than some blood found at the scene, there's no proof that Dexter is dead. *None.* He would have hung on to that weapon and waited until the right time to sell it. Three days ago was apparently the right time for him because it appeared."

Marin took a moment to rein in her emotions. Despite his sometimes selfish behavior, she loved her brother and didn't want to believe he was capable of doing something like this. She'd grieved for him, and she missed him. Would Dexter have put the family and her through all that pain just to cover himself?

Maybe.

And if so, then maybe Lucky was telling the truth. "Assuming you're right, then what does this case have to do with you?"

"Dexter pissed off the wrong people, Marin," Lucky explained. "And I'm one of those people."

That didn't sound like something a PI would say about one of his cases. It sounded personal. "What do you mean?"

His jaw muscles stirred. He eased back down into the chair and scrubbed his hands over his face. "My sister was fresh out of her doctoral program at the University of Texas, and her first and only real job was working for Dexter."

Marin sucked in her breath. This was starting to move in a direction that she didn't want to go. "Not Brenna Martel?" Brenna had been a colleague, one of the women who went missing and was presumed dead. But Brenna hadn't just been Dexter's business associate. She'd been his lover.

"No. Not Brenna. His lab assistant, Kinley Ford." He waited a moment. "My dad died right after Kinley was born, my mom remarried shortly thereafter, and Kinley took our stepdad's surname."

That's why Marin hadn't immediately made the connection between Lucky and the woman. She hadn't met Kinley Ford, but since her brother's disappearance, she had seen a photo of the young chemical engineer who'd assisted Dexter on his last project.

Kinley Ford had her brother's eyes.

And those storm-gray eyes were drilling into her, waiting for her to answer.

"The police believe your sister was killed that night," Marin whispered. "And unlike Dexter, there's evidence to point to that."

He nodded. And swallowed hard. "The cops think Brenna was killed, too. They found blood from all three of them. Just a trace from Dexter. More than a pint from Brenna. Triple that from my sister. There's no way she could have lived with that much blood loss."

"But the police didn't find the bodies of either woman," she pointed out.

Lucky shrugged. "Dexter probably hid them somewhere before he gave up and set the explosives to blow up the research lab. There was evidence that someone had tried to clean up the crime scene."

Yes, she'd read that, as well, and along with the fact that there'd been no lethal quantities of her brother's blood found, she could understand why some people believed he was still alive.

And guilty.

Though Lucky hadn't convinced her that Dexter was alive, he had convinced her of something—the pain he was feeling over the loss of his sister. She understood that loss because she'd grieved for Dexter. "I'm sorry Kinley was killed."

"Yeah. So am I." She heard the pain. It was raw and

still so close to the surface that she could practically feel it. "Your brother murdered her."

Marin didn't want to believe that, either. But she couldn't totally dismiss it. However, if Dexter was responsible, then it must have been an accident.

"You followed me because you thought I'd lead you to Dexter," she concluded.

He nodded. "I've been monitoring you for months. When I learned you were going to the ranch to see your grandmother, I figured Dexter would do the same."

A chill went through her. "You've been *monitoring* me? What the heck does that mean?"

He didn't get a chance to answer.

There was a tap at the door a split second before it opened. Marin didn't want the interruption. She wanted to finish this conversation with Lucky. But then, she saw that it wasn't her parents returning for round two. It was Nurse Garcia, and she had Noah in her arms.

The anger and frustration didn't exactly evaporate, but Marin did push aside those particular emotions along with her questions so that she could stand and go to her son. Just seeing him flooded her heart with love.

"Stay put. I'll bring this little guy to you," Nurse Garcia insisted. "I told the doctor you were awake and anxious for this visit. He was going to be tied up with another patient for an hour or so, but he agreed to let you see your son before the examination."

Noah smiled when he spotted Marin, and he began to pump his arms and legs. He babbled some excited indistinguishable sounds. Marin reached for him, and

he went right into her arms. Nurse Garcia excused herself and left.

Marin didn't even try to blink her tears away. It was
a miracle that she was holding her son, and an even
greater miracle that he hadn't been hurt.

Noah tolerated the embrace for several seconds
before he got bored. He leaned back and reached for the
bandage on her head. Marin shifted him in her arms, and
her son's attention landed on Lucky.

Noah immediately reached for him.

Her son had given her a warm reception, but it was
mild compared to the one he gave Lucky. Noah
squealed with delight and laughed when Lucky stood
to give him a kiss on the cheek.

"I told you that your mom was okay, buddy," Lucky
said to Noah.

When Noah's reach got more insistent and he began
to fuss, Marin handed her son over to a man who was
feeling more and more like her enemy.

"Sorry about that," Lucky mumbled, gathering Noah
in his arms. "I've hardly let him out of my sight since
the explosion. I guess he's gotten used to me."

"I guess." And she didn't bother to sound pleased
about it.

"I wasn't sure what to feed him so I called a doctor
friend and got some suggestions for formula and food.
He said to go with rice cereal. I hope that was okay."

"Fine," she managed to say. "I guess you didn't have
any trouble getting him to sleep?"

"Not really. But he's got a good set of lungs on
him when he wants a bottle. Don't you, buddy?" Lucky

grinned at Noah, the expression making him a little more endearing than she wanted at the moment.

Marin watched as Noah playfully batted at Lucky. Her son was at ease in this man's arms. More than at ease. The two looked like father and son. And they weren't. Lucky was simply a temporary stand-in.

Now, it was time to deal with reality.

The replacement father act had to be over soon, because she and Lucky obviously weren't on the same path. He not only hated her brother, he wanted revenge for his sister's death, and he'd been willing to use her to get to Dexter.

"Earlier you said you'd monitored me," she reminded him. "How?"

His grin evaporated, and even though he kept his attention on Noah, his expression became somber. "I rented the condo connected to yours."

The chill inside her got significantly colder. "You watched me? You listened in on my conversations?"

He nodded. "The walls between the condos are thin. It's not hard to overhear, if you're listening. And I was. I wanted to know if you were in contact with Dexter."

She silently cursed. "So you know I didn't. Still, you invaded my privacy."

"I did," Lucky readily admitted. "Because I had to do it. Whether you want to believe it or not, your brother's a dangerous man."

Marin groaned softly, looked at her son and blinked back more tears. "First, you save my son. You save me. And then you tell me that you've not only been spying on me, you want to kill my brother if by some miracle he's still alive."

"I don't want to kill him. I want him arrested so he can stand trial, be convicted and then get the death penalty."

"Oh, is that all?" The sarcasm dripped from her voice.

With Noah still gripped lovingly in his arms, Lucky stood back up. There was emotion in his eyes. But even though she owed this man a lot, she had just as much reason to despise him.

Marin hoped like the devil that she was keeping her temper in check because of her headache and Noah. Not because she was feeling anything like attraction for Lucky Bacelli.

But just looking at him gave her a little tug deep within her belly. She didn't want that tug to mean anything. She wanted it to go away. It was a primal reminder that no matter what he wanted from her brother, she was still hotly attracted to him.

"I'm not the only person after Dexter," Lucky continued. "Have you met Grady Duran?"

Oh, yes. And unlike what she was feeling for Lucky, there was no ambivalence when it came to Duran. She loathed Duran as much as she was afraid of him. Judging from their brief, heated encounters he thought she was a liar.

"Duran and my brother were in business together on the chemical antidote project. He believes Dexter is alive," she supplied. "For the past year he's been harassing me because he thinks I know more than I'm saying. The man's a bully, and he's dangerous."

"Did Duran hurt you?" Lucky immediately asked.

Marin's gaze rifled to his. Lucky's tone set off all sorts of alarms. That sounded like the tone of a man who was concerned.

About *her*.

Marin rethought that when she studied the ease he seemed to have when interacting with Noah. Maybe the alarm wasn't for her but for her son. That led her to another question.

Was there reason for concern?

"Duran didn't physically hurt me," Marin explained. "But he's one of the reasons I've tried to keep where I live secret. I was in Dallas for a while, but when he showed up, I moved to Fort Worth. The man frightens me because his desperation seems almost as intense as his determination to find Dexter."

Lucky's mouth tightened. "Duran probably knows about the chemical weapon's components surfacing on the black market. He might try to contact you again."

He paused, took a step toward her, halving the distance between them. "Marin, you have a lot to deal with, and you're not a hundred percent. Right now, just concentrate on recovering and getting through the interview that your parents set up."

Marin wanted to argue, but he was right. She also wanted to turn down Lucky's offer to pose as Noah's father. But she couldn't do that, either. She couldn't let her anger and pride cause her to lose custody. However, there was something she could do.

Something to put some distance between her and Lucky.

"All right," Marin agreed. "I'll check with the doctor and see how soon I can be discharged. Then, once he gives me the okay, I'll call a cab to take Noah and me to the ranch. When I know the exact time and place of the interview, I'll phone you and you can meet me at the psychologist's office. If all goes well, maybe it won't take more than an hour or two."

Lucky pulled in a deep breath and eased down on the bed beside her. The mattress creaked softly. "I should be at the ranch with you."

"No." Marin didn't even have to think about that— the tug in her belly had convinced her of that. "My parents will be expecting us to be a loving couple. In fact, they won't just be expecting it, they'll be looking for anything they can use against me to force me to return home for good."

"You need me there with you," he insisted.

She met his stare. The tug got worse. So, Marin dodged those lethal gray eyes. "I don't want to be coddled."

"Good." He leaned in, so close that it forced her to make eye contact again. "Because I'm not the coddling type."

No. He wasn't. There was a dangerous edge about him, and despite the gentleness he was showing her son, Marin didn't think this was his normal way of dealing with things. Lucky Bacelli was a lifetime bad boy.

The tug became a full-fledged pull.

Marin drew back. She had to. Because there was no

room in her life for a man, especially this man who could make her feel things she didn't want to feel.

He inched even closer. "Marin, I'm not giving you a choice about this. I'm coming to the ranch with Noah and you."

His adamancy didn't sit well with her. Especially after all the things he'd just admitted.

Then, it hit her.

She finally got why Lucky was so adamant. "You think Dexter had something to do with that explosion on the train?"

He gave a crisp nod. "Who else?"

"Not Dexter. My brother wouldn't hurt me," she informed him.

"If not him, then someone who was trying to stop me from getting to him. And that person didn't care if you or Noah got hurt in the process."

Lucky snared her gaze. "Marin, what I'm saying is that Noah and you could still be in serious danger."

Chapter Six

Lucky caught on to Marin's arm to help steady her as she walked through the door of her old room at her parents' ranch. But Marin would have no part of accepting his help. With Noah clutched in her arms, she moved out of Lucky's grip and tossed him a warning glance.

He tossed her one of his own.

"We aren't going to pull this off if you're shooting daggers at me," he mumbled.

She'd been giving him the silent treatment since they left the hospital an hour earlier. And because Noah had hardly made a peep the entire trip to the ranch, it'd been a very quiet drive in the rental car she'd arranged so that they wouldn't be in the same vehicle with her parents.

Lucky wasn't sure what to say to her anyway. Truth was, he had let her down. He'd gone onto that train to follow her, and even though he'd gotten Noah and her out of the burning debris, that wasn't going to negate one simple fact.

Marin didn't trust him.

Heck, she didn't even like him.

And that would make these next forty-eight hours damn uncomfortable.

His opinion about that didn't change when he glanced around the room. There were plenty of signs of Marin's life here. Her earlier life, that is, when she was still her parents' daughter. Several framed pictures of her sat on the dresser. In one she wore a pale pink promlike dress; in another, a dark blue graduation gown. But the photo in the middle, the one most prominently displayed was a shot of her standing between her parents. It was the most recent of the photographs, probably taken just shortly before her move to Dallas–Fort Worth.

She looked miserable.

"I figured all of this stuff would have been put in storage," Marin grumbled. "Instead, they've made it a sort of shrine."

They had indeed.

From the background investigation Lucky had run on her, Marin had left Willow Ridge in a hurry after a bitter argument with her parents over her relationship with Randall, the jerk her parents had thankfully never met. Before that, she'd lived and worked just a few miles away, running her CPA business from an office on Main Street in Willow Ridge. Her apartment had been over her office, and according to a former town resident that Lucky had interviewed, Marin's parents had visited her every day.

Marin had then met Randall while on a short business trip to New Orleans. The problems with her parents had started when Marin began dating him and had refused to bring him home so they could meet him. Maybe she'd done that because subconsciously she hadn't trusted Randall, but it probably had more to do with the fact that her parents had disapproved of all of her previous relationships.

This fake one would be no different.

"Obviously, we can't ask for separate rooms," Marin grumbled.

She was right about that. But at least the suite was big, thank goodness. Probably at least four hundred square feet, with a bathroom on one side. On the other there was a sitting room that had been converted to a nursery—complete with a crib and changing table.

There was only one bed though, covered with a garnet-red comforter.

Lucky followed the direction of Marin's gaze—the bed had obviously caught her attention, as well.

"Only two days," he reminded her.

Her heavy sigh reminded him that those two days would seem like an eternity. It was also a reminder that he should at least try to do some damage control because Lucky was positive that things could get a lot worse than they already were.

Lucky took off his leather jacket and placed it over the back of a chair that was perched in front of an antique desk. He adjusted the compact-size handgun that he had tucked in a slide holster at the back of his jeans.

Marin's gaze went racing to his holster. "Is that a gun?" she asked.

"Yes. I always carry it. I'm a PI, remember?"

She opened her mouth, closed it and turned away.

Great. Now, they had another issue. "We have to talk," Lucky insisted.

Another sigh. Marin sank down onto the edge of the bed and lay Noah next to her. The little boy didn't stay put, however. He rolled onto his stomach and tried to crawl away, but Marin caught on to him. Soon the tiny floral pattern in the comforter caught his eye, and Noah stopped crawling and began to pick at the embroidery.

"There really isn't anything to talk about," Marin countered. "I think you've made everything perfectly clear."

But then, her gaze came to his again. Lucky didn't exactly see a carte blanche acceptance there, but he did see and feel a slight change in her. She probably knew her animosity, though warranted, wasn't going to do them any good.

"You really think Noah and I are still in danger?" she asked.

He considered his answer. "Yes. And if I could do anything to change that, I would."

She wearily pushed her hair away from her bandaged forehead. "So would I. I even thought if I distanced myself from you that the danger would go away." Marin waved him off when Lucky started to respond to that. "But if the danger is connected to Dexter and the people who might want him and that chemical weapon, then no matter where I am, the danger will find me."

Marin stared at him. "How do I stop the danger from finding Noah?"

Since this wasn't going to be an easy answer, Lucky sat down beside her. "I won't let anything happen to Noah, understand?"

She shook her head. Then, swallowed hard. "I can't lose him."

"I know." And because he truly understood her concern and fear, Lucky reached out and slid his arm around her.

Marin stiffened, and for a moment he thought she might push him away. She didn't. But she didn't exactly melt into his arms, either. Still, this contact was better than the silent treatment.

Wasn't it?

Lucky rethought that when she looked at him. Just like that, he felt the hard punch of attraction. A punch he'd been trying to ward off since the first time he'd watched Marin with his surveillance equipment. Of course, he hadn't spoken to her then. At that time, he'd merely thought of her as Dexter Sheppard's sister who might have been hiding her brother's whereabouts. But she was more than that now.

And that wasn't good.

Lucky couldn't lose focus. He owed it to Kinley to find her killer, and he owed it to Noah to keep him safe. He couldn't do either if he was daydreaming about having sex with Marin.

But that little reminder didn't really help.

Next to him, Marin was warm, soft, and her scent was stirring things in him that were best left alone.

"On the train, you said you were hitting on me," she

commented, her voice practically a whisper as if discussing a secret. "Why did you lie about that?"

Now, that riled him. "Who said I lied?"

"You were following me to find Dexter."

"And I was hitting on you. Despite what you think of me, I can do two things at once."

She frowned and glanced down at the close contact. "Is that what you're doing now—hitting on me?" And it wasn't exactly an invitation to continue.

The knock at the door stopped anything stupid he was about to say. Or do. Like kiss her blind just to prove the attraction that was already way too obvious.

"It's me," the visitor called out.

"My grandmother," Marin provided, and she got up to open the door.

The petite woman who gave Marin a long hug was an older version of Lois, Marin's mother. Except unlike Lois, this woman had some warmth about her. Of course, Marin had come all this way to see her, so obviously there wasn't the tension she had with her parents.

Lucky got to his feet, as well, though he didn't move far from the bed in case Noah crawled closer to the edge.

"I'm Helen," the woman said, introducing herself to Lucky. Her dusty-blue eyes were as easy as her smile. "Welcome to Willow Ridge."

Her eye contact was hospitable, unlike the frostiness he'd gotten from Marin's parents when they'd arrived minutes earlier. Helen's scrutiny lasted only a few seconds though before the woman's attention

landed on Noah. She smiled again. No. She *beamed* and
went to the bed to sit next to her great-grandson.

"My, my, now aren't you a handsome-looking young
man," Helen concluded. Noah stared at her a moment
before he returned the smile. That caused Helen to
giggle with delight, and she scooped up the little boy
in her arms. "Why don't we go out on the patio and have
a little visit."

Lucky was about to question whether Marin was up
to going outside, but she followed her grandmother to a
pair of French doors that thankfully led to a glass
enclosed patio. No sting of the winter wind here. It was
warm, cozy and had an incredible view of the west
pasture that was green with winter rye grass. With the
sun just starting to set, the room was filled with golden
light.

"How are you feeling?" Helen asked, her attention
going back to Marin. The older woman dropped down
into one of the white wicker chairs.

"I'm fine," Marin assured her, taking the love seat
next to her grandmother and son.

Everyone in that sunroom knew that was a lie. The dark
smudgy circles beneath Marin's eyes revealed her
draining fatigue. And then there was that bandage on her
forehead, a stark reminder of how close she'd come to
being killed. It would take Lucky a lifetime or two to
forgive himself for not being able to stop what had
happened.

"How are you feeling?" Marin countered.

Helen gave her a short-lived smile and showered

Noah's cheeks with kisses. "I figured the only way to get you here was to tell you I was under the weather."

Marin mumbled something under her breath. Then, huffed. "When you called Lizette earlier this week and asked her to give me a message, you said you were sick, not under the weather. *Sick.* I was worried about you."

"I know, and considering what happened on the train, I'm sorry. But I'm not sorry you're here." Helen paused a moment. "All of these problems with your folks need to be worked out, and this was the only way I could think to do it."

"Grandma, it didn't resolve anything. Mom and Dad are trying to take Noah from me."

"I know, and I'm sorry about that, too. I did try to stop them, but you know how your mother is when she gets an idea in her head." The smile returned. "But they'll forget all about custody and such when Dexter comes home."

That grabbed Lucky's complete attention. "You think Dexter's alive?"

"Of course. And he won't miss the chance to see his sister and nephew. I figure Dexter's been waiting for the best time to make his homecoming, and that time is now."

Lucky was about to agree, but Helen continued before he could speak. "I don't guess you'll be joining the family for dinner tonight?"

"No," Marin immediately answered. "Mom and Dad might have blackmailed me into staying here, but there's nothing in that judge's order that says I have to socialize with the people trying to take my son."

"I thought you'd feel that way. I'll make sure the cook brings in some trays for you two and some baby goodies for our little man here." Helen tipped her head toward the bedroom. "It's my guess that your folks have your suite bugged."

Lucky and Marin just stared at her.

Helen continued, "I heard them talking when they got back from the hospital after they saw you. Don't know where the bug is, but I'll bet my favorite broach that they put one somewhere in the bedroom."

"Why would they do that?" Lucky asked.

"Because they're suspicious. I don't know where Howard got the notion, but he thinks Lucky here is only out to break your heart. My advice, be careful what you say. And be just as careful what you do. Don't give Howard and Lois any ammunition to take this little boy. Because with a judge who's your dad's fishing buddy, they already have enough."

Marin groaned softly and started to get up. "I'll look for the bug."

Lucky put his hand on her shoulder and eased her back down. "I'll do it."

"You might not want to do that," Helen volunteered. "I mean, you could think of a bug as a golden opportunity to give Howard and my often misguided daughter a dose of their own medicine. After all, they're using deceit to try to force Marin back here. Why don't you prove to them that you have nothing to hide, that you are what you say you are?"

Lucky could think of a reason—because it would be damn impossible to stay "in character" 24/7. He would have to disarm that eavesdropping device.

His cell phone rang. He considered letting it go to voice mail. Until he spotted the name on the caller ID.

"I have to take this," he told Marin, and since he couldn't go into the bugged bedroom, he stepped outside so he could have some privacy.

Winter came right at him. The wind felt like razor blades whipping at his shirt and jeans. But that didn't stop him. This call was exactly what he'd been waiting for.

"Cal," Lucky answered. As in Special Agent Cal Rico from the Justice Department. Just as important, Cal was his best friend and had been since they'd grown up together in San Antonio. "Please tell me you have good news about that train explosion."

"Some." But Cal immediately paused. "It looks as though someone left a homemade explosive device in a suitcase in one of the storage lockers near the lounge car."

The car where they'd been sitting.

"I don't suppose you saw anyone suspicious carrying a black leather suitcase?" Cal asked.

"No." But then, Lucky had been preoccupied with Marin. He'd allowed the attraction he felt for her to stop him from doing his job. And his job had been to make sure that no one had followed him while he'd been following Marin.

Obviously, he'd failed big-time.

"Did any of the other passengers notice the suitcase-carrying bomber?" Lucky leaned his shoulder against the sunroom glass, hoping he'd absorb some of the heat. Inside, Marin and her grandmother were still talking.

"No, but I'm about to start reviewing the surveillance disks."

That caught Lucky's attention. "What exactly was recorded?"

"All the main areas on the train itself, and the two depots where the train stopped in Fort Worth and then in Dallas."

Good. It was what he wanted to hear. "So anyone who boarded should be on that surveillance?"

"Should be. Of course, that doesn't rule out a person who was already on the train. The person could have been hiding there for a while just so they wouldn't be so obvious on surveillance."

Hell. But Lucky would take what he could get. These disks were a start.

"We'll scan the disks using the face recognition program," Cal continued. "And also check for anyone carrying a suitcase that matches the leather fragments we were able to find at the point of origin of the explosion. We might get something useful."

Lucky didn't like the possibility that they might not succeed. He had to find that bomber. Better yet, he had to prove the bomber was either Dexter or someone connected to him. And then, he had to stop this SOB before Marin and Noah were put in harm's way again.

From the other side of the glass, Noah grinned at him, a reminder of just what was at stake here.

"I want a copy of those surveillance disks," Lucky requested.

"I figured you would. And I thought about how many different ways to tell you no. You're no longer a cop, Lucky. I can't give you official authorization to see them."

Lucky cursed. "Then I hope you've worked out a way to do it unofficially because I need those disks. Someone tried to kill me, and I want to know who."

Cal groaned heavily enough for Lucky to hear it. "And that's how I'm going to get around the official part. A set of the disks are already on the way to the local sheriff there in Willow Ridge. He'll bring them out to you so you can view them as a witness looking for anything that you would consider suspicious."

Lucky released the breath that he didn't even know he'd been holding. "Thanks, Cal. I owe you."

"Yeah. You do. You can repay me by finding our unknown suspect on those disks." And with that assignment, Cal hung up.

Lucky didn't waste any time. He went back into the sunroom so he could question Helen about Dexter. So far, she was the only person who seemed to want to talk about Marin's brother. But when Lucky saw Marin's face, he immediately knew his questions about Dexter would have to wait.

"What's wrong?" he asked. He hadn't thought it possible, but she was even paler than she had been when they first arrived.

Marin exchanged an uneasy glance with her grandmother, who still had Noah in her arms. "There was a message left for me." She pointed to the phone on a wicker coffee table.

"It's a private line," Helen supplied, taking up the explanation. "Lois didn't have the line taken out when Marin moved. And since no one other than the cleaning lady ever goes out here, we didn't notice the message until just now."

Since this "message" had obviously upset both women, Lucky went to the phone and pressed the play button. It took a couple of seconds to work through Marin's old recorded greeting and the date and time of the call. Two days earlier at nine fifty-three in the morning. About the same time Marin had been on the train en route to Willow Ridge.

The answering machine continued, and a man's rusty voice poured through the sunroom. "Marin Sheppard, this is Grady Duran."

The very person who'd hounded Marin when she first moved to Dallas–Fort Worth.

"I'm tired of waiting for you to get chatty about Dexter," Duran continued. "And I'm tired of warning you of what could happen if you don't tell me where your brother is. My number will be on your caller ID. Get in touch with me. That's not a suggestion. Keep ignoring me, and you'll regret it."

Lucky felt the inevitable slam of anger. How dare this SOB threaten Marin, especially after everything she'd been through. But then, something else occurred to him.

Had Grady Duran been the one to set that explosive? Lucky couldn't immediately see a motive for that, since Duran would want Marin alive. Well, alive until he got the info about Dexter's whereabouts. But maybe the explosion had been meant to scare her.

If so, it'd worked.

"Has Grady Duran ever been here at the ranch?" he asked Helen and Marin.

Marin shook her head. "I don't think so." Helen echoed the same.

Lucky took out his wallet, fished out the dog-eared photo and handed it to Helen. "Does he look familiar?"

Helen brought it closer to her face and studied the picture. Marin leaned in and looked at it, as well. Lucky had already studied it so long that he'd memorized every little detail. Kinley had sent it to him just a month before she was murdered.

The last picture taken of her.

Kinley was smiling, as usual. It was a victory photo of sorts, she'd said in her brief e-mail to Lucky. An office party to celebrate her boss getting a new research contract, which meant she'd be employed at least another year.

In the posed shot, her boss, Dexter, was on her right. Tall, blond and toned, he looked as if he'd be more at home on a California beach than a research lab. He was sporting a thousand-watt smile—smiles like that had probably gone a long way to helping him with the ladies.

Lucky also knew something else about that photo: Dexter had his arm slung a little too intimately over Kinley's shoulder.

On Kinley's left was a woman with light brown hair.

Brenna Martel, Dexter's former lover and other lab assistant. And then there was Grady Duran, standing just off from the others. Wide shoulders, imposing dark stare, he wasn't looking like a man in a festive mood.

Odd, since of the four he was the only one who wasn't missing or dead.

"I remember her," Helen tapped Brenna's image. "Dexter brought her here a time or two. She's dead."

"Looks that way. Either that or she disappeared from the face of the earth. No one's touched her bank accounts or her other personal assets since the night of the explosion at the research facility. What about the other guy, Grady Duran? Ever seen him?"

"He wasn't at the ranch," Helen concluded. "But I'm pretty sure I saw him in town. He was in the parking lot of Doc Sullivan's office when I came out from having my blood pressure checked. That was Monday. I noticed because we don't get many strangers in Willow Ridge, especially this time of year."

Helen turned back to Lucky. "Is it a bad thing that this man's in town?"

"A suspicious thing," Lucky supplied. He didn't like the timing of Duran's reappearance. Monday was the day before the train explosion. "Did he say anything to you?"

"Not a word. In fact, he looked away and turned his head when I spotted him."

Lucky didn't care for that, either. Except that it could mean that Duran was here because he knew Dexter was nearby. That was both good and bad.

He looked at Noah, who had hardly been out of his

arms for two days. Two days wasn't that long. But it was more than long enough. Lucky loved Noah. He couldn't have loved him more if he were his own son. With Dexter's possible return, that meant Lucky would have the additional challenge of protecting Noah in case something went wrong.

"You need to tell the sheriff that you saw this man," Lucky instructed Helen. "And while you're doing that, I'll ask him to keep a watch out for Duran in case he makes a return visit. I don't want him anywhere near here."

Helen's forehead bunched up. "You think there could be trouble?"

"Maybe."

But the truth was trouble was already on the way.

Jaime's Secret?

Chapter Seven

Frustrated, Marin shut the dresser drawer with far more force than necessary. "Where is it?" she mumbled.

She'd looked at every inch of the furniture and still hadn't found an eavesdropping device. She glanced at Lucky, who was still examining her closet, but he didn't seem to be having any better luck than she was.

With Noah now asleep in his crib in the sitting room, Marin walked toward the closet. "Maybe Grandma was wrong about the bug," she whispered.

Lucky, too, was obviously frustrated, and he stopped his search to stare at her. "We could be going about this the wrong way," he said under his breath. "Maybe we should just blow off this bug and concentrate on making sure this place is as secure as it can be."

"You've already done that," she pointed out.

The sheriff, Jack Whitley, had already been alerted about Grady Duran possibly being in town, and he'd agreed to send out a deputy to patrol the ranch. The ranch hands had been instructed to keep an eye out for Grady, as well. And her parents had agreed to turn on the security system that they'd had installed but almost never used.

"I could arrange to have surveillance cameras brought in," Lucky explained, his voice not so soft now. "Then, I could monitor the perimeter of the ranch."

"The ranch is huge. Well over a thousand acres and with more than a dozen outbuildings." She glanced back at Noah to make sure he was okay. He was. Her son was on his side and still asleep. "Besides, we only have two days here. After that, I can make other arrangements for security."

Marin was still undecided about her future living arrangements. But returning to Fort Worth probably wasn't a wise move. She'd need a new place, a new home, far away from danger and from her parents. First though, she had to fight this custody challenge.

And she had to keep Noah safe.

Of course, Lucky had taken over that task as if he'd been ordained to protect her son. She couldn't exactly fault him for that. Yes, he'd lied to her about Dexter. Probably lied about hitting on her, as well. But she couldn't doubt that he had her son's best interest at heart.

"So, what do we do about this bug?" Marin mouthed.

Lucky glanced around. Scowled. "Howard and Lois?" he called out. "If you're listening, and you probably are, maybe the judge and the shrink would like to know how perverted you are. Eavesdropping on your daughter having sex with her fiancé. How sick is that, huh?"

Lucky stepped closer to her, placed his palm on the

wall just behind her head, and made a throaty grunting sound. It was the exaggerated sound of a man in the throes of sex. He grunted some more, and Marin couldn't help it, she smiled.

Since she figured this was an impromptu outlet for all that pent-up frustration about her parents' antics, she added some moans of her own.

Lucky laughed. It was husky, low and totally male. And she didn't know why—maybe it was the sheer absurdity of their situation—but their charade did indeed help ease some of the frustration.

Well, for a moment or two.

Then, the frustration returned and went in a totally different direction. Or rather, a too familiar, dangerous direction.

Their eyes met and their gazes held. There it was again, that jolt of attraction that'd hit her when she first met him. Lucky was hot. But Marin remembered he was hands-off. He wanted her brother, and he'd been willing to use her to find him.

That reminder was still flashing through her head when Lucky lowered his head. She saw it coming. He was making a move on her. Slick. Effortless. Still, even though she saw it coming, she didn't do anything to stop it. She leaned closer into him, and his mouth found hers, letting the dreamy feel of his kiss wash over her.

He was gentle. A surprise. She'd thought he would be rough and demanding. A bad boy's kiss. But his mouth was as easy as his smooth Texas drawl.

Marin slipped her arms around his neck. First one, then the other. Everything inside her slowed to practically a crawl. Except her heart. It was racing, and she could feel it in her throat.

The slow crawling feeling didn't last long. It couldn't. Not with his clever kiss. When she'd first seen Lucky's face, she'd thought of him being in a bar brawl, of his rough exterior. Of those snug jeans that hugged all the interesting parts of his body. Now, all of that came into play. All of those had drawn her in.

Her body went from mindless resistance to being flooded with raging heat. His chest brushed her breasts. It was enough to urge her closer, to feel more of him. He was solid, all sinew and muscle, and she felt so soft in his arms.

He hooked his arm around her waist and snapped her to him. The gentleness vanished. Thank goodness! Because what good was it to lust after a rough and tumble bad boy if he held back one of the very things that made him bad?

Their bodies met head-on, a collision of sensations. The thoroughness of his touch. The firmness of his grip. His taste. The undeniable need of his mouth as he took the kiss and made it French.

Yes! she thought. Yes. This was her fantasy. Him, taking her like this. Not treating her with kid gloves.

And Lucky didn't disappoint.

His left hand went into her hair. Avoiding her injured forehead, he caught the strands of hair between his fingers and pulled back her head gently, but firmly so that he controlled the angle of the kiss. So that he controlled her.

Marin moved into the kiss, against him. Lucky

moved, too, sliding his hand down her back, over her butt. He caught on to the back of her thigh, lifting it, just a little, to create the right angle so that his sex would touch hers.

Her breath vanished, and her vision blurred. She mumbled a word of profanity that she'd never used.

Every part of her responded. A slow, melting heat that urged her to take this farther. She wanted Lucky. Not just his French kiss. Not just the clever pressure created by his erection now nestled against her. She wanted it all.

Right here. Right now.

Senseless and thinking with her body, Marin fought to regain control. It wasn't easy. She had to fight her way though the mindlessness of pure, raw desire and a fantasy she'd been weaving for hours. She remembered that having sex just wasn't a good idea. Thankfully, she got a jolt of help when she heard the bedroom door open.

"Noah," she said on a rise of breath.

Just like that, the heat was gone, and even though she turned to race back into the bedroom, Lucky launched himself ahead of her and beat her to it. However, the threat Marin had been prepared to face wasn't there.

Well, not exactly.

With a large thick envelope tucked beneath her arm, her mother, Lois, waltzed inside. Marin made a mental note to keep the door locked from now on—and to keep some distance between Lucky and her.

Lois glanced over at her grandson in the sitting room and gave the sleeping baby a thin smile. Her scrutiny of Lucky and her though lasted a bit longer, and Marin didn't think it was her imagination that her mother was displeased about something. Probably because both Lucky and she looked as if, well, they'd gotten lucky. For the sake of the facade, Marin tried to hang on to the well-satisfied look. It wasn't hard to do. That kiss had been darn memorable.

Which was exactly why she had to forget it.

Her mother snapped her fingers and in stepped a young dark-haired woman carrying a large tray of plates covered with domed silver lids. She set the tray on the desk in the corner and made a hasty exit.

"Your dinner," Lois announced. "Since you made it clear that you wouldn't be dining with us. There's some rice cereal and formula there for Noah, as well."

"Thank you," Lucky responded. "But Noah's already had his dinner—Grandmother brought it in. Oh, and next time, knock first."

Her mother looked as if she wanted to argue with that, but she didn't. Instead, she extracted the envelope and thrust it at Lucky. "Sheriff Whitley had his deputy bring this over for you. I suppose it's connected to the explosion?"

Neither Lucky nor Marin confirmed that. Nor would they. But it was no doubt the surveillance disks from the train that Lucky had told her about. Lucky examined the red tape that sealed the envelope, and Marin could see that someone had written their initials in permanent marker on that tape.

The sound her mother made was of obvious disapproval. "The sheriff apparently packaged it like that. He said if the seal was tampered with that he'd arrest my husband and me for obstruction of justice."

"Good for Sheriff Whitley," Lucky mumbled.

"The man isn't fit to wear that badge," Lois declared. But her expression softened when she looked at Marin. "You should at least eat dinner with your family."

"I would if my family were really a family." Marin paused a moment to put a chokehold on her temper. She didn't want to shout with Noah in the room. "Drop this interview. Apologize. Back off. And then I might have dinner with you."

"The interview has to happen, for your son's sake," her mother said without hesitation. "And it's for his sake that I can't back off."

"Neither can I," someone echoed. It was her father who stepped inside to join forces with her mother.

"Oh, goody," Marin mumbled.

Lucky placed the envelope on the foot of the bed and positioned himself closer to her, so that they were literally facing down her parents.

"By the way, did either of you know about the threatening phone message that Grady Duran left Marin on her private line?" Lucky asked.

It was a good question. One that Marin should have already thought to ask.

"*That message,*" her father grumbled. "Marin's grandmother told us about it after her visit with you. No. We didn't know. But the sheriff does now. For all the good that'll do."

Apparently, her father wasn't any happier with the sealed envelope than her mother. Marin didn't care. She wanted the authorities to know about Grady Duran because it was her guess that he was the one responsible for that explosion, and she wanted him off the streets and behind bars.

Her father propped his hands on his hips. "I thought you should know, I just heard from your brother."

Marin could have sworn her heart stopped.

Lucky must have had a similar reaction because he didn't utter a word. Neither did her mother. And the three all stood there, staring at the man who'd just made the announcement she'd never thought she would hear.

"Dexter's not dead?" Marin finally managed to say.

"Obviously not. He just e-mailed me," Howard explained.

Lois pressed her hand to her chest and pulled in several quick breaths. "What did he say?"

"That he's alive and he wants to come home to see his family."

"Where is he?" Lucky demanded.

"Even if he had said, I wouldn't tell you. Dexter's worried about his safety, as he should be. He knows someone killed two of his employees and an agent who was posing as a security guard at the research facility. Whoever did that is trying to set him up to take the blame."

Marin figured Lucky wasn't buying that or this entire conversation.

Her father's eyes narrowed when he looked at Lucky. "But Dexter says he won't come while you're here, Randall. And he wants you to leave immediately."

It was another shock. Not that Dexter wanted to

come home. But that he'd even mentioned Randall, Marin's dead ex-boyfriend.

"I want to see that e-mail," Lucky insisted.

"I'm sure you do," her father snarled. "But first I want you to answer one question. Since you've supposedly never met anyone in Marin's family, mind explaining how the hell my son knows you?"

Chapter Eight

How the hell does my son know you?

Lucky hadn't been able to provide an answer to Howard Sheppard, nor had he speculated to the man. He'd ended the inquisition by walking away. Now, two hours later, he still didn't know the answer to Howard's question.

Was the e-mail bogus? And if it was real, did that mean Dexter knew who Lucky really was and why he was at the ranch?

Of course, another possibility was that Howard had asked Dexter to make that demand. After all, what better and faster way to get Lucky off the ranch than to tie Dexter's homecoming to his departure? It would give Howard and Lois everything they wanted.

Their son's return.

And their daughter and grandson at the ranch with no ally, other than Marin's grandmother, who was too old to put up much of a fight. After all, Helen hadn't been able to stop the Sheppards so far. That's why Lucky had refused to leave and then ordered Marin's parents out of the room.

Well, it was one of the reasons anyway.

That kissing session with Marin was another.

Pushing that uncomfortable thought aside, Lucky concentrated on the images from the surveillance disks on his laptop. So far, he hadn't seen anything or anyone suspicious, and he'd been looking for well over an hour. He'd hoped to have spotted Dexter doing something incriminating by now.

He heard Noah stir, and Lucky got up from the desk to check on him. But Noah was still sleeping peacefully in the crib in the sitting room.

Lucky leaned down, gave Noah a light kiss on the cheek and turned to go back to the bedroom, but another sound stopped him. Marin came out of the bathroom. Toweling her damp hair, she was dressed in a turquoise-blue robe that was nearly the same color as her eyes.

She didn't look so pale now, probably because the hot steamy shower had given her skin a pinkish flush. She'd changed the bandage on her forehead, replacing it was a Band-Aid that covered the stitches. It was less noticeable, even though it still exposed the bruise left from the impact.

"Everything okay?" she asked in a whisper.

He nodded. "Just making sure he's all right."

Marin walked closer, close enough for him to catch her scent. Lucky hadn't remembered strawberry shampoo ever smelling that good.

"It's probably best that you try to distance yourself from him," she said, her voice still soft. "Since you'll only be around him a couple more days, I don't want him to get too attached."

Lucky thought it might be too late for that. For both of them. But Marin was right. Noah wasn't his to claim, even though his feelings for Noah were the most real thing he'd felt since his sister's death. Noah was young and wouldn't remember him, but Lucky would certainly remember the little boy.

"The same applies to us," Marin added, scratching her eyebrow. She shifted her position and adjusted the sash on her robe. "That kiss in the closet shouldn't have happened."

He had to agree with that, even though saying it to himself didn't make the sensations go away.

"I want to kiss you again," he admitted.

Her shoulders snapped back. "But you won't," she insisted, sounding about as convinced as Lucky felt. "We need to keep our hands off each other."

"It's not my hands you should be worried about," he mumbled, causing her to laugh.

"Tell you what, if the kissing urge hits us again," she said, "let's make ourselves count to ten. That might give us just enough time to realize what a huge mistake we'd be making."

Right.

The side of her bathrobe slipped a little, easing off her shoulder. Her *bare* shoulder. And he got just a glimpse of the top of her right breast and her nipple.

"Oh, man. You're not wearing anything beneath that bathrobe?"

She jerked the sides together to close the gap. "I came out to check on Noah. Then, I was going to get dressed."

"So you're naked?"

Why couldn't he just let this subject drop? Because he was suddenly aroused beyond belief.

So, he did something totally stupid. He reached out, caught on to her shoulders.

And yeah, he kissed her again, all the while convincing himself that if he stopped, she'd give into the emotion caused by the danger and the adrenaline. She'd get worried and depressed again. He also tried to convince himself that he wasn't enjoying it, that it was therapeutic.

A bald-faced lie.

He was enjoying the heck out of it. The feel of her mouth against his. The way she fit in his arms. The hot-as-sin scent of hers stirring around him. Yes, he was enjoying it.

And he wasn't the only one.

Marin moaned in pure pleasure. That's when he knew he had to stop. With Noah only a couple of inches away, this couldn't continue.

He pulled away from her, ran his tongue over his bottom lip and wasn't surprised when he tasted her there. It was a taste that might be permanently etched into his brain.

"We shouldn't have done that, either," she grumbled. "With all the emotional baggage that each of us has, it wouldn't work between us. Every time you look at me, you'll see my brother, the man you blame for your sister's death."

"You're right," he said. Except it was partly a lie. Marin would always be Dexter's sister, but she was also her own woman.

And he was attracted to her.

Still, Marin was correct. They shouldn't be kissing. Maybe if he said it enough to himself, his body would start to listen. Heaven knows it hadn't listened to anything else he'd demanded it not do.

Lucky tried to get his mind back on business. "While you were in the shower, I got another call from my friend Cal Rico. He's a special agent in the Justice Department, and he's the one responsible for getting those surveillance disks to the sheriff who got them to me."

"Have you found anything?" she asked.

"Not yet. I'm still looking. But Cal let me know that he's using department resources to look into the e-mail Dexter sent your father."

"I think that e-mail was a hoax. It might be my father's way of trying to get you to leave."

Marin and he were obviously on the same page. "Either way, Cal will find out the origin of the e-mail."

Lucky didn't doubt his friend's ability, but verifying the e-mail was a long shot. If Dexter had indeed sent the e-mail, then he would have almost certainly covered his tracks.

Marin turned and tipped her head toward his laptop. "So, what have you seen on those surveillance disks?"

"A lot of people. Not Dexter though. But if he came onto the train, he was probably wearing a disguise." He paused. "Maybe you could take a look at them and see if you can spot him."

She frowned, then nodded. "All right. But for the record, I don't expect to see him. I think we should be looking for Grady Duran."

"Absolutely. But since you know what he looks like, as well, this might go faster with both of us going over the surveillance." But he rethought that when he glanced at the bandage on her head. "Then again, why don't you get some rest, and I'll finish reviewing the disks."

"I'll help," she insisted, going straight for the desk.

Lucky huffed, but he knew it wouldn't do any good to try to talk her out of this. He was quickly learning that Marin was as stubborn as he was.

That only made him want her more.

"By the way," he whispered, just in case there was a bug in the room. "Are there any extra linens around?" He glanced at the bed as they walked past it. "I'm thinking it's not a good idea if we share the same mattress."

She understood completely. "The extra bedding's in the linen closet. Next to my parents' room. Probably not a good idea to advertise the fact we need two sleeping areas."

True. They already had enough issues with Howard and Lois. "No problem. I'll just take the floor."

"We could build a barrier with the pillows—"

He stopped and stared at her mouth. "I get your point," she conceded. "Pillows wouldn't be much of a barrier."

Heck, he wasn't sure being on the floor would be much of a barrier, either, but Lucky knew he wouldn't get a minute of sleep next to her. And he needed a clear head along with a little sleep to get through the next two days.

Lucky clicked the resume feature on the surveillance

disk, and images immediately appeared on the screen. Marin dragged a chair next to his, and they sat, silently. Since Lucky figured a visual aid might help Marin, he took out the photo of Dexter, Grady Duran, his sister and Brenna Martel and positioned it next to his laptop.

"This is the station in Fort Worth, where we both got on," he explained. "The security cameras were on the entire time that passengers were boarding." He backtracked the disk to show her the recorded image of Noah and her.

Lucky was about ten yards behind them.

Several times during that brief walk from the terminal to the train, Marin glanced back, but each time Lucky tried to make sure he disappeared in the crowd.

"Well, if I didn't notice you," she remarked, "then I could have missed Grady Duran."

"Or your brother."

That earned him a scowl that he probably deserved, and they continued to watch the disk. "Okay, this is where I left off before I went to check on Noah. The train is about to leave. There are only a couple of people left at the terminal door. And none of them look anything like Grady Duran or Dexter."

"None of those people are carrying a large suitcase, either."

Without taking her attention from the screen, Marin got up, opened a bottle of pills that she'd placed on the dresser and took one of the tablets, washing it down with a glass of water she took from their dinner tray.

"Pain meds?" Lucky questioned.

"No. I took one of those earlier. This is for my

seizures. I have to take them twice a day—a small price to pay for being as normal as I can be."

Yes. It was. But he wondered how all of this additional stress was affecting her health. "How old were you when you had your first seizure?"

"Twelve. I was riding a roller coaster at an amusement park. Scared the devil out of everyone, including myself. Before that, my parents were only overprotective. After that, they got obsessive."

He shrugged. "But you said you haven't had a seizure in years. That should cause them to back off."

"You'd think." She gave a heavy sigh and sank down next to him again. "They do love me in their own crazy way. I know that. But they just can't seem to give up control. They're scared I'll have another seizure, and they won't be around to help me."

Lucky understood that. He'd felt that way about his sister. And now Noah.

Hell, Marin was on that list, too.

Since it was starting to feel like one of those moments where he wanted to pull Marin in his arms and protect the hell out of her, Lucky just turned his focus back the surveillance images.

And then he saw it.

Just as the train was about to close the boarding doors, a passenger carrying a black suitcase hurried forward. Dressed in a bulky knee-length denim coat, the person wore jeans, gloves and a Texas Rangers baseball cap. With that cap sitting low on the forehead and with the bulky clothes, it was hard to tell who the person was.

Lucky backtracked the disk to the point just prior to boarding, froze the frame and zoomed in.

"Does that look like Dexter?" Lucky asked.

Marin moved even closer to the screen and studied it. "No. The body language is wrong. Dexter didn't slump like that."

"Maybe he would if he was trying to keep his face from being seen." Lucky advanced the disk one frame farther and got a better view of the face. Well, the lower part of it anyway. That cap created a strategic shadow.

Marin shook her head. "It's not Dexter. Maybe Grady Duran?"

That was the next possibility that Lucky had planned to consider. He rewound even more of the disk, looking for the best face shot possible. When he thought he'd found it, he zoomed in again. And this time, he didn't have to ask if that was Dexter or Grady Duran.

Because it wasn't either of the men. It wasn't a man at all.

He was looking at the face of a dead woman.

His sister, Kinley.

Chapter Nine

From her chair in the sitting room, Marin finished her scrambled eggs and watched her grandmother feed Noah. Noah and her gran were doing great, but she couldn't say the same for Lucky.

He still hadn't moved.

He'd been at that desk in the adjoining bedroom for at least two hours, and it didn't appear he was going to move anytime soon. Right now, he was on hold, waiting for Agent Cal Rico to come back on the line. With his cell phone sandwiched between his shoulder and ear, his fingers worked frantically on the keyboard of his laptop. What he wasn't doing was eating his breakfast.

Marin stood, put her mug of tea aside and blew Noah and her grandmother a kiss. She went into the bedroom toward the desk. "Why don't you come with me for a walk?" she suggested to Lucky.

He didn't even glance up at her. He kept his attention superglued to the e-mail he was typing on the computer screen. "You should be resting."

"It's 9:00 a.m. I've already rested. You, on the other

hand, haven't. I know for a fact that you didn't get much sleep. You were in the bathroom talking on your cell phone most of the night."

"I'm sorry I kept you up," he grumbled.

She huffed. "I'm concerned about you, not me."

He huffed, too. "I'm not tired."

Oh, yes, he was. And he was frustrated and confused. Marin totally understood why. Before last night, all the evidence pointed to his dead sister having had no part in the wrongdoing at the research facility. But yet there she was in that surveillance video.

"I'm still here," Lucky quickly said into the phone. Agent Cal Rico had obviously come back on the line, hopefully with some answers.

Lucky paused. "I need your lab to keep trying to enhance that image from the disk." Another pause. "Yeah, I'm asking the impossible, but I have to know if that was Kinley getting onto the train."

Another pause, but she could see that Lucky was processing something. "Bits of money?" he questioned. "And you're sure that was in the suitcase, along with some clothes. Just how big was that explosive device anyway?"

Marin couldn't hear the agent's answer, but after several terse answers from Lucky, he jabbed the end-call button and cursed. He lowered his voice to mumble profanity, however, when his attention landed on Helen feeding Noah rice cereal for breakfast. Marin figured there was more cereal on her son and her grandmother than in Noah's tummy.

Noah grinned when he realized he had everyone's

attention, and Lucky gave him a half-hearted smile in return before he groaned and rubbed his eyes.

That did it. Marin caught on to his arm, and in the same motion, she took his leather jacket from the back of the chair. "We're taking that walk," she insisted.

Lucky stood but didn't move. His stare was a challenge, and it let her know that he had no plans to budge.

"There are things we need to discuss," she whispered. "And I'd prefer not to do that in a room that's bugged. Plus, I could use some fresh air."

He glanced at his laptop, his silent cell phone and then at Noah.

"A *short* walk," Lucky finally conceded. "I don't want you out in that cold very long."

Marin didn't argue with the restriction. She turned toward the sitting room, but before she could even ask her grandmother if she'd watch Noah for a couple of minutes, the woman was already nodding. "Go ahead. Take as much time as you need."

She thanked her grandmother, grabbed her coat from the closet, put it on and led Lucky out the enclosed patio exit before he could change his mind.

Thankfully, it wasn't nearly as cold as it had been the day before. Still, it was in the low fifties, and Marin hugged her coat close to her so that she wouldn't get a chill.

"About an hour ago, I called a lawyer that I know in Fort Worth," Marin explained. "I asked him to contact the psychologist to see if he'd cancel the interview since I don't feel it's necessary."

"Don't count on that happening. The psychologist is probably in your parents' pockets, as well."

That might be true, but Marin had to try. Lucky wasn't in the right state of mind for that interview. Neither was she, and Marin hoped there was still some way to prevent it from happening.

She spotted her mother staring at them from the window, and Marin maneuvered him away from the yard and onto a trail that would take them to the edge of the one of the pastures. "Either way, I want you to leave this morning so you can find your sister."

He tossed her a puzzling glance. "Leave? If I don't do that interview, Marin, you could lose Noah."

Yes, and that terrified her. Still, she couldn't make Lucky stay, not when he had so much at stake. "But if you don't look for your sister before the trail goes cold, you might not find her."

"If that's really my sister."

So, he had doubts, as well. "You're thinking it's a look-alike?"

He shrugged. "I'm thinking if my sister had been alive for the past year, then she would have already contacted me."

"I seem to remember saying the same thing to you about Dexter."

"But my sister wasn't doing anything illegal." Then, he frowned. "At least, I don't think she was."

Neither was Marin. Anything was possible. "Let's assume then that it was a look-alike, maybe even someone in disguise. Brenna Martel, maybe?"

"No. I'd recognize Brenna." He said it so quickly that he'd obviously already considered it. "Plus, there's also the issue of the blood. Both Brenna's and my sister's blood was found all over the floor in Dexter's research lab. The CSI guys said there was little chance that the women could have survived after losing that much blood."

But survival was possible. And that led Marin to the next question. "Was the suitcase the woman was carrying the one that contained the explosives?"

"It appears to be. It also contained money and clothes. Agent Rico believes the explosives were hidden in a concealed compartment."

Since they'd already ruled out the logical explanations, Marin tried out one that was unlikely but still possible. "So, maybe your sister is alive. Maybe she has amnesia from her injuries at the research facility? That would explain why she hasn't contacted you."

"But it wouldn't explain why she got on that train."

Good point. Marin quickly tried to come up with something to counter that. "Maybe she didn't know she was carrying explosives?"

"I considered that at about 1:00 a.m. when I checked the records of everyone injured. There was no injured woman fitting my sister's description. If she hadn't known she was carrying explosives, then she would have been sitting near the suitcase."

"Perhaps not. She could have gone to the bathroom or something. She could have changed seats for a variety of reasons. Like maybe some guy was hitting on her."

The corner of his mouth lifted for a very short smile.

He stopped at a small rocky stream that cut through the pasture. The water created a miniature valley and was banked with chunks of white limestone and slate-gray clay. It was a peaceful spot where she'd spent a lot of time as a kid. A bare pasture was on one side and in the spring would be filled with Angus cattle that would graze there. On the other side was a barn that stored equipment, tractors and massive circular bales of hay.

Lucky could have easily stepped over the stream, but instead he stared into the water. "I want to believe she's alive and that she's done nothing wrong. That'd be the best-case scenario. But even if Kinley has amnesia or whatever, she obviously needs help."

If Grady Duran was gutsy enough to press Marin for answers about Dexter, how hard would he press Kinley? Lucky's sister could be in danger.

"Let's go back to the house," Marin insisted. "I'll have someone drive you to the train station, the airport or wherever you need to go to find her."

He continued to look into the water. "That would make your parents very happy. They'd have you right where they want you. Here, alone and in fear of losing your son."

"I won't lose Noah," she promised. "I'll figure out a way to postpone or cancel that meeting." Though Marin didn't have a clue how she was going to do that. "Besides, the lawyer in Fort Worth is sending someone down to talk to the judge and the psychologist."

"If all that fails, you'd be giving up a lot," he said. "Just so I can leave."

He was thinking of her. Well, maybe more Noah than her. But whichever, he was putting himself and his needs after hers.

And Marin couldn't help but appreciate that.

There it was. That weird intimacy again. It was growing. They seemed to be racing toward some heated passionate encounter that neither of them seemed capable of stopping.

Worse, she wasn't sure she wanted to stop it.

He reached out and brushed his hand over her arm. Even through the wool coat, she could feel his touch. Then, he trailed those clever fingers over her cheek. The moment was far warmer than it should have been.

But then, Lucky's hand froze.

"What's wrong?" Marin asked.

He didn't answer. He didn't have to. Marin heard the thick roar of the engine and looked in the direction of the sound. A large rust-scabbed tan-colored truck with heavily tinted windows bolted out from the barn.

Her first thought was a ranch hand had loaded the truck bed with hay to take out to one of the other pastures. But there was no hay. The driver, hidden behind all that dark glass, gunned the engine.

The truck came right at them.

LUCKY'S HEART DROPPED. This couldn't be happening.

He drew his weapon and hooked his arm around Marin's waist. He didn't wait to see if that truck was the threat that he thought it was.

Waiting was too big of a risk.

Firing shots through that windshield might not be the best idea, either, because shooting would mean stopping to take aim. The driver could be low in the seat, or leaning far to the side, out of range. Lucky couldn't stand there and shoot when he might not even hit the guy. He had to get Marin out of the path of the oncoming vehicle and then figure out if he needed to stop the driver.

They jumped the shallow stream, and ran like hell. He hoped the soggy clay banks would be enough to slow down the truck.

It wasn't.

The four-wheel drive went right through it, sloshing rocks and water out from the mammoth-size tires.

So Lucky did the only thing he could do. He continued to run and pulled Marin right along with him.

Glancing back over his shoulder, Lucky tried to assess their situation. It damn sure wasn't good. That truck was closing in fast. And there was literally no place to hide in an open pasture. Their best bet was to try to double back and get to the barn.

Easier said that done.

The truck was in their path and coming straight for them. And it was quickly eating up the meager distance between them.

"Go right," Lucky yelled to Marin, hoping that she heard him over the roar of the engine.

Just in case she didn't, Lucky dragged her in the direction he wanted her to go.

The driver adjusted, and came at them again.

"Who's doing this?" Marin shouted.

But Lucky didn't have to time to speculate. Marin and he had to sprint to their right. The truck was so close that Lucky could feel the heat from the engine. And the front bumper missed them by less than a couple of inches.

Marin stumbled. Lucky's heart did, too. But he didn't let her fall. A fall could be fatal for both of them. Instead, he grabbed her and zigzagged to their left.

It wasn't enough.

The driver came right at them, and to avoid being hit, Lucky latched on to Marin even tighter and dove out of the way.

They landed hard on the packed winter soil.

Lucky came up, ready to fire. "Run!" he shouted to Marin.

Thankfully, she managed to do that and started sprinting toward the barn. The truck had to turn around and backtrack to come at him again. Those few precious seconds of time might be the only break they got.

So, Lucky took aim at the windshield and fired.

A thick blast tore through the pasture, drowning out even the sound of the roaring truck engine. The bullet slammed into the safety glass and shattered it, but it stayed in place, concealing the identity of the driver.

Maybe someone from the house would hear the shot and come running. But the house was a good quarter of a mile away, and it might take Marin's parents or the ranch hands a couple of minutes just to figure out what was going on.

By then, they could be dead.

Lucky dodged another attempt to run him down, repositioned himself and fired again. This bullet skipped off the truck's roof and sent sparks flying when it ripped through the metal. What it didn't do was stop the driver.

The truck came at him again.

Lucky dove out of the way. But not before the front bumper scraped against his right thigh.

He fired another shot into the windshield and prayed he could stop the SOB who was trying to kill them.

From the corner of his eye, Lucky spotted Marin running toward the barn. She looked over her shoulder at him, and he could see the terror on her face. Still, she was alive, and the driver didn't appear to be going after her.

Lucky dove for the ground again, but just like before, the driver adjusted and swung back around. He figured if he could keep this up until Marin got to the barn, then maybe she could call for help.

But on the next turn, the driver changed course. He didn't come after Lucky. He did a doughnut in the pasture and slammed on the accelerator.

Hell. He was going after Marin.

She was still a good thirty feet from the barn, and even once inside, she might not be protected. This SOB might just drive the truck right in there after her. If that happened, she'd be trapped.

There was no way he could outrun the truck and get to Marin first, so Lucky took aim again and fired. This time, the back windshield blew apart, and he got just a glimpse of the driver.

Whoever it was wore a dark knit cap.

Lucky fired again. And again. Until he saw the truck's brake lights flash on. Maybe one of the shots had hit him. Lucky hoped so. But just in case this was some kind of ploy to make them think he was hurt, Lucky kept his gun aimed, and he raced forward.

Ahead of him, with the truck at a dead stop in between them, Marin ducked into the barn. Thank God. She might be safer there.

Lucky raced forward, keeping his eye on the driver and looking out for any weapon the guy might have.

Lucky slowed when he neared the truck and kept his gun ready. "Step out of the vehicle," Lucky warned.

He needed the guy out in the open because he could be just sitting there waiting for his best opportunity to kill Lucky so he could go after Marin.

Nothing.

No reaction. No sound.

Not even any movement.

Lucky inched forward. And with each step he prayed he wouldn't look inside that vehicle and see his sister. If she'd been the one on that train, if she'd set those explosives, then she might want him dead. Why, he didn't know. And he didn't want to have to find out.

He took another step, then another—aware that between the pulse hammering in his ears and the drone of the engine, he couldn't hear much. But he didn't need to hear well to realize that the driver was about to do something that Lucky was certain he wouldn't like.

The brake lights went off. In the same second, the driver jammed the accelerator again.

"No!" Lucky yelled.

He added another prayer that Marin had found some safe place in the barn.

To his right, he heard voices. Someone shouting their names. Two of the ranch hands were making their way across the pasture. Neither was armed, but because they were closer to the barn, Lucky figured they would stand a better chance of getting to Marin in time.

The driver must have thought so, as well. Because he didn't head for the barn.

Instead, he made a beeline for the back of the pasture, obviously trying get away.

"Take care of Marin," Lucky shouted to the ranch hands as he started sprinting after the truck.

Chapter Ten

Marin glanced at the clock on the nightstand next to her bed. It was less than a minute since the last time she'd checked. It felt like an eternity, but it had only been a little over an hour that Sheriff Whitley and Lucky had been searching for the driver of that truck.

Maybe Lucky and the sheriff had already caught the man. Maybe he was already on his way to the jail, ready to tell the sheriff why he wanted her dead.

"Maybe," she mumbled.

She hugged Noah to her chest and rocked him. After nearly being killed in the pasture, she needed to hold her son and try to deal with the adrenaline shock and the aftermath.

"He's asleep," her grandmother whispered. "Want me to put him in his crib?"

Marin was about to decline, to say she wanted another minute or two to hold Noah, but then she heard footsteps. Because the overwhelming sense of danger was still with her, she bolted from the bed, ready to run so that she could protect her baby. But running wasn't necessary.

Lucky appeared in the doorway.

"The driver got away," he announced.

So much for her wish. "But the truck left tracks. The sheriff will be able to follow him."

Lucky shook his head. "The truck drove through a fence in the back of the pasture, and Sheriff Whitley thinks he escaped using an old ranch trail."

So, he was gone. Gone! And that meant Lucky, Noah and she weren't safe. There could be another attack.

Her grandmother came and took Noah, gently removing him from her arms, and carried him into the sitting room. Since Marin didn't want to wake him and they obviously had to talk, she grabbed on to his arm and led him into her walk-in closet.

"I'm sorry," Lucky mumbled. "I should have caught that SOB while he was still in the pasture."

His frustration and anger were so strong they were palatable. Marin knew how he felt. "He was in a truck. You were on foot. Catching him was a long shot at best."

She hoped her words comforted her as much as she was trying to comfort Lucky. This wasn't his fault. In fact, he'd done everything in his power to stop her from being hurt. He had literally put himself in harm's way to protect her.

"Are you okay?" he asked. He leaned away from her and checked her over from head to toe.

"I'm fine." Marin checked him, as well, and wasn't pleased to see grass and mud on his jacket and jeans. But then, he'd had to hit the ground several times to dodge the truck. "Were you hurt?"

"No." There was a thin veneer of bravado covering all the emotion that lay just beneath the surface. Lucky held on to his composure for several seconds before he cursed. "First the explosion. Now, this. I brought all of this to your doorstep."

"I doubt it." She touched his arm and rubbed gently. "Since this particular doorstep at the ranch is also Dexter's, the danger might have happened whether you were here or not."

She saw the flash of realization in his eyes, and he glanced over his shoulder in the direction of the sitting room, where her son was sleeping. When Lucky's gaze came back to hers, there was a different emotion. One she understood because she was a parent.

Lucky cursed again and pulled her to him. His grip was too tight. His breath, hot and fast. She felt his heartbeat hammer against her chest.

He mumbled something she didn't understand. The words came out as mere breath brushing against her hair.

"I didn't get a good a look at the driver of that truck," he said. "Did you?"

"No. But I don't think it was Dexter." Marin immediately reexamined the images racing through her head. "Still, I can't be sure, especially since I didn't see the driver's face." She paused. "First there was that e-mail from Dexter. And then you see Kinley on the surveillance video. Two of the people we thought were dead might not be."

He nodded. "Now the question is, are they responsible for what's happening to us?" Lucky also paused. "But just like you can't believe Dexter would do this, I can't believe Kinley would, either."

Neither of them could be objective about the situation. Marin knew that. But it didn't mean they were wrong. Maybe both of their siblings were alive.

And innocent.

There was a sharp knock at the bedroom door, and Lucky drew his gun from his shoulder holster. He headed out of the closet. Fast. He obviously wasn't taking any chances. But the vigilance was unnecessary because the person on the other side of the door was Sheriff Jack Whitley.

Marin had known Jack most of her life, and he hadn't changed much. A real cowboy cop. Tall and lanky with dark hair and gray eyes, Jack had on jeans and a white shirt with his badge clipped onto a leather belt.

Since Jack obviously wanted to talk to them, Marin thought of the bug, and her parents who were probably trying to hear every word. "We'll have some privacy out here," she told him, and Jack didn't say anything until they walked into the enclosed patio.

"My deputy wasn't able to find the truck or the driver," Jack announced, causing Lucky to groan. The sheriff volleyed glances at them and kept his voice low. "You're sure this guy tried to kill you?"

"Dead sure," Lucky insisted.

Jack nodded and seemed to accept that as gospel truth. "The ranch hands said the truck wasn't used very often and was put in the barn for the winter. Keys were almost certainly in the ignition, and the barn wasn't locked, either. They didn't see anyone around that part of the pasture."

"I guess that means no one saw the driver?" she asked.

"No one," Jack Whitley verified. "But there were footprints in the barn, and there's a Texas Ranger coming out from the crime lab. He'll take impressions and try to see if that'll tell us anything." His attention landed on Marin. "I spoke to your dad. He says this has nothing to do with Dexter."

It took Marin several long moments to figure out how to answer that. "I want to believe that."

Jack didn't answer right away, either. "Yeah. I understand. But since I have a job to do and since I'm sure you don't want to dodge any more trucks, I have to say that the circumstantial evidence is pointing to Dexter."

"Why do you say that?" Lucky wanted to know.

The sheriff took out the envelope he had tucked beneath his arm. "A visitor who just arrived and this." He extracted a photo from the envelope and handed it to Lucky.

Marin leaned in so she could see the photograph, as well. It was a grainy shot, taken from what appeared to be the surveillance camera outside the bank on Main Street. But even with the grainy shot, it wasn't hard to make out the woman's face.

"That's Brenna Martel," Lucky confirmed. "She's someone else I thought was dead."

Jack made a sound of agreement. "While I was looking around for that truck driver, I had the Justice Department give me a case update." Now, his attention turned to Lucky. "I know who you really are. And it seems your sister and now this woman might both be alive. Dexter, too."

Three people, all presumed dead. Now, all alive. Innocent people didn't usually let their friends and families believe they were dead unless something bad, very bad, was going on.

"You said something about a visitor?" Lucky prompted.

Marin held her breath. God, had one of those three come to the ranch?

"The visitor is the other player in the case," Jack explained. "Grady Duran."

"He's here?" And Lucky didn't sound any happier about it than Marin was.

"Duran's here," the sheriff verified. "And he's demanding to speak to both of you now."

LUCKY WOULD HAVE preferred to delay this meeting.

After all, Marin was just coming down from a horrible ordeal. The last thing he wanted was to add any more tension to her already stress-filled day. But this chat with Duran might give them answers, and right now, answers were in very short supply.

"I'd rather you waited in the bedroom," Lucky repeated to Marin. But like the other two times he'd said it, she didn't budge. She walked side by side with him toward the front of the ranch house where the sheriff had said Grady Duran was waiting to see them. Sheriff Whitley was right behind them.

"If Duran's the one who just tried to kill us, then I want the chance to confront him," Marin insisted.

That's what Lucky was afraid of. That Duran had indeed been behind the wheel of the truck. And that Duran would try to kill them again.

But why?

Lucky kept going back to that critical question. If Duran was on the up and up and simply wanted answers as to Dexter's whereabouts, then he wouldn't want Marin

and him dead. He'd follow them, demand to talk to them.
But it would serve no purpose for Duran to kill them.

Well, at least no purpose that Lucky could think of.

Still, he couldn't take any more risks when it came
to Marin. As they approached the great room of the
ranch house, Lucky drew his weapon. He checked over
his shoulder and saw that the sheriff had placed his
hand over the butt on his own service revolver. Good.
They were both ready in case something went wrong.

Duran was pacing in the great room. The man was
just over six feet tall and solid. He wore a perfectly
tailored suit. Cashmere, probably. He impatiently
checked his watch at the exact moment his gaze connected with Lucky's.

Duran wasn't alone. On the other side of the massive
room near the stone fireplace stood Lois and Howard
Sheppard. They didn't look happy about their unexpected visitor.

"He said it was important, that it's about Dexter,"
Lois volunteered. "I was hoping he'd know where my
son is. That's the only reason we let him in." She didn't
go any closer to her daughter. Probably because both the
sheriff and Lucky moved protectively in front of Marin.

However, Marin would have no part in that. She
merely stepped to the side. "Were you the one who tried
to kill us?" she demanded.

"No," Duran readily answered, though the denial
hadn't come easily. The muscles in his jaw were so
tight that Lucky was surprised the man could even
speak. "I could ask you the same thing. Someone
planted an explosive device in my rental car."

Lucky glanced at the sheriff who confirmed that with a nod. "The device was on a timer, but failed to detonate. If it had, I would have been blown to smithereens."

"Well, neither Lucky nor I set an explosive," Marin grumbled. "But I'm sure you're not short of suspects. With your caustic personality, you've made your share of enemies."

Duran didn't react to her insult. He whipped his gaze toward Lois and Howard. "What about you two? Either of you into blowing things up to protect your son?"

Lois made a slight gasp and flattened her hand over her chest. Howard hardly reacted, other than a slight narrowing of his eyes. "I think you've already worn out your welcome."

Duran shook his head. "I'm not leaving yet. Not until you tell me where Dexter is."

"We thought you knew," Lois accused.

Lucky waited for someone to respond, but the room fell silent.

"All right. I'll get this conversation rolling," Duran continued a moment later, aiming his comment at Howard and Lois. "Here's my theory. You want me out of the picture because when I find Dexter, I'm going to haul his butt off to jail. Then, I'll figure out how to get back every penny he owes me. And by the way, that's a lot of pennies. Your son is in debt to me for the tune of nearly six million dollars."

Six million. Lucky had no idea it was that much. That was a big motive for murder. It also explained why Duran was desperate to find Dexter.

Howard took a menacing step forward, but Duran held out his hands. Then, he pulled an envelope from his pocket and slapped it onto the coffee table. "That's a copy of the letter my lawyer sent to the state attorney general and the Justice Department. I haven't had the best relationship with those two groups in the past, but I've decided to help them with their ongoing investigation."

"So?" Howard challenged.

But Lucky knew what this meant, and it had just upped the stakes.

So far, Duran had tried to find Dexter on his own. He'd not only refused to assist the Justice Department, he had likely withheld critical evidence. Now, Duran's cooperation could blow this case wide open, and it could lead them directly to Dexter or at least to the truth of what'd really happened in that research facility.

"So," Duran repeated, "I'd rather deal with Dexter on my own, but I'm willing to cut a deal with the Feds. I'm also willing to hang your son to get revenge for what he did to me. Understand?"

"We understand," Lois snapped.

The corner of Duran's mouth lifted. "I'm not going away. And I'm not backing down. I'm staying in Willow Ridge, and I plan to haunt you, your daughter and her fiancé until you lead me to Dexter."

"Just make sure your threats stay verbal," the sheriff warned Duran. "Because you'll be the one arrested if you cross the line."

Duran mumbled something and turned to leave. Lucky followed him. Marin would have no doubt done the same, but the phone rang, and several seconds later, one of the housekeepers announced that the call was for Marin.

Lucky went to the porch and caught Duran's arm before he could head down the steps. "Talk to me about Kinley Ford. What do you know about her?"

"She's dead." He paused, studied Lucky's expression and then shook off his grip with far more force than necessary. "At least the police think she is. You have any information to the contrary?"

"No," Lucky lied.

Duran kept staring. "Kinley Ford was at the research facility the night of the explosion. I know, because I was there, too."

"You saw her?" But Lucky already knew the answer. Or rather the answer that Duran had given the investigators when they had first interviewed him.

"I did see her. Dexter, Brenna and Kinley." Duran glanced around the grounds. The vigilant glance of a man who was wary of his surroundings. "Something was off, but I didn't know what. Dexter was acting even less normal than usual. I mean, he was forever pulling that prima donna genius crap where he'd say he couldn't be interrupted. But that night, he was wound up so tight that I could see he was about to snap."

Probably because Dexter was about to put his plan into action. "Did you ask why he was on edge?"

He lifted a shoulder, glanced around again "The prototype of the chemical project was due within forty-eight hours. Dexter kept saying it was ready, but that I couldn't see it until he'd given it one final test." Duran cursed. "I should have forced him to show it to me."

Lucky gave that some thought. "So, if the prototype wasn't ready, you think Dexter could have set the explosion, run with his research project and then faked his death?"

Duran met him eye to eye. "I think he faked not only his own death but maybe Kinley Ford's and Brenna Martel's."

Yes. After seeing his sister on that surveillance video, Lucky had toyed with that idea, too. Still, there was all that blood. "Why would Dexter have done that?"

"Simple. Because he needed their help to finish the project. Plus, he knew what a fortune that chemical weapon would make, and he didn't want to hand it over to the investors. Maybe he thought he could get away with it if everyone associated with the project was presumed dead. Then, he could wait a year or two and use an alias when he tried to sell it on the black market."

"There's a big problem with that theory. Kinley Ford wouldn't have cooperated with Dexter's illegal plan. She wasn't a criminal," Lucky insisted.

Duran shrugged. "Maybe she wasn't a willing participant."

Hell. That theory raced through and left him with more questions than when he'd started this investigation. "What could Dexter have used to force her to cooperate?"

"Right off the top of my head, I'd say maybe she was a fool for love. Brenna certainly was." Another glance around. "But I know that Dexter had already broken things off with Brenna."

Lucky hated to even put this out there, but it was something he had to know. "And you think that Dexter then started an affair with Kinley?"

Another shrug. "Something was going on between them. Hell for all I know, maybe Kinley Ford was the mastermind of that explosion. Or Brenna. *Women*," he added like profanity.

Lucky dismissed his sister's involvement. He had to. Because he couldn't deal with the alternative. "But if Dexter and both women are alive, why haven't they surfaced?"

"Maybe they have." Duran extracted a set of car keys from his pocket. "My advice? Don't trust anyone around here."

"You think Dexter wants me dead, too?"

Duran blinked. "He has no reason to kill you. Does he?"

Oh, Lucky could think of a reason. If Dexter knew who he really was, then he might try to eliminate him. Dexter would figure out that Lucky wouldn't stop until he had justice for Kinley.

If Kinley needed justice, that is.

Lucky hated that he was beginning to doubt her.

"But I think Dexter's parents would do anything to keep you out of their daughter's life," Duran continued. "The stories Dexter used to tell me about them. They're manipulative enough to be very dangerous." He headed down the steps.

Like Duran, Lucky wasn't certain that Howard and Lois's parental concerns were all just threats.

He turned to go back inside, but as he reached for the door, it opened. Marin was there, and he instantly knew something was wrong. She'd probably gotten some bad news from that phone call.

"Is it your brother?" he asked.

She shook her head. "The psychologist, Dr. Ross Blevins. He called to let us know that the judge ordered that the interview be completed today."

"Impossible." Lucky didn't even have to think about it. "The driver of that truck might be sitting out there, waiting for round two." He glared at Lois and Howard. They'd no doubt tried to orchestrate scheduling the interview when both Marin and he were not mentally ready.

"I know, and that's what I told the psychologist. But he said the judge insisted. He wants a preliminary report on his desk by close of business today."

Lucky cursed under his breath and intensified the glare at the Sheppards. Lois at least had the decency to look a little uncomfortable. Howard, however, couldn't quite contain his pleasure. To him, this was the next step in regaining control of his daughter.

But that wasn't going to happen.

"I'll call the psychologist," Lucky told her. He hooked his arm around her waist so he could lead her back to the bedroom. "I'll work out all of this."

But Marin didn't budge. "It's too late. Dr. Blevins is already on his way over here to conduct the interview. He should be here any minute."

Chapter Eleven

"Marin was nearly murdered today," she heard Lucky say to Dr. Blevins. Lucky had called the psychologist despite the fact the man was already en route. "The sheriff and his deputy are still here checking out the crime scene. Plus, she just got out of the hospital yesterday."

Marin continued to feed Noah his bottle, and she tried not to react to what was going on around her. Impossible to do. She still had dirt on the knees of her jeans. Dirt she'd gotten from trying to dodge that killer truck.

Lucky's appearance wasn't much better. He had triple the mud and dirt that she did, and unlike her, he was definitely reacting with anger. From what she could judge from the one side of the conversation she could hear, the psychologist wasn't going to postpone the interview.

Apparently aware that she had her attention elsewhere, Noah bucked a little and reached for her face. He pinched her chin, automatically causing Marin to smile.

Looking down at him, seeing that precious little face, was all the reminder she needed that somehow she had to muster enough energy and resolve to get through this ordeal.

"This meeting needs to be rescheduled," Lucky continued. "Marin's attorney hasn't arrived." He paused again. "Yes, I know it's not necessary for her attorney to be there, but we'd like him to be."

Judging from his expression, that didn't go over well with the doctor.

"I couldn't change his mind," Lucky growled a moment later. He jabbed the end-call button and shoved his phone back into his pocket. "He's already here at the ranch and is waiting for us in your father's office."

That didn't surprise her. Her father would want to listen in on the interview, as well. "As soon as I'm finished feeding Noah, we'll go ahead and get this over with."

"Take your time. Let the guy wait." Lucky sat down on the bed beside her and brushed his fingers across Noah's hair. Her son responded with a smile and turned to face Lucky. Noah no longer seemed interested in the bottle and instead reached for Lucky. Marin let her son go into his arms.

"No barfing, okay, buddy?" Lucky teased. He put Noah against his chest and patted his back to burp him.

It was such a simple gesture, something she'd done dozens of times. Still, today it seemed, well, special. Maybe because of the near-death experience. But it also had to do with Lucky. With the way he held her son. The genuine pleasure in his eyes from doing something that many would consider mundane and even a little gross.

"Thank you," Marin heard herself say. Mercy, she was actually tearing up.

Lucky met her gaze over the top of Noah's head. "For what?"

"Everything."

But she immediately regretted that. It sounded gushy. As if she wanted this arrangement to be permanent. She didn't. They were on opposite sides of an important issue: Dexter. Plus, after her ordeal with Randall, she wasn't ready to risk her heart again.

Or Noah's.

Lucky had too much personal baggage of his own to be a real father to Noah.

"The kissing has screwed things up. It gave us this…connection. And it's complicating the heck out of this situation."

Since Marin couldn't deny that and since she had no idea what to say, she figured it was a good time to just sit there and listen.

"If this interview goes well…" Lucky continued a moment later. But he didn't finish it. He didn't have to.

"You'll be leaving the ranch right away," Marin finished for him. "I know. You need to find your sister."

He brushed a kiss on Noah's cheek. "I can't leave until I'm certain you're both safe."

It was tempting to try to keep him there, but she didn't have the right. Or the courage to make a commitment. Besides, he really did need to find his sister. She could be in serious danger. And if she was the person who'd tried to kill them, he might need to stop her from setting another explosive.

"Once the interview is done, I'll leave the ranch, as well," Marin assured him. "I have enough money to hire a bodyguard. Once I'm back in Fort Worth, I'll move again. I'll make sure no one finds Noah and me."

Lucky stared at her. "You can't be sure of that."

"True. But I can't be sure of it if you're with me, either." And then she played her trump card, the one thing that she knew would convince Lucky to leave. "Besides, if Dexter is behind this, Noah and I could be in even more danger just being around you."

It stung to say that, because she didn't believe it was true. She didn't honestly believe Dexter would come after her, even if he was trying to get to Lucky. Still, she needed some leverage to get Lucky to budge in the only direction he should go.

Lucky made an unhappy sound deep within his throat and gave a crisp nod. That was it. No more conversation. No rebuttal of what she'd just said. That nod was all she got before he stood and started for the door.

Marin followed, of course. "We can leave Noah with my grandmother."

He didn't comment on that, either. Lucky merely went down the hall and knocked on her grandmother's door. "Time for the interview," Helen commented, taking Noah from Lucky. "Don't let that head doctor bully you."

Marin assured her that they wouldn't and thanked her grandmother for watching Noah.

The walk down the hall had an ominous feel to it that only got worse when they passed the living room, and saw her parents.

"This is for your own good," her father insisted, again.

"Is it?" Marin fired back, but she didn't give them more than that. She didn't want them to get any satisfaction from seeing her upset. But underneath she was well past being upset.

Dr. Ross Blevins waited in the office. She'd seen him before around town, but had never been introduced. Too bad they had to meet under these circumstances.

Wearing a dark gray suit that was almost the same color as the winter sky and his precisely groomed hair, the doctor stood in front of the bay windows, the sprawling pasture a backdrop behind him. He looked like an inquisitor with his probing blue eyes and judgmental frown.

"Mr. Davidson," the doctor greeted Lucky. It made Marin cringe a little to hear Lucky labeled with the name of Noah's birth father. "Ms. Sheppard. Why don't you two sit so we can get started?"

But Lucky continued to stand, staring at the doctor. "I don't suppose it'd do any good to object to this on the basis that Marin has already been through enough for one day."

Dr. Blevins shook his head and remained perfectly calm. He sat at her father's desk. "This matter should be addressed immediately."

"Why?"

The doctor blinked. Hesitated. "Because the safety of a child is at stake."

"Noah's fine," Lucky insisted. "But this entire witch hunt of which you're obviously a major participant— or a pawn—isn't."

Marin took up the argument from there. "How much are my parents paying you?"

That caused a slight ruffle in his cool composure. A muscle tightened in his jaw. "The county is paying me for what will be an independent, objective assessment. But I have to tell you, you're not off to a good start."

"Neither are you," Lucky fired back.

Dr. Blevins got to his feet. "At least I am who I say I am, *Mr. Davidson.*"

The room went silent, and Marin held her breath because that comment had a heavy punch to it. Coupled with the doctor's now almost smug glare, she knew this was about to take a very ugly turn.

"Sit down," the doctor insisted. He took his own advice and returned to her father's chair. "And then you can explain why you two lied about your relationship."

Marin lost her breath for a moment. Yes, this was an ugly turn. And it would no doubt get even uglier.

Lucky caught on to her hand and eased her into the chair across from where the doctor was seated. Then, he sat, as well, and they stared at the man who could ultimately take Noah away from her.

"You're not engaged," Dr. Blevins continued. "In fact, I suspect you're practically strangers."

"Why do you think that?" Lucky asked. Marin was glad he did. Her throat seemed to have snapped shut.

The doctor propped his elbows on the desk. "Because I know the truth."

"The truth?" Lucky repeated. "I doubt that. What you know is what Marin's parents have told you."

"Her parents didn't tell me. Someone else tipped me

off, and then I did some investigating. I know you're not Randall Davidson. He's been dead for well over a year. I have a copy of his death certificate, though it wasn't easy to get since Randall was his middle name. The certificate was filed as Mitchell R. Davidson."

Since Marin couldn't deny any of this, she just sat there and wondered where this was leading. Would the doctor try to use this to challenge her custodial rights? And if so, how could she stop that from happening?

She glanced at Lucky, and in that brief exchange, she could tell he was as concerned as she was. But there was something else beneath the surface. Resolve. "It'll be okay," he promised in a whisper.

But Marin wasn't sure how anyone could make this okay.

Dr. Blevins stared at Lucky. "Since I know you're not Randall Davidson, would you like to tell me who you really are?"

"Quinn Bacelli." He paused a moment. Leaned forward. And returned the steely stare. "Marin's fiancé."

Marin hoped she didn't look too surprised. But the doctor certainly did. "You're lying."

Lucky shook his head and slid his hand over hers. "Why would I do that?"

"To help Marin keep her son."

"Marin doesn't need my help for that. She's a good mother who's been railroaded by parents who want to control her life." Lucky stabbed an accusing finger at Blevins. "And you're helping them do that."

The doctor shook his head. "I'm trying to get to the truth."

"You have the truth. No, I'm not Noah's biological father, but he's my son in every way that matters."

Lucky sounded sincere. Because he probably was. He did care deeply for her son. But would that be enough to get Dr. Blevins to back off?

"Why did you lie to everyone about who you were?" Blevins asked Lucky.

"Because I asked him to," Marin volunteered before Lucky could answer. "I came to the ranch to visit my grandmother. I wanted the trip to be short. And I didn't want to have to answer what I knew would be a litany of my parents' questions about my personal relationship. I figured it would keep things simple if they thought he was Randall."

The doctor obviously didn't like her quick response. His forehead bunched up, and he was no doubt trying to figure out a way to challenge what she was saying because that's what her parents had told him to do.

Marin pushed harder. "Lucky took care of my son while I was in the hospital. Do you think I'd trust a stranger to do that?" She didn't wait for him to respond. "Do you think I'd have a stranger sleep in my bed?"

"Well?" Lucky challenged when the doctor only stared at them.

"I'll have to tell the judge that you lied about your real identity," Blevins finally said.

"Go ahead. I'll have my attorney contact the judge, as well. And the state attorney general. Because, you see, you might think you're doing the right thing, but I don't believe your motives will hold up under scrutiny from someone who's not beholden to Howard and Lois Sheppard."

The doctor scrawled something on the paper in front of him. "Judge Carrick will get my report today. You should hear something as early as tomorrow."

Marin wasn't sure what that meant, but she had to hope that it would all turn out all right despite this horrible meeting.

She and Lucky stood, but the doctor spoke before they could even take a step.

"Judge Carrick tends to be conservative, even old-fashioned, when it comes to his cases," Blevins said. It sounded as if he were choosing his words carefully. "He wants me to tell you that you're to remain here at the ranch until you hear his decision."

"Lucky has to leave," Marin volunteered. "A family emergency."

The doctor made a sound to indicate he understood. But, of course, there was no way he could. "It could take weeks or even months for someone like the state attorney general to intercede. In the mean time, Judge Carrick could give temporary custody of your son to your parents."

Marin was glad that Lucky still had his arm around her. Still, she didn't want Blevins to see that she was on the verge of losing it. "You can stop that from happening," she told the doctor.

Blevins pulled in a long, weary breath and shook his head. "You were born and raised here, Marin. You know how things work."

That chilled her to the bone. She knew how much power and influence her wealthy parents had. This session had been nothing more than a square filler, the prelude to her parents getting what they wanted—her back under their control.

"I'll help if I can," Dr. Blevins finally conceded. But his tone and demeanor said that his help wouldn't do them any good.

Lucky led her out of the room. "I'll call my lawyer and get her out here."

Marin was so tired from the adrenaline crash and the stress that she nearly gave in. It would be so easy just to put all of this on Lucky's shoulders. But that's what had gotten her in trouble in the first place.

"I'll contact that attorney again in Fort Worth, and while I'm at it, I'll phone my friend Lizette, too. If she's back in town, I know she'll come right away."

Lucky nodded and caught on to her chin to force eye contact. "Are you okay?"

"No. But I will be, after I confront my parents."

"You think that'll help?"

"It'll help me," she insisted. She paused and moved closer so that her mouth was right against Lucky's ear. "I'm thinking about taking Noah and leaving tonight."

He didn't stiffen, nor did he seem surprised. Lucky simply slipped his arm around her and pulled her closer. He brushed a kiss on her cheek. That kiss went through her. Warm lips against cold cheek.

"Your parents won't give up. From the sound of it, neither will this judge. They'll look for you. No matter where you go, they'll keep looking."

"What other choice do I have? I can't let them have Noah. You heard what Dr. Blevins said about temporary custody. It could take me months to sort out everything and get Noah back. In the mean time, I'd be here, right where my parents want me to be."

"There is an alternative, something that might help you keep custody."

"What? I'll do anything." Marin was certain she sounded as desperate as she felt.

Lucky looked her straight in the eyes. "You can marry me."

LUCKY WATCHED HIS marriage proposal register in Marin's eyes. He'd dumbfounded her. She didn't utter a sound. Her mouth dropped open a little, and it stayed in that position while she stared at him.

"It makes sense," he insisted. "If we're married and I make it known that I intend to legally adopt Noah, then how could a judge object?"

But Lucky could think of a reason: Marin's parents were paying the judge so well that the man would find a way around the law. However, a maneuver like that would be temporary at best and highly illegal. Even this judge couldn't be out of reach from the state attorney general or Justice Department. Just like Duran, Lucky intended to use both if it came down to it.

"Marriage?" Marin finally mumbled. "That wasn't something I'd considered."

"I know. We've been in overload mode since we first met." Unfortunately, there were worse things to think about than temporarily losing custody of Noah.

Marin and Noah were in danger.

Marriage wouldn't keep them from a killer, but it would give Marin a little breathing room. He also hoped it wouldn't create a new set of problems. After all, Marin and he were attracted to each other. A marriage of convenience would muddy already murky waters.

She shook her head, but Lucky couldn't tell from her stunned expression exactly what she was thinking. She opened her mouth to answer, but she didn't get to utter a word before his cell phone rang.

"Blocked number," he mumbled, glancing down at the caller ID screen. And he immediately thought of his sister. Was she trying to contact him? "Bacelli," he answered.

But it wasn't his sister's voice he heard.

"Mr. Bacelli, this is Brenna Martel. Your sister and I worked together for Dexter Sheppard."

Well, that was certainly a voice he hadn't expected to hear. But it was welcome.

"I know who you are." He didn't want to put the call on speaker in case Marin's parents were still around, but he motioned for Marin to move closer so she could hear this. "I thought you were dead."

"A lot of people think that."

Of course, Lucky wondered why she was calling and if this call was related to the attempts to kill Marin and him. But right now, he had a more pressing question. "Is Kinley alive?"

Silence. Lucky held his breath. Beside him, Marin was doing the same.

"I'd rather not say anything about Kinley," Brenna finally answered.

"You don't have a choice. I want to know if my sister is alive, and you're going to tell me."

"Not over the phone," Brenna maintained, though her voice was shaky and hardly there. "It isn't safe. The less I say, the safer it will be for me. Someone wants me dead."

"Welcome to the club," Lucky snarled. "Your safety isn't my top priority, so start talking. I want to know if Kinley is alive and if so, where she is."

"No answers over the phone. I want to meet with you and Marin Sheppard."

Lucky didn't bother to suppress a groan. "I'll just bet you do. That way you can get another crack at trying to kill us."

"It isn't me who wants you dead." Despite that whispery, weak voice, Brenna sounded adamant. However, that didn't mean she was telling the truth. Killers were often very convincing liars.

"If not you, then who?" Lucky demanded.

"I don't know. Dexter, maybe. Or someone connected to him. Possibly even Grady Duran. God knows he's furious with everyone right now. I have information, or rather pieces of information, and I don't know how they all fit. That's why I need to see you. We have important things to discuss that involve both of you."

Lucky had to pause a moment to gather his composure. He wanted to know about Kinley, but this sounded a lot like suicide. "You must think Marin and I are fools. Meet with you so you can ambush us?"

"Fool or not, if you want to know about your siblings, you'll see me. Tomorrow morning, 6:00 a.m., at the abandoned drive-in theater. You must arrive together, without the sheriff or anyone else. And if

you're carrying a weapon, hold it high so I can see it.
Because I don't want to be ambushed, either."

With that, Brenna Martel hung up.

"The drive-in is on the edge of town," Marin immediately supplied, letting him know that she'd managed
to hear the conversation. "It's surrounded by a flat field.
Last time I saw it, the big screen and the concession
stand were still there, but little else. In other words,
there aren't many places a person could hide to ambush
us."

Lucky was already shaking his head before Marin
even finished. "I can't risk taking you out there. Heck,
I can't risk taking you out of this house after what
happened on our little walk this morning."

She caught on to his shoulders. "You can't miss this
meeting, either. Lucky, this could be your best chance
to find your sister and for me to know once and for all
what happened to Dexter."

He made sure there was plenty of sarcasm in his
voice. "You want to meet a potential felon who might
have not only faked her own death and stole a chemical
weapon, but also tried to kill us twice?"

Marin lifted her shoulder. "What's the alternative?
Not ever knowing? Running? Hiding? Brenna Martel
might have what we need to stop all of this. She could end
the danger so that I can safely get out of here with Noah."

He couldn't argue with that. "Then, I'll go meet
with her. I'll hear what she has to say and come back
here to tell you."

She cocked her head to the side. "You heard what she
said. This meeting will only happen if we're both there."

"Yeah, so it'll be easier for her to kill us."

"Not if we take precautions. I know that drive-in. We used to go there when I was a kid." Marin caught on to his arm when he started to move away. "We can arrive ahead of time, hours before Brenna will be expecting us, and stake out a safe place to wait for her."

Lucky couldn't believe what he was hearing. Or what he was thinking. God, was it even something he should consider?

How could he not?

Judging from the determined look in Marin's eyes, she felt the same. He cursed under his breath. "It's still too dangerous."

"Yes. But you can make it less dangerous. This is what you do. You know ways to minimize the risk."

"Yeah. And you staying here at the house is the best way to do that."

"No." Marin let that hang in the air. "Nowhere is safe until we learn who's trying to kill us. And if it's Brenna, then maybe it's time for a showdown."

"A showdown?" He threw his hands in the air. "With you in the frickin' middle?"

"With us in control of the situation." She pressed her fingers to his mouth to stop more of his protest. "We have to do this, so no more arguing. Instead, let's figure out how we can make this as safe as possible."

He saw it then. The sheer determination on her face. Marin wasn't going to back down from this. Worse? He couldn't let her back down. Because she was right— they had to know the truth.

"I'll set up a safety net. Some security," he said

thinking out loud. "I'll get someone to provide backup so we're not out there alone."

"Does that mean we'll meet her?"

Lucky cursed again. There was really only one answer he could live with. "Yes."

He only hoped that he wasn't leading them straight to their deaths.

"I need to make lots of calls," he explained. "I have a PI friend who can get us some monitoring equipment so that no one can sneak up on us out there."

He would have added more if he hadn't heard footsteps. At first he thought the doctor was coming out of the office, but the footsteps came from the other direction.

Lucky pushed Marin behind him and drew his gun.

Just as Howard and Lois stepped into the hallway.

Lucky didn't put his gun away, and he hoped his glare conveyed his displeasure over what the two were trying to do to their daughter.

"Dr. Blevins just called me on my cell," Howard announced. He kept his attention nailed to Lucky. "He's writing his report now, but he wanted to give us a heads-up about the lie you told. Now, who the hell are you? I know for a fact you're not Randall Davidson."

"Guess there's no such thing as confidentiality when it comes to Blevins," Lucky grumbled. That was something else he could mention to the state attorney general. "My name is Lucky Bacelli."

"Marin, how could you do this?" her mother asked, snapping her attention to her daughter. "You hired this man, this imposter, so that we'd think Noah had a father?"

Lucky spoke before Marin could. "Noah does have a father. *Me.* My feelings for Noah aren't based on DNA. Good thing, too. Because after meeting you guys, I think that whole DNA connection thing is highly over-rated."

Lois stiffened while her husband just stood there and stewed. "Judge Carrick will hear about your lies," she threatened. "You're obviously not thinking straight." She kept her eyes trained on Marin. "If you had been, you wouldn't have brought this imposter into our home. I don't care what he claims his feelings are for Noah. This is a sham of a relationship."

"A sham?" Marin stepped out from behind him and faced her parents. "For the record, Lucky asked me to marry him."

With Brenna's phone call, Lucky had nearly forgotten that. Though it was another critical cog in this complicated wheel they were building.

"You turned him down, of course," her father issued like a warning.

Marin's chin came up. "Actually, I hadn't given an answer yet. But now is as good a time as any." She turned, leaned in and kissed him. A real kiss like the one they'd shared in the closet.

"Yes, Lucky," Marin said. "I'll marry you."

Chapter Twelve

Marin waited, something she seemed to have been doing for hours.

Lucky was on the phone. She only hoped his efforts paid off and that this meeting with Brenna Martel ended with them alive and with crucial answers about Dexter and Kinley.

Lucky had certainly taken every conceivable precaution to assure their safety. It was midnight, a full six hours before the scheduled meeting. They weren't at the drive-in, but rather parked across the field, with their car nestled in some trees. Marin was armed with one of the handguns she'd taken from the ranch. Lucky had his own weapon and a backup that he'd slipped into an ankle holster.

To make sure they were safe and not sitting ducks in the field, Lucky had rigged the area around the car with a motion detector that he'd had delivered to the ranch. With the detector activated, no one would get close enough to ambush them without him finding out.

Lucky had called Dr. Blevins and the judge. There

was no word yet on the outcome of the so-called hearing. No decision about custody. It was a reprieve, but it wouldn't last. Marin needed to make some decisions before the judge made them for her and took her son.

But what were the right decisions?

Lucky was obviously on the same wavelength because in the middle of all this chaos, he'd made wedding plans. Right after announcing to her parents that she'd accepted Lucky's proposal, he'd taken her to town to see the justice of the peace and arranged for a marriage license. And he'd done that without so much as a flicker of emotion. If was as if he'd gone on autopilot.

Get safety equipment. Check.

Call the PI. Check.

Set up security for meeting. Check.

Marry Marin. Check.

It was stupid for that to sting. After all, Lucky was doing her a huge favor by marrying her. Or rather letting her parents *think* he was going to marry her. She wasn't sure he'd actually go through with it. After all, he wouldn't exactly jump at the chance to have a loveless marriage all because he cared for her son.

Marin wondered if there was more to his feelings.

Those kisses had confused her. And they'd made her burn. There was definitely physical attraction there between them. But that would only give her hope about having a real relationship with Lucky, which just wasn't a good idea. The timing was all wrong. She already had too many things to deal with. Lucky did, as well.

"You're positive there's no one around the drive-in?" Lucky asked.

Though Marin couldn't hear the answer, she knew that Lucky was talking to Burney Rickman, a San Antonio PI who had arrived earlier with a carload of security equipment. Lucky had told her that he trusted this man with his life. That was good because even though they had no choice about this meeting, they might need assistance to stay alive.

Thankfully, Noah was back at the ranch with her grandmother and a deputy that Sheriff Jack Whitley had sent over to guard them and the rest of the place. As a backup, her grandmother had an old Smith & Wesson that she definitely knew how to use. Still, Marin was eager to get this meeting over and done so she could get back to Noah, especially since her parents were also at home.

"Burney doesn't see anyone around the drive-in or in the concession stand, and he's searched the entire place," Lucky relayed to her when he finished the call. "He's also using equipment to make sure no one has set up surveillance cameras. If they have, he said it must be low-tech because his equipment's not picking up anything."

"Maybe the meeting is just that. A meeting. Maybe Brenna doesn't have anything up her sleeve." But Marin couldn't trust that. They had to stay vigilant when and if they ever went into that drive-in to talk to her.

It was entirely possible that Brenna wouldn't show.

And if so, they were back to square one.

Lucky's phone rang again, and he immediately glanced down at the caller ID screen. "It's Cal Rico from the Justice Department. I asked him to call if he found out anything about Brenna or Kinley."

Apparently, he had.

"I see," Lucky said to the Justice Department agent a moment later. Lucky sounded puzzled. "But it was my sister's blood on the floor of that research facility."

The comment had Marin moving across the front seat so she could hear what was being said. Unfortunately, the wind didn't cooperate. Winter had decided to return in full force, and the wind was howling right out of the north. Added to that was the sound of the overhead swishing tree limbs, so she didn't catch a word.

Lucky finally pressed the end-call button and slipped the phone back into his jacket pocket. "Cal Rico ran the surveillance disk from the train through some facial recognition software. It was a high percentage match for Kinley."

No wonder Lucky looked so shell-shocked. "You said something about the blood on the floor?"

Because of the full moon, she had no trouble seeing his expression. That call had not been good news. "Cal had the blood from the research lab retested. It belonged to Brenna and Kinley all right, but there was a preservative present. They didn't find the preservatives in the earlier tests because they weren't looking for it."

Marin shook her head. "What does that mean?"

"Someone could have stockpiled their blood, possibly without their knowledge if they thought they were donating to a blood bank. Then the person could have used it to fake their deaths." Lucky paused. "Of course, they could have faked it themselves."

Oh, mercy. That put his sister not only alive, but in the thick of what could be the cover-up to a crime. "It doesn't mean she's behind the attempts to kill us," Marin pointed out. "She could be a pawn in all of this."

Anything was possible, including the prospect that her own brother was the one who was manipulating this situation. Though she didn't want to believe that, Marin had to at least consider the possibility. To do otherwise might be a fatal mistake.

"Just focus on what we can control," Lucky said. But it seemed as if he was trying to convince himself along with her. "Once we know the outcome of this meeting, we'll deal with the individual issues."

"Like the wedding."

Marin hadn't intended to say it aloud. It just sort of popped out of her mouth. And it earned her a puzzled stare from Lucky.

Since the subject was out there, seemingly coiled and ready to strike, and since they appeared to have several hours of free time on their hands, Marin continued. "You know a wedding might not do any good. I mean, my parents will probably just look for another way to challenge me for custody of Noah."

He made a sound that could have meant anything. "You're afraid of marrying me."

She thought about that a moment. "I'm afraid of us."

Lucky had apparently thought about that, too. "Yeah."

Marin thought it best to leave that comment alone. But she didn't. "I can't fall for you."

"Same here."

Surprised at his blatant honesty, she took a deep breath. "Good." They were in agreement.

Then, she made the mistake of looking at him. There he sat, looking hotter than any man had a right to look. He certainly had her number. He could take her mind off anything and move it straight to where it shouldn't be.

Specifically, on having down-and-dirty sex with him. She wasn't exactly the dirty-sex type, but he certainly put some bad ideas in her head. They must have crept into his mind, too, because he cursed. Something sexual and rough.

"I'm thinking about kissing you," he said.

"I'm thinking about it, too," Marin admitted. It was a stupid admission, but he could no doubt see and feel the need inside her.

He gripped the steering wheel. "How much are you thinking about it?"

She noted his white knuckles. His rapid breath. "As much as you are."

He squeezed his eyes shut. Groaned. And when he opened his eyes again, he reached for her.

It wasn't a slow, fluid motion. It was frantic and hungry and totally out of control. Exactly the way that Marin wanted it to be. Their arms tangled around each other, and lowering his head, he placed his mouth solidly on hers.

Lucky nudged her lips apart, though it didn't take

much effort. She was ready to give him everything, even though she knew that wasn't possible here in the car. This car was her safety net. A way of counting to ten. Because Lucky wouldn't let things go too far.

Would he?

The whole forbidden fantasy thing spiked the heat. Lucky was the ultimate forbidden fantasy.

He pushed open her coat and slipped his hand inside to cover her breast. His touch was clever, wonderful, and he somehow managed to caress her nipple through her bra. Coupled with the fiery effects of his mouth, it sent her need soaring.

"We're in the car," she reminded him when he paused long enough for her to catch her breath.

"Yeah. I'm keeping watch."

She opened her eyes to see if he was truly managing to do that. He was. Damn him, he was. Here she was, body on fire, wishing she could strip him naked, and somehow he was kissing her, pinching her nipple *and* keeping watch.

For some reason, that riled her. Or maybe it just made her feel as if she weren't doing her part. "I'll watch," she insisted.

And because of her aroused, ornery mood, she slid her hand down his chest to his stomach. But her wrist brushed against the most aroused part of him.

Lucky sucked in his breath. "You can't do that."

"I'm keeping watch." Oh, it felt so good to say that and see the tormented pleasure on his hot face.

"We can't have sex in this car," he insisted.

"No. We shouldn't even be kissing."

She couldn't argue with that. So, they sat there. Staring at each other.

"Stupid, stupid, stupid," she mumbled. It seemed the threat of danger wasn't enough to cool them down. "Someone could come at us any minute," Marin reminded him.

"The PI would alert us." His mouth inched toward hers again. "And while I'd like nothing more than to be inside you right now, I don't want to have to multitask while we're having sex."

He continued to stare at her. His mouth moved a little closer. His hand slid up her jeans-covered thigh. Her breath stalled in her throat as his fingers touched her.

Marin could have sworn that her jeans dissolved off her. His touch felt that intimate, like breath against skin. She melted, her body preparing itself for more.

Which it wasn't going to get, of course. She repeated that to herself.

"Keep watch a second," Lucky instructed.

Before she could ask why, Lucky pushed her against the inside of the door, lowered his head and replaced his fingers with his mouth.

True, there was denim between his mouth and her sex, but he managed to make her feel ready to climax.

"Keep watch," Lucky repeated.

"I can't see," she warned.

He chuckled, and his warm breath and the vibration of his laughter creating some very interesting ripples in her body.

Lucky made his way back up. Kissed her mouth

again. Then, her cheeks. All the while, he continued surveillance around them.

"This is driving me crazy," she said. "You know
that?"

His phone rang, the sound slicing through the car and
causing Marin to jump. Just like that, the lightness and
the heat between them evaporated. Her heart immediately went into overdrive, and they pulled apart.

Lucky blew out several quick breaths to clear his
head, and answered the call, clicking the speaker
function. "It's Burney Rickman," the PI said. "A car's
headed this way."

Thank God at least one of them was actually keeping
an eye on things.

Marin fixed her clothes, tried to fix her brain and
peered out into the darkness. "I don't see anything."

"The driver has the car headlights turned off," the
PI provided.

In other words, the person didn't want anyone to
know she was approaching. Did that mean Brenna had
arrived five hours early so she could set a trap for them?
Or like them, was she getting a head start to ensure she
didn't die tonight? After all, Brenna probably didn't
trust them any more than they trusted her.

There was a slight clicking sound. "I have another
call," Lucky told the PI. "Stay low. I don't want you
spotted." He pressed the button to answer it.

"I know you're here," the caller said. It was a woman.

"Brenna Martel," Lucky supplied to Marin.

"I set up some small surveillance cameras in the
surrounding area before I even phoned you for the meet-

ing," Brenna explained. "So, I know what's going on. Who's the big guy with the gun trying to hide in the drive-in?"

Lucky hesitated and looked as if he wanted to curse. "A PI friend. He won't hurt you."

"I'm not willing to take that chance. Tell him to leave now."

"I will if you'll tell me what this meeting is all about."

Now, it was Brenna's turn to hesitate. A moment later, Marin heard another voice. Another woman.

Definitely not Brenna.

"Lucky?" the woman said, her voice little more than a raspy whisper. "It's me. Kinley."

Lucky's sister.

"I need you to do exactly as Brenna says," Kinley warned. "If not, I'm afraid she'll kill us all."

Chapter Thirteen

"Kinley?" Lucky practically shouted into the phone. That was his sister's voice all right—or else a very good imitation. "Is it really you?"

"Yes. You have to tell that man to leave. You have to come now."

He wanted to do just that. But he had to think of Marin and her safety. "How do I know it's really you?"

Lucky heard some whispered chatter between the women on the other end of the line. The woman next to him, however, sat silent and frozen. She was probably as stunned as he was.

"When I was six," the caller said, "you made me a dollhouse out of Popsicle sticks. You painted it lime-green."

Hell. It was Kinley.

Now, the question was, what was he going to do about it?

"We'll be there in a few minutes," Marin said, making the decision for him. His gaze snapped to hers, but she offered no apology. "We have to do this."

They did. But how?

"Sixty seconds," Brenna said, coming back on the line. "Tell your PI friend to get lost and come to the drive-in. Park just beneath the movie screen. Oh, and Bacelli, if you do anything stupid, your sister is the one who'll pay the price."

"Let's go," Marin said the moment that Brenna ended the call.

Lucky tried to push aside all his doubt, but he couldn't. He was taking Marin directly into the line of fire.

"Get in the backseat," he instructed Marin while he called Burney Rickman. "Burney, make it look as if you're leaving. But stay nearby, hidden, just in case I need you."

"Will do."

Lucky started the engine and drove toward the drive-in.

"There's no reason for me to stay in the backseat," Marin insisted. "I have a gun." She took the snub-nosed .38 from her purse. "And I'm not a bad shot."

"Doesn't matter. I don't intend for you to be doing any shooting."

She mumbled some protest, but thankfully did as he said. The backseat wasn't bulletproof, but if something went wrong, she wouldn't be an easy target.

Lucky didn't turn on the car headlights. Though Brenna had him under surveillance, he didn't want to announce his arrival to anyone else. This was a complicated game with a lot of potential players, and what mattered most was surviving this so that he could get Marin and his sister out of there.

He approached the drive-in slowly. Cautiously. On one side was the concession building and projection room. The windows were all shattered. No doors. The concrete-block building was blistered with what was left of flamingo-pink paint.

On the other side of the drive-in was a thirty-foot-wide screen, that had essentially been a white wall, but it was now pocked with baseball-size holes. Moonlight spewed onto the ground, which was littered with metal poles that had once held speakers. Now, though, it looked more like some eerie haunted obstacle course.

Lucky checked his mirror to make sure Marin was staying down and came to a stop where the speaker rows began. He waited, the seconds ticking off in his head.

The phone rang again, and he snatched it up while keeping a vigilant watch on their surroundings. "Drive forward," Brenna instructed. "Stop directly in front of the center of the movie screen."

Of course. The center. The most vulnerable spot. Too vulnerable. And that meant it was time to set some ground rules of his own.

"I have a better idea. You drive forward, too, and meet me halfway. We both stop in the center." He made sure it wasn't a suggestion.

More seconds ticked by. He could hear the rapid jolts of Marin's breath. The wind. The pounding of his own heartbeat in his ears.

"All right," Brenna finally conceded. "But remember, I have your sister."

"And remember that I have something you want or you wouldn't have demanded this meeting."

Though Lucky didn't have a clue what it was that he had. Hopefully, it was something he could use to bargain so he could get his sister and Marin safely out of there.

Brenna ended the call again, and Lucky proceeded to drive forward.

"You think this is a trap?" Marin asked.

"I just don't know." He had a bad feeling, but then it would have been worse if he'd decided not to come.

He spotted the other car. A black two door. It crawled across the grounds toward him, and they stopped at the same time. About ten feet apart.

"Stay put for now," Lucky told Marin. He drew his gun and held it against his leg. After saying a quick prayer that firing wouldn't become necessary, he stepped out of the car, using the door for cover.

A moment later, the door to Brenna's car opened. There was a shuffle of movement, and two women emerged from the driver's side. A tall blond with a sturdy build who dragged the other woman from the vehicle. The other woman, a brunette, was practically frail in comparison, at least six inches shorter and twenty pounds lighter.

Because the brunette had her head hung low, it took him a moment to realize it was indeed Kinley. His sister was there, right in front of him.

And Brenna had a gun pointed at Kinley's head.

His sister had lost some weight, but other than that she looked the same. Short dark brown hair. The Bacelli eyes. One thing was for certain, unless this was some kind of hologram, she was very much alive.

He wanted to go to her. To hug her. To tell her how relieved he was that she was alive. All these months he'd grieved for her and blamed himself for not doing more to save her. But she'd already been saved.

Well, maybe.

After all, Brenna was holding the gun, and it was clear that Kinley was her hostage.

"I'm sorry, Lucky." Kinley was hoarse, and judging from the puffiness around her eyes, she'd been crying.

It took Lucky a moment to find his breath and another moment before he could speak. "What happened to you?"

But Brenna didn't let her answer. "I think Kinley's the one who's been trying to kill me."

Kinley shook her head, her hair swishing against the gun. "No. I didn't try to kill anyone. But someone tried to murder me. Many times."

Lucky wanted to know every detail about what'd happened the last year, but first things first. "Brenna, you need to put down the gun so we can all talk."

"Where's Marin Sheppard?" she asked, obviously ignoring Lucky's request.

He tipped his head to the backseat. "There's no reason to bring her into this. Marin just got out of the hospital, and she's not up to another confrontation."

Brenna jammed the gun harder against Kinley's head. "There are plenty of reasons to bring her into this. Get her out here now, or this meeting is over."

Lucky believed her. Apparently so did Marin because she stepped from the car and lifted her hands in a show of surrender. However, when she joined Lucky behind the door, he could see that she had her gun tucked in the back waist of her jeans. Maybe Marin wouldn't need to use it, but he hated that she was right back in the middle of danger.

"I want to know where Dexter is," Brenna demanded of Marin.

"Is he alive?" Marin demanded right back.

A sound of pure frustration left Brenna's mouth. "I figured you'd be the one person who could tell me that."

"I honestly don't know," Marin assured her. "In fact, I thought all three of you were dead. But now that you're here, I'd like to know if my brother is alive."

"So would we," Kinley agreed. "If he is, he hasn't shown his face. Not to me, anyway. Brenna thought you'd been in contact with him."

Kinley's comment earned her another jab from Brenna's gun, and it took every ounce of Lucky's willpower not to charge at the woman to stop her from further hurting his kid sister. But he couldn't do that. It would put them all at risk. Brenna was obviously on the edge.

"Why don't you put down that weapon," Lucky tried again. "We're all in the same boat here. Someone's tried to kill all of us, and we need to figure out who the enemy is."

Brenna continued to grip the weapon. "Well, it's not me."

"Nor me," Kinley insisted.

"I'm not a killer. I didn't try to run myself down with a truck," Lucky clarified.

Marin glanced at all of them. "I wouldn't have risked

my son's life in a train explosion." Then, she stared at Kinley. "But maybe you did?"

"No!" And Kinley continued to repeat it.

"But you were on the train," Lucky reminded her. God, he hated to do this, to accuse her, especially under these circumstances while she was held at gunpoint. But it had to be done. And if she had endangered Noah and Marin, then heaven help her. Being his sister wouldn't give her immunity from his rage.

"I got on the train because of a note that threatened to kill you. And someone else," she added in a whisper. "But I didn't set those explosives. Once I got on, I checked the suitcase, and it was empty."

"Someone sent you on the train with an empty suitcase?" Marin clarified, though it was more like an accusation.

"Yes," Kinley insisted.

Brenna shook her head. "There's too much missing information from her story. And it just doesn't make sense. A threatening note. An empty suitcase. An explosion, and she comes out of it without a scratch." Brenna spoke in raw anger, but Lucky thought she had a valid point.

"Who threatened to kill me, Kinley?" Lucky wanted to know. But his sister didn't answer. Apparently stunned by his demand and his rough tone, she just stared at him. "Dexter? Who?" Lucky pressed.

His phone rang again. He cursed. It was the worst timing possible. Still, he had to answer it in case something had gone wrong at the ranch.

"It's Rickman," the PI said. "We have a visitor. He

arrived on foot and is coming up on the side of the concession stand. Judging from those pictures you e-mailed me, it's Grady Duran, one of your suspects."

Not just a suspect. The primary one.

"You want me to detain him?" Rickman asked.

Lucky snared Brenna's attention. "Grady Duran is here. You want him to join this meeting so we can get everything out in the open?"

"No," Brenna said at the same moment that Kinley said, "Yes."

"We need to know the truth," Kinley added.

Lucky agreed with her. "Escort him to where we are. Disarm him first, and if he does anything stupid, pound him to dust."

"You can't trust Duran," Brenna said the moment he hung up.

"I can't trust you, either," Lucky reminded her. "Now, while we're waiting, how about an answer to my question. Kinley, who threatened to kill me?"

"I don't know. The threats came by anonymous e-mail."

"And you believed them?" Lucky asked.

Her eyes filled with tears. "I had to believe them. You weren't the only one they threatened. They threatened the child, too."

"Noah?" Marin immediately asked.

"No. *My* child."

Lucky damn sure hadn't expected her to say that.

"She had a baby four months ago," Brenna supplied. "Dexter's baby."

The tears began to spill down his sister's cheeks. "I left him with someone for safekeeping. Someone had been trying to kill me, and the person said he'd go after my son. I couldn't risk it."

Lucky waited a moment, hoping to process all of that. Here he'd just learned his sister was alive, and now there was another child involved in all of this mess?

"And this person threatened to hurt your child if you didn't carry that suitcase onto the train?" Marin asked.

"It's me, Rickman," the PI called out before Kinley could respond. "I've got Grady Duran with me."

Everyone's attention shifted in the direction of his voice. Lucky didn't have any trouble spotting the two men. The bulkier, meaner looking Rickman had a death grip on Duran, but Duran wasn't protesting. In fact, he seemed pleased to be present.

And that made Lucky very uneasy.

Lucky looked at Marin to see what her take was on all of this. Her too-fast breathing said it all. This had turned into a nightmare. But at least it had the potential to put an end to the danger.

"Keep a close watch on Duran," Lucky warned the PI.

"Finally, we're all together," Duran said, sparing each of them a glance before he settled on the gun Brenna was still holding on Kinley. "Either you two have learned how to return from the dead or else you've been hiding because you're guilty of stealing the plans for the chemical weapon. Which is it?"

"I didn't steal anything," Kinley insisted.

Brenna didn't deny it. "Are you the one who's trying to kill all of us?"

But any one of them could have asked the same question.

The corner of Duran's mouth hitched. "If Dexter's behind this, then he must be somewhere nearby laughing his butt off. He gets us all to turn against each other. Or better yet, kill each other. When the dust settles, he'll be the last man standing. And he'll have the plans for my chemical weapon."

"You don't own that weapon," Brenna pointed out.

"I'm the primary shareholder. Or maybe I should say, I'm the one who got stuck holding the proverbial bag when all of you decided to go into hiding." He rammed his thumb against his chest. "I'm the one who'd put up the most money, and I'm the one who had to answer the threatening lawsuits and letters from the silent partner that Dexter conned into investing in this project."

"Silent partner?" Lucky questioned. This was the first he was hearing of this.

As if she'd noticed something, Brenna suddenly jerked her head to the right, toward the old screen. Lucky looked in that direction, as well, though he'd heard nothing other than the wind and the normal sounds of the night.

Hell. Was Dexter about to join them? It didn't sound like footsteps. More like a click. Like the wind catching a piece of that tattered movie screen.

Brenna shook her head. Cursed. She curved her forearm around Kinley's neck and began to maneuver her back toward the car.

Lucky couldn't let them leave. For one thing, Brenna

might truly kill his sister. And for another, he was going to get answers.

"Brenna," he said, trying to soothe her. He stepped away from the meager protection of the car door and inched his way toward the two women. Unfortunately, Marin was right behind him. "Don't leave."

She didn't listen. Brenna shoved Kinley into the car, pushing her into the passenger's seat.

"It's probably just the wind," Lucky let her know, going even closer. "But I'll check it out, just to make sure."

Lucky turned to do that, but before he could shout out the order, he heard another click. At first he thought it was Brenna putting the keys in the ignition because a split second later, her car engine roared on.

But that sound was soon drowned out by the deafening blast to his left.

He had just enough time for his brain to register that it was an explosion. He turned, dove at Marin, trying to get her back into the car.

It was too late.

The explosion ripped through the massive movie screen, and it came tumbling right at them.

MARIN DOVE ACROSS the front seat as a chunk of the screen slammed into the car and missed Lucky by what had to be less than an inch. He scrambled inside, and in the same motion, he started the car just as a massive slab crashed into the windshield.

The safety glass cracked and webbed, but it thankfully stayed in place.

With Duran still in his grip, the PI turned and began to race toward the concession stand.

Lucky shifted the car into reverse, turned to look over his shoulder and hit the accelerator. Even though Marin couldn't see Brenna's car, she heard the woman make her own getaway. But the screen was enormous, stretching across nearly the entire width of the drive-in. It would take a miracle for all six of them to escape without being crushed to death.

"Keep your gun ready," Lucky warned her.

That didn't help steady her heart. Of course, nothing would steady it at this point. It was a terrifying thought to realize that if they made it out of this situation, there might be someone waiting for them. After all, someone had set that explosive.

But who?

Marin took out her gun and waited.

Debris continued to rain down on them. The chunks pelted the car as Lucky maneuvered his way through the obstacle course of metal speaker poles. It seemed to take an eternity, and the seconds clicked by keeping time with the pulse pounding in her ears.

"Take my phone," Lucky instructed. "Call the sheriff. Tell him what happened and that I need him or one of his deputies to meet us at the ranch."

With all the horrible things that could happen zooming through her head, she made the 9-1-1 call and reported the explosion to the sheriff's dispatcher, who assured her that someone would be sent out immediately. Good. It was a crime scene and needed to be secured and examined. Maybe the person responsible had left something incriminating behind.

"Now, look through the recent calls to get the PI's number. Find out if Duran and he made it out," Lucky insisted.

Another lump of the screen smashed into the front windshield, dumping the sheet of broken safety glass onto their laps. With the glass obstruction now gone, she could see Brenna's vehicle on the other side of the drive-in. The roof of her car was bashed in on the passenger's side where Lucky's sister was sitting.

While she located the PI's number, Marin kept her attention pinned to the other car, but she also sheltered her face in case any debris came through what was left of the windshield. A moment later, she watched as Brenna's car disappeared into the darkness. Lucky noticed it, too, and cursed.

"You two okay?" Rickman immediately asked when he answered.

"We're alive." Marin put the call on speaker so that Lucky could hear.

"I want you to go after Brenna," Lucky ordered.

"I'm already on the way to my vehicle," was the PI's answer. "Should I take Duran with me?"

"No. He'll only slow you down, and you can't trust him." Lucky didn't hesitate, either. "By any chance, did you see who set that explosive?"

"I didn't see anyone near that movie screen. But once I catch up with Brenna, I'll check it out." With that, Rickman hung up.

Once they were clear of all the metal poles, Lucky did a doughnut to turn the car around. He slammed on the accelerator again and got them back onto the road.

He slowed when he got to the connecting road, and his gaze darted all around, looking for Brenna's car.

"Are you going after her?" Marin asked. She wrapped her arms around herself to stave off the cold wind that was now gushing through the glassless windshield.

He shifted his posture slightly. "I can't. Too big of a risk." Lucky sped up again.

"Because of me?" But she knew the answer. He didn't want to put her at further risk. Even if that meant not trying to follow Brenna and his sister.

Lucky increased the speed even more, and even in the darkness she could see the troubled look on his face. "We need to get back to the ranch," he said.

That comment chilled her more than the brutal winter wind that was assaulting them. When Lucky had requested that the sheriff or the deputy go to the ranch, she'd thought it was so the person could take their statement. "You don't think this bomber would go to the ranch, do you?"

He glanced at her. Just a glance, but it said volumes. "If this person wants leverage against us, what better way to get it than to go after Noah."

Oh, God. He was right. If this person had no hesitation about blowing up four people, he wouldn't think twice about going after a child.

Marin grabbed the phone to call the ranch, and prayed they weren't too late.

Chapter Fourteen

Lucky had his car door open before he even came to a full stop in front of the Sheppard ranch.

With his gun ready, he hit the ground running. But he didn't have to go far to find proof that everything was okay. Deputy Reyes Medina was right there on the front porch, standing guard.

"Like I told you on the phone," the deputy said, "there's no reason to panic. No one's tried to get anywhere near the house. There are two armed ranch hands out back. Three more are patrolling the grounds on horseback."

"You're sure Noah's okay?" Lucky pressed.

"He's fine," the deputy assured them. "I told Ms. Helen to call me if she heard anything suspicious. Plus, I reset the security system after your mom headed out a little while ago."

That temporarily stopped Marin, who'd already reached the front door. "Where did my mom go?"

"Wouldn't say. But she got a phone call and left not long after you two did."

Maybe that phone call had been from Dexter? Mercy. Was Lois meeting with her son right at this moment? Or was this late night visit somehow connected to the explosion?

"Marin's father didn't go with his wife?" Lucky wanted to know.

The deputy shook his head. "No. He's not here, either. From what I gathered from Ms. Helen, he's been gone for hours."

"Hours?" Marin repeated.

That was troubling, but it didn't overshadow her need to check on her son. She hurried past the deputy, threw open the front door, disarmed the security system and began to run toward her grandmother's room.

Lucky was right behind her.

Her grandmother must have heard the footsteps in the hall because she answered the door after Marin knocked just once and called out her name.

"Noah's safe," Helen said immediately.

But Marin had to see for herself. She rushed across the room and checked the crib Lucky had moved there. He checked Noah, as well, and discovered the little guy was sound asleep. Not that surprising since it was a little after 1:00 a.m.

Marin mumbled a prayer of thanks, lowered the side of the crib, leaned down and lightly kissed Noah's cheek. Lucky couldn't help himself. He did the same, and he felt relief flood through him.

"Let him sleep out the night here," Helen whispered. "No need to wake him."

Lucky agreed, and he was a little surprised when

Marin did, too. That probably had a lot to do with fatigue. She leaned against him, and he felt her practically collapse.

"She needs to rest," her grandmother insisted. "Stress can sometimes trigger a seizure."

Oh, man. Marin didn't need that tonight. He slipped his weapon back into his shoulder holster and scooped Marin into his arms.

"I can walk," Marin insisted.

But he ignored her and headed toward her bedroom. He only got a few steps into the hall when he saw Deputy Medina headed their way.

"Is Marin hurt?" Medina asked.

"No," she answered, trying to wiggle out of his arms, but Lucky held on tight.

"She's exhausted," Lucky explained. "The sheriff will want us to give a statement about what happened at the drive-in, but it's going to have to wait until morning." He didn't ask for permission. Besides, it'd take Sheriff Whitley hours just to process the massive crime scene. "I take it you'll be standing guard all night?"

Medina nodded. "I'll be here until the sheriff says otherwise. The ranch hands, too. I went ahead and reset the security system, and I'll be posted right by the monitor at the front door. That way I can see if anyone tries to open a window or anything."

Lucky thanked the man and carried Marin to her room. He eased her onto the bed, locked the door and took off her shoes.

"No need to treat me like glass," she said, sitting right

back up. "I haven't had a seizure in years. But if you're squeamish about the possibility of it happening, I can go into the sitting room."

Now, that just made him mad. "Squeamish?" he challenged.

He pulled off his boots and practically threw them on the floor. He wasn't much gentler when he removed his slide holster and dropped it onto the nightstand.

She lifted a shoulder and pushed her hair from her face. "We've already been through enough without you having to be on seizure watch."

That also didn't help cool down his anger. "Marin, you might not have noticed, but I'm not here because someone forced me to be here. And hell's bells, I don't want you to have a seizure, but I imagine it'd be a cakewalk compared to what just happened to us."

"Then why exactly are you here?" she snapped. But she immediately waved it off. "What I'm trying to do— and failing at miserably—is giving you an out."

"An out?" There was still a lot of anger in his voice.

She groaned softly and stood. "I think after tonight we both know that Dexter is behind these attempts to kill us."

Lucky shook his head. "How do you figure that?"

Marin gave him a flat look. "He was the only key player not at the meeting. And he was the only one whose life wasn't in danger tonight."

He couldn't argue with the last part, but he sure as hell could argue with the rest of her theory. "So, why would I need an out? If your brother wants us dead, he won't stop just because we're no longer together. Our best bet is to catch the person responsible. And if it turns out to be Dexter, nothing changes. You need my help to keep Noah, remember?"

She looked exhausted, but ready to continue this ridiculous debate. Something Lucky instantly regretted. He'd brought her in here to lessen her stress, not to cause more by arguing with her.

With that reminder, he ditched his own anger, and eased down on the bed next to her. "I'm not treating you like glass. I'm not leaving. I'm not blaming you because of Dexter. And if you have a seizure, I can deal with it. Okay?"

The emotion in her seemed to soften, too, and she sighed and leaned against him. The physical contact was a strong reminder that no matter what the devil was going on, his body always seemed to react to her.

"Now, what about you?" he asked. "How are we going to deal with your concerns?"

She looked up at him just as he looked down at her. "I'll calm down. I won't blame myself because of Dexter. Well, I'll try not to. And I'll continue to try to make you understand that you're not responsible for Noah's safety. Or mine."

The seriousness of the conversation was getting mixed up with all the physical stuff he was feeling for her. Or at least that was the explanation Lucky wanted to believe. He couldn't fall for her. Not with everything ready to crash down around them.

But he was.

"I *am* responsible for your safety," he concluded, causing her to frown.

"Why?"

Good question. He considered dodging the truth but decided against it when he looked into her eyes. He automatically leaned in. "Because I love Noah. And because I want you."

She blinked. "Want?"

He cringed. "Yeah. That shouldn't come as a surprise to you. Not after what happened in the car."

Another blink. "No. Not a surprise. I'm just trying to figure out why your desire…" She stopped. Shook her head. "How *our* desire for each other would make you feel that you need to protect me."

He brushed a kiss on her forehead and hoped he could change the subject with a little humor. "It's a guy thing. You wouldn't understand."

The corner of her mouth lifted. A weary, exhausted half smile. And a damn sexy one at that.

Before he could warn himself to back off from her, which he almost certainly wouldn't heed, his cell phone rang. He fished it from his pocket, glanced at the caller ID and answered it.

"Rickman," he said to the PI. Because he knew Marin would want to hear this, he put the call on speaker phone. "Please tell me you have Brenna and my sister."

"Sorry. I lost them. Or rather, I never found them. By the time I ditched Duran, got to my car and went in pursuit, Brenna and Kinley were gone."

Marin and he cursed at the same time.

"What do you want me to do?" Rickman asked.

Lucky scrubbed his hand over his face. "Go back to the drive-in. The sheriff should be there by now. Try to figure out what the heck happened. If either you or the sheriff find any answers, call me."

"Will do."

"If there's a lull, I also want you to check on what my sister's been doing for the past year," Lucky added. "See if you can confirm if she had a child."

"I'll see what I can do."

When Rickman hung up, Lucky turned his attention back to Marin. No more hot, sexy smile. She looked alarmed again. And stressed. He caught on to her wrist to check her pulse.

"I'm fine," Marin insisted.

He took her pulse anyway and confirmed what he already suspected. "It's been a while since my EMS training at the police academy, but your pulse seems fast to me. Do you have something you can take to make yourself relax?"

"I'm not sure I want to relax."

Lucky understood that. He wouldn't be doing any relaxing, but Marin was a different matter. "Noah is safe, and it'll be hours before he wakes up. Security measures are in place. You're safe, Marin, and rest is the best thing for you."

She nodded, and got up from the bed. She took a pre-scription bottle of pills from her cosmetic bag on the dresser, popped one of the capsules into her mouth and went into the bathroom to get some water. A moment later, she reappeared. She stopped just short of the bed where he was still sitting and she stared at him.

"What are we going to do, Lucky?" she asked.

Since that sounded like the start of another stressful

conversation, he caught on to her hand and pulled her onto the bed. But since he wasn't totally stupid, he draped the comforter over her so there'd be a barrier between them.

"Get some sleep," he insisted, turning off the light.

He started to move away from her, but she caught on to him and pulled him to her. And in doing so, she revved up his already interested body.

"One," he said, remembering the counting rule. "Two."

Marin pulled him even closer until their mouths were mere inches apart. His breath touched her mouth when he mumbled, "Three. Four."

"Does it help to count?" she asked, her voice like sin and silk.

"Yes," he lied.

Right before he lowered his head and kissed her.

MARIN IMMEDIATELY FELT a sweet tangle of heat in her stomach, and it spread like a wild blaze. Her nipples drew into peaks, the sensitive flesh contracting so that even a brush from Lucky's chest seemed like a thorough, eager caress from a lover's hand. And he kept right on kissing her.

Now, this was the ultimate way to relieve stress.

She didn't hesitate. Didn't give herself time to think. Because if she had, she would have stopped, opting for the more logical approach. But she didn't want logic tonight. She didn't want to think.

She wanted Lucky.

"Are you sure we should be doing this?" he asked with his mouth still against hers.

"I'm sure." She went after his shirt.

He went after hers.

It didn't take much for him to strip her stretchy pullover sweater off her. With his kisses now wild and frantic, he went after the zipper of her jeans while she still fumbled with the buttons on his shirt.

"What about a condom?" He groaned, stopped and stared at her.

"I'm on the pill."

She nearly cheered when she finally managed to open his shirt. And she wasn't disappointed. His body was perfect. All toned and naturally tanned. She gave herself the pleasure of touching him.

Lucky groaned and stripped off her jeans. He slid his hand down her breasts and then her stomach until he reached his goal, working his fingers into the wet entrance to her body. With the skill of an artist, he touched her so perfectly, so intimately that Marin thought she might unravel right in his hand.

Within moments he had her starving for him. What she had been unable to say in words, her body said for her. She wanted more. And she wanted it now. Marin pushed herself against his fingers, trying to relieve the desperate hunger that he had created.

She went after his zipper. Not a simple task. He was already huge and hard, which didn't make it easy for her to free him from his jeans and boxers.

Repositioning her, Lucky removed his hand and pushed himself into the slickly soft heat of her body.

Marin wrapped her legs around him and caught on to his shoulders to bring him even closer. Her body adjusted—no one else had felt this way inside her, no one else belonged inside her.

Marin realized that she had gone a year and a half without a man.

And a lifetime without a lover.

He drove into her. Treating her not like glass, but like a lover that he desperately had to have. Each new stroke, each assault of her mouth with his wildfire kisses became more urgent.

She heard herself moan. Felt herself go right to the edge. She considered trying to pull back, to wait for Lucky. But when she looked into his eyes, she realized, he truly was right there with her.

Marin gave in to the unbearable heat and pleasure.

Lucky did the same.

He kissed her hard and deep as they went over that edge together.

Their breaths were the only sounds in the room, though Marin could feel her heartbeat. And his. It would have been wonderful just to lie there in his arms and let her sated body drift off to sleep. But she wanted to remain alert in case anything else went wrong.

Lucky didn't give into the moment, either. Breaking the intimate contact, he stared down at her. Their limbs were tangled together, their bodies slick with sweat. Marin felt so fragile that she thought she might shatter into a thousand pieces. Nothing could have prepared her for what had happened. Nothing could have been more beautiful, more perfect than what she had just experienced with Lucky.

She relaxed the harsh grip she still had on him, letting

her fingers slide over the tightly corded muscles of his chest. She resisted the urge to ask how he felt about what they had just done. *Was it good for you?* She smiled. Anything she could ask would seem so clichéd, so ordinary.

But surely this couldn't be ordinary.

"Next time, I'll remember to count to ten," he said.

She laughed. A very short-lived moment. She knew he was right—they should have backed off. But she refused to regret this. Especially since this might be the only time they would be together like this.

Lucky moved off her, dropping on the mattress next to her and staring up at the ceiling. Silent. Thankfully, he didn't remind her that this probably hadn't been a good idea.

His phone rang, the sound slicing through the room. Lucky snapped up his jeans, dug his cell from the pocket and glanced at the screen. "The caller's ID is blocked."

The last time that'd happened, the call had been from his sister. Lucky hurriedly answered it and put it on speaker.

But it wasn't his sister this time.

"It's Grady Duran," the caller said. "There's been a murder."

Chapter Fifteen

"Who's been murdered?" Lucky asked. And he held his breath and prayed it wasn't his sister.

"I don't know," Duran insisted. "The sheriff just found a body in the drive-in debris."

Lucky pressed harder for information he wasn't sure he wanted. "Is it Kinley?"

"They haven't identified the body, but it's definitely not Kinley. She's with me."

He felt the relief, followed by a slam of new concern. "How'd that happen?"

"I'd put a GPS device on Brenna's car this afternoon before I ever walked into that drive-in and encountered your PI. I knew Brenna would run if things didn't go her way in this meeting, and she did. When I caught up with them, she pushed Kinley out of the car. I nearly ran over her. And when I stopped to make sure she was okay, Brenna got away."

Oh, man. Lucky did not want to hear this. "Bring Kinley to the ranch," he demanded.

"She's already here. All you have to do is come out and get her."

Marin shook her head and mouthed, "No."

But as dangerous as Duran's offer sounded, Lucky couldn't just dismiss it. "Where are you?"

"In the hay barn on the east side of the pasture. I want you to come here and get your sister."

Lucky cursed. "You mean the same barn where someone nearly ran over Marin and me with a truck?"

"The very one." There was ton of cockiness and danger in his tone.

Before Lucky could even respond, there was another voice. One he recognized. "Duran says to tell you this isn't a trick," Kinley said. "All he wants in exchange for me is information." She hesitated. "Don't come, Lucky." Her voice was frantic, and it sounded as if she were crying. "I don't know if this is a trap—"

There was a shuffling sound. Definitely some frenzied movement. "It's not a trap," Duran said, coming back on the line. "And I'm not giving you a choice. Come now, or I'll make sure you don't see your sister again."

That punched Lucky hard, and he had to force himself not to panic. "What, are you going to kill her?" he calmly asked.

"No, but she'll make a good bargaining chip. You heard what she said. She had Dexter's kid. Dexter hasn't shown any interest in contacting her or the baby, but you never know. He might cave, especially if I remind him how his parents would feel about him casting off his own son. It might shame Dexter into cooperating and coughing up what he owes me."

That would put his sister right in the line of fire. "Kinley's not responsible for what Dexter did."

He hoped.

"Just come," Duran demanded. "We need to get to the bottom of all of this."

Lucky couldn't agree more. "Why should I trust you?"

"For the same reason I have to trust you. Because we have to learn the truth."

He couldn't disagree with that, either. "How will meeting with you accomplish that? According to you, you don't know the truth. Neither do I, and that means this little get-together wouldn't accomplish much."

"There has to be something, some bit of information that we're overlooking. And I'm tired of waiting for it," Duran snapped. "You've got ten minutes. If you're not here, I'm leaving. Oh, and Lucky? Don't alert the deputy or the ranch hands patrolling the place. Because if you do, this *little get-together* will be over before it even starts."

Before Lucky could bargain for more time so he could set up a plan, Duran hung up.

"You're not thinking about going," Marin said. She hurriedly put on her clothes.

While Lucky dressed, he went through his options and realized he didn't have any. Ten minutes wasn't enough time to get the sheriff out there. Of course, he could take the deputy with him, or the ranch hands, but that would leave the house itself vulnerable.

And that might be the real trap.

Duran could be using this meeting to lure Lucky out of the house so that he could get inside.

"If you leave, I'll go with you," Marin insisted. "I can be your backup."

Lucky shook his head, zipped up his jeans and put on his shirt. "You can't. For one thing, it's too dangerous. For another, you just took that sedative, and you're sleepy."

"Not so sleepy that I can't help you."

"You can help me by staying here." Then, he played dirty because the stakes were too high to take her with him. "Think of Noah. You need to be here in case Duran tries to get in the house."

Her breath froze. But there were no more head shakes. She knew he was right.

"I have to hurry," Lucky said, putting on his boots. "I don't think Duran will wait around past that ten-minute time limit he set."

"Then at least let me call the sheriff," Marin pleaded.

"He wouldn't be able to get here in time. Besides, I don't want him to do anything that might spook Duran. Okay?"

She nodded, eventually, though she didn't seem sure of any of this. Neither was Lucky. "I'll be careful," he promised. "I'll approach the barn from behind. I won't let Duran get the drop on me."

Another nod as tears watered her eyes.

"I'm going out the front door," he explained. "So the deputy can reset the security system."

Lucky wanted to give Marin more reassurance, but there wasn't time. The seconds were literally ticking away. So, he kissed her and hoped this wasn't the last time she'd ever see him alive.

Marin watched from the window of the sitting room.

With the curtain lifted just a fraction and with the lights off so that no one could see her, she waited and finally spotted Lucky. He glanced in the direction of the window and hurried toward the meeting with Duran.

She had a very bad feeling about this.

They couldn't trust Duran—this might all be a trap. Even Kinley had thought so. But Marin also understood Lucky's need to try to save his sister. If their positions had been reversed, she would have done the same. She just wished she could have gone with him.

Yawning, she leaned against the window frame and kept her gaze on Lucky until he disappeared into the night. Mercy, why had she taken that stupid sedative? It was clouding her mind at a time when she needed to think clearly about this meeting and the body that'd been found at the drive-in.

Should she call the sheriff?

Lucky had insisted that she not do that, but what if he was ambushed?

He'd need help.

She reached for the phone. Stopped. Rethought the whole argument. And while she was arguing with herself, she saw movement. It was a person walking along the fence, headed in the same direction that Lucky had just gone.

She froze. God, was someone trying to follow him?

Marin searched through the darkness, and when the silhouette stepped from the shadows of some mountain laurels, she saw who it was.

Her mother.

Marin blinked. At first she was certain she was seeing things. But it was indeed her mother. Lois was looking around as if she expected someone to jump out of those bushes.

What the heck was going on?

It was nearly two o'clock in the morning, and it was bitterly cold—hardly the time or the weather for her mother to take a stroll. That meant she was up to something.

But what?

Marin grabbed her coat and the gun she'd taken earlier to the drive-in, and she hurried out of her room toward the front door. "My mother's out there," she said to the deputy. "I need to see what she's doing."

Deputy Medina hesitated. "Lucky said I wasn't to let you leave."

Of course he had. Because he would have suspected that she might try to follow him.

Marin silently cursed. If she didn't get out there, her mother might already be gone, and Marin knew instinctively that something critical was going on. Her mother wouldn't be out there unless it involved her father or Dexter.

"I'll only be a minute, and I won't go far," Marin bargained with the deputy.

He frowned and mumbled his displeasure under his breath. "I'll go with you."

"No." To save further argument, she disarmed the security system. "Stay here. I don't want my son and grandmother left alone."

Marin hurried out before the deputy could stop her, and ran across the front lawn to get to the side of the house. Thankfully, the moonlight cooperated. She saw her mother on the trail just ahead.

Marin shook her head to fight off the dizziness from the sedative. Just in case, she kept her gun ready.

"Mother?" she called out, trying to keep her voice low. They were still far enough away from the barn that Duran shouldn't be able to hear them, but Marin didn't want to take any chances.

Her mother stopped and turned. "No," she whispered. Her warm breath blended with the frigid air and created a wispy surreal haze around her. "You shouldn't be here."

"Neither should you. What are you doing out here anyway?" Marin asked.

"Taking a walk."

It wasn't a convincing lie, and coupled with the troubled look on her mother's face, Marin knew that something was terribly wrong.

"Why don't you come back inside," Marin suggested. "I'll make you a cup of tea. We can talk."

Lois frantically shook her head. "I'm too antsy for tea. I need to walk. But you look exhausted. Go back to your room, Marin. I meant what I said—you shouldn't be out here."

That sounded like a warning.

Marin didn't want to bring up Lucky and the meeting with Duran, so she took a different approach in the hope of learning what was going on. "Mother, is Dexter alive? Are you about to meet with him?"

She dodged Marin's stare. "I don't know if he's alive."

"You're lying again."

Lois looked around. Her breath was too fast. Her eyes, almost wild now. "You'll turn him in to the police."

Marin felt everything inside her go still. "Dexter's really alive?"

Her mother nodded and then groaned. "He didn't want you to know. He said you'd go to the police."

And she would have. Marin couldn't deny that. Her brother had put her son in danger, and Noah's safety came ahead of her brother's desire to go unpunished for the things he'd done wrong.

"He faked his death?" Marin asked.

Lois hesitated so long that Marin wasn't sure the woman would answer. But she finally did. "He faked his death, Brenna's and Kinley's."

"Kinley had his child."

Her mother's eyes widened. Her reaction was too genuine for it to be fake. "He didn't tell me that. He's been in Mexico. The people who invested in his project wanted to kill him."

That was not good to hear. Marin glanced back at the house to make sure it looked safe and secure. Thankfully, it did.

"But the investors are dead now," Lois continued. "Dexter took care of them."

Oh, mercy. "He killed them?"

"He had to. Don't you see? If he hadn't, they would have killed him. And he could have never come home."

That tightened the knot in her stomach. "But he's home now?"

Lois smiled and touched Marin's arm. "He's home," she said with all the joy of a mother who was about to see her son. Marin could understand that on some level—she had a son. But unlike her son, Dexter was a killer. "He called this afternoon to tell us that he was back. Soon, we'll all be a family again."

Not a chance. Dexter would know that she wouldn't want him anywhere near Noah.

Then, it hit her. "Lucky," Marin whispered under her breath.

God, was Dexter going after him? Did he plan to eliminate Lucky, too?

Blinking back another wave of dizziness, Marin considered running toward the barn. Maybe Dexter was there, waiting to ambush Lucky.

Her mother stiffened and whirled around to face the other direction. The direction of the barn. Her gaze flew to her watch and the lighted dial. "I have to go. It's time."

Marin caught on to her arm. "Time for what?"

"To meet Dexter. He should be waiting in the truck that I left for him at the hay barn. But you can't come. If he sees you, he'll leave." Lois began to run, staying on the trail.

Marin considered following her directly. But that would be a dangerous move, especially if Dexter wanted her dead. Instead, she waited several seconds until her mother had a head start, then went off the trail, using the mountain laurels for cover. She slapped aside the low hanging branches and began to run. She'd get to the barn taking the same path that Lucky had likely taken.

She prayed she wasn't too late to save him from her brother.

Chapter Sixteen

Lucky eased his way through the darkness and the meager shrubs. There wasn't a lot of cover once he got close to the barn.

He was a sitting duck.

And there wasn't much he could do about it.

He kept telling himself that if Duran wanted to kill Kinley, he would have already done it. So, now the trick was to get to this meeting and come up with some kind of resolution that would set his sister free.

A twig snapped beneath his boot, spiking his heartbeat and causing his finger to tense on the trigger of his gun. Lucky paused, waiting to make sure the twig hadn't alerted anyone. It apparently hadn't. He continued forward one cautious step at a time.

There was no light on in the barn, but the entire structure was visible because of the watery white moonlight. The wind was still stirring and that made it next to impossible to know if he was about to be ambushed.

He saw a truck parked at the back of the barn. It wasn't the same one that'd been used to try to kill him, but he was certain he'd seen the vehicle on the ranch.

Lucky walked toward it, keeping vigilant. He wanted to be sure he was mentally and physically ready for whatever was about to happen.

When he was within twenty feet of the barn, he picked up the pace. He practically ran until he got to the north side of the structure, and then to the passenger's side of the truck. He paused there and listened for any sound to indicate something was wrong.

Everything was quiet.

Too quiet.

He glanced inside the truck. It was empty. No keys in the ignition. There was no one in the back, either. Which meant the person who'd driven it, Grady Duran probably, was already inside the barn. If Duran had truly been the one who'd tried to run them down, then Lucky intended to make the man pay.

Trying not to make his presence known, he maneuvered his way to the back entrance, a double set of high wooden doors, one of which was slightly ajar. He peeked in, but it was too dark to see anything.

He stepped inside.

The toe of his left boot rammed into something soft and pliable that didn't budge when Lucky gave it a light shove with his foot.

He waited a moment, until his eyes could adjust to the darkness. Lucky saw the bales of hay stacked on both sides of the barn in staggered piles. They seemed to extend to the ceiling, and there was only a narrow path that cut through the middle of the barn.

And then he looked down.

What he'd walked into was no bale of hay.

It was a body.

"Hell," he cursed.

Without taking his attention off his surroundings, he stooped and fumbled around until he located the person's neck. He shoved his fingers against the carotid artery.

Nothing.

Not even the hint of a pulse.

Frantic now, he prayed this wasn't his sister. He turned over the body. Not Kinley.

Grady Duran.

There was blood. Lots of it. It spread out across the entire front of Duran's shirt.

Both the blood and the body were still warm.

That just had time to register in his head when he heard a muffled scream. But it wasn't so muffled that he couldn't figure out who'd made that blood-chilling sound. Kinley. He was certain of it.

With his gun ready and aimed, he stepped over Duran and began to make his way through the maze of hay bales. He had to find his sister. She was in trouble. The person who'd killed Duran might have already gotten to her.

There was another sound.

Lois Sheppard.

And Marin.

He couldn't understand exactly what Marin was saying, but she sounded close, probably just outside the barn. His first instinct was to shout for her to stay back.

To tell her to run. To get away. But he didn't have time for that.

Then pain exploded in his head.

Lucky felt himself falling, but there was nothing he could do to stop it. He hit the hay-strewn floor of the barn hard just as the world went blank.

His last coherent thought was that he wouldn't be able to save Marin.

"DEXTER?" LOIS CALLED out again.

Marin caught up with her mother just outside the barn and tried to stop her from shouting Dexter's name.

"This could be dangerous," Marin warned. There were no signs of Lucky. Nor his sister or Grady Duran.

Not Dexter, either.

No signs of anyone. A meeting should be taking place, but where were all the parties? Where was Lucky?

"Dexter's in there," her mother said, and she bolted for the barn.

Since it was obvious her mother wasn't going to stop her quest to see Dexter, Marin got her gun ready and followed her through the front entrance. The place was pitch-black. She reached for the overhead light, only to realize that wasn't a good idea. She grabbed a flashlight from the tack shelf instead and turned it on.

She fanned the circle of light over the darkness, and the first thing she saw was Kinley.

Lucky's sister was tied to a post, gagged and blind-folded with rags. She was struggling to get free and mumbling something.

And that's when Marin noticed Lucky.

Lying on the floor.

"Lucky?" Even though it occurred to her head that it might be a trap, she couldn't stop herself from running to him. God, he couldn't be dead.

He wasn't moving.

Her panic soared when she saw blood on his head. Not a gunshot wound. At least she didn't think it was. The wound was small, and he wasn't gushing blood. It looked as if someone had clubbed him across the back on the head.

"Lucky?" she repeated.

With the gun in her right hand and the flashlight in her left, she stooped down, rolled him onto his side and made sure he was breathing.

He was.

Thank God. But he still needed medical attention. She reached for her cell phone, only to realize she'd left it in her room.

"Mother, do you have your phone with you? I need you to call for help."

Her mother didn't answer. She looked behind her, turned the flashlight in that direction and saw nothing.

Her mother was gone.

Marin got up to run to Kinley, to see if the woman had a phone, but then she felt something.

Lucky gripped on to her arm. "You need to get out of here," he warned, forcing his eyes to open. He winced in pain and touched his fingers to his injured head.

Despite his weak voice, she felt relief. He could speak. However that didn't mean he didn't have serious injuries. "I need to get you to the hospital. You're hurt."

Lucky shook his head. "You have to leave. *Now.* Duran's dead."

An icy chill went through her. "Dead, how?"

"Shot."

Mercy. Was Dexter responsible? Probably. But she didn't have time to point fingers now. "Can you stand up? I have to get you to the hospital. Kinley, too."

"Where's Kinley?" He sat up and wobbled, so Marin helped him to his feet. Somehow. She cursed her own dizziness and weak legs.

"She's here in the barn. Alive." Marin hadn't seen any obvious injuries, but that didn't mean there weren't some.

And where the heck was her mother?

With Lucky leaning against her and with her gun clutched in a death grip, they made it through the hay bales to the front of the barn.

The moment Lucky saw his sister, he reached for her, and though he was clumsy from his injury, he pulled the gag from her mouth.

"Watch out!" Kinley immediately shouted.

From the corner of her eye, Marin saw the movement. And the gun. It was aimed right at Lucky.

"No!" she yelled and automatically turned the flashlight and her gun in the direction of the shooter.

White light slashed across the barn like a razor, blinding the shooter. That didn't stop him from shooting.

Kinley screamed.

But it took Marin a second to realize the bullet had missed her and that it had smacked into a hay bale on the other side of the barn. Bits of dried grass burst into the air.

Praying that the dizziness from the sedative would go away, Marin readjusted her aim and braced herself to return fire. And then she saw the shooter.

Her father.

He re-aimed and pointed his gun right at Lucky.

Marin didn't think about the situation or anything else. She just reacted. She dove in front of Lucky, just as he tried to pull her behind him. They collided, both ending up right in the line of fire.

"Get out of the way, Marin!" her father ordered.

There was no chance of that. In fact, she moved back in front of Lucky. Well, as much as Lucky would allow her to do.

"Dad, what are you doing?" she shouted.

"Saving you. You need to get out of here." His gaze was frozen on Lucky. And Marin knew in that moment what her father was doing.

He intended to kill Lucky.

"Did you murder Duran?" Lucky asked her father.

Howard moved to the side, obviously trying to position himself for a better shot. He had a set of keys hooked to his belt that jangled when he moved.

Marin didn't believe her father would kill her to get to Lucky. But she couldn't be sure. She couldn't be sure of anything right now. Her world had just tipped upside down.

"I had to get rid of him. He got in the way."

Oh, God.

Her father was a killer.

"You've gotten in the way, too," Howard continued, aiming his comments and his gun at Lucky. "And like Duran, you're getting too close to finding out the truth about Dexter."

Blinking back tears and trying to deal with the horrific image of her father as a cold-blooded murderer, Marin moved, intending to use herself as a shield.

"And what truth would that be?" she asked.

"That Dexter's alive," Kinley provided. That hung in the air for several seconds. "Howard helped him fake our deaths that night in the research lab because Dexter took money from the wrong people. Not just from Duran, but from other investors. Dexter promised both he'd deliver a weapon I learned that we couldn't deliver. We only had the technology for components of the weapon, not the entire package."

"So, Duran and the other investor were going to get their money back any way they could," Howard supplied. "One of them put a contract on Dexter's life. That's when I knew I had to help my son."

"You helped him by blackmailing me into staying quiet," Kinley fired back. She looked at Lucky. "I'm so sorry."

Lucky glanced at her, but like Marin, he kept his attention on Howard.

And on his trigger finger.

"Now that Duran's dead and I've discovered the identity of the other investor who's after Dexter," Howard continued, "the only thing I need to clear up is this mess." He tipped his head first to Kinley and then to Lucky.

"You aren't going to try to kill them," Marin insisted.

"I won't try. I'll *succeed*. I have to, for Dexter's sake." Turning to the side so he could still keep an eye on them, her father pulled the barn door shut and, with his left hand, used the key on his belt to lock them in. Of course, the back entrance was still open. If possible, they could use that way to escape.

Because she had no choice, Marin tried again. She had to make her father see that what he was doing was crazy. "You'll be arrested. You'll go to jail for murder."

"No. Brenna will take the blame for this. She has to be eliminated, too. After I'm done here, I'll find her and plant this gun on her."

Lucky inched closer to her father. "The deputy's at the house. You plan to kill him, too?"

"No. He won't hear a thing," he said, waving the silencer at Lucky. "Neither will the ranch hands that I asked to patrol the place. I told them to stick to the front of the ranch. They won't come back here."

Mercy. He had planned all of this. She had to do something to stop him. It would have been easier if he were ranting and out of control. Then, maybe she wouldn't have seen the small part of her father that still remained.

"Why would you risk killing your own daughter?" Marin asked.

He looked genuinely insulted. "I don't want to hurt you. I'm only doing what I have to do to save your brother."

"But you nearly killed Marin and Noah on the train

and then again at the drive-in," Lucky pointed out. He took another step closer.

"I didn't set those explosives. Dexter did. And even though I was furious when I learned what he did, I forgave him because he was desperate. *I'm desperate.*"

Marin didn't doubt that. She could see the pain etched in his face. That meant she might be able to talk him out of this insanity.

"And what about Mother? Is she in on this with you, too?" Marin asked, wondering if her entire family had gone stark raving mad. She also wanted to keep her father occupied so that maybe he wouldn't notice that Lucky was maneuvering himself closer.

"Not a chance. Your mother has no idea. That's why I sent her back to the house. I told her that Dexter would meet her there. That's the plan, anyway."

With his gun still aimed right at Lucky, her father walked closer and latched on to her arm. "I don't want you to see this. It might trigger a seizure."

She wanted to laugh at the irony. Her father didn't want to trigger a seizure, but he was willing to kill the man she loved.

In that moment, Marin realized that she loved Lucky. Talk about lousy timing.

"I can't let you do this," Marin said.

But before the last word left her mouth, her father reached out, lightning fast. With a fierce grip, he knocked the gun from her hand. Lucky bolted forward, but her father turned his gun in Kinley's direction.

"Back off," Howard warned.

Lucky froze and stared at Marin. She could see him

process their situation. He couldn't risk killing his sister, or getting himself killed. Because every minute he stayed alive was another minute he had to get them all out of there.

Only then her father latched on to her and started dragging her toward the back exit of the barn, away from Lucky.

Chapter Seventeen

For Lucky, this was a nightmare.

Marin's father was ready to kill him and Kinley, and
now Howard was literally dragging Marin away from the
crime scene. God knows what the man would do to her
when she didn't cooperate with his plan to protect Dexter.

And Marin wouldn't cooperate.

Lucky was certain that it was that lack of cooperation that would get her killed. Because despite Howard's
assurance that he wouldn't hurt her, the man would obviously do anything to protect his precious son. Lucky
understood that on some level. He loved Noah and
would protect him. But not like this.

"Stop," Lucky warned Howard, and he stepped
toward the man cautiously. Lucky didn't want Marin's
father accidentally firing that gun and hitting her.

But Howard didn't stop.

Marin didn't stop struggling, either.

"Don't come any closer," Howard threatened Lucky.
"You and your sister better stay put, or Marin will pay
the price. I'll kill her if you try to escape."

Marin dug in her heels and punched at him, trying to knock the gun from his hand. Cursing, Howard finally gave up and pushed her at Lucky. The impact sent them both crashing into a wooden post.

Howard aimed his gun again, this time at Marin.

"Put down your weapon," Howard warned him, "or I'll shoot her."

Lucky wanted to believe it was a bluff, but he could tell from the stony look in Howard's eyes that it wasn't. Howard had chosen which child to protect.

It wasn't Marin.

"You're doing this for nothing," Lucky insisted.

"Put down the gun," Howard repeated. He took a step closer to them. At this distance, he wouldn't miss, and the shot would be fatal.

Lucky dropped his gun onto the floor and inched himself in front of Marin and Kinley. "Dexter is dead." It was a bluff. A calculated one.

Howard shook his head and stepped even closer. "You're lying."

"No. I'm not. A little while ago Sheriff Whitley found a body at the drive-in. It's Dexter. He died when he set the explosions to kill us."

Marin's father froze.

"Think about it," Lucky continued, hoping that if this was a bluff, it'd stand up to scrutiny. "You haven't heard from Dexter since the explosion, have you?"

"That doesn't mean he's dead."

No, it didn't. But Lucky had put enough doubts in Howard's head. With his hand shaking, Howard unclipped his cell phone from his belt and pressed a button.

The seconds crawled by.

Because the barn had gone deadly silent, Lucky could hear the rings to Dexter's number. No one answered.

Howard's concern kicked up considerably, and while volleying nervous glances between them, he pressed in another set of numbers, looking for someone who could verify Dexter's whereabouts.

Just in case Dexter happened to be alive, Lucky got ready to launch himself at Howard. It would be a risk, of course, but doing nothing would be even a bigger risk. Even if Howard changed his mind about killing Marin, there was no chance he'd let him and Kinley go.

Lucky kept a close watch on Howard's body language while he waited for an opportunity to strike. He glanced at Marin and hopefully conveyed that when the time came, he wanted her to get down.

Marin shook her head, just a little, but enough to let him know that she wasn't going to let him do this alone.

Hell.

"Think of Noah," he mouthed. "He needs you."

It was the second time tonight he'd used the little boy to get her to cooperate, but if this was the only way to save her life, then Lucky didn't feel the least bit guilty. He wanted Noah's mom alive so she could raise him.

"Sheriff Whitley," Howard said when the person on the other end of the line answered the call. "Tell me about the body you found at the drive-in."

Lucky shut out everything else but Howard Sheppard. He watched his face, and Lucky knew the exact moment that the sheriff confirmed exactly whose body had been found.

A hoarse sob tore from Howard's throat. A wounded, helpless sound. But Lucky didn't let it distract him. Nor did he let it allow him any sympathy for the man who'd been about to kill them all.

He launched himself at Howard, plowing into him with full force and knocking him to the ground. Howard's phone went flying.

His gun didn't.

Howard somehow managed to keep a firm grip on it. He could fire at any second, and the bullet could hit Marin or Kinley.

"Get out here now, Sheriff!" Lucky shouted so that Whitley would hear him.

Lucky heard Marin move, first to recover her gun, and then to join the battle. Not good. He wanted her far away from this, but Marin obviously wouldn't have that. She pushed at her father, trying to force them apart.

Howard threw out his hand, and the gun. Lucky was certain he lost ten years of his life when he saw the barrel aimed at Marin.

"Get down," Lucky yelled.

The imminent threat gave him the extra jolt of adrenaline he needed. Despite being bashed in the head, Lucky gathered every ounce of strength he had, grabbed on to Howard's right wrist and slammed his hand against the barn floor. It took three hard jolts.

Then, the gun skittered across the floor.

Lucky didn't waste any time. He drew back his fist and landed a punch to Howard's jaw. Howard stopped moving, stopped fighting.

He surrendered.

"Make sure the sheriff is on his way out here," Lucky instructed Marin. He grabbed Howard by his shoulders and flipped the man onto his stomach. "And then untie Kinley so I can use those ropes."

He didn't want to risk Howard having second thoughts and trying to come at them again. Lucky didn't want to have to shoot the man, especially not in front of Marin.

With the cell phone sandwiched between her shoulder and her ear, Marin worked frantically to set Kinley free. Once Marin had her unbound, she tossed him the rope. Lucky reached up to catch it when he heard something.

He whirled around toward the sound. It'd come from the back of the barn, from the path he'd taken between the stacks of hay.

Someone was there in the darkness, directly behind Marin. Because she was still working to free his sister's feet, she probably hadn't heard the sound or noticed the other person.

Lucky aimed his gun at the newcomer and tried to make sure Howard didn't get free. He was obviously having second thoughts about his surrender because he began to struggle.

"Marin," Lucky warned. "Watch out."

She, too, spun around, just as their visitor stepped from the shadows. The illumination from the flashlight was more than enough for him to recognize the person.

Brenna Martel.

She had a gun clutched in her right hand, which she held just beneath a bulky blanket.

Lucky's heart dropped to his knees when he saw what Brenna had in that blanket.

Noah.

MARIN FELT THE SCREAM rise in her throat.

Her son wasn't moving.

Noah was just lying there bundled in the blanket in Brenna's arms. It took Marin several terrifying seconds to realize that he was asleep, that Brenna hadn't hurt him.

Both Lucky and Marin bolted toward Brenna, but Brenna merely raised her gun. "I wouldn't do that," she warned, her voice hardly louder than a whisper. It didn't need to be any louder for them to understand that Brenna meant business.

And that she had the ultimate bargaining tool.

"Give me Noah," Lucky insisted.

Marin tried to demand the same, but her mouth was suddenly so dry that she couldn't speak.

Her father, however, had no trouble responding to the situation. Without Lucky bearing down on him, he got up from the floor.

Brenna shifted the gun in Howard's direction. "You're not going anywhere. Back on the floor. While you're at it, I want the key to the front door."

Her father actually looked ready to argue, and that infuriated Marin. And terrified her.

"Do as she says," Lucky warned Howard, giving him a chilling glare that seemed much more threatening than Brenna's gun.

Mumbling something under his breath, her father

tossed the keys in Brenna's direction. They landed, clanging, just at her feet.

Howard sat back on the floor. He'd be able to strike easily from this position. If he'd been on their side, Marin wouldn't have minded that, but she had no idea what her father would do if cornered.

"Did you hurt my grandmother?" Marin asked Brenna.

"No." Brenna picked up the key, slipped it into her pocket and checked her watch. "I didn't hurt anyone, not even the police officer guarding the place. I covered my face with a stocking cap so he wouldn't see who I was and then sneaked up on him and held him at gunpoint. I tied him up after I forced him to disengage the security system. I found your grandmother, tied her up and took Noah."

Marin wasn't sure she could believe her, but she held onto the possibility that her grandmother was safe. She had to be alive and well.

"Please," Marin said to Brenna, "give me my son."

"I won't harm him," Brenna promised though she didn't seem convincing. Actually, she seemed disoriented. Her eyes were red and puffy. "I just wanted him here to make sure you would cooperate."

Oh, she'd cooperate, all right. First chance she got, she would get Noah away from this woman.

"Dexter's dead," Brenna whispered a moment later.

"Yes," Marin confirmed. "I think he died while trying to kill us." This wasn't a conversation she wanted to have right now. All she wanted to do was run to her son and get him out of Brenna's arms.

Brenna shook head. Then, the tears welled up in her

eyes. "Dexter didn't mean to hurt me." Just as quickly though, she blinked those tears away and shot Howard a look that could kill. "But you wanted to hurt me. You were going to murder Kinley, Marin and Lucky and set me up to take the fall. Thanks a lot, you miserable piece of slime."

Howard didn't deny it. In fact, he seemed defiant.

"I can't let any of you live," Brenna continued. She glanced at Howard. "Especially you." And then another glance at Kinley. "And you."

"Kinley has nothing to do with this," Lucky insisted.

"She has everything to do with it. Dexter slept with her. He cheated on me—"

"He broke things off with you," Kinley volunteered. "I would have never gotten involved with him while he was still with you."

The pain and tears in Brenna's eyes instantly went away, and in their place was raw anger. Marin had already been terrified for her son, but that look took her beyond that. It took every ounce of her willpower not to launch herself at Brenna.

"Don't," she heard Lucky say. Obviously, he knew what she was thinking. He had the same need to protect Noah.

"So, what are you going to do?" Howard snarled.

"I'm leaving."

"Leaving?" he questioned. "And what makes you think I won't come after you?"

"Noah," Brenna answered without a shred of doubt in her voice. "He lives if all of you stay put. It's as simple as that."

Mercy. Brenna would use Noah to save herself.

"You mean if we stay put and die?" Howard countered.

"I mean if you're willing to sacrifice yourself for the life of a baby. For your grandson," Brenna added. She looked at Kinley. "Your death will be quick. Painless. Because in five minutes or so, this place will be a fireball. That'll happen with or without Noah here inside. Your decision."

"Oh, God." Marin pressed her fingers to her mouth and tried to figure out how to get away from this. "Please don't hurt Noah."

"Don't worry," Brenna said almost calmly. "I'll make sure he's raised by a good family."

And with that, she started to back out of the barn.

"You don't have to do this," Lucky said.

He took a step toward her, but Brenna lifted her gun. She didn't quite aim it at Noah, but she sure as heck implied that's what she would do.

"I do," Brenna said, spearing Howard's gaze. "Don't I?"

"What does she mean?" Marin demanded when her father didn't say anything.

"I'm a wanted woman, thanks to your dear ol' dad. The man I love is dead. I'm flat broke. I don't even have the components to the chemical weapon that I helped create. Why? Because Dexter sold them on the black market to make some money, and when he did that, he leaked my identity to Howard."

"Brenna Martel is the other investor that the Feds are looking for," Howard supplied. "She used every penny of a trust fund her grandmother set up for her." That helped put the puzzle pieces together.

Brenna continued, "I'll be wanted for murder of the security guard who was killed in the explosion at the research facility once the authorities find out I'm the one who actually set the explosives. I'll be looking at the death penalty."

So Brenna had nothing to lose.

"Without money, where will you go?" Marin hoped it would make Brenna rethink this lethal plan.

"Somewhere I can start fresh." Brenna took another step back. It wouldn't be long before she was out that door. With Noah as a hostage, there was no way Lucky could stop her with his gun.

Plus, seconds were ticking away. It wouldn't be long before the explosives went off. And as much as Marin wanted to live, she didn't want her son anywhere near the place if it blew up.

"Wait," Lucky said to Marin. "Let everyone leave. Give Noah to Marin. I'll go with you. I'll be your hostage. And everyone here will be sworn to secrecy. No one will know you're the investor. I'll use my contacts in the Justice Department to help you clear your name."

But that didn't stop Brenna. She continued to move back. Faster now. While volleying her attention between them and her watch.

How much time did they have? A minute, maybe two? Was that enough time to get Noah from Brenna and save themselves?

Marin didn't think so.

Knowing she had to do something, fast, Marin

glanced at Lucky. He looked at her at the same moment. A dozen things passed between them, and with that look, he promised her that he would save her son.

Even if it cost them their lives.

Marin nodded. And braced herself to do whatever it took to get Noah to safety.

A deep growl came from Lucky's throat. It was the only warning she got before he charged at Brenna. The woman had just glanced at her watch again. It took her several seconds to re-aim her gun. She managed to do that, just as Lucky got to her and wrenched Noah from her arms.

Marin was right there, behind him, ready to take her son.

"Run!" Lucky yelled.

Noah yelled, too. The sudden movement and the shout woke him up, and he began to cry. His screams blended with the sound of the struggle.

Somehow, Marin made it past Lucky and Brenna, though their arms and legs seemed to be blocking every inch of the narrow path between the stacked hay bales.

Marin wanted to help Lucky. She wanted to help him get that gun from Brenna. But it was too huge of a risk to take. She had to get Noah out of there.

So, she ran. Just as she reached the back door of the barn, a shot rang out.

Chapter Eighteen

Lucky ignored the deafening blast from the shot that Brenna fired. He wasn't sure, but he thought it'd landed in the barn loft. He had Brenna's right hand in a death grip and had purposely turned the weapon upward in case she fired.

Which she did.

Lucky ignored the shot so he could keep up the fight to gain control of the weapon. But Marin, Noah and his sister still weren't safe. Worse, Howard might use this particular battle to subdue Kinley so he could use her as a bargaining chip. But there'd be nothing to bargain for if those explosives went off.

"Get out," Lucky shouted to his sister.

From the corner of his eye, he saw Kinley try to do exactly that. Howard, too. Marin's father charged at them while he was still trying to free himself from the ropes that Lucky hadn't had time to secure tightly enough.

Lucky bashed Brenna's hand against one of the posts, and the impact dislodged the gun from her grip.

He pinned her against the hay long enough for Kinley to get by. His sister went running to the back exit.

With Brenna in tow, Lucky grabbed her gun and followed his sister.

Behind him, he heard Howard, and Lucky tried to keep watch to make sure the man didn't ambush him. But thankfully, Howard must have realized they were in dire straits because he was as eager to get out of the barn as Lucky was.

Brenna, however, was a different matter. She continued to fight, scratching at him, while he maneuvered her through the hay. Once he reached the exit, he latched on to her and started to run into the cold night air.

"Marin?" Lucky called out.

"Here," she answered.

She sounded a lot closer to the barn than he wanted her to be, and he spotted her running toward the pasture. She had Noah clutched to her chest, and the little guy was still crying.

Kinley followed Marin, and since Lucky needed to put some distance between the barn and him, he wasn't too far behind. He glanced over his shoulder though and saw something he didn't like.

Howard wasn't anywhere in sight.

Lucky didn't have time to react to that because behind them, the barn exploded into a fireball.

Brenna finally quit struggling, thanks to a chunk of the roof that nearly landed right on them. Lucky latched on to her even harder and raced them across the pasture to safety.

Ahead of him, Marin stopped and looked back. She

was far enough away, he hoped, to avoid being hit with any of the fiery debris. He caught up with Kinley, and the three of them raced to join Marin. Out of breath now and unnerved with adrenaline, they stopped and looked at the blaze that had nearly claimed their lives.

"How dare you endanger my child!" Marin warned Brenna. Her eyes were narrowed, and her breath was coming out in rough jolts.

Lucky checked Noah to make sure he was okay. He appeared to be, despite the crying. They'd been fortunate. A lot could have gone wrong in that barn.

He pulled Marin and Noah into his arms for a short but much needed hug before he turned back around to face Brenna. He was about to add to Marin's warning when he heard the sound of an engine.

Slowly, he looked behind them, fearing what he would see. His fears were confirmed.

A truck was coming right at them.

"It's my father," Marin announced.

The interior truck cab light was on, and the driver's door was partly open, clearly revealing the driver.

"Run," he instructed the others.

However, Lucky didn't move. The man was obviously hell-bent on killing them. Lucky was hell bent on making sure that didn't happen. Noah, Marin and his sister had already been through enough, and this had to end now.

Kinley latched on to Brenna's arm and got her moving.

"Run!" Lucky repeated when Marin stayed put.

He looked at her, to make sure she understood that

he wasn't going to let her and Noah die. She said a lot with that one look. A look that made him realize he would do anything to protect her. That look also made him realize that this could be goodbye.

With the truck closing in on them, she nodded. "I love you," she said. And she turned to run.

I love you.

Powerful words. Words that would have normally shaken him to the core. But he'd have to deal with Marin's admission later. Because right now, he had to do something to stop Howard Sheppard.

Lucky lifted his hand. Took aim at the truck. And waited. Behind him, he could hear Marin running with Noah. His sister and Brenna weren't too far ahead of them. Yet something else to concern him—he didn't want Brenna doing anything stupid.

But for now, he speared all of his attention on Howard.

He watched the truck barrel over the pasture. Howard no doubt had his foot jammed on the accelerator. Pedal to the metal.

Everything inside Lucky stilled. Focused. He adjusted his arm. And when the truck was within range, Lucky double tapped the trigger. The windshield shattered, and Lucky dove to the side so he wouldn't be run over.

He immediately got up and raced into position for round two, so that Howard couldn't get anywhere near Marin and Noah.

But it wasn't necessary.

The truck careened to the left, going right into the

rocky stream. Just yards on the other side, it came to a stop. No brake lights. No signs that the driver had tried to bring the truck under control.

Lucky soon learned why.

With his gun ready, he approached the vehicle. But his vigilance and caution weren't necessary.

Howard was slumped in the seat.

Dead.

"Hell," Lucky cursed.

Now, he was going to have to tell Marin that he'd killed her father.

Chapter Nineteen

The morning sun was too bright, and it glared directly into Marin's eyes.

She didn't move from the glass-encased patio off her bedroom. She couldn't. There seemed to be no energy left in her body so she stayed put on the wicker love seat.

This was the aftermath of a nightmare.

And in some ways, the continuation of one.

Seemingly oblivious to the fact that he'd recently been kidnapped and endangered by Brenna Martel, Noah was playing on a quilt at her feet. He batted at her leg with a small stuffed dog and laughed as if he'd accomplished something phenomenal. Marin couldn't even manage a weak smile in response, though with every fiber of her being, she was thankful that her child hadn't been harmed.

In the bedroom, she could hear the conversations that were going on. Lucky and the sheriff were discussing what had happened. Her grandmother was talking to her mother.

Consoling her.

After all, her mother had only hours ago learned that her husband was a killer and that both her son and husband were dead. That was a lot for anyone to absorb.

Marin, included.

It'd been years since she'd felt real love for her father, and she had already grieved her brother's death a year earlier when she thought he'd been killed. Still, it hurt. It hurt even more that Dexter and her father had been willing to risk her life, Noah's and Lucky's just so they could cover their tracks. It would take a very long time for Marin to get over what had happened. If ever.

"Lucky wanted me to check on you," she heard her grandmother say. She was now in the doorway, examining Marin. "He'll be finished up with the sheriff soon."

"Good." Because she didn't know what else to say, she repeated it.

Her grandmother walked closer and dropped down into the chair next to her. "Your mother says to tell you that she's sorry."

Marin peered into the bedroom. Her mother was no longer there. "Why didn't she tell me herself?"

"The wound's too fresh. Give her time."

Maybe it was her mood or the fact that she didn't trust her mother, but Marin didn't like the sound of that. "I hope that doesn't mean she'll try to get custody of Noah."

"Not a chance. She'll be lucky if she doesn't get jail time for aiding and abetting Dexter. Your brother was a fugitive, and the federal agents aren't happy that she kept his whereabouts a secret from them."

Neither was Marin.

But then, she wasn't pleased about a lot of things.

"What about Lucky?" Marin asked, almost afraid to hear the answer. "Has he said anything about when he'll be leaving?"

"Not to me." Her gran hesitated. "I'm guessing from your tone that you expect him to go?"

Marin didn't trust her voice and settled for a nod. Lucky would have to tend to his sister and tie up the loose ends of this investigation. Without a custody hearing, there was no reason for him to hang around.

Or was there?

So what if she and Lucky had slept together? That didn't obligate him to be part of her life. But God help her, that's what she wanted. Still, she couldn't cling. She'd spent a lifetime being coddled, and if this brush with death had taught her anything, it was that she was strong enough to stand on her own two feet.

She heard the footsteps, glanced in the direction of the sound and saw Lucky making his way toward them. Marin straightened her shoulders and lifted her chin. She doubted that she could completely erase her gloom-and-doom expression, but she tried. She didn't want this conversation to turn into a pity party.

"How's your sister?" Marin asked when Lucky joined them.

"She's fine. She's at the Justice Department office in San Antonio. There won't be any charges filed against her, but she needs to give her statement about what happened the night of the explosion and assist them with the case against Brenna. Once she's done with that, she can leave and get her baby. My nephew," he added, causing a brief smile to bend his mouth.

"Good." Marin winced. It sounded like a token well-wishing. It wasn't.

Looking totally uncomfortable, Lucky stared at her a moment, moved closer and sank down on the floor next to Noah. He immediately got a bop on the forearm from Noah's stuffed dog, and her son giggled.

"Are you playing with your da-da?" her gran asked Noah. She goosed his tummy, causing Noah to laugh even more.

Marin frowned at the question. Her grandmother knew the truth. Lucky and she had lied about, well, pretty much everything—he wasn't Noah's father or her fiancé.

Helen stood. "I think I need a nap. Let me know if you need me to babysit." And with that, she kissed all three of their cheeks and left the room—but not before she winked at Marin.

With her exit came plenty of silence.

Noah volleyed glances between them, trying to figure out what was going on with the sudden silence. Marin wanted to know the same.

"Brenna was arrested, of course," Lucky informed her. He sounded as grim as his expression.

Marin choked back a laugh. "Between your sister and her, maybe we'll learn the truth about what happened at that research facility."

He grunted. "From what Brenna said before they took her away, Dexter couldn't deliver the chemical weapon so he forced her and Kinley to fake their deaths, and then spent the last year trying to eliminate them so there'd be no witnesses as to what he'd done."

Now, it was her turn to make that sound. "And Dexter used your sister as a decoy for the train explosion."

Lucky nodded. "The Justice Department thinks Dexter used a disguise when he got on the train. They'll take a harder look at those surveillance disks."

They'd no doubt take a harder look at all the evidence. But in the end, it would lead them back to Dexter and her father. "I figure that's why Dexter was trying to kill you. Because he knew that between you and Grady Duran, you were close to figuring out the truth."

She paused because she had to and then added, "I'm sorry."

"I'm sorry," Lucky said at the exact moment.

Marin stared at him and blinked. "Why are you sorry? My brother terrorized your sister, forced her to put her child in hiding, and then my father and Dexter tried to murder you."

Lucky held the stare for several moments and then looked away. "I killed your father."

She heard it then. The pain in his voice. It cut her to the bone. Because Lucky was obviously agonizing over something he couldn't have prevented.

"My father didn't give you a choice. And I don't blame you for his death. In fact, if you hadn't killed him, he would have done the same to us. You saved my life, again."

Tears threatened, but Marin blinked them back. She needed to stay strong.

So she could tell Lucky goodbye.

He already had enough guilt without her adding more. The trick was to make this quick. She couldn't make it painless. But she could do Lucky this one last favor.

"As soon as the sheriff gives me the all clear, I'll call a taxi to take me to the airport." She reached for Noah, but he batted her hands away and climbed into Lucky's lap.

Her son grinned up at Lucky. "Da-Da," he said with perfect clarity.

Marin groaned and buried her face in her hands. It was Noah's first word. And it couldn't have come at a worse time.

"I think my grandmother taught him that," Marin said as an apology. She risked looking at Lucky then.

He was glaring at her. "You'll call a taxi to take you to the airport."

It wasn't a question. It was more like a snarl.

"Your rental car is wrecked from the drive-in explosion," she reminded him.

Just then, Noah said, "Da-Da" again. In fact, he began to rattle it off, stringing the syllables together while he snuggled against Lucky.

"You'll call a taxi?"

Both Lucky and Noah gave her accusing stares as if they were waiting. But waiting for what? Marin couldn't give Noah the nod of approval for his Da-Da mantra. Nor could she back down on calling that taxi. She couldn't be clingy. She had to be strong.

Even though her heart was breaking.

Lucky kissed Noah on the forehead and mimicked what her son was saying nonstop. "Da-Da is right." And then Lucky turned those sizzling gray eyes back on Marin. "I might have started out as a replacement father, but as far as Noah and I are concerned, I'm the real deal. Any objections?"

She glanced at her son's happy face and then at Lucky. Not happy, exactly. Hot and riled.

"No objections," she managed to say.

The silence came again.

Marin just sat there. What was she supposed to say or do? The right thing was to give Lucky that out.

Wasn't it?

He had a life, one that hadn't included her before he started investigating Dexter. But then, she'd had a life, too. A life she no longer wanted—it didn't include Lucky.

"You about got it figured out?" Lucky asked.

Marin frowned at his question, which seemed not only eerily insightful, but also like a challenge. Yes, she'd figured out what she wanted. Marin wanted the life in front of her. Lucky as Noah's father. And Lucky as her lover.

No, wait.

She wanted more than that.

The corner of Lucky's mouth lifted. "Count to ten and tell me what you want."

"One," she mumbled. Marin slid down out of the love seat and sat on the floor next to him. She was about to move on to two, but it seemed rather pointless.

"I'm in love with you, Lucky," she confessed. "I don't

want a taxi, and I don't want to go to the airport unless you're with Noah and me."

The other corner of his mouth lifted for a full-fledged smile. "And?"

She leaned in and kissed him. "And I want to be your lover and your wife. I want to marry you."

A chuckle rumbled deep within his chest. "And?"

Marin wasn't sure what he wanted her to say. She'd already poured out her heart. But what she hadn't done was take the ultimate risk. "And I want you to be in love in with me, too."

She held her breath.

Waited.

Heck, she even prayed.

"Then, you have everything you want, Marin. I'm crazy in love with you."

Lucky slid his arm around her neck, pulled her to him and kissed her, hard.

The kiss might have gone on for hours had it not been for Noah. He bopped them with the stuffed dog and laughed when they pulled away from each other.

"Da-Da," Noah announced.

Noah certainly knew a good thing when he saw it. And so did Marin. She pulled her family into her arms and held on tight.

* * * * *

Texas Paternity *continues in February 2010, only from Delores Fossen and Mills & Boon® Intrigue!*

HIS 7-DAY FIANCÉE

BY
GAIL BARRETT

Gail Barrett always dreamed of becoming a writer. After living everywhere from Spain to the Bahamas, raising two children and teaching high-school Spanish for years, she finally fulfilled that lifelong goal. Her writing has won numerous awards, including Romance Writers of America's prestigious Golden Heart. Gail currently lives in western Maryland with her two sons, a quirky Chinook dog and her own Montana rancher turned retired coast-guard officer hero. Write to her at PO Box 65, Funkstown, Maryland 21734-0065, USA, or visit her website, www.gailbarrett.com.

To my wonderful editor, Susan Litman, with
appreciation for all that you've done.
Thank you so much!

Acknowledgements
I'd like to thank the following people for their help:
Destry Labo for answering my questions about
Las Vegas; John K Barrett, for his information about
guns; Mary Jo Archer for her usual super help;
and, as always, Judith Sandbrook, critique partner
extraordinaire. Thank you all!

Chapter 1

He was watching her again.

Fear razored through her belly like the slash of a switchblade—swift, hot, deep. It rippled through her awareness, stripped away her composure, shattering the illusion of safety she'd so desperately built.

Leaving her weak, defenseless, exposed.

No. Amanda Patterson wheezed air past her strangled throat, pressed her palm to her rioting heart. She wasn't weak, not anymore. And she refused to be vulnerable again.

She jerked her gaze past the line of stretch limos, inhaled deeply to steady her nerves. Cars idled by the casino on the gridlocked Strip, their horns blaring, stereos booming. Neon lights beckoned and flashed. And people streamed past, an endless parade of humanity—laughing, fearless people out to have fun on a warm April night.

She let out her breath, eased the death grip she had on her wrist, forced her shoulders to relax. She was imagining things. Wayne wasn't watching her. He wasn't even in Las Vegas. Her ex-husband was in Maryland, in prison, exactly where he belonged.

She was safe. *Safe.* She was thousands of miles away from Wayne, rid of him forever. She was in a new house, getting a new job, starting a new life.

Her sister, Kendall, finished paying the taxi driver and flashed her a smile. "Ready to rock?"

She dragged in another breath, tugged up the corners of her mouth. "You bet."

Kendall tilted her head. Her thick, honey-brown hair slid over her sculpted dancer's arms. "What's wrong? You're not worrying about Claire already are you?"

Her sister knew her too well. "No, of course not. Mrs. Schmidt seems great."

"She is great. And you warned her about Claire's allergies a dozen times. So stop worrying. Claire will have a great time. Mrs. Schmidt will spoil her to death."

To death. Amanda's heart squeezed. Dread shivered through her veins, but she shook off the gloomy thought. This was ridiculous. She was safe. Her three-year-old daughter was safe.

And she wasn't going to let her old fears ruin her new life.

"Then what is it?" Kendall probed. "It better not be Wayne because if you're going to let that creep—"

"It's not him. And I'm fine, really," she lied, embarrassed to let her sister know how rattled she was, how hard it was to quell that horrible feeling that he was spying on her, controlling her, even after all these months.

Kendall studied her with those perceptive hazel eyes.

Then her mouth softened. "Nothing's going to happen. You know that, right?"

"Right." She wouldn't let it. No matter how badly she'd mucked up the past, she owed her daughter a safe and stable life. Heck, she owed it to herself. She'd endured a hellish marriage, the terror of being stalked.

Now she was done with the past, done with the paranoia and fear—and on to a much better life.

She straightened her shoulders, tugged the hem of the tight red minidress Kendall had insisted she wear and tried for a lighter tone. "But getting arrested for indecent exposure isn't exactly what I need right now. Are you sure this dress is legal?"

Kendall tossed back her head and laughed, her trademark exuberance drawing the gazes of passing men. "Mandy, this is Vegas. The place where anything goes."

"Yes, I know, but—"

"But nothing. That dress is fabulous—although I still say you should have lost that ugly purse. Now, come on," she continued when Amanda opened her mouth to defend the huge, battered bag. "Lighten up. This is your lucky night out, remember?"

"Luck. Right." She latched on to Kendall's arm, turned toward the arched entrance to the famed Janus casino. "But walk slowly. I'm not used to these skyscraper heels."

"You're not used to having fun. Which is exactly why we're here. You're going to let loose for once— gamble, meet some hot men, have a ball."

Amanda grimaced. She had no intention of meeting men, hot or otherwise. She knew her limits too well. But Kendall was determined to light up the town, and the least she could do was try.

"Wait until you see this lobby," Kendall added as they

walked by a gleaming Bentley, then climbed the marble steps. "You're going to love it. It's right up your alley."

"My alley? Since when is gambling my thing?" She'd never placed a bet in her life.

"You'll see." The uniformed doorman swung the door open, and Kendall shot Amanda a knowing smile.

Amanda dutifully followed her inside. She gave herself a mental pep talk, tried to resist that constant urge to scan the crowds and monitor her surroundings for Wayne—a habit born of the need to survive. But she didn't need to worry about Wayne anymore. And she was *not* going to let him ruin this night.

She stepped past the doorway into the lobby, looked up and abruptly stopped. A huge, vaulted ceiling soared above her. Beneath it towered an enormous stone aqueduct, its tri-level arcades a marvel of ancient times.

"Oh, my," she murmured, and every thought of Wayne fled her mind. Captivated, she twirled in a circle, ignoring the people streaming around her, intent on absorbing every detail—the statues of Roman emperors, the decorative medallions and columns, the chariot perched on a marble dais.

"I told you," Kendall said while Amanda still gaped, trying to take it all in.

"You were right." This place was amazing. Fabulous. She felt as if she'd been dropped into ancient Rome.

Her gaze lingered on the colorful murals, the display of early black-glazed pottery, and the closet archaeologist in her thrilled. Whoever designed this place deserved an award. She couldn't believe how authentic it looked.

A woman brushed past, jostling her, and Amanda staggered to stay on her feet. She knew that she needed to move, that she was blocking the entrance, but she couldn't seem to budge. She wanted to absorb everything—the gurgling fountains, the flickering torches on the walls, the lions pacing restlessly behind glass. *Lions.* She shook her head, incredulous. This place was unreal.

Then her eyes settled on a plaster relief of Janus, and the tight ball knotting her belly began to slide loose. Janus, the Roman god of doorways and gates, endings and beginnings—the perfect symbol for her new life.

And for the first time in ages a sliver of optimism surged inside her, a long-buried glimmer of hope. She really was going to be all right here. She'd find a new job. Her daughter would thrive. She'd finally find the peace she deserved.

She smiled then, inhaling the soothing scent of moisture from the splashing fountains, the heavenly aroma of roses and gladioli brimming from urns. Still smiling, she turned to join her sister. The tang of a man's aftershave teased her nose.

Wayne's aftershave.

Her heart tripped. She stumbled, anxiety drumming through her. She glanced around, frantic to find the source of the scent, but a crowd formed around her, blocking her view.

Calm. Stay calm, she urged herself sternly. Wayne wasn't here. This had nothing to do with him.

She hauled in air, struggled to swallow around the tension gripping her throat, determined not to overreact. She stepped to the side, tried to work her way through the noisy throng to find where her sister had gone. But the people shifted and trapped her in.

"Get out of my way," a man in a white shirt shouted beside her, and his rough, raised voice agitated her nerves.

"The hell I will," another man answered.

Amanda glanced up, caught the first man's glowering face and took another step back. They were too close. Too close. Trying to beat back the onrush of panic, she cleared her throat. "Excuse me."

They ignored her. Her anxiety building, she prodded the nearest man with her elbow, intent on getting past. But another whiff of aftershave curled through her senses, and her heart made a frenzied throb.

Stop it, she lectured herself. She had no reason to be afraid. This man had nothing to do with Wayne.

And these people were not going to hurt her. She had to get over the irrational fear, this wrenching need to escape.

She pivoted, wobbled on her too-high heels, determined to get free of this mess. But then a fistfight broke out. Someone shoved. The white-shirted man pushed back, sending the beefy man into her side. Thrown off balance, she gasped, dropped her purse, and nearly fell. The contents of her handbag spilled over the floor.

Great.

Her hands trembling, urgency making her head light, she knelt, scooped up her cell phone and keys. The man in the white shirt squatted beside her. "Sorry," he muttered, his voice gruff. His aftershave assailed her, setting off a spurt of panic, unleashing a bone-deep reaction she couldn't control.

"Just leave it. Please. It doesn't matter," she pleaded, needing him to move far away. But he snatched up her wallet and tissues with his thick, stubby fingers, and stuffed them into her bag. Desperate now, unable to meet his eyes, she grabbed her purse, clutched it to her chest and rose.

"Break it up!" someone shouted as she turned and stumbled away from the arguing men. She searched through the crowd for her sister, found her waiting a few yards away.

"There you are," her sister said. "What are you doing?"

"Nothing." Her voice came out high and rushed, and she sucked in a calming breath. "I just got bumped and my purse spilled."

"I told you not to bring that bag."

"I know." She reopened the drawstring top, pawed through the jumbled contents, double-checked that her wallet was there. Relief flooded through her, and she blew out her pent-up breath.

"Well, try to keep up this time," Kendall said, and shook her head.

Feeling foolish, berating her loss of control, she trailed her sister across the room. So she'd smelled Wayne's aftershave. Big deal. He'd worn a popular brand. She'd let her imagination run away from her.

And she had to stop it. She couldn't keep letting him do this to her. Every time she thought of him, he won.

But as they crossed the enormous lobby—past the restless lions, past the Roman arches leading to intriguing gardens and baths—that feeling of trepidation crept through her again, as if eyes were boring into her back. She straightened her shoulders, determined not to assume that submissive hunch, and tried to shrug the sensation off. But it only intensified, crawling up her spine, her neck, growing stronger with every step.

Her temper flared. This was ridiculous. She didn't deserve this constant fear. She had to put an end to the lunacy now.

"Wait a minute," she said to Kendall. Defiant, she stopped, whipped around.

And met the dark, searing eyes of a man.

But not the one who'd bumped her. This man stood apart from the rest, his feet planted wide, his hands braced low on his hips, like an ancient conqueror surveying his realm.

His thick black hair gleamed in the lights. Heavy beard stubble shadowed his jaw. He had black, slashing brows, taut, masculine cheeks and a mouth so sensual it made her breath catch. A black suit gloved his tall frame.

He was handsome, riveting—shockingly so. But more than his dark looks commanded attention. He had a stillness about him, a feral intensity that exuded intelligence, authority, power.

Her heart thumped, made a funny zigzag in her chest. The word *predator* flashed through her mind.

The edge of his mouth kicked up at her blatant inspection. His eyes smoldered even more. Then his own gaze dropped, making a long, slow slide over the length of her, trailing a firestorm of heat in its wake.

Her knees trembled. A zap of awareness sizzled her blood. And a completely different type of tension arose in her nerves.

Her face burning, she whirled back toward her sister.

"Whoa, when I said hot men, I didn't mean that hot," Kendall said.

"What?" Breathless, mortified that she'd responded so outrageously, she grabbed her sister's arm and hauled her away.

"You know who that was, don't you? That was Luke Montgomery. *The* Luke Montgomery. Oh, for goodness sakes," Kendall said when she shot her a blank look.

"Don't you know anything? He's the billionaire who owns this place."

"You're kidding." She'd been ogling a billionaire? How ridiculous could she get?

"No, I'm not kidding. And I can't believe you haven't heard of him. He's been in the news for weeks. You know, because of that woman who was murdered, that casino heiress, Candace Rothchild?"

"No." Amanda slowed to navigate the steps into the gaming pit. She'd been too worried about her own precarious situation to follow the news.

Her sister paused at the bottom of the stairs and huffed out her breath. "You're hopeless. It's a good thing you're in my hands now. I'll get you caught up on tabloid gossip and have you living in sin in no time."

"Great." A wry smile nudged the corner of her mouth. "Just what I need. My own personal guide to corruption."

Kendall grinned back. "Hey, don't knock it."

"I'm not." Her sister might not lead a conventional life, but she did know how to have fun. And at least she hadn't screwed everything up like Amanda had.

Determined to forget all that, she glanced around at the flashing lights and jangling machines, the kaleidoscope of colors and noise. "All right, what's first?"

"Slots. Once you win a little, gain some confidence, we'll graduate to blackjack."

Amanda sighed. She was pathetic. Even her sister knew she couldn't just plunge in and enjoy herself. She had to be coaxed in slowly, teased into having fun.

Her sister took her arm, led her down the aisle to a couple of empty stools. "Here. These machines are loose. They pay out more often."

"How do you know that?"

Kendall propped one slim hip on the stool, squirmed to keep her own short dress from creeping up. "They do it on purpose. They figure if you win here, they can lure you back to the tables and steal your shirt. Now sit down and listen up."

Amanda slid onto the next stool over. She placed her purse on her lap, her amusement growing as her sister gave her a crash course on gambling with slots.

Not that her sister's expertise surprised her. Growing up, Kendall had been everything Amanda was not—confident, popular, outgoing. She'd been the star of every party, the diva on every stage. And she hadn't been afraid to pursue her goals. The day after high school ended she'd hopped on the first bus to Vegas and landed her dream job dancing in a show.

Whereas the far-too-cautious, ever-responsible Amanda had become a teacher and married Wayne.

"Got it?" Kendall asked.

Amanda pulled her thoughts from the past. "I think so." She tugged a twenty dollar bill from her wallet and fed it into the machine, saw the credits appear.

"Here goes." She inhaled, selected the maximum number of coins, and pushed the button to spin the machine. Bars whirred, then stopped. More credits appeared, and she widened her eyes. "Hey, I won."

"I knew you would." Kendall's smile was smug. "I told you your luck was going to change tonight."

"Maybe so." Buoyed by that small success, she pushed the button again. Three lemons. Getting the hang of it now, she threw herself into the game. Cherries combined with sevens. Lemons were followed by bars. Bells dinged. Colored lights flashed. Credits accumulated, then disappeared. Beside her, Kendall cheered, groaned and clapped at her own progress. And a half hour and a free margarita later, Amanda felt like a seasoned pro.

"Ready for the blackjack table?" Kendall called over the noise.

Amanda glanced up. "Go ahead. I'll be there in a minute. I've just got a few pulls left."

"Okay. It's in the back." Kendall drained her drink, hopped off her stool and then jiggled her legs to straighten her dress. "Don't forget to take your ticket. We'll cash out before we leave."

Amanda waved her off and returned her attention to her machine. In the periphery of her vision, she saw Kendall collect her ticket and leave.

She pulled the lever. Lemon-bar-seven. *Drats.* She pushed the button again and won. She grinned, pleased with her take so far. Not too shabby for her first attempt at gambling. She was ahead by fifteen bucks.

And she had to hand it to her sister. It was fun to do something mindless for once, to forget her problems and relax. Kendall had been right to insist that they come.

She gave the button a final press, then waited for the tumbler to stop. "Come on, jackpot," she murmured. A seven stuck. Then another. She held her breath, her hopes rising, her eyes glued on the machine.

The scent of Wayne's aftershave drifted past.

Her heart went still. Every cell in her body tensed.

The machine stopped. She stared at it blindly, her palms suddenly sweating, her pulse pounding so hard she could barely hear.

Wayne wasn't here. He couldn't be here.

Then why was this happening to her?

She gripped her purse like a lifeline, fought the urge to glance over her shoulder and check. She couldn't keep doing this. She couldn't keep panicking and falling apart. Dear God, it had to stop.

But the need to look back grew even stronger—the instinct to protect herself, take cover. *Survive.* Unable to stand it, she leaped from the stool and whipped around.

No one was there.

She didn't move.

Lights flashed on another machine. A woman squealed and laughed down the aisle. Amanda hitched out her breath, ran her gaze up and down the rows, but there was no sign of the man who'd bumped her, no sign of Wayne.

Thoroughly rattled, she turned back to her machine and printed out her credits with trembling hands. Had she imagined that scent? Was that even possible? Her mentally ill mother had hallucinated before she'd—

No. She was not losing her mind.

Maybe it was a flashback, a delayed reaction to stress. The past few years had worn her down completely—Wayne's abuse, the constant fear for her daughter's safety, the painful divorce and move. No wonder she was suffering now.

And she would conquer this fear. *She would.*

Her heart still racing, she inhaled to calm her nerves. Then she walked deliberately toward the back of the casino, refusing to let herself rush. There was nothing to be afraid of. Nothing.

She paused at the end of the aisle, unsure which way to go. Taking a guess, she turned right.

The scent of aftershave hit her again.

Her stomach balled tight. Her heart sped into her

throat. She picked up the pace, walking faster now, even though she knew there was nothing wrong. She was safe, *safe*.

She hurried past a group of noisy gamblers. A bell dinged, and someone cheered. Knowing she was acting foolish but unable to stifle the fear, she walked as fast as she could on the spindly heels. *Run, run, run* bludgeoned her nerves.

She reached the end of the aisle, turned again, then reached some swinging doors. Oh, no. She'd gone the wrong way. The blackjack tables had to be across the pit.

She stopped, started to turn, but Wayne's scent swarmed her again. A hard, narrow object bit into her back, and she froze.

"That's right," the man said. "Stay quiet, and you won't get hurt."

Her knees buckled. A dull roar invaded her skull. The obscene smell of aftershave permeated the air.

"Walk over to the doors. Slow now." He rammed the gun deeper into her back, and she stepped forward, trying to battle through the hysteria and think. It wasn't Wayne. He had the wrong voice. But then what on earth did he want?

"Stop," he demanded when she reached the double doors. "Now give me the ring. And no fast moves."

"R…ring?" He wanted her jewelry? But she didn't wear any. She wheezed in the too-thick air. "But—"

"Now." His voice turned harsher. He prodded her again with the gun.

"But I don't…"

The double doors swung open. A waitress stepped out, balancing a tray.

Now or never.

She lunged, slammed into the waitress. The woman shrieked, staggered back and dropped the tray.

Amanda didn't hesitate. She ran.

Chapter 2

The soft buzz of his private telephone line cut through the silence—muted, deceptively quiet, like the rattle of a Mojave Desert Sidewinder preparing to strike. Luke Montgomery stared out his penthouse window at the Las Vegas skyline shimmering against the dark velvet sky. He'd left instructions not to be disturbed. A call now could only mean one thing.

Trouble. Just what he didn't need.

He exhaled, knowing he couldn't postpone the inevitable, and padded across the carpet to his desk. He punched the button to answer the phone. "Yeah."

"Mr. Montgomery. Frank Ruiz in security. I'm sorry to bother you, but there was an armed robbery attempt in the gaming pit. I thought you'd want to know."

"I'll be right there."

Luke disconnected the phone and frowned. An armed robbery attempt. Interesting timing with the investment consortium scheduled to vote in just two weeks. A coincidence or something more?

Thoughtful, he pulled his suit jacket from the chair where he'd tossed it, slipped it on as he strode to the door. Coincidence or not, he couldn't afford the bad publicity. Candace Rothchild's murder had caused enough problems.

Not that being suspected of murder had hurt his business. He exited his penthouse, the edge of his mouth ticked up in a cynical smile. Crowds flocked to his casino, whipped up by lurid rumors in the tabloids, hoping to glimpse the man who'd supposedly clubbed the heiress to death.

But his consortium investors weren't nearly as intrigued. The murder—combined with the downturn in the economy—had made them nervous. Too nervous. More problems now would cause them to bolt.

And no way could he let that happen.

His gaze hardening, he crossed to his private elevator, then leaned back against the mahogany panels as it started down. He had everything riding on this project. He'd spent twenty years meticulously constructing his empire, amassing money, power.

Twenty years plotting revenge.

The elevator doors slid open, and he headed toward the security office, ignoring the employees scurrying out of his way. Nothing could jeopardize this project. Nothing. If this robbery attempt was legit, he'd hush it up, keep it out of the papers until the deal went through. And if it wasn't...

He mentally shrugged. Whoever had planned this escapade had made a mistake, a big one. No one played Luke Montgomery for a fool.

A lesson the Rothchilds should have learned long ago.

He entered the office, met the eyes of the guard on duty behind the desk. The balding man leaped to his feet. "Mr. Montgomery." He tugged at the tie dangling from his beefy neck.

Luke nodded, got straight to the point. "What's going on?"

"A woman said she was held up at gunpoint near the slot machines. I've pulled up the surveillance tapes. She's in the next room."

"Let's see the tapes." He rounded the desk as Ruiz lowered himself into his chair and keyed the bank of monitors to the proper time.

The screens flickered, and suddenly a woman strolled into view from a dozen angles. Her full hips swiveled with a seductive swing. Her high breasts shifted and swayed.

Luke's gaze cut to her face, and his heart made a sudden swerve. Well, hell. It was the blonde he'd admired earlier in the lobby.

He studied her now with frank appreciation. She was on the tall side, slender, but the tight dress revealed her ample curves. She had long, shiny hair, sweetly rounded hips, the kind of killer legs that could fuel his fantasies for years.

He slanted his head. She wasn't the usual overblown Vegas type, despite the skimpy dress. She seemed more natural, unstudied—a rarity in Sin City, a place where illusions ruled.

She stumbled on the mile-high heels, regained her balance and glanced around. The cameras caught her darting gaze, and his gut went still.

She looked furtive. Guilty.

Bad move, babe. Better to look nervous *after* the guy with the gun shows up.

As if on cue, a man appeared on scene. The newcomer kept his head bent low, his face carefully hidden from the camera's view. His long, stringy hair swung past his jaw, hiding his features even more.

Luke's gaze narrowed on the man's pleated blue shirt and black bow tie—the uniform his dealers wore. "Is he one of ours?"

"We don't know yet. We're checking the records now."

He rubbed his stubble-roughened jaw, watched the episode play out. The galley doors swung open. A waitress stepped out, carrying a tray. The blonde crashed into her, then bolted off, while the man ran the other way.

He raised a brow. The blonde thought fast on her feet, he'd give her that much. "Who is she?"

The guard consulted his notes. "Amanda Patterson. Said she arrived in Las Vegas last week. She's staying with her sister, Kendall Patterson, a dancer in your ten-o'clock show."

Luke thought back to the brunette he'd seen with her in the lobby. A dealer and a dancer. An inside job, then? Probably a scam to sue the casino.

The spurt of disappointment took him by surprise. He knew better than to expect the blonde to be innocent. This was Vegas. Everyone was on the make. Even the prettiest face masked a conniving heart.

The guard switched to another screen, and Luke watched the man exit the casino, still hiding his face. He checked the time on the tape. Twenty minutes ago. No point looking for him now.

"Let me know what the employee search brings up. Contact legal, call the police. Get Martinez over here if you can." He and Martinez went way back to their child-hood in Naked City, the slums beyond the Strip. He could count on him to keep the story hushed until the Phoenix deal went through.

He turned, headed down the hall to interview the blonde. Chances were that this was an inside job, but he couldn't rule out the Rothchilds. Harold Rothchild was buried in debt, his empire on the verge of collapse. Luke's project would seal his doom.

Which was exactly what Luke planned.

Of course, if the Phoenix project failed, he would suffer instead. He set his jaw. Good thing he didn't intend to fail.

He pushed open the office door, spotted the blonde standing by the desk. She turned toward him as he entered the room.

His gaze met hers. A sudden awareness shivered between them, and he hesitated in midstride.

She was even more attractive close up. Her eyes were a deep, startling blue, as vibrant as the desert sky. She had pale, creamy skin, a smattering of freckles on her feminine nose. Her lips looked soft and lush.

She was pretty, damned pretty—stunning if he factored in those world-class legs.

But this close he could also sense an aura of vulnerability about her. She stood with her shoulders hunched, her arms crossed tightly across her chest. Dark circles shadowed her eyes.

The sudden urge to protect her caught him off guard.

He frowned, shook himself out of his daze. This woman didn't need his protection. For all he knew, she was here to swindle him. "Amanda Patterson?"

"Yes." Her low, smoky voice slid through him, doing strange things to his insides.

He crossed the room. "I'm Luke Montgomery."

"Yes, I know, I…" A blush crept up her cheeks. "My sister pointed you out earlier."

He'd bet. He reached out his hand. She hesitated, then gripped his palm. The smooth, silky feel of her skin arrowed through him, deleting his thoughts. He was held immobile by those amazing blue eyes. His heart beat hard in his chest.

After several long moments, he realized he was still holding her hand. He scowled, pried his fingers loose, annoyed by the effort it took. What the hell was that about? He hadn't been that affected by a woman in years.

And this one could be trying to deceive him.

"Have a seat." Anxious to put some distance between them, he retreated to the desk, then leaned back against it and folded his arms.

She perched on the leather chair in front of the desk and crossed her legs. His gaze fell to her lean, bare thighs, traced the elegant curve of her calves. Realizing his thoughts were derailing again, he lifted his eyes.

"So what happened?" His tone was more brusque than he'd intended, and she blinked.

She sat up straighter, flexed her wrist as if it ached. Her chest rose as she drew in a breath. "I was going to the blackjack tables to find my sister, but I got lost. I've never been here before. I started to turn around but then a…a man came up behind me."

Her voice trembled convincingly, but he was determined to stay objective. "He was armed?"

"I think so. He jabbed something into my back. I thought…it felt like a gun."

"Then what?"

"He said…he wanted my jewelry, my ring."

His gaze cut to her unadorned ears, to the cleavage bared by the plunging dress, and his mind flashed back to the tapes. He hadn't noticed any jewelry before the attack. A slipup there.

"So you handed it over?" he asked, knowing damned well she hadn't.

But she surprised him by shaking her head. "No, I…I don't have any jewelry, not anymore." She lifted one slender shoulder and lowered her eyes. "I sold everything a while back when I needed the money."

So she was short on cash. Good motive to run a scam.

He pinched the bridge of his nose and sighed. No matter how attractive she was, he didn't have time for this farce. He'd make sure the Rothchilds weren't involved, keep this damned thing out of the news, then let the police handle the rest.

"So you're saying a man held you up with a gun you didn't see, and demanded jewelry that you don't have."

A small frown creased her brow. "You don't believe me? You think I made this up?"

"We have cameras all over the casino. I saw the tapes." He raised his brows. "You looked nervous even before the man showed up."

Her smooth lips parted. The color drained from her face. "But that's because I thought…I thought…" She pressed her fingers to her lips and closed her eyes.

"You thought what? That you'd pretend to be attacked and sue the casino?"

Her eyes flew open, and she gasped. "You think I'd pretend about something like that? Are you joking?"

She let out a high-pitched laugh. "Oh, God. This figures. I thought…" She shook her head, gathered her bulky purse and rose. "Forget it."

"The hell I will." He pushed himself away from the desk and blocked her path. "You thought what?"

"Nothing. It doesn't matter." She tried to step around him, but he reached out and grabbed her upper arm. She flinched, jerked back. "Let me go."

He dropped her arm, stunned by the urgency in her voice, the flash of fear in her eyes. She quickly scuttled away.

He studied her, taken aback. She couldn't be this good of an actress. She was actually afraid of him.

He eased apart his hands, made his expression neutral, his voice nonthreatening so she wouldn't bolt. "Look, I'm not trying to hurt you. I just need to know what happened."

"I…" She nodded, sucked in her breath, as if to pull herself together. "I didn't really… It was just…my ex-husband. Wayne Wheeler. I thought he was here."

He eyed the distance she'd put between them, the wary way she watched him—defensive, alert, like a cornered animal ready to run. And anger stirred in his gut. He had no patience for abusive men. And unless he was wildly off base, this woman had been attacked.

He struggled to keep the emotion from his voice. "Your ex lives around here?"

She shook her head, sending her silky hair sliding over her arms. "He's in Maryland, in jail. It wasn't him. It wasn't even his voice. But I thought, earlier… I was just nervous. I overreacted. I'm sorry." She rubbed her forehead with a trembling hand, sank back into her chair.

He frowned. He didn't doubt her story. Her fear looked real… And the facts would be easy to check.

So what should he do about it? Assuming she was telling the truth, this still didn't eliminate the Rothchilds' involvement. Or her sister's. It wouldn't be the first time an unsuspecting family member had been an accomplice to a crime.

Which led him back to his original problem. He paced across the room, pivoted, then returned to lean against the desk. He had to contain this, keep it out of the news. He couldn't let that consortium implode.

Which meant making sure Amanda Patterson didn't talk.

But somehow the thought that anyone would hurt this gentle woman made it hard to stay detached.

"I need to go." Her eyes pleaded with his. "My sister will be wondering where I am. I left her a voice mail that I'd meet her in the lobby."

"You can leave as soon as you talk to the police." A knock sounded on the door, and he rose. "That's probably the detective now. I'll walk you out to the lobby when you're done."

"All right." Their gazes held. The vulnerable look in her eyes tugged at something inside him, urging him to shelter her, to keep her safe.

He shook it off. Her life, her problems were none of his concern. The only thing he needed to do was convince her not to talk. But she had been attacked in his casino. He could at least alleviate some of her fear. He turned, strode out the door.

Ramón Martinez from the Las Vegas Metropolitan Police Department was waiting for him in the hall. "Martinez." Luke shook his hand, briefed him on the situation, and the need to keep it quiet for now. "Could you check on the ex and make sure he's still in jail?" he added. "The name's Wheeler. Wayne Wheeler."

"No problem." The detective flipped open his cell phone, called in the information. "It'll take a few minutes to run him through the system. I'll get a statement from the Patterson woman and get back to you on that."

"Thanks." Luke returned to the main office, had his security guard run the tapes again as he waited for the detective to finish up. Now that he'd heard Amanda's version of events, the anxiety in her eyes made sense.

His gaze lingered on the seductive flare of her hips, those endless legs. It was too bad she wasn't his type. She was a damned attractive woman. But he only dated celebrities, supermodels, women willing to hang on his arm for an evening in exchange for a fancy meal.

He didn't have relationships, and he didn't mix dating with business. And that's all Amanda Patterson could ever be—a business concern. One he needed to wrap up now.

She emerged from the office a few minutes later. "I heard back about Wheeler," Martinez said from behind her. "He's still in jail."

"Good." He caught Amanda's gaze, and that disturbing attraction rocked through him again. His eyes dipped from her face to those killer legs, and he had to struggle to remember his plan. "I'll walk you out."

He nodded to the detective, held the door open for Amanda, then accompanied her down the carpeted hall. He liked how her long strides kept pace with his, how her height made it easy to meet her eyes.

"Thanks for checking on Wayne for me," she said, her voice subdued. "It helps to know he's far away." Her eyes held his, and the worry lurking in those vivid eyes bothered him more than he cared to admit.

"No problem. I have a favor to ask, though." They reached the door to the lobby, and he paused. "I'd like to keep this incident out of the news—at least for a couple of weeks. I'm in the middle of some negotiations right now, and I don't want the publicity. So if anyone calls you—any reporters, the tabloids—I'd appreciate it if you didn't talk."

"Okay."

"The paparazzi can be persistent," he warned her. "I doubt they'll get wind of this, but if they do they'll call, show up at your door, follow you around."

"But that's ridiculous." Her forehead wrinkled. "Why would they care what happened to me?"

"They won't. But I'm big news these days."

"I see." She bit her lip, made that flexing motion with her wrist again.

He frowned. "Did you get hurt back there?"

"What?" She looked at her wrist. "Oh. No, it's an old injury. It aches sometimes."

He nodded, tugged his business card from his inside pocket and held it out, determined to make sure she complied. "Here's my number. Call me if they show up. I'll top whatever they're willing to pay."

She blinked, shot him a look of disbelief. "You're offering to pay me not to talk?"

"I told you that I don't want the publicity right now."

"Well, neither do I." Stunned outrage tinged her voice. "I have a daughter to protect. I don't want to be in the news."

But money had a way of changing minds. And the tabloids' pockets were deep. "Take the card, Amanda." He pressed it into her hand. "Just call me if they contact you."

She glanced at the card and shook her head. "There's really no need. I told you that I won't talk."

He let out a cynical laugh. "Promises don't mean much when money's involved."

"Well, mine does."

Her eyes simmered with indignation.

He tilted his head, impressed. Despite her air of fragility, the woman had courage. He liked how she held her ground.

Hell, he liked a lot of things about her. His gaze lowered, traced the sultry swell of her lips, then flicked back to her brilliant blue eyes. And hunger pulsed inside him, the slow, drugging beat of desire.

But this woman had no place in his plans. He stepped away, crushing back the urge to touch her, giving them some much-needed space.

She cleared her throat. "I'd say good-night, but it hasn't really been good, has it?"

"No, not good." Especially with this disturbing attraction between them.

"Farewell, then." She turned, pushed open the door.

He followed her into the lobby, then stopped, inhaling deeply to clear his mind. His eyes tracked the alluring swivel of her hips as she continued across the marble floor. She joined her sister, and the two women walked to the door.

But suddenly she paused, glanced back. Her eyes met his, and another bolt of electricity zapped his nerves. Then she pivoted on her high heels and went out the door.

For a long moment, he just stood there, the image of

those lush lips and long legs scorched in his brain. Then he slowly eased out his breath.

So that was done. She was gone. He had no reason to see her again. His security chief and the police could handle the investigation from here.

He hoped her ex-husband left her alone, though. He hated to think of her afraid, cowering before some brute.

And he hoped that he could trust her. Amanda Patterson was a wild card, an unknown, someone beyond his control.

Someone, he had a feeling, it would take a very long time to forget.

Chapter 3

The telephone was ringing again.

Amanda sat motionless on her sister's patio, her muscles tensing, the teaching application she'd filled out forgotten in her hand.

"Phone, Mommy," Claire announced from her turtle-shaped sandbox in the yard.

"I know." Amanda tried not to let fear seep into her voice. "But Aunt Kendall's at rehearsal. We'll let the answering machine pick it up." And hope to God it wasn't another hang-up call.

The answering machine kicked on, and her sister's perky voice floated through the open sliding glass door. The machine beeped. The abrupt silence of the disconnected line made her stomach churn.

She set down her papers and rubbed her arms—chilled now, despite the heat. It was just another wrong number or a junk phone call. There was nothing sinister about people calling and hanging up. Annoying, yes. Dangerous, no.

Even if the hang-up calls had only begun three days ago, after the casino attack. Even if they now got a dozen such calls a day. Even if whenever she answered the phone, there was only heavy, ominous breathing— nothing more.

It couldn't be reporters. They would talk to her, ask questions, not just breathe and hang up.

This was something Wayne would do—something he had done to unsettle her nerves. But Wayne was in jail. That detective had checked.

She set her pen on the table and rose, placed a rock over the job application so it wouldn't flutter away. Regardless of who was calling, she wasn't going to let this get to her. And she wasn't going to let Claire sense her fear. She'd moved here to give her daughter a safer, more peaceful life, and she would succeed.

"It's time to get the mail and have our snack." She struggled to make her voice cheerful, but Claire still looked at her and frowned. "How about some apple juice and animal crackers today?"

"Okay." Claire trotted over, and Amanda brushed the sand off her daughter's bottom and hands, adjusted the sun hat flopping around her sweet face.

"Wait. Brownie." Claire grabbed the bear she'd propped on the patio chair and hugged it close. Too close. Had Claire picked up on her fear?

She forced a smile to lighten the mood. "Is Brownie going to help us get the mail?" She knew the answer, of course. Claire didn't go anywhere without her bear. Brownie ate with her, slept with her, played with her.

She'd hugged off most of its fur, kissed the color from its once-black eyes. Amanda prayed that bear never got lost, or Claire would be destroyed.

"You two can lead the way," she added, and followed her along the walkway to the gate. Her sister lived in one of the new developments that had sprung up during the recent building boom. It was a modest, family-oriented neighborhood with two-story stucco homes, a far cry from Wayne's luxury condo at the Ritz Carlton in DC. And thank goodness for that. Wayne had been all about status, appearances. He didn't care that there'd been no place for Claire to ride a bike or play.

She unlatched the gate, waited for Claire to toddle through. She couldn't even begin to imagine how Luke Montgomery lived. She'd read up on him during the past few days, learned that he was a notorious playboy, a megabillionaire developer who owned casinos and resorts throughout the world. That suit he'd worn had probably cost more than her car.

An image of his broad, muscled shoulders, the dark, sexy planes of his face flashed into her mind. She didn't doubt the playboy part. The man was lethally attractive with his deeply graveled voice and intense eyes. And that moment in the hallway when she'd thought he was going to kiss her…

She shut the gate behind her with a forceful click. Surely she'd imagined his interest in her. Luke Montgomery operated completely outside her orbit—which was fine with her. She had all she wanted in life right here. Maybe she didn't hobnob with billionaires, and maybe she'd once dreamed of a more exciting life, but she had a great sister, a daughter she adored. And soon she'd have a job and her own house, too.

She just needed to lose this constant fear.

"Wait for me," she warned Claire. She grabbed her daughter's hand to make sure she didn't dart off, then walked with her toward the mailbox. The warm sun shimmered off the neighbors' red-tiled roofs. Palm fronds rustled in the breeze. Laughter and the thump of a bouncing basketball came from some teens shooting hoops down the street.

She let Claire open the mailbox and pull out the advertisements and bills. She lunged forward to catch a sheath of junk mail tumbling loose.

"Mine," Claire cried and clutched the mail.

"I'm just getting the stuff that fell." She scooped up the ads and stray letters and then closed the box. A plain white envelope in her hand caught her eye.

She paused, turned it over. No name. No address.

A sliver of foreboding snaked up her back.

She shook it off, exasperated by her overreaction. She was getting ridiculous, imagining danger at every turn. It was probably an advertisement. She tore open the back flap, pulled out the contents—a piece of white paper, some photos.

Photos of Claire.

Her heart stopped.

She flipped through the photos. Claire riding her pink tricycle. Claire eating at the kitchen table. Claire sleeping next to Brownie in her bed.

The air turned thick. Her hands shook as she unfolded the note. *"Put the diamond in the mailbox or else."*

Her lungs seized up. Sheer panic roared through her veins. She fought to maintain her composure, but every instinct screeched at her to snatch Claire up and flee.

Calm down, she ordered herself fiercely. Don't let Claire see your fear.

Forcing her feet to move slowly, normally, she followed her daughter back to the house. She looked casually to the neighbor's windows—no movement there. She opened the gate and let Claire through, then snuck a glance at the street. Empty.

But someone was spying on them, taking photos of Claire.

Her panic intensified, threatening to overwhelm her, but she ruthlessly crushed it down. She ushered Claire calmly into the house and locked the sliding glass door. She lifted Claire to the sink and washed her hands. Still working on autopilot, she took out the juice, helped Claire into her chair, opened the animal crackers and propped up the bear.

"What's wrong, Mommy?" Claire asked, her voice tight.

"Nothing. Nothing at all." Her falsely cheerful voice sounded too far away. "It's just a little hot in here. I'm going to close the drapes to keep it cool. I'll be right back."

She forced her lips into a brittle smile, closed the blinds on the sliding glass door and strolled sedately into the hall. Then she raced around the house like a maniac, locking the windows, yanking the drapes closed, scrambling up and down the stairs, rushing from room to room to room, throwing the deadbolts on every door.

She returned to the kitchen, sank into a seat across the table from Claire and covered her face with her hands. What on earth was going on here? What diamond? She'd sold her wedding ring as soon as she'd left Wayne.

Besides, Wayne was in jail. It couldn't be him.

Unless he'd hired someone else to harass her.

Trying to compose herself, she scrubbed her face with her quivering hands. God, she was sick of this. So bloody tired. All she wanted was a life without fear. Was that too much to ask?

The phone rang.

She jerked up her head, stared at the phone. Her palms started to sweat.

The ringing stopped. The answering machine turned on. Her sister's message ended, and the machine made its high-pitched beep.

And then there was heavy breathing.

"Tonight." The single word cleaved the silence, detonating her nerves. The machine clicked off. The tape whirred softly as it rewound.

Her adrenaline surged. Panic wiped out her thoughts. She had to run. Flee. Go somewhere, anywhere, and keep her daughter safe.

She looked at Claire, saw her daughter's lower lip quiver, the anxiety pinching her face. And she knew with dead certainty that she couldn't run. If this was Wayne, he'd only find them again. For Claire's sake, she had to end this terror now.

And if there was one thing she'd learned about her ex-husband, it was that he thrived on power and control. He wanted to see her run, plead, whimper with fear. And she'd be damned if she'd play his sick games.

She rose, her knees knocking so hard she could barely stand, and crossed the kitchen to the answering machine. She ejected the tape, slipped it into her pocket and disconnected the phone.

Then she grabbed her purse from the counter and

fumbled through her wallet for Detective Martinez's card. She found Luke Montgomery's number instead.

She hesitated. Should she call him? If the letter and phone calls were related to the casino attack, he would want to know.

But her priority was Claire, keeping her safe. Which meant reporting this to the police—no matter what Luke Montgomery might want.

Still, the memory of the skepticism in his eyes made her pause. He hadn't trusted her; that had been clear. He thought she'd sell her story to the highest bidder, even though she'd given him her word.

And maybe she was a fool to care, but there was something sad about a man that cynical, who thought that money always talked. And if she didn't call him now, she'd only confirm his jaded beliefs.

So maybe she should warn him. Maybe she should update him on this latest threat first and then inform the police.

And pray that whoever was watching them didn't see them go.

She met her daughter's frightened eyes, and a frigid pit formed in her gut. Claire was right to be afraid. Because if their watcher learned what she was up to, her daughter would pay the price.

The Las Vegas police were certainly thorough. Three hours later, Amanda still hunched on a folding metal chair in the Las Vegas Metropolitan Police station while Claire dozed on her lap. She'd turned over the evidence, given multiple statements, submitted fingerprints so they could exclude her prints from the note. Now several people crowded around her in the air-conditioned room—the detective she'd met in the casino, a petite police officer named Natalie Rothchild, several others whose names she couldn't recall.

And Luke Montgomery. He'd arrived shortly after she had, to her surprise. Now he sat in the chair beside her, the sleeves of his crisp white shirt rolled up, his dark forearms braced on his knees, listening intently while Natalie Rothchild summed up the case.

The police officer tucked her short brown hair behind her ears, then cleared her throat. "All right, then. In light of these developments, I think we have to consider the possibility that the ring isn't lost after all."

"Damn," Luke muttered.

Amanda glanced around at the circle of grim faces, confused. "What ring?"

Detective Martinez shifted his bulky frame in his seat. "We had a murder case recently—a woman named Candace Rothchild. You might have read about it in the news."

"Yes." She'd read up on the sensational case after she'd met Luke.

"She was Natalie's sister," he added.

"Oh." Amanda shifted her gaze to the other woman. "I'm sorry."

Natalie nodded. A pained look shadowed her eyes. "The night she was killed, Candace was wearing a diamond ring, a family heirloom we called the Tears of the Quetzal. We never found it, so we assumed it was lost. But we'll have to rethink that now."

Amanda frowned. "You think my note is related to that ring?"

"I think we have to consider that possibility, yes."

"But I just moved here. How could I possibly be involved?"

"That's what we need to find out. And it might not be related. But we can't rule it out, especially since the man who held you up demanded a ring. And that note is similar to the one my father received." She turned her head, spoke to one of the men. "Get that note to Lex Duncan at the FBI, will you?"

Amanda's head whirled. She gaped at the nodding men. Surely they were joking. She was tangled up in a diamond theft? It didn't make any sense.

She gave her head a sharp shake, tried to recall the facts of the case. From what she'd read, Luke had hosted a jewelry convention in his casino a few weeks back. Celebrities from around the globe had attended the glitzy event—including the casino heiress Candace Rothchild. Later that night she'd been murdered, her ring stolen. The priceless diamond ring—rumored to be under a bizarre curse promising the wearer love at first sight—had never been found.

Luke had originally been a suspect, although he'd later been cleared of the crime. She cut her gaze to his harsh profile, noted the rigid line of his jaw. No wonder he'd come here. He was as involved in this case as she was.

She pressed her hand to her throat, still unable to process it all. It was bad enough to think Wayne could be watching her. But a vicious murderer…

"There's something else I need to tell you," Natalie said gently.

Dazed, Amanda jerked her attention from Luke. The other police officers rose and began filing out. "I'm sorry. What?"

"Your ex-husband was released from jail last week."

Shock rippled through her. She tightened her hold on Claire. "But…Detective Martinez said he was in jail."

Natalie made a face. "I'm sorry. There was a computer glitch, and some of the data didn't get entered on time. Wheeler reported to his parole officer in Maryland yesterday, though, so you shouldn't have to worry about him."

"You don't know Wayne." He was clever. Cunning. And he knew her habits, her fears. She closed her eyes, felt her skin go cold. Her worst nightmare had just returned.

Natalie stood. "We've increased our patrols in your neighborhood, and we'll have someone monitor the house tonight in case anyone goes near that mailbox. We've also told Maryland to alert us if Wheeler breaks his parole."

It wouldn't do any good. Wayne had gotten around those measures before. A tight ball of terror knotted her gut.

Natalie shook her hand. "We'll be in touch."

"Thank you," she whispered, knowing there wasn't much else the police could do. She'd learned that fact back East.

"Claire, honey." She nudged her daughter gently to wake her. "It's time to go."

She roused her daughter, helped her to her feet, then left the room on quivering legs. Behind her, Luke and Natalie began to talk.

So Wayne was out of jail. He would come after her, if he hadn't already. He'd promised her he would. And if that weren't enough, she had a killer on her heels, demanding a ring she didn't have. Hysteria gurgled inside her. Could her life get any worse?

And what on earth should she do? Clutching Claire's small hand, she exited the building, then squinted in the blinding sun. She had to go home, warn Kendall. But then what? Should she leave town?

Would it do any good? Running from Wayne was hard enough. How could she flee an enemy she didn't know?

"Mommy," Claire said, her voice anxious.

Realizing she'd been squeezing Claire's hand, she relaxed her grip. "Don't worry. Everything's okay," she lied. She knelt, ignored the pavement sizzling her bare knees, and gave her daughter a hug. She buried her face in her hair, inhaled her little-girl scent, held her small, warm body tight against hers.

But a terrible dread lodged inside her, a wild, desperate fear that seeped like ice through her bones. How could she protect her daughter from a killer? She'd never felt more terrified in her life.

But she had to succeed. Claire's life was in her hands. She opened her eyes, smoothed the silky strands of hair from her daughter's cheeks, then eased her grip and rose.

"How about macaroni and cheese for dinner?" she suggested. This was definitely a comfort food night. "And then we'll watch a movie, maybe *Mary Poppins.* Would Brownie like that?"

Claire whispered to her bear, then held it up to her ear. Her big blue eyes met hers. "*The Little Mermaid,* too."

"Sure, we can do that." They might as well watch movies all night. No way would she fall asleep knowing a killer was lurking outside. She grabbed Claire's hand and stepped off the curb.

"Amanda, wait." She glanced back, surprised to see Luke Montgomery hurrying toward her, his black hair glinting in the sun.

He caught up to her and stopped. He glanced at Claire, then leveled his whiskey-brown eyes at hers. "We need to talk."

"Sure." Although she couldn't imagine what he'd have to say. She motioned to her green Honda Accord across the lot. "I parked in the shade. Why don't we talk over there?"

"All right." She started across the lot with Claire, and he slowed his pace to theirs. Without her high heels on, she was more aware of his height, the power in his fluid stride.

She slid a glance at the hard male planes of his face, that sexy, carnal mouth. His eyes captured hers, and a sudden tension sparked between them, igniting a flurry of nerves. She quickly turned away.

They stopped in the patch of shade beside her car. He leaned back against it, folded his muscled arms across his chest. His gaze caught hers again, touching off another rush of adrenaline, and she forced herself to breathe.

"What kind of security system do you have?" he asked.

"On the house?" She frowned, led Claire around the car to the rear passenger door, hoping the distance would quiet her nerves. "We don't have one, just locks on the windows and doors."

"That's what I figured." He turned to face her, propped his forearm on the roof, drawing her gaze to the black hair marching across his tanned arm. "If that killer's out there, you need better protection than that."

Her stomach clenched. "I know." But it would take time to get a security system installed—time she didn't have.

"I have a place you can stay," he said, and she raised

her brows. "A house. It's in a gated community on the north side of town. It has an alarm system, round-the-clock security guards. You'll be safe there."

She stared at him over the roof. He was offering her the use of his house? "That's nice of you, but—"

"I'm not doing it to be nice. Not entirely." The edge of his mouth quirked up. "You and your daughter need protection. I don't want any bad publicity right now. If you're in a safe place, the attacks will stop. It solves both our problems.

"The house is comfortable enough," he continued. "It has a pool, tennis courts, a home theater. If there's anything else you need, you can let me know."

Comfortable enough? He had to be joking. She'd seen pictures of the mansion in the tabloids. It put a sheikh's desert palace to shame. "Comfort isn't the issue."

"Then what is?"

She made an exasperated sound. "Well, for starters, I don't even know you."

He lifted one broad shoulder in a shrug. "You'd hardly see me. I spend most of my time in my penthouse. And it's only until they find this guy."

"Even so…" She shook her head, opened the car door for Claire. It was impossible, crazy. "What if the tabloids find out? Won't that make things worse?"

"I doubt they'll find out. They won't expect it, and I pay my staff not to talk. Although…" He drummed his fingers on the car roof, and a calculating look entered his eyes. "That's not a bad idea. We could spin it, play that angle up. Hell, the consortium might even approve."

"I'm afraid you've lost me."

"If the media thinks we're engaged, it would give

them something to speculate about besides the murder. I'd need you to attend a few events with me, though."

"Engaged?" Her jaw dropped. He wanted her to pose as his fiancée? "But…that's ridiculous. No one would believe it. I'm not even your type."

Amusement crinkled his eyes. "They'll believe whatever story we feed them. Besides…" His gaze dipped, making a long, heated slide over her breasts, and her heart fluttered hard. "I think I know my own type."

"Right." Her voice came out breathless, and her face turned warm. This was nuts. She had to get a grip and control herself before she totally embarrassed herself. "Except that if I'm in the news, Wayne and that murderer will know where I am for sure."

"But at least you'll have better security."

She couldn't argue that. She and Claire were vulnerable right now. She'd even dragged her sister into this mess. But moving into Luke's mansion…

"I appreciate the offer," she said carefully. "I really do. But I'll have to think about it."

His expression turned sharp. "You think I murdered Candace Rothchild? Is that the problem?"

"What? No, of course not." She ducked, helped Claire into her car seat to avoid his scrutiny. Truthfully, she didn't know what to think. According to the tabloids, Luke had argued with the murdered woman that night, and they'd had a tumultuous, romantic past. But the police had cleared him of the crime. And she couldn't imagine him killing anyone, considering how gentle he'd been with her.

But she was a lousy judge of men.

She straightened, flexed her wrist—a stark reminder of just how flawed her judgment was.

Luke's gaze stayed on hers. "I didn't do it. I despised the woman, but I didn't kill her. That's part of the problem, though. If they reopen the case, I'll be back in the news. The police might investigate me again."

"I'm sorry. It's just…this is pretty sudden. I need to think." She closed Claire's door, walked around the car to the driver's side. Luke straightened and stepped out of her way.

"You'd like the house. You both would," he said as she climbed inside. She nodded, closed the door, then rolled down the windows to let in air.

He bent down, putting his face just inches from hers. She tried to ignore the virile beard stubble coating his jaw, the disturbing effect of his riveting gaze. "It's a safe place, Amanda." His deep voice caressed her nerves. "No one will bother you there."

Except him. "Thank you. I really will think about it."

Of course she couldn't accept the offer. It was beyond ludicrous. She'd already moved in once with a man she'd barely known, and that had been a disaster. She couldn't compound her mistakes.

She backed out of her parking space and drove to the nearest exit. While she waited for a break in traffic, she glanced in the rearview mirror. Luke stood by a gleaming black Jaguar convertible, watching her with those arresting eyes.

She shivered. No wonder the women flocked to him. Just being near him had a devastating effect on her nerves.

And he was wrong about the media. Even if she agreed to the fake engagement, they would never buy it. She spotted a break in the traffic and gunned the car, anxious to leave Luke behind. She'd seen photos of his dates in the tabloids—gorgeous, voluptuous women, the kind who wore designer clothes, shoes that cost more than most people's mortgage payment. A-list women who vacationed on exotic beaches and sun-bathed on yachts.

Whereas she was a high school history teacher. A single mother with a three-year-old child. And she couldn't forget that fact.

She sighed, changed lanes, then worked her way through the city streets toward home. That was the mistake she'd made with Wayne. She'd been flattered when he'd asked her out, impressed that a rich, charming man had showered attention on her. She hadn't cared about his money, but it had been so darned nice to have some-one pamper her for once. All her life she'd worked to put food on the table, to keep sanity in their unstable lives. Wayne had made her feel sheltered, cared for. She'd even admired his self-control.

Big mistake. One she couldn't afford to repeat.

She turned into her sister's street, pushed thoughts of the past from her mind. She neared the house and slowed the car, and every cell in her body tensed. She inhaled, blew out a long, slow breath, trying to stay calm. But what if Wayne was nearby? What if the killer was here? Her knuckles turned white on the wheel.

She pulled into her driveway and idled the car, hardly able to breathe. She scanned the neighbors' bushes and yards, watched for movement around her house. Nothing. She pried her hand from the wheel, hit the button on the remote to open the garage door, checked the street in the rearview mirror.

Everything was fine. No one was there.

The garage door swung open, and she drove inside,

her pulse flaying her skull. God, she hated this fear, this constant anxiety, the need to listen, watch, run. She cut the engine and set the brake. Still scanning the garage, she unlatched her seat belt and opened her door.

The side door burst open. A masked man lunged toward her, a crowbar in hand.

She shrieked, slammed her door shut and hit the locks. Her heart rioting, her hands fumbling, she jammed the key back into the ignition. But the man leaped around the car and smashed Claire's window.

Claire wailed. Amanda's heart went berserk.

She cranked the engine, rammed the gearshift into Reverse, shaking so hard she couldn't think. She yanked off the brake, slammed the accelerator to the floor. The car rocketed out of the garage backward, shot down the driveway into the street—and crashed.

Amanda screamed, her voice merging with the din of twisting metal and shattering glass. The car jumped forward from the impact, hurling her against the steering wheel, and she gasped at the sharp jab of pain.

The car rocked backward again, then stopped. The sudden silence rang in her ears. Stunned, she looked up. The man in the garage ran off.

She swiveled around in panic. Claire still sat in her car seat, sobbing, clutching her bear, her face streaked with tears. But she was all right. She was all right. They'd both survived.

But who had she hit? She looked out the rear window. A cop emerged from his crumpled car.

She closed her eyes, rested her throbbing forehead against the steering wheel, ignored the blood trickling down her cheek. The cop banged on her door. She gestured for him to wait.

And the horror of it all washed through her. She'd nearly lost Claire. That man had tried to abduct her. She'd nearly failed to protect her child.

She sucked in her breath and knew she no longer had a choice. Whether she knew Luke or not didn't matter. They were moving into his mansion tonight.

Chapter 4

Luke had a reputation for being ruthless in business—
a reputation he deserved. He crushed all opposition,
never let emotions interfere with a decision and never
lost sight of his goals.

Which didn't at all explain the turmoil now roiling
through him, this odd hesitation to involve Amanda
in his plans.

He prowled across his sunny patio toward the pool,
the Italian tiles warming his bare feet. He watched
Amanda steer her daughter through the sparkling blue
water, the kid's arms buoyed by inflatable wings.

Bringing Amanda here made sense. She needed
security, which he could provide. In exchange, she
would lend him an air of stability, help pacify the consortium until they voted on the project next week. It was
a logical arrangement, mutually beneficial—vital now
that he'd read the morning news.

He scowled, skirted one of the twenty-foot Canary Island palm trees ringing the pool, tossed the offending newspaper onto a chair. He needed her help, all right. His project's success hinged on this plan.

Hell of a time for a crisis of conscience.

She glanced up from the pool just then and shielded her eyes from the sun. "Luke."

"Mind if I join you?"

"Of course not. Come on in." She steered her daughter to the side of the pool.

He dropped his towel on the chair and dove in, then swam underwater to where she stood in the shallow end. He surfaced near the others, shook the water from his eyes. The kid giggled and ducked behind her mother's back.

"Say hello to Mr. Montgomery," Amanda told her.

"Luke," he corrected.

Amanda smiled, her blue eyes warming, and his heart made a sudden lurch. "Say hello to Luke then."

The kid peeked out. "Luke then," she whispered and giggled again.

Luke grinned back and gently splashed her, and she squealed with delight. Claire was a miniature version of her mother with that angel-white hair and big blue eyes. A little shy, cute as hell.

Her mother wasn't cute. She was a knockout. Thick, dark lashes framed her dazzling eyes. Her hair was wet from the swim, slicked back, emphasizing the feminine lines of her face. Water glistened on her lips and shimmered in the hollow of her throat.

He looked at her shoulders, over the tantalizing cleavage bared by the scoop-necked suit. Water lapped over her breasts, bringing them in and out of focus like a desert mirage, tempting him to peel down that conservative suit, lick the sparkling drops from her skin.

Aware that he was staring, he jerked his mind to why he was here. "I've got news."

Her full lips pursed, and she glanced at Claire. "Let me get Claire settled down for a nap. It won't take long."

"Take your time. I'll swim some laps." He watched her maneuver her daughter to the steps. Water streamed from her shoulders and back as she climbed from the pool. His eyes followed in the water's wake, skimming her naked back, her perfect butt, the taut, creamy skin of her thighs.

She picked up a towel and quickly wrapped it around her waist. The modest gesture amused him, piquing his interest even more.

But it was an interest he couldn't indulge in right now. He plunged back into the water and began counting laps, relying on the exertion to settle his mind. A mile and a half later, his arms and shoulders tired, and the tension pounding in his temples eased. Feeling more controlled now, he touched bottom and waded to the side of the pool.

Amanda waited in a nearby lounge chair. She'd changed, and her snug, sleeveless T-shirt hugged her round breasts. Her hair had dried, and wispy blond tendrils fluttered around her face. Her shorts bared her elegant legs.

So much for regaining his focus.

He sighed, braced his hands on the edge of the pool and heaved himself out. He caught her eyes wandering over his shoulders and arms, down to his abdomen, and below. She bit her lip, looked away.

So she felt the attraction, too. Good to know, even if the timing sucked. He grabbed his towel, shook the water from his hair, then pulled up the chair next to hers.

Her blue eyes met his, and that unnerving sizzle jolted through him again. "I want to thank you again for letting us stay here," she said. "The house is beautiful. And this view…" She waved at the mountains beyond the golf course. "It's fabulous."

"You're comfortable then?"

She shot him a look of disbelief. "This place is amazing. It's like a palace. I've never stayed anywhere so nice."

He nodded absently, blotted the water still trickling down his jaw. "I talked to my security chief this morning, Matt Schaffer. He's engaged to Natalie Rothchild, the police officer you met yesterday."

"What did he say?"

"No one showed up at the mailbox last night."

Her forehead creased. "So they didn't catch the guy who attacked us."

"No, but the FBI thinks the note matches the one Natalie's father got. They won't know for sure until they run tests, but on the surface it looks the same."

Her face paled, making the freckles stand out on her nose. "So the man who tried to kidnap Claire… You're saying he might have been the killer?"

"Maybe."

Her eyes searched his. "You think he'll figure out where we are?"

He handed her the morning newspaper. She unfolded it, glanced at the headlines, and blanched even more. "Oh, God."

"Yeah." The lead story rehashed the missing ring

and murder, his possible role in the crime. Beneath that was a photo of Amanda with Claire.

"But how did they get this photo?" She sounded bewildered.

"Hell if I know."

She gnawed her lip. Stark fear shone in her eyes. "So he knows where we are now. He'll come after us for sure."

"He can't get in. Even a pro would have a hard time cracking this system. And I'm hiring extra guards, just to be safe.

"This was always a risk," he continued, wanting to reassure her. "I thought we'd have more time before the news broke, but it shouldn't affect our plan."

"Our plan?" She sounded numb.

"To pass you off as my fiancée. There's a charity event at the Rothchilds' tomorrow night. My investors will be there. If you're up to it, it's a good place to make your debut."

She passed her hand over her face, turned her gaze to his. "I'm sorry. I'm a little lost here. Investors in what?"

"A project I'm building—a casino and high-rise complex called the Phoenix. It was all set until the real estate market flatlined. Then Candace got murdered, and all hell broke loose." Every damned investor had threatened to bolt. "I've been making progress, getting the investors back on board, but they're still nervous. They're not going to sink money into this project if they think I'm going to jail."

She frowned. "What exactly do you want me to do?"

"Nothing hard. Just hang on my arm and smile, act unconcerned. If you're not worried about the rumors, it will calm them down. They vote on the project next week."

Her forehead furrowed, and for a moment she didn't speak. The warm breeze rustled the palm fronds overhead, dappling shadows over her face.

"Security's tight at these events," he added. "You'll be safe enough." But there was no guarantee. Unease wormed through his gut again, setting off that inconvenient feeling of guilt.

And he knew he had to be honest. No matter how important this project was, no matter how much he needed her help, he couldn't force her to risk her life.

"Look," he said. "You don't have to do this. I can send you somewhere else until this thing blows over—on an extended cruise or to some resort. You might feel safer that way."

Her troubled gaze met his. And then she rose, walked to the hedge along the patio wall. She stopped with her back to the pool and hugged her arms. She looked so lonely, so in need of protection that he had that damned urge to comfort her again.

He picked up his towel and joined her at the wall. For a long moment he just looked at the mountains beyond the golf course, their brown peaks shimmering in the rising heat. And the irony of his predicament made his lips curl. All his life, he'd stared at those mountains. When he was a kid in the slums, they'd seemed huge to him, formidable, like everything he wanted to become—powerful, bigger than the rest. And he'd vowed that someday he *would* be someone, that he'd have money, respect…revenge.

Now it was finally within his grasp. His plans would come to a head next week. But he couldn't put this woman's life at risk, no matter how important the goal.

Amanda turned to him then, and this close he could

see the fatigue tightening her eyes, the dark circles bruising her skin. She looked delicate, wounded, as if she hadn't slept in days.

"I'm serious," he told her. "I can have you and Claire out of here and halfway around the world by tonight."

She sighed. "Thanks, but it won't do any good."

"Sure it will."

"You don't understand." She looked toward the mountains again and flexed her wrist. "My ex-husband, Wayne... He was violent, volatile. I lived in fear of him for years. It was like living in a war zone. I was always on edge, afraid that something would set him off and make him explode. And I...I can't live like that anymore."

"But this isn't about your ex."

"Maybe not, but it doesn't matter. It's exactly the same thing. If this guy thinks I have the ring, he's not going to give up. No matter where I go, he'll follow me. I'll always be looking over my shoulder, wondering if this is the day he finds me, if this is the day he attacks. Wondering if he's watching, waiting."

She rubbed her arms, her eyes frightened, trying to be so brave it made Luke's chest hurt. And he couldn't resist the need building inside him, the need to defend her, protect her. Touch her.

He stepped close. He reached out slowly, giving her time to react, but she didn't flinch, didn't move away. He stroked the velvet skin of her jaw with his thumb, brushed the feminine line of her throat. She was so soft, so gentle. And yet, she was determined to stand her ground.

And something stirred inside him. Something beyond sympathy. Beyond the instinctive need to protect. The realization that this woman was different, special.

Her eyes turned dark. Her pulse raced against his thumb. He leaned closer, so close that his thighs brushed hers. Her warm breath feathered his face.

He knew he should let go, back away, put some space between them. He couldn't move.

His gaze dropped, traced the lush, sultry swell of her lips, then flicked back to her mesmerizing eyes. And a deep ache surged inside him, the need to pull her into his arms, fit that sweet, curving body to his, taste the provocative heat of her lips.

But this woman needed comfort, protection—not sex. He fisted his hand and stepped back.

"You're sure about this?" His voice rasped in the quiet air. "It's not too late to change your mind."

"I'm sure. I'll stay." Her voice was as throaty as his.

"Good." They were committed now, their bargain struck—until his deal went through and the killer was found. "Then I'll pick you up tomorrow at nine."

She hesitated. "I need to check with Kendall first and see if she can get the night off. Claire might not stay with anyone else, especially in a strange house."

"I'll clear it with her boss. She can go on paid vacation for the next few weeks."

"All right then."

He frowned, wishing he could reassure her, wanting to erase the concern from her face. But there were no guarantees. And he didn't trust himself to stay.

Before he could reconsider, he strode across the patio to the house, then paused at the door and looked back. She still stood by the hedge watching him, her eyes worried.

And he knew he had to be careful. There was something different about this woman. Something too compelling. If he didn't watch out, she'd slip under his guard, become far more than a means to clinch the Phoenix deal.

And that was a risk he couldn't afford.

Amanda stood beneath the chandelier in the private ballroom of the Rothchild Grand Casino, her sister's dire warnings about Luke still ringing in her ears. He was an incorrigible playboy, cutthroat in business, possibly even a murderer—a dangerous, worldly wolf to her naive and innocent lamb.

But dangerous or not, he'd been the epitome of charm tonight. He'd introduced her to his investors, hovered attentively at her side, acting the enamored fiancé to the hilt.

He leaned close, and the scent of his warm male skin, the sight of his white teeth flashing in his handsome face made her heart rate climb. "Champagne?" he asked, and his deep voice rumbled through her nerves.

"Sure." Now that she'd survived the first round of introductions without a major faux pas, she could relax.

Luke motioned to a passing waiter and scooped a drink from his tray. The motion tightened his black tuxedo jacket across his broad back. She admired his freshly shaven jaw, the strong lines of his corded neck. And images paraded through her mind like an erotic slideshow—his biceps flexing as he surged from the pool, the dark hair arrowing down his muscled chest. And that delirious moment when his eyes turned to molten gold and she thought that he might kiss her... She inhaled, pressed her hand to her belly to subdue the jitters rising inside.

He turned to her, held out the drink and their eyes locked. And tension ignited between them again, that electric spark of desire. She took the drink with trembling hands, struggled to act composed. They were only pretending, for goodness' sake. The worst thing she could do was start spinning fantasies about Luke. She'd end up mortifying them both.

But just one glance from those carnal eyes and everything inside her went wild.

"I see someone I need to talk to by the bar," he told her.

She cleared the thickness from her throat. "I'll wait here." She could use a moment to compose herself.

He nodded. "I'll only be a minute."

She sipped her drink, watched him work his way across the room. Women latched onto his arm like long-lost friends. Men greeted him with deference and shook his hand. These were the high rollers of Las Vegas, the elite. And they all kept their eyes on Luke.

She drained her glass, hummed to the piano music lilting in the background. A burst of laughter broke out nearby. Waiters in crisp white jackets wove past, scooping up discarded glasses and refreshing drinks.

How many events like this had she attended with Wayne? Not that he'd moved in quite these circles, but they'd been lofty enough. And at every party, he'd worked the crowd, charming clients with that smarmy smile, arranging illicit affairs with the wives. And she'd had to smile through her teeth, play the role of the devoted wife—until she'd finally squirreled away enough money to escape.

A waiter materialized at her elbow. "Another drink, ma'am?"

Goosebumps rose on her arms at the sound of his voice. She cut her gaze to his face, but he just stood there, his expression polite.

She pulled in a breath, forced herself to relax. She didn't know him. He was just a waiter doing his job, wanting to swap out her empty glass. Feeling foolish, she thanked him, exchanged her flute for the full one left on his tray. He bent, picked up a stray glass from a table and strolled away.

She sipped her champagne, determined not to revert to survival mode and start scanning the crowd. She had to stop jumping at shadows. Luke had promised she'd be safe here. She had to forget her fears and calm down.

She looked for Luke, spotted him talking to a gorgeous brunette. Jenna Rothchild. Amanda had met her earlier. The woman clung to his arm, her pose intimate, suggestive, and whispered into his ear. Luke flashed her a wicked smile, then turned to watch her walk away.

Amanda's head throbbed. So much for the enamored fiancé.

But she didn't care. She didn't. Her relationship with Luke was an act, a ploy. He could flirt as much as he liked.

She didn't plan to stand here and watch, though. She drank more champagne, lifted her wrist to check the time, but she'd left her watch at the house. No sporty watch, no bulky purse allowed tonight, her sister had decreed, only the small, sequined clutch that matched her borrowed dress.

Suddenly weary, she pasted a smile on her face, nodded to one of the investors—a balding man she'd met earlier—and wandered toward the corner where the pianist played. She glanced around for a chair, did a double take when she spotted the pianist's face. Silver Rothchild, the former teen pop star. Her career had fizzled as she'd aged, but Amanda had always loved her songs. And goodness, that music she was playing took her back—back to a time when she'd had dreams, her whole life still ahead.

Before she'd met Wayne.

She grimaced and pushed away that depressing thought. She hummed a few bars of the song, glanced at Silver again and noticed how exhausted she looked. Her face was pale. Dark smudges shadowed her eyes. Amanda could relate. She hadn't slept well in days.

A wave of dizziness hit her, and she pressed her hand to her pounding head. Talk about tired. And this headache was getting worse. She pushed back the fatigue, drank the last of her champagne, then glanced around for Luke, but he still chatted across the room.

A man stepped into her path, his dark eyes hard on hers, and her heart made a sudden swerve. But it was just the waiter, the same one she'd seen earlier. She was getting paranoid now.

And Lord, she was tired. Her head whirled. The entire room seemed to tilt. She set the empty glass on his tray, but it fell off and bounced on the rug.

"I've got it," he murmured.

"Thanks," she said, her voice slurred. Oh, God. Was she drunk? That was all Luke needed, for his fiancée to act like a fool. But how could she be drunk? She'd only had two tiny flutes of champagne.

Her face grew hot. Sweat trickled down her scalp and beaded her upper lip. The waiter still stood there, looking expectantly at her, and she used her purse to fan her face.

What did he want? Why was he staring at her like that? She lurched past him, searching for the ladies' room, desperate to find a place to sit down.

But her heart started to race. Her skin felt clammy,

then chilled. She staggered, bumped into the wall, narrowly missing a huge gilded frame. She paused, her face burning now. How could she be sweating when she felt so cold?

She fumbled with the clasp on her clutch purse, searched for one of the tissues she'd stuck inside. The purse was empty.

She frowned. She'd folded up three blue tissues and tucked them inside, next to her lipstick and blush. And she hadn't opened her purse since she'd left the house.

Confused, she veered to a nearby table, grabbed a cocktail napkin from the stack, knocking the rest to the floor. Too dizzy to pick them up, she dabbed her streaming face.

"Ma'am?" someone asked. She turned her head, and the waiter's face wove into view. "Do you need help?"

"Help?" Was that her voice coming from so far away? She stared at him, shocked when his face morphed into Luke's. She blinked, and the waiter's vaguely Hispanic face reappeared.

Someone grabbed her arm. "No," she whispered, and the waiter laughed. Luke's golden eyes seared into hers. The room faded, began to twirl.

And then everything went black.

Chapter 5

Her eyelids refused to open. A dull pounding buffeted her head. *Claire. Where was Claire?* She had to make sure she was safe.

Amanda wrenched open her eyelids, then squinted at the blast of bright sun. Her gaze landed on the copper-colored bedspread, the Navajo rug on the wall. Luke's mansion. She'd made it home. She slumped against the pillows in relief.

"You're awake." Luke's deep voice rumbled from the corner of the room.

She turned her head as he heaved himself from an armchair, then prowled across the room to her side. His thick hair was tousled, his eyes somber. He had on loose, faded jeans, a wrinkled shirt that he'd left undone, inviting glimpses of his muscled abs. Morning whiskers darkened his jaw, giving him a virile, gunslinger look.

She sank deeper into the pillows and closed her eyes. He looked sexy as sin, conjuring thoughts of torrid nights and sweaty sheets. Whereas she probably had raccoon eyes from her makeup and rat's nest hair.

"How do you feel?" he asked.

As if she'd been dragged through a garbage chute. "Not great." She turned her head to the side, winced at the pulsing pain. "What time is it?"

He perched on the edge of her bed near her hip, and she scooted over to give him more room. "Noon. You've been out since I brought you back last night."

She shut her eyes, massaged the ache between her brows. Her eyes felt gritty, and she desperately needed to bathe. "Where's Claire?"

"In the kitchen with your sister. We told her you were tired and needed to sleep. She left you something, though."

Amanda opened her eyes, saw Brownie propped on the pillow beside her head and a huge rush of love warmed her heart. She picked up the bear, pressed the threadbare fur to her cheek. "I hope she didn't see me come in."

"She was asleep."

"Thank goodness." The last thing she wanted to do was frighten Claire. But what must Luke think of her? She'd passed out at the reception, created a scene. "I'm so sorry," she said. "I didn't mean to embarrass you last night."

He lifted one massive shoulder, his expression inscrutable. "Don't worry about it."

"But people must be talking."

"It doesn't matter."

"Of course it does." He'd wanted to avoid bad publicity and give the impression of settling down. Instead, she'd made things worse. "The investors... They must have seen me." And who knew what they'd think?

"We'll adjust." His eyes wandered over her face, her lips. She felt the heat rising from his body, the tantalizing scent of his hair. She fiddled with the bear, her breathing suddenly labored, her heart fluttering in her chest. Lord, he was sexy. The sheer maleness of him made her body hum.

She peeked under the covers, relieved to see she had on her knee-length T-shirt. Kendall must have undressed her. At least she hoped it was Kendall and not Luke. Her face turned hot at the thought.

"So what happened?" he asked.

Good question. She set down the bear and frowned, trying hard to think back. "I'm not sure. I felt fine, a little tired. I saw you talking to Jenna Rothchild."

She eyed his chiseled mouth, the lean, masculine planes of his face. She couldn't blame Jenna for flirting. If he weren't so far out of her league she'd be tempted herself. "I had some champagne, and then I felt dizzy."

"How much did you drink?"

"Two glasses, hardly enough to make me drunk. Plus, I'd eaten a lot of hors d'oeuvres."

Brackets deepened around his mouth. "You think it was food poisoning?"

"I doubt it. That wouldn't make me black out. And I didn't feel sick, just dizzy and tired."

His eyes narrowed, and she could tell he was flipping through possibilities, calculating the odds. "Had you taken any pills? Anything that could have reacted with the alcohol?"

"Nothing. Not even an aspirin." He slanted his head, his eyes turning grimmer yet, and the sudden realization of what he was thinking took her aback. "You think it was drugs."

"They can knock you out fast."

"But that's ridiculous. Who would want to drug me at the gala? The gunman wasn't there."

He rose, paced to the window, then stood facing out, his hands braced low on his hips.

"Luke?" He didn't answer, and her voice rose. "Why would anyone there want to hurt me?" What kind of mess was she in?

He turned and met her gaze. "To get you out of the picture, cause the investors to balk. This project will hurt the Rothchilds' business. Harold's trying to stop it from going through."

"Even so... You really think he'd drug me? Isn't that extreme?"

"He's done worse. In fact, I should have expected a move like this. There's a lot at stake here. He's probably getting desperate by now."

Her mind reeled. This was all she needed. She had a murderer on her heels, an abusive ex-husband who'd vowed to hunt her down—and now a deranged businessman might be drugging her drinks.

She had to admit that the drug explanation made sense, though. That dizziness had come over her fast. And there'd been something about that waiter's voice... But he couldn't be the same man who'd attacked her in the casino. Why would he be at the Rothchilds' event?

For that matter, Luke could have drugged her. She eyed the tight set of his jaw, the intelligence in his amber eyes. She really knew nothing about him, except the little she'd gleaned from the news.

And what if the rumors were true? What if he had

murdered Candace Rothchild and was now after the ring? Just before she'd blacked out, she had seen his face.

But that was absurd. If Luke had wanted to harm her, he'd have done it here, in his house, not in a public place. And certainly not in front of the investors he hoped to impress.

She rubbed the ache pulsing between her brows, struggling to sort through the confusion. Luke wouldn't hurt her. He wasn't a brute, not like Wayne. He was cynical and tough in business, but he'd been nothing but gentle with her.

So had Wayne at the start.

She flexed her wrist, trying not to go off the deep end and imagine the worst. Besides, there was another explanation for her blackout, one that had nothing to do with drugs.

One she dreaded even more.

She glanced around, spotted the sequined clutch on a chair, and her heart struck an uneven beat. She didn't want to look, but she had to find out the truth.

She tossed off the covers and rose, tugged her long T-shirt over her hips. Then she slowly advanced on the purse.

Her pulse pounded as she picked it up. She undid the clasp, hardly able to breathe. She jerked the sides apart. Her heart faltered. The tissues were there, tucked next to her lipstick, exactly how she'd placed them last night. Her hand rose to her throat.

"What's wrong?" Luke asked.

Her purse had been empty. Those tissues had been gone. But then how had they reappeared? "Nothing. I thought I lost my lipstick, that's all."

She set down the purse, her hands shaking. Had she imagined that they'd disappeared? Her mother had hallucinated, suffered from dizzy spells and blackouts...

She thought of the waiter morphing into Luke and back and quickly blocked off the thought. No. This couldn't be happening. She wouldn't let it. If she had inherited her mother's mental illness, she might have to give up Claire.

But what else could have happened? Who had moved the tissues, and why? The only people who'd been near her purse were her sister, Claire and Luke.

She swallowed hard, battled the hysteria surging inside her. She didn't know which was worse—thinking someone had drugged her or losing her mind.

Luke stalked toward her from across the room. She looked up and met his eyes. "I think... I was just overly tired." She made her voice firm. "And then the champagne... I'm sure that's all it was."

He stopped. Deep lines wrinkled his brow. "Do you want me to call a doctor?"

"No." The last thing she wanted was a doctor documenting this.

"He could do a blood test, find out if you'd been drugged."

And what if the answer was no? "I just need to rest. Really. I'll be fine."

"You're sure?"

"Yes." He moved closer, tipped up her chin, and his rough fingers tingled her skin. He studied her with narrowed eyes, as if to discern the truth. She struggled to look convinced.

"You'd better be all right," he said. "You scared the hell out of me last night."

He'd worried about her? She blinked, touched. She couldn't remember the last time anyone had worried about her. She'd always been the responsible one, the dependable one, the one who'd had to take charge and cope.

"Thank you," she murmured. "For everything. For bringing me back here, for helping—"

"Shh. Forget it." He pressed his thumb to her lips. The slight touch set off a storm of sensations, turning her insides to liquid heat. His hand slid to her cheek, cradled her jaw. His eyes didn't move from hers.

The moment stretched. She couldn't think. She was lost in his hot, hot eyes. He slanted his head, tilted her jaw up and she dropped her gaze to his mouth.

Would he kiss her? Her pulse raced. Excitement hammered her nerves. She tried to swallow, but her throat refused to work.

And then his lips touched hers and her heart jack-hammered to life.

His lips were warm, smooth. Pleasure sizzled and rushed through her veins. She gripped his steel-hard arms, slid her palms up his powerful neck, thrilled to the erotic rasp of his jaw.

He felt so strong, so rough, so male. She wanted him closer, wanted that tough, muscled body hard against hers.

As if reading her mind, he tugged her against him, then prodded her lips with his tongue. She shuddered at the sensual invasion, at the deep, pulsing hunger she could barely contain.

He tasted like sin, her darkest temptation, a lure to excitement that she'd never known. The warm, male scent of him ignited her senses. The taste of him shorted her brain. And a sudden urgency consumed her, a desperate need to pull him close. She wanted his hands on her breasts, her naked skin. She wanted to throw off caution and live.

He groaned, widened his stance. The thick, massive feel of him scorched through her blood. She tightened her grip on his neck, bringing her aching breasts tighter against his chest. And still it wasn't enough.

But he stopped, pushed himself away, and she swayed at the sudden loss. And for several long seconds he just stared at her, his eyes glittering with hunger, arousal. Regret?

She blinked, dazed, tried to think through the thick fog of lust. What had come over her? She never acted that impulsive. And the door was open. Claire could come in at any time. She glanced at the doorway, appalled.

"I, uh…" He grimaced, lifted his hands, as if to ward her off. "You'd better rest."

"Right." Her face flamed. Her behavior mortified her. What must he think of her now?

His frown deepened. He inched closer to the door. "About the investors. We'll figure something out." He strode to the door, glanced back. His hot eyes blazed into hers. "And Amanda… Don't worry. I'll keep you safe."

He fled the room, and she sank onto the bed, her whole world spinning apart. What had just happened? How could a kiss affect her like that? She'd never felt such brazen urgency, so frantically turned on in her life.

Sex with Wayne had been tepid at best, revolting later on. She'd assumed that the problem was her, that she wasn't the physical type. Wayne had told her as much.

But that kiss… Dear God. She closed her eyes, pressed her hand to her still-throbbing lips, unable to believe her response.

Luke said he'd keep her enemies at bay—but who would protect her from herself?

As mistakes went, that kiss ranked up with the big ones.

Luke paced across the kitchen two nights later, watching Amanda at the table with Claire. He'd had no business touching Amanda. He'd only intended to offer comfort and calm his raging fear. Because the thought that someone had drugged her… His blood still congealed at the thought.

But giving comfort was one thing. Surrendering to those soft, sweet lips had been totally out of line.

He pivoted at the sink, stalked back toward the table, listening to the lilt of her voice. Even worse, no matter how many numbers he'd crunched, no matter how hard he'd worked in the past two days, he couldn't get her out of his head. He kept veering back to those warm, moist lips, the erotic brush of her breasts. That kiss had left him so knotted up that he'd do anything to touch her again.

Which was crazy. She wasn't even his type. He dated fast, jaded women. Women out for a night of hot sex. Amanda was too innocent, too vulnerable. She even had a kid.

She glanced up as he passed her again and blushed. *Blushed.* He shoved his hand through his hair, appalled. He didn't get involved with women who blushed. He'd lost his friggin' mind.

"Time for bed," she told her daughter. She rose, bent to help Claire from her chair, and his gaze zeroed in on her hips. She wore those shorts again, the ones that hugged her lush behind, exposing the tempting skin of

her thighs. And images flashed through his mind—
Amanda naked, stretched seductively over his bed,
dressed in nothing but a pair of high heels.

"Say good-night to Luke," she said, and he jerked his
mind from that scene.

"'Night, Luke." Claire trotted over and lifted her
bear. "Give Brownie a kiss."

"A kiss?" Caught off guard, he frowned at the scruffy
bear. But the kid was watching him with those huge,
blue eyes, and he hated to let her down. Feeling awkward, he took the bear, pressed it to his cheek, then
flipped it into the air. It spun, started down headfirst, and
Claire made a startled gasp. He caught it on his knee,
juggled it several times like a soccer ball and launched
it back in the air. He snagged it on the down curve and
handed it to Claire.

Her eyes were wide, her mouth open. But then she
giggled, clutched the bear and ran back to her mom.

Amanda's eyes crinkled. Her lips curved into a
smile—a warm, easy smile that softened his heart. Not
his type, he reminded himself firmly. He turned, tracked
those killer legs as she sauntered away, mesmerized by
the swing of her hips.

When she'd disappeared from view, he leaned
against the counter and crossed his arms. Okay, this was
getting out of hand. He prided himself on his self-
control. Hell, he was famous for it. So why was she getting to him?

He frowned out the window at the darkening sky. If
she were different, he'd indulge in a brief affair. That
always got a woman out of his system and took the edge
off his sexual needs.

But there was something special about Amanda,

something he'd felt from the start. She threatened his distance, kicked up feelings he'd long suppressed.

And that was dangerous.

He gave his head a hard shake. He only had one more week until the consortium voted. One more week to masquerade as her fiancé. He could control himself until then.

Determined to regain his focus, he crossed the room to his wine vault, selected a bottle of *Riserva* he'd picked up in Tuscany the previous spring. He popped the cork, set the bottle on the counter to breathe while he waited for her to come back.

She strolled into the kitchen a moment later, then started gathering her papers into a pile.

"What are you working on?" he asked to get his mind off the intriguing way her breasts swayed as she reached for a paper that fell.

"My teaching credential." She set the wayward paper on the stack. "I need to get it validated in Nevada. They have a reciprocal agreement with Maryland, so I don't need to retake the tests. I just have to file the forms."

He pulled two wine glasses from the cupboard and held them up. "Wine?"

"Thanks, that would be nice."

He set down the glasses, watched as she stuffed Claire's crayons into the box. The overhead lamp made her blond hair shine and highlighted the curve of her cheeks. "What do you teach?"

"High school history." Her gaze met his. "I love your casino, by the way. You did an amazing job on the lobby."

He shrugged. "I didn't do it. I told the interior designer to make it look like Rome, then left the rest to her."

"Well, it's wonderful…magical. Ancient Rome must have looked exactly like that."

A wistful smile softened her face, and another spurt of warmth curled through his chest. He realized that he liked pleasing her, liked basking in her approval.

He scowled, turned back to the wine. Since when did he care what anyone thought? He worked alone, rarely asked for opinions. The only approval that mattered was his.

"Speaking of casinos, we need to make another appearance together." He poured the wine, crossed to the table and handed her a glass. "I'd like to do it soon. The consortium meets again early next week to review the final plans."

"All right."

"We should probably include Claire this time. She'll help us look more settled." Especially with the rumors now swirling around. Half of Vegas thought Amanda had an addiction that made her black out at the gala. The rest believed he'd tried to do her in.

But there was no point worrying her with that.

"I'm not sure about Claire." She sat and sipped her wine, her expression doubtful. "She gets shy around strangers, especially if we go somewhere new. Could we invite them here instead?"

He lowered himself into the chair next to hers. "I don't see why not." In fact, it was a good idea. It would give them a more domestic look. He leaned back in the chair, sipped the rich, dark wine, tried to ignore the tempting scent of her skin. "There are six investors, their wives and us. Fifteen people. I'll contact the caterer first thing."

"I don't mind cooking. In fact, I'd like to." She glanced around, and her lips turned up. "You have a fabulous kitchen to work in. And I make pretty good Mexican food—unless you want something fancier."

"No, Mexican's great." And having her cook would add to the homey look. "You're sure you don't mind?"

"I need to do something. I can't just sit here and worry all day."

The anxiety in her voice caught his attention. "Has something else happened?"

"No." She shook her head, but her eyes didn't quite meet his. "It's just the stress, not knowing where the killer is. There hasn't been any word?"

"Last I heard they were still waiting for the lab report."

She nodded, looked away, but this close he could see the fatigue shadowing her eyes. He took a swallow of wine, still studying her face. She was worried, no doubt about it. "You're sure there's not a problem?"

"No, nothing. Everything's fine."

He didn't buy it. She looked as if she hadn't slept in days. But he'd couldn't force her to talk. He nodded toward the papers stacked near her glass, decided to lighten the mood. "So you've never been to Rome?"

"I've never been anywhere. I've never even left the country."

"Why not?"

She shrugged. "Money, life. When I was younger, my mother…wasn't well. She couldn't work, and the disability checks didn't go too far, so I worked to help pay the rent. Then Kendall left for Vegas, and I stayed to help my mom."

He raised a brow. "That doesn't seem fair."

"Kendall sent money, and she came home when she could. Later she offered to move back so I could leave. But it didn't seem right to make her give up her dream. I mean, you can only dance when you're young, right? And I could study any time."

He didn't agree, but nodded for her to go on.

"I didn't mind teaching," she added. "It wasn't as exciting as being an archaeologist, but I liked the kids, and I had enough time off to take care of my mom."

He frowned. Her childhood sounded a lot like his with a mother who couldn't work. And no matter what she said, he doubted her sister had helped much. Amanda had probably taken charge of her mother like she now did Claire.

Disturbed by that thought, he drained his wine, then rose and paced to the sink. It was better if he didn't get involved with her, didn't know her past. It made her too sympathetic, too real.

Too damn hard to resist.

But when she came up behind him, he had to ask. "So where did Wheeler come in?"

She didn't answer at first. She rinsed her glass, wiped her hands, then finally leaned against the counter and sighed. "I met him after my mother died. I was planning to go to graduate school so I could study archaeology and get a job in the field. But he kept pressuring me to move in with him.

"I didn't want to. I hardly knew him. But then…well, I got pregnant, and I didn't want Claire to grow up without a father like I did." She grimaced. "Obviously, he wasn't the man I thought."

"No." He knew Wheeler's type. He'd seen a few violent men when he was growing up—bullies who fed their egos by terrorizing the weak. They were all about power, control. In fact, Wheeler had probably knocked her up just to keep her in his control.

That thought needled him, and he clenched his jaw. He didn't like knowing she'd suffered abuse at the hands of a scumbag. He didn't like knowing she lived in fear of the man.

And he sure as hell didn't like how she stood watching him with those big blue eyes, looking too damn defenseless as she clutched her wrist. His hold on his temper slid. "What happened to your wrist?"

"Nothing."

Like hell it was. "And that's why you hold it all the time?"

She flattened her lips, as if reluctant to talk, but then she let out a heavy sigh. "It was Wayne. He flew into a rage and broke it." Her eyes filled with remembered fear. "I found drugs in the house and confronted him. It was dumb. I never should have challenged him like that."

His mouth thinned. He didn't want to picture it. He didn't want to think of her cowering before that thug. And if he ever got his hands on Wheeler... Anger blazed through his gut.

"That's when I knew I had to leave," she added. "I didn't want drugs or violence around Claire."

That fit. She'd cared for her mom, sacrificed for her sister. And now she protected her child. But who'd ever protected her?

He caught hold of her injured wrist. She tugged back, but he stroked the delicate skin of her wrist with his thumb, felt the frantic beat of her pulse. And emotions swirled inside him. Respect, admiration, desire.

He slowly lifted her wrist, pressed his mouth to the sensitive skin, heard the sudden catch in her breath. Her seductive scent wrapped through his mind.

"Luke..." she whispered.

"I know." His voice came out too deep. "It's a bad idea."

"Very bad." Her pulse sped under his thumb. Her gaze didn't budge from his.

Get out, he urged himself. *Don't let this happen.* He didn't want to get involved with her. He didn't want to know her worries, her pain.

And he sure as hell didn't want to hear her plead for his touch, watch her eyes turn blurry with need or sink into that warmth and make her his.

She tugged her arm. He let her go. "I can't," she said, sounding desperate. "It's too complicated. Claire... There's too much else going on."

"Right." *Distance.* That was what he'd wanted. That was what he'd come for—to forget this attraction, to regain control, to prove that he could resist.

To stay detached.

But as he stared into her eyes, his gut roiling with hunger, he had a feeling it was already too damned late.

Chapter 6

The cilantro had disappeared.

Amanda stared into the refrigerator, unwilling to believe her eyes. She'd put it on the top shelf, right next to the artichoke dip. So where on earth had it gone?

She pawed through the vegetable drawers, her anxiety rising, then checked behind the enchiladas and rice. But the cilantro was nowhere in sight.

She straightened, pushed the refrigerator door closed with her hip and tried to keep herself calm. Okay. She knew she'd bought it. She'd ticked it off her grocery list. She remembered putting it on that shelf. But then how had it disappeared?

A sliver of dread trickled through her, but she struggled not to overreact. So she was acting a little bizarre these days, getting absentminded. She'd left her wallet in the bathroom, her comb in the silverware drawer.

She'd turned off lights, only to later find them switched back on.

But that didn't mean she had a mental illness. Anyone would forget things under this kind of stress.

She barely ate. She hardly slept, thanks to that awful paranoia that nagged her again, the feeling that someone was watching…waiting. And when she did give into exhaustion and nod off, memories of Luke invaded her dreams, leaving her breathless and aching with need.

"Mom. Help me," Claire called from the table, where she was coloring clothes for her paper doll.

"Not right now. We need to run to the store. I forgot something, and the guests will be here soon." She glanced at her watch, then gasped. Yikes. It was later than she'd thought. She had to get that cilantro fast.

She grabbed her purse from the counter, hustled Claire from the table to the garage and set the alarm. Luke wouldn't approve of the errand. Neither would Kendall. They'd both urged her not to budge from the house. But there was a grocery store just outside the entrance to the gated community. She could get there and back in fifteen minutes tops.

She strapped Claire into her car seat, backed quickly out of the garage. It felt good to get out, she decided moments later as she followed a gardening truck down the street. Luke's house was gorgeous—like a luxury resort—but after nearly a week, the confinement was starting to chafe.

She kept the windows rolled down, and the warm desert breeze ruffled her hair. Despite her current danger, she had to admit that she liked Nevada. She liked the wide-open spaces, the mountains jutting against the brilliant blue sky. There was something adventurous about the west. Even the air seemed to pulse with excitement, as if anything were possible here. It was a great place to start a new life—or it would be, once she escaped her current mess.

The supermarket sat in a small, modern strip mall just outside the community's gates. She found a parking space close to the cart return and rushed Claire into the store. She just prayed that they had cilantro, or she'd have to drive across town.

"I'm cold," Claire said, shivering in the air-conditioned store.

"I know. So am I. We'll hurry." She hustled her through the produce section, giving wide berth to a bin of peanuts that would trigger an allergic reaction in Claire. To her relief, there was plenty of cilantro. She shoved a fresh bunch into a plastic bag, grabbed a *jicama* to slice up for the dip. Seconds later, she'd led Claire through the checkout line, then exited to a blast of dry heat.

She pulled out her keys and checked her watch. Oh, God. She had to rush. Taking a firm grip on Claire's hand, she hurried up the row toward her car.

It was gone.

She stopped, whirled around, glanced up and down the row. This had to be the right spot. She'd parked by the cart return, right where a blue Corvette now sat. Bewildered, she scanned the spaces again, then walked between the cars to the next row. But there was still no sign of the car.

Where could it have gone? Had someone stolen it? But who'd take her old Honda with all the BMWs around? The repair shop had done a great job fixing the damage from that accident, but it was still hardly a prize.

"Mom," Claire complained, and she realized she was squeezing her hand.

"I'm sorry, honey. I just can't find our car." She turned in another circle, frantically searching the lot. And then she spotted it two rows away—nowhere near the cart return.

Her heart fumbled a beat. Her breath grew shallow and fast. She didn't remember parking there, had no memory of it at all. But no one could have moved it. No one else had a key.

Still clutching Claire's hand, she warily walked toward the car, feeling as if she were approaching a bomb. Dread pounded her skull. Her palms moistened with sweat. The car had Maryland plates on the brand-new bumper, Claire's car seat in the back. It was hers, all right. And it was locked.

But how could she not remember parking it here?

Her head buzzing, she unlocked the doors, buckled Claire in her seat and started home. Sprinklers swished on the nearby golf course. Laughing children bicycled past. She drove down the road like a zombie, her eyes glued straight ahead, too numb to process it all.

Still dazed, she parked the car in the garage, carried the groceries into the house, trying to focus on the evening ahead. Luke was depending on her to make a good impression tonight, and she couldn't mess up again. She'd think about the lost car and missing cilantro later, after the guests had gone.

She rinsed the cilantro, put it in the colander to drain, went to get the jalapeños from the fridge. She swung the door open, then froze.

The cilantro was back. Right where she'd left it on the shelf.

Her head felt light. The air turned hot and thick. She whipped around, searched the kitchen for signs of intrusion. But the windows were closed. Claire's paper dolls and crayons sat undisturbed at her place. Everything was fine.

Except for her.

Dear God. She was losing her mind.

Something was bothering Amanda.

Luke studied her as she fidgeted with the napkins on the patio table and smiled at Fletcher Coddington, their last, lingering guest. He doubted anyone else had noticed how nervous she was. She'd been the perfect, gracious hostess all night—smiling, keeping the conversation going, making sure everyone stayed comfortable and involved.

And the investors had fallen for her hard. They'd devoured the food she'd made, listened avidly to her stories about local history. Even Claire had behaved like a model child, giving him a stable, domestic appearance.

A car door slammed in the distance, and Amanda's head jerked up. His eyes narrowed. That was it, right there—the way she jumped at routine noises, the way her eyes tightened with the same anxious look he'd seen on that surveillance tape. All evening long her voice had been a little too high, her smile too bright.

Something was wrong, all right, and he intended to find out what. But first he had to get Fletcher Coddington to leave.

He headed toward her, and she glanced up. She straightened, her eyes going wide.

"You must be tired," he said smoothly. He slid his

arm around her waist and pulled her soft, curving body against his.

She stiffened. "I...I'm fine."

"You're sure?" He leaned down and nuzzled her neck, and she didn't quite stifle her gasp.

The hug was for show, part of the charade they'd been playing all night. But the scent of her skin, the feel of her full, round breasts brushing his arm sent a jolt of heat through his blood.

"Luke," she whispered when he nibbled her jaw. "Fletcher will see."

"I hope so." He moved his mouth to her ear, inhaled the aroma of her perfume. "I'm trying to make him leave."

It worked. Coddington set down his whiskey tumbler and glanced at his watch. "Montgomery, it's been a pleasure."

Amanda extracted herself from his arms and rushed to their guest. "I'm so sorry your wife couldn't make it tonight."

Coddington offered her his arm, and Luke followed them through the house. Amanda kept up the chatter until they reached the door.

"You'll have to stop by and see my arrowhead collection," Coddington told her. "I used to dig around the *pishkuns* in Montana when I was young. They frown on that now—can't dig in historical places, you know. I'll probably donate them to a museum some day."

"I'd love to see them," she said, sounding sincere, and Luke frowned at a sudden thought. They'd never discussed their eventual breakup, or exactly how long they'd keep up this charade. But they'd have to continue at least until that killer was found, and Amanda was safe.

Coddington turned to him then. "I take it you heard about the protests?"

He turned his mind back to business. "It's not a problem."

"I don't want a lawsuit tripping us up."

"Don't worry. It won't get that far." He'd make sure of that.

The investor nodded and smiled again at Amanda. "Tomorrow, then." He stepped outside.

"Good night," Amanda called, and he closed the door.

For a minute, neither moved. Luke's eyes settled on hers. Ticks from the nearby grandfather clock rent the air. It seemed strangely intimate standing together like this, as if they really were a married couple, alone in their home at last.

His gaze swept her face. The hall light grazed the curves of her cheeks, showing the deep smudges under her eyes. "I meant what I said earlier. You look tired."

"I guess I am, a little." She turned and headed to the kitchen, and he trailed her there, admiring the way her dress molded her hips.

"You did a great job. The investors liked you."

"It was fun. I told you I like to cook." She picked up a stack of plates from the table and yawned.

"Give me those." He tugged the plates from her hands. "Go sit by the pool and rest. I'll bring you a glass of wine."

"It will only take a minute to clean up."

"Amanda, you're dead on your feet." Not to mention nervous as hell—and he intended to find out why. She opened her mouth to protest, but he held his ground. "Go."

"All right. I'll just check on Claire first."

He stacked the dishes by the sink and poured the wine, then went out the patio door. She sat on the low wall near the myrtle hedge, cocooned by the malibu lights. A cool breeze had sprung up, swishing the palm trees by the pool and tousling the ends of her hair.

He handed her the glass, then sat on the wall beside her, wondering where to begin. If he asked her outright what was bothering her, she'd either deny it or claim to be tired.

"So tell me more about your project," she said.

He sipped his drink, decided to bide his time. Talking about the project might relax her, get her to open up. "What do you want to know?"

"Where are you building it?"

"Naked City. It's not actually a city," he said, when she arched a brow. "It's just an area past Sahara Avenue, outside the Strip."

The corner of her mouth edged up. "Interesting name, though."

"Yeah." He took another swallow of wine. "But that's the only interesting thing about it. It's a slum, one of the worst in Vegas. It's where I grew up."

"Really?" She looked surprised, and he didn't blame her. He never talked about his childhood, couldn't imagine why he'd mentioned it now. But there was something soothing about Amanda, something that invited confidence, trust.

"I figured you always had money," she said.

"Hardly. But the Strip was only a few blocks away. I could see it from our apartment. It might as well have been on Mars, though. It was a world apart, all that luxury and wealth." Completely out of his reach.

"So what was your family like?"

He shrugged. "Small. Poor." He frowned down at his glass. "My father split before I was born. My mother was a cocktail waitress in Harold Rothchild's casino."

The old emotions roiled through him before he could block them—bitterness, helplessness, rage. Restless, he set down his glass and walked to the hedge. Then he stood with his arms crossed and stared out at the night.

Amanda joined him a moment later. Maybe it was the quiet way she stood beside him, her shoulder brushing his arm. And maybe it was the darkness, the intimacy of the night. But suddenly, he wanted to tell her, wanted her to know.

"Her back went out," he said. "She couldn't work. She needed surgery, but we couldn't afford it."

"You didn't have insurance?"

"No. The Rothchilds blocked the unions back then, so benefits were scarce. She tried to get another job but kept missing work because of her back. And then she got hooked on pain pills. She went downhill from there."

Amanda didn't answer, but he found her silence comforting, more soothing than anything she could have said. And he realized that she understood exactly what he'd gone through. She'd also cared for her mother at an early age.

"So what did you do?" she finally asked.

"Lived on welfare. But then the rent went up and we couldn't pay. We got evicted." By their ever-compassionate slumlord, Harold Rothchild.

That moment had changed his life. He'd been twelve years old, fighting off the street gangs, scouring the garbage for food. He'd gazed at the mind-boggling luxury of the nearby Strip, the towering casino that

Rothchild owned, and he'd vowed right then that he'd be rich and powerful someday.

And that he'd avenge his mother's death.

In one more week he'd finally do it. The Phoenix would rise from the ruins of that old apartment and crush Harold Rothchild for good.

"It's not easy being poor," Amanda said gently, and he switched his attention to her. He observed her soft, wide eyes, the sympathetic set to her lips.

"No," he agreed, his voice huskier now. "It's not easy." He reached out and brushed the curve of her cheek, traced the delicate bones of her jaw. And he wondered how she had coped. She'd had a mother to support, later a kid. But she was a lot like him, a survivor. Every time life knocked her down, she'd fought back.

He ran his thumb down the bridge of her nose, over the velvety skin of her cheek. His eyes roamed her face, her curving throat, down to the tempting vee of her dress.

She was amazing, all right. Determined, protective, arousing.

"You look good in this dress." His voice deepened. "Too damned good. If Coddington hadn't stopped ogling you, I was going to slam his face into the flan."

She blinked, then let out a laugh. "Don't be silly. He wasn't ogling me."

"The hell he wasn't."

"Oh, come on. He has to be seventy years old. I probably reminded him of his granddaughter."

"He's been married five times. His current wife is twenty-one."

Her jaw dropped. "You're joking, right?"

He shook his head.

"Oh, my. You do run with a fast crowd."

"Yeah. Fast. Bad." He brushed his hand down her arm, and her smile abruptly disappeared. Sudden tension vibrated the air.

He shouldn't touch her. He was pushing the limits, testing his already strained self-control. For hours he'd been watching her smile and talk, worry and frown. He'd memorized the provocative way her lips quirked and her forehead creased, how her hair shimmered over her back. And all night long he'd been holding her, stroking her, inhaling her feminine scent as he played the part of her fiancé.

It had been four hours of exquisite torture.

And if he didn't get away from her now, he was going to break. "It's late. You'd better go inside."

"I know." Her voice came out breathless. She stayed rooted in place.

He shifted closer, drawn to the heat in her eyes, the lure of her lush, sultry lips. He stroked his hands up her arms, his blood pumping hard. Hunger built in his veins.

Kissing her would be a mistake, a complication he couldn't afford. He needed to protect her, find out why she was worried, not muddy their relationship more.

Besides, they'd agreed to keep their distance. They'd agreed this idea was bad.

But her gaze stalled on his mouth. Her breath made a provocative hitch, and the small sound tore through his nerves.

To hell with control. Ignoring her gasp, he hauled her against him. He plunged his hand in her hair, slanted his mouth over hers. And then he devoured her with a hot, urgent kiss that demolished his self-control.

He was too rough, too urgent, he knew that, but he

couldn't be gentle or nice. The whole evening had been hours of tormenting foreplay, and he was already over the edge.

She wrapped her hands around his neck and sagged against him. He inhaled the erotic heat of her skin. He gathered her closer, giving vent to his unruly hunger, and his entire body turned hard.

She moaned and wriggled against him, sending a bolt of lust to his groin. He broke the kiss, blazed a path down her velvety neck with his tongue, and his desperation surged.

He had to see her, feel her. He caught the shoulder strap of her dress in his teeth, tugged on the bow. The fabric slid down, exposing one breast. She wasn't wearing a bra.

His mind went blank. Stark need roared through his blood. She was beautiful. So damned beautiful. All ripe, perfect curves and sultry skin.

And he wanted to take her, take all of her, make her writhe and quiver and scream. He wanted to hear her breath catch, feel her heart race, make her mindless and whimpering with need.

He cupped her breast with his hand and lowered his head, loved the smooth, creamy skin with his tongue.

"Luke." She moaned and clutched his hair. Then he kissed her again, knowing he was moving too far, too fast.

But she was kissing him back, running her hands over his shoulders, his back. And he needed to feel her right where he ached.

His hands went to her bottom, and he pulled her against him, and the sweet, hot feel of her made him groan.

"Mommy?" a small voice called.

Amanda instantly stiffened. He lifted his head, lust still hazing his brain, and tightened his grip on her hips.

They couldn't stop. Not now. He was too damned aroused.

"I'm coming," she called, and tried to wriggle from his grasp. He inhaled, reluctantly let go. She jerked up her dress and retied the strap.

Her eyes were dark, her lips swollen. Her hair was a tangle of silk. He wanted to sling her over his shoulder and drag her to bed.

"I have to go," she said, sounding breathless.

"I know." But this wasn't finished, not by a long shot. And he still needed to find out what had her on edge.

He shoved his hand through his hair, made a decision. "Get your sister to babysit tomorrow. We're going hiking."

"What? Where—"

"Not far from here. I've got something to show you. And a trip will do you good."

"But…you have a meeting. I heard you talking about it tonight."

"I'm rescheduling it."

She glanced at the house, looking torn. "All right," she finally said. "If you're sure." She turned and hurried into the house.

Sure? He scoffed at that. He wasn't sure of anything right now—least of all what he'd just done. He was canceling a meeting to go hiking? Was he completely out of his mind?

He didn't know. But keeping his distance from her wasn't working. It was time for a change of plans.

Chapter 7

She was a wreck.

Amanda trudged up the trail behind Luke the next morning, so exhausted she could hardly move. All night long, she'd tossed and turned, too wound up to sleep. She'd relived every second of the thrilling evening, from Luke's heated looks to his blistering kiss. And the feel of his mouth on her breast…

She flushed, dodged a twisting juniper pine tree, then hurried to pick up her pace. She'd lectured herself for hours during the restless night, trying desperately to regain her good sense. Their engagement was fake. They had no future together. He was a billionaire play-boy, and she had a daughter to raise.

But none of that seemed to matter. All it took was the sound of his husky voice, one glance from those piercing golden eyes and she wanted to throw herself into his arms.

And if Claire hadn't interrupted them when she had…

She skidded on a patch of loose stones, and Luke whipped around and steadied her arm. "Are you all right?"

"I'm fine." Except that her heart was sprinting again. His eyes swept her body, her face, and her breath took an erratic turn. She tore her gaze away to calm her nerves.

"It's not much farther." He adjusted the pack he'd slung over his back and started walking again. She skirted a clump of cactus, knew she had to watch her step. But her eyes kept returning to the broad, strong ledge of his shoulders, his black hair gleaming in the sun. He wore loose, faded jeans—worn white in intriguing stress spots—and he looked so virile, so blatantly male that she ached to touch him again.

He stopped a moment later at a lookout point. She wiped her forehead on her sleeve, pulled her attention from his muscled biceps and looked out at the view. Directly beneath them was a small valley. A weathered wooden ranch house and derelict barn stood in the overgrown yard.

But the spot was spectacular, the views amazing. Blood-red sandstone lined the surrounding foothills. Smoky green sagebrush punctuated the rocks. The desert shimmered in the distance, topped by that startling, azure sky.

Luke glanced at her. "So what do you think?"

"It's beautiful." She inhaled the scent of juniper pines and sun-drenched earth. "How did you find this place?"

They'd driven for nearly two hours out of Vegas, most of it over teeth-jarring, washboarded roads. They'd eventually turned off the county roads onto private property and bumped along a tractor trail riddled with ruts. Then they'd hiked.

"I own it."

She blinked up at him. "This land is yours?"

He folded his muscled arms across his chest and looked out at the valley below. "I bought it about ten years ago. It's good land, a little isolated, but there's room for an airstrip near the house. There's a river and a small lake over that hill."

She glimpsed at where he was pointing, stunned. She never would have expected him to own a ranch. "What are you going to do with it?"

"Nothing, at the moment. I haven't really made any plans."

That was a relief. She'd hate to see him build a mega-resort or golf course here. She scanned the hills, absorbing the rugged, untamed beauty. The place had almost a spiritual feel.

"Did you buy it as an investment, then?"

"Not exactly." He frowned, shifted his attention back to the landscape.

Long seconds passed, so she tried again. "So why did you buy it?"

He shrugged. "It was a gift of sorts. I told you about my mother."

"Yes." She studied his profile, confused.

"She always talked about buying a ranch. You know, one of those 'when we win the jackpot' dreams. All the years I was growing up, that's all I heard about, how we were going to buy a ranch when we hit it big. So when this came on the market…"

He frowned. "It was dumb. She was already gone, and I sure as hell didn't need more land. But I don't know. It just seemed like the right thing to do."

He resumed hiking, and she followed more slowly,

her mind reeling from what he'd revealed. He'd bought this gorgeous ranch for his deceased mother. Oh, God. Emotions piled inside her, and a huge lump thickened her throat. Who would have guessed that this ruthless, powerful man had a tender side?

But she'd seen glimpses of it from the start. He'd checked on Wayne's whereabouts to ease her worries. He'd offered her the use of his house. He'd helped her when she'd blacked out, even canceled his meeting today so she could relax.

And this side of Luke scared her to death. The physical attraction was dangerous enough. But this softer side touched her heart and made her care.

And the last thing she needed now was to fall for Luke—he was a guaranteed broken heart.

But how was she going to stop?

"Be careful. This part is steep." He leaped down a small incline, then reached back and grabbed her hand. Awareness shimmered through her at the contact, and she sucked in a startled breath. Their eyes met, held. For a heartbeat, neither moved.

But then he dropped her hand and kept walking, and she struggled to regain her good sense. Maybe she was falling for Luke, but he probably just wanted sex.

And why was that so bad?

He stopped in front of a boulder. "Here it is."

Still unsettled, she glanced at the rock. An Indian petroglyph. "Oh, wow," she breathed, her turmoil abruptly forgotten. She rushed to the chunk of brown sandstone, captivated by the crudely drawn lizard etched into the rock. "I can't believe it. It's amazing."

"There are more."

"More?" She glanced around. "Where?"

He motioned ahead, and her heart skipped. Glyphs covered the surrounding boulders—etchings of deer and snakes, horses and human hands. She roamed through the rocks, entranced. "Luke, this is wonderful." To think that centuries ago, people had stood on this very spot, carving their messages into the rocks.

She studied a wavy design that might have meant water. "This probably marked a migration route or game trail." Especially since there was water nearby.

"Maybe, but there's another possibility."

Her face lifted to his. "What's that?"

"I'll show you, as long as you're not claustrophobic."

Her excitement built. "Are you saying there's a cave?"

A smile played at the edge of his mouth. "It's tight at the start, but it opens up. I'll go first with the flashlight. Just watch where you stick your hands. Rattlesnakes are active now."

Startled, she checked the ground, but not even the threat of a poisonous snake could deter her. Luke rolled aside some stones, pulled the pack off his shoulder, then squeezed through a cleft in the rocks.

She quickly followed. The opening wasn't too tight at the start, but Luke's shoulders were wider, and he had to angle them more. The air grew mustier as they entered the cave, the light dimmer. After a dozen yards, they both stooped over, then had to crawl. The walls squeezed in. There was no room to turn around. But Amanda couldn't remember when she'd enjoyed herself more.

"Almost there," Luke called back. Seconds later, the space opened up. He scrambled to his feet, still ducking, and helped her stand. "Watch your head," he cautioned. "It's low in spots." He raised the flashlight and shined it around the spacious room.

"Oh, my," she whispered, too overwhelmed to move. Primitive hunt scenes covered the walls. Hundreds of artifacts littered the ground. There were baskets, carved wooden implements, piles of arrowheads and shafts. It was incredible. She wanted to examine everything at once.

Thrilled, she twirled around.

"Easy." Luke caught her arm. She grabbed his shoulder and laughed.

"Luke, this is amazing."

"Yeah, amazing." He brushed a smudge from her cheek and angled his head. His gaze dropped to her mouth, holding her in place. And suddenly, the Indian artifacts faded away.

And then he kissed her. His mouth was warm and hard, sending waves of pleasure skidding along her nerves. And she melted into the kiss, overjoyed. This was what she'd dreamed of, longed for during that restless night.

His tongue swept her mouth. His big hand caressed her back. She moaned at the drugging sensations, the way her body pulsated with heat. She shifted closer, hoping he wouldn't stop.

But after a moment, he pulled away, then rested his forehead against hers. Her heart hammered fast. Her breath came in uneven rasps.

"Take a minute to look around, and then we'll go," he said, his voice rough.

She nodded, straightened, struggling to shift her attention back to the ruins. But she was far more interested in kissing Luke.

Still, this was the dream of a lifetime. He handed her the flashlight, and she roamed the cave, careful not to disturb anything. "Has this site been surveyed?" she asked as she examined an ancient atlatl.

"Not that I know. I've never seen it in any records. I don't think anyone knows it exists."

She skirted a stack of woven baskets, peered at a deer painted on the wall. The cave might have been a storage site, or maybe a ceremonial place, although she didn't see any remnants of fires. And it looked remarkably intact with no signs of digging or looting. The archaeologists would go berserk. "How did you find it?"

"The farmer had drawn a map. I found it with some old papers in the house."

She took another pass around the cavernous room, absorbing every detail. This was what had drawn her to archaeology—the thrill of discovery, wanting to see how ancient people had lived, wondering what they'd dreamed of, thought about and who they'd loved. The minutes passed by too fast.

"We'd better go," Luke finally said, and she reluctantly followed him from the cave. While she squinted in the blinding sunlight, he rolled the rocks into place and concealed the entrance with brush.

A short time later, they spread their picnic blanket in a patch of shade at the lookout point. Luke pulled out bottles of water and wraps.

Suddenly ravenous, she devoured her vegetable wrap, then dropped back on the blanket and sighed. She inhaled the soothing scent of sagebrush, watched a hawk ride the thermals in the sky. And for the first time in weeks, she felt relaxed, almost carefree.

"Thank you so much for showing me this, Luke. It's spectacular." To think she was one of the few people alive who'd seen it—and that Luke had realized what this would mean to her, how much she'd enjoy exploring the cave.

He stretched out beside her. "You looked tired last night, worried. I thought you could use a break." He lifted himself to one elbow, and leaned over her, kicking off a flurry of anticipation. She studied the hollows of his cheeks, the strong, masculine lines of his neck. A hint of emerging whiskers darkened his jaw.

"So what's been bothering you?" he asked. "And don't tell me it's nothing. You've been acting too jumpy for that excuse."

She sighed, knowing she could trust him, but reluctant to tell him the truth. She didn't want to reveal her mother's illness. If anyone suspected she'd inherited her mental problems, she could lose custody of Claire. And she'd die if she lost her child. Claire mattered more to her than the world.

But she also had to keep Claire safe. And if there was any chance she wasn't imagining things...

"I'm not really sure what's happening," she admitted. "It started the night I blacked out. I've been misplacing things, getting forgetful. But I really think it's just due to stress."

His eyes narrowed. "What kinds of things?"

"Small things mostly." She told him about the missing tissues and cilantro, the other bizarre events. His mouth turned hard as she talked, his eyes grim.

"And why didn't you mention this before?" His voice had a dangerous edge.

"There was no reason to. What could you do about it? You can't keep me from forgetting things."

"What if it's not you? What if someone's getting into the house? Have you thought of that?"

"Of course, I have. But you told me yourself that security system is good. And who would be getting in?

The cleaning crew hasn't been there all week. The gardeners don't come near the house. And Kendall doesn't know the code, so that just leaves me."

He leaned over her, looking predatory suddenly. "I can get in."

"And what would be your point?" She shook her head and scoffed. "You wouldn't hurt me."

His eyes bore into hers. "You're sure about that?"

The anger in his voice confused her, and she frowned. "Of course, I'm sure. You've helped me, let me stay in your house. I trust you."

His hand slid over her throat, and her heart beat fast. He looked powerful, angry…deadly. His voice dropped deeper yet. "A lot of people think I murdered Candace Rothchild."

He looked capable of murder. His eyes burned dark. His mouth was a lethal slash. Any hint of tenderness or vulnerability had disappeared.

But this was the man who'd made Claire giggle. This was the man who'd fulfilled his mother's dream, even when she wouldn't know. This was the man who made her heart race and her blood heat, who with just a kiss brought her more pleasure than she'd ever known.

This was the man she was falling for fast.

She tried to swallow. She lifted her hand to his face and traced the harsh lines framing his mouth. "You're a good man, Luke."

His eyes blazed. "The hell I am."

And then his mouth was on hers, and he was kissing her again—hot and hard and deep. She gasped at the delicious invasion, thrilled at the rough, sensual feel of his skin. The kiss was harsh, giving vent to his sudden temper, as if he wanted to prove she was wrong.

But the grinding kiss stirred her senses. She plunged her hands in his hair, roused by his delirious feel, abandoning herself to desire.

The kiss deepened, lengthened, spinning her further beyond control. She knew she should pull back, think things through, but he felt so darned good. And just once, she wanted to forget her worries, just once, she wanted to do something impulsive and surrender to the rampaging need.

He made a low, rough sound deep in his throat and shifted his weight over hers. He trailed his mouth down her neck, sending streams of pleasure rippling over her skin. She moaned.

He captured her lips again, making her head whirl. She clutched his shoulders and back. Urgency mounted inside her, and she made soft, mewling noises of need.

Then he slowed and softened the kiss, and excitement skidded through her veins. And she realized with a daze that he was an expert at this. He knew exactly when to charge and when to withdraw, how to tease and make her feel crazed. He was a connoisseur, a master of this sensual craft, and he was driving her out of her mind.

And she wanted to let him. She knew that this would change nothing. She couldn't spin this interlude into more than it was. This was sex, just sex, a brief respite from danger, a magical moment out of time.

But she needed this, wanted this. She wanted to submit to the mind-boggling pleasure, yield to the tempting bliss. All her life she'd been the responsible one, the hardworking one, the one who'd borne the weight of the world. Now, just for this moment, she wanted to forget all that—forget the fear, forget the threats, not think, not worry, just feel.

His kisses hypnotized her. The need to touch him grew frantic, overwhelming, urgent.

She gripped his shoulders and tried to pull him against her, but his mouth roamed to her throat. Then he slid his hand under her T-shirt, and his palm scorched her breast. She shuddered, growing insistent. He groaned against her throat.

He rose then and tugged off her shirt. His eyes stalled on her breasts.

Her face turned hot. She felt unprotected and exposed, even in the lacy bra. Embarrassment mingled with pleasure. His heated gaze incited her nerves.

"You're beautiful," he growled, and her breath caught. She knew it wasn't true. She wasn't gorgeous like the women he dated. And Wayne had dwelled on her shortfalls enough. But as Luke's gaze swept the length of her, she felt beautiful and desired.

Then suddenly, a gunshot shattered the silence. The sharp report thundered through the hills. Her heart froze, and she gaped at Luke. "What—"

He dove over her, mashing her into the blanket, covering her head with his chest. Her pulse scrambled. Panic seized her. Someone had shot at them, and they were out in the open, exposed.

"Behind the rocks. *Now.*" Luke rolled to his feet and yanked her upright. She scooped up her T-shirt and ran. A bullet whined past. Tension screamed through her nerves as they swerved through the scattered pines.

The edge of the cliff was littered with boulders. Luke ducked behind one, pulling her with him, and she huddled beside him and struggled to breathe. She jerked her T-shirt over her head, stuffed her arms through the sleeves, then searched for a way to escape.

The slope below them was steep and covered with sagebrush. Luke pointed to a distant cluster of pines. "Run to those trees. The trail's back there. Go straight to the car and wait. And don't stop, no matter what."

Her gaze flew to his. "But what—"

"I'm going to head him off. Now go!"

She bit her lip, reluctant to leave him. But they didn't have time to argue. The gunman could show up at any time. Luke gave her a nudge, and she leaped off the edge of the cliff.

She hit the ground and nearly fell but managed to stay on her feet. Fighting to keep her balance and control her momentum, she angled across the hill toward the trees.

She skidded in the loose dirt, plowed into some sagebrush and let out a muffled cry. But she couldn't slow, couldn't stop. She had to reach the safety of those trees.

But what was Luke doing? Had their attacker seen him? How could he stop a man with a gun?

Then another shot rang out. She zigzagged in alarm.

She reached the pine trees and whipped behind one, then whirled around to look. The hillside was empty. Luke was nowhere in sight. Where on earth had he gone?

And where was the gunman? *Who* was the gunman? Why had he been shooting at them?

She hauled in a ragged breath, forcing those thoughts from her mind. She'd worry about all that later. She had to get to the car and wait for Luke.

But the path wound below her across the open slope, visible from above. She hesitated, still struggling to catch her breath. What if the gunman had her in his sights?

She fought back a spurt of dread, trying to decide

what to do. Luke had told her not to stop. He was buying her time to reach the car. But then how was he going to get down?

Another shot barked out. Sheer panic bludgeoned her nerves. What if Luke had been hit?

She couldn't leave him. She had to go back and check. But both the hillside and trail were too exposed. She had to find another way up.

The only other route was over the rocks. She darted to the nearby boulders, scrambled through the silvery sage. A chuckwalla scurried past, and she bit back a startled shriek.

Calm down, she told herself firmly. The lizard wouldn't hurt her. She climbed over some rocks, eased around a yucca plant, then eyed the long stretch of sandstone above.

She had no choice. She had to climb it. At least it wasn't too steep, and there were bushes and ridges to grip. As long as she went slowly, she would be fine.

She clambered up, then crept across the rock face, the hot sun scorching her scalp. Her heart beat fast. Sweat beaded and trickled down her jaw. She grabbed a plant, boosted herself up, then reached for a nearby ledge.

An ominous rattle stopped her. Unable to move, she jerked her gaze to the side.

A rattlesnake hissed at her, preparing to strike.

Chapter 8

The wild scream shattered the silence, sending adrenaline streaming through Luke's blood. *Amanda*. She was in danger. He had to get to her fast. But he couldn't move yet, not with the shooter just a few yards away. Even the soft snap of a twig could tip him off.

He sucked air through his tightly clenched teeth and crushed back the mushrooming fear. He had to stay calm, think through the haze of panic, stay smart or he'd get them both killed.

Insects buzzed in the bushes around him. A turkey vulture soared overhead. Blood dripped down his left arm from where the bullet had grazed him, and his shoulder hammered with pain. He adjusted the handkerchief he'd knotted as a makeshift bandage, shifted his gaze to the bushes ahead.

Concentrate. Be patient. The man who stayed focused was the one who survived. He'd learned that lesson on Las Vegas's deadly streets.

He just wished he had a handgun or knife.

The bushes rustled, and his vision tunneled. His body shook with the need to attack.

His pursuer rose, crept into the open with his pistol drawn. Then he turned in the direction of Amanda's scream.

Big mistake.

Luke leaped out, slammed into his side. They hit the ground grunting and rolled.

Luke landed on top. The man twisted, thrust back his elbow. Luke took the jab to his chest. He groaned, shook off the pain and fought for an opening, landed a punch to the man's gut.

The man wheezed and quickly recovered, then raised his pistol to shoot. But Luke lunged, tackled him again, scrambling for an advantage in the thick cloud of dust. He grabbed the man's wrist and rammed it against the ground.

His muscles strained as he battled to hold him. Sweat burned into his eyes. He grappled for dominance, straining and shoving, until the man's hand finally went slack. The pistol skidded loose.

But the man butted his head into Luke's injured shoulder. Luke went dizzy with the fierce waves of pain. *Damn.*

He hauled back, slammed his fist into his attacker's head and the sickening thump vibrated through his arm. The man slumped against the ground and went still.

Luke wheezed in the dusty air, shook the stinging sweat from his eyes. He pushed himself up, his muscles trembling from the adrenaline dump. Then he staggered over and picked up the gun.

A 9mm Glock. He released the magazine to count the rounds, slammed it back home and racked the slide. Feeling less vulnerable now, he stuffed it into the waistband of his jeans.

But he couldn't go to Amanda yet. He strode back to his attacker and kicked him over, then lowered himself to one knee. He rifled through the man's pockets but came up empty. No identification, not even a damned set of keys. He took a long look at his face— Hispanic, swarthy complexion, high cheekbones. Late thirties, early forties, judging by the receding hair.

He scowled. Too bad he'd left his cell phone in the car. He could have photographed this thug.

Frustrated, he exhaled and glanced around. He didn't have a rope to restrain him, and he couldn't waste any more time. He'd have to leave him, hope the police picked him up later on.

His urgency mounting, he leaped up and ran down the trail, the memory of that scream echoing through his mind. He shouldn't have left her alone. What if she'd been captured or worse? He immediately pushed aside that awful thought, needing to focus on finding her fast.

At the top of a hill he paused and scanned the landscape, searching for movement, or anything out of place. The sun sizzled off the blood-red sandstone. A hawk passed by, dragging a shadow over the earth.

Then a speck of blue in the sagebrush snagged his attention, and his heart careened to a stop. She'd been wearing a blue T-shirt and jeans.

His gut balled tight now, he raced across the parched hillside, hurdling creosote bushes and rocks. Had she been shot? He hadn't heard another gun fire. But then why had she veered off the trail?

He reached her seconds later. She lay facedown in the dirt surrounded by yucca plants and sagebrush. He dropped to his knees, leaned close to check her pulse. "Amanda. Amanda."

"Luke." She groaned, lifted her head.

She was alive. Thank God. He sagged, closed his eyes and exhaled, his own pulse running amok. He snapped his eyes open again. "What happened?"

She propped herself on her elbows and hung her head. "There was a snake."

Oh, hell. "Where did he get you?" he demanded, running his hands over her back.

"He didn't. I fell down the rocks. I hit some cactus, and my ankle…"

She'd fallen? He scowled up at the wall of sandstone. "What were you doing up there?"

"I heard that gunshot. I thought you might have been hurt. I was trying to go back to see."

His jaw turned slack. He stared at her in disbelief. "So you tried to climb the cliff?"

She didn't answer, and he bit back a curse, his fear for her out of control. But he'd have it out with her later. He needed to get her to safety first.

With effort he held on to his temper and managed to gentle his voice. "Where did you hit the cactus?"

"The back of my leg." She groaned again. "My right thigh."

He scooted closer, wincing when he spotted a dozen thick spines embedded in her jeans. No way could she ride in the car like that. Taking off her pants might jar the spines loose—or twist them and torture her more.

"I'll have to pull them out," he told her. He rose,

quartered the area for sticks, finally found two the right size. "This is going to hurt like hell, though."

He knelt beside her again, caught hold of a spine with the sticks. "Brace yourself." He jerked it from her thigh, flicked it away. She bit off an anguished cry.

He grimaced, sorry to be causing her more pain, but he didn't have much choice. Working as fast as he could, he pulled out the spines and tossed them a safe distance away. Then he ran his hand carefully over her thigh. "I think that's it. We'll check you out better when we get back."

"Thanks."

He shook his head. She hardly owed him thanks. His big attempt to help her relax today had only made things worse.

"Here. Hold on to me," he said as she struggled to rise. He grabbed her waist, slung her arm over his shoulder and helped her to her feet.

She took a step, nearly collapsed. "My ankle." She tried again and gasped. "I think I sprained it."

"Lean on me more." He helped her adjust her grip, glanced at her dirt-streaked face. She looked a wreck—her long hair wild, one cheek bleeding, her blue eyes shimmering with tears. But despite the grime—despite her pain—her soft, natural beauty wound through him, touching his heart.

He'd never had anyone try to save him before. He lived in a high-stakes, cutthroat world—a world where money ruled, the strong survived and every man looked out for himself. It was a world he understood, a world he'd mastered. He'd clawed his way to the top, stopping for no one, and now he was the one with the power.

Or he would be, once that project went through.

But Amanda was different. She was loyal, gentle, protective—even of him.

And that thought disturbed him. It brought back memories of his childhood, the way he'd once been before reality had smacked him down, feelings he'd buried for years. Because gentleness weakened a man. It left him vulnerable, ripe for attack.

"Luke, you're bleeding."

Still unsettled, he shook his head. "It's just a graze. I'll take care of it when we get back to town."

She gnawed her lip, glanced around. "Where's the gunman?"

"Still up there. I knocked him out and took his gun." And hopefully, gained them some time.

But he couldn't afford to take chances. As they worked their way to the car, their breaths rasping in the quiet air, he focused again on the hills. They'd had a close call, too close, and he wouldn't be caught off guard again.

A few minutes later, they reached his Land Rover, only to find that the tires had been slashed.

"Oh, no." Amanda turned to him. "What are we going to do now?"

"We don't have much choice. We'll drive on the rims, at least until we can pick up a cell phone signal and call for a tow."

He helped her into her seat, climbed into the driver's side. Despite his denial, his left arm throbbed. It was going to be a long ride back for them both.

Ignoring the pain, he cranked the engine, relieved when it started up. He drove along the rutted tractor trail, jolted through a dried-out creek bed. The ruined tires slapped against the dirt.

The slashed tires bothered him. It felt personal, more

like an act of rage than an attempt to strand them—especially since the engine had been left alone.

He looked at Amanda. "What does your ex look like?"

"Wayne? He's about five ten, blond, a heavy build. Why? Was it him back there?"

"No. This guy looked Hispanic, maybe part Indian."

"Oh. I'd hoped…" She turned her gaze to the windshield and hugged her arms.

"What?"

"Nothing."

"Have you seen him before?"

She frowned, shook her head. "I don't think so. The guy who tried to kidnap Claire was wearing a ski mask, so I didn't see his face. I didn't see the man in your casino, either."

He swerved to avoid a hole. "I saw the surveillance tape. His hair was longer than this guy's, and lighter brown. It wasn't him."

She looked at him again. "The waiter the other night… He might have been Hispanic."

That didn't mean much. Half the western population had Hispanic roots. But if this was the same man, it meant Harold Rothchild had hired this guy. But then where did the casino gunman come in?

He scowled. Damn, this was complicated. And another thing bothered him—how had their attacker found them today? Few people knew he owned this land, and he hadn't announced his plans. Unless the gunman had been watching and then followed them here. He could have hung back, followed their dust trail. Without a breeze to disperse it, they'd probably raised dust for at least five miles.

He was still mulling that over when he reached the

barbed wire gate at the end of the tractor path. He idled the engine and hopped out. But as he dragged the gate open, he spotted a Jeep by the trees down the road.

His spirits rising, he jogged back and turned off the engine, then grabbed his cell phone and keys. "We found a replacement car. Come on."

"But how are you going to drive it without a key?" She opened her door, and he helped her out.

"Don't worry." He'd picked up more than just survival skills on the streets.

And this job turned out to be easy. The dashboard had already been torn apart, the wires exposed. "It looks like he stole it." No point searching the vehicle for clues about his identity, then.

He touched the wires and started the engine. "Ready?" She nodded, and he drove off. They hit a bump, and she moaned.

He kept his attention on the sun-baked road, trying to avoid the worst of the washboard and ruts. But as he drove toward the highway, a cloud of dust billowing in his wake, the memory of Amanda's scream shuddered through him, that god-awful moment when he'd feared that she could be dead.

This situation had grown more dangerous today. This wasn't just about the ring anymore, or even an ex-husband bent on revenge. Someone had tried to kill them. Someone had followed them into the hills and hunted them down. They'd only survived due to luck.

But Luke knew better than to trust in luck. He'd built his fortune on the harsh reality that luck didn't last, that every gambler eventually lost.

So how could he keep Amanda safe? She wouldn't leave town; he'd already tried that tack.

He glanced sideways, took in her dusty clothes and tousled hair, the way her full lips flattened with pain. And he realized he didn't have a choice. He had to stay close to protect her. This had gone beyond lust, beyond mutual favors, two people helping each other out. Amanda's life was at stake.

And from now on—whether she liked it or not—he wasn't letting her out of his sight.

Amanda stared out Luke's penthouse window later that night, watching the city lights glitter against the sky. She'd gone from extreme highs to terrible lows today, from the ecstasy of nearly making love to Luke to barely escaping death.

But at whose hands? Certainly not Wayne's—which was terrible news. Not that she wanted Wayne after her. But at least he was a known enemy, one who she could fight. And it would have explained the bizarre events in the house. Wayne was vindictive, controlling. It would be just like him to try to mess with her mind.

But that hadn't been Wayne on that hill.

Her stomach in turmoil, she adjusted her grip on her crutches and hobbled back to the couch. She sank into the soft, creamy leather, propped her bandaged ankle on the ottoman and closed her eyes.

What a disaster moving here had been. Her life had spun completely out of control. She'd escaped an abusive ex-husband only to land in an even worse mess.

And to top it off, she'd discovered that she might have inherited her mother's mental illness.

But she couldn't wallow in self-pity or dwell on her fears. She had Claire to keep safe. She exhaled again, trying to purge the anxiety from her voice, then punched in Kendall's number on her phone.

"It's about time," Kendall complained when she picked up. "Where are you?"

"Luke's penthouse."

"How's your ankle?"

"Just sprained." She'd phoned Kendall earlier from the urgent care clinic to update her on the news. "But I'm staying here tonight."

Silence greeted that statement. "It's not what you think," she added. Although it nearly had been back in the hills.

"Mandy…"

"You don't have to say it. I know."

"But you don't even know this guy." Amanda opened her mouth to argue, but her sister forged on. "I know he's rich, and I know he's letting you stay here, which is nice. But for God's sake, Mandy, get real. Luke Montgomery isn't your type."

Her temper stirred. The last thing she needed after her hellish day was a lecture from her sister about men. "So who is my type? Wayne?"

"Don't be ridiculous. You know I never liked that creep. But that's the problem. Luke might be just as bad."

"He's not—"

"It was all over the news today. He had a restraining order on Candace Rothchild."

Amanda's temper abruptly deflated. *A restraining order.* Her belly churned even more. She glanced over her shoulder at the hall to Luke's bedroom and lowered her voice. "That doesn't make him a killer."

"But you don't know what might have happened

that night. They argued in his casino—everyone saw it. And maybe she provoked him later on. Maybe he flew into a rage."

Amanda shuddered and rotated her wrist, remembering Wayne. But Luke wasn't like that. Yes, he was a hard man, a powerful one. But he'd saved her life today. He'd taken a bullet to keep her safe.

She shoved her hand through her freshly washed hair and sighed. "Listen, you don't have to worry about me. I know what I'm doing."

"Do you?" Kendall's voice went flat. "Look, I know I'm always after you to take more chances, but not this one."

"Don't worry. I'll be fine." She hoped. Gathering her courage, she fiddled with the tie on the thick, fluffy bathrobe from the spa downstairs. She dreaded asking but needed to know. "You're all right, aren't you? I mean, nothing strange has happened at the house today?"

"No, why?" Suspicion tinged Kendall's voice. "Is there something I need to know?"

"No." She closed her eyes, pressed her fingers to her temple. There went her last remaining long shot—that someone was targeting the house. "I just wanted to make sure you were both all right."

"We're fine. We've been swimming, coloring, reading books… Hold on." There was a muffled commotion in the background. "Here's Claire now."

"Hi, Mommy." Claire's voice chirped over the line. She babbled about Aunt Kendall and Brownie, the minutia of the day's events.

Amanda's throat turned thick as she listened. It would kill her to lose custody of Claire. But if she did have her mother's illness, she couldn't endanger her child. She had to do everything she could to keep her safe, even if it meant giving her up.

And she knew exactly how the illness would progress—the paranoia and delusions, the tormenting voices and suicidal thoughts. Not one medication on the market had helped her mother cope.

She beat back that frightening thought, then forced a peppy note into her voice so she wouldn't scare Claire. "Be good for Aunt Kendall tonight. And eat all your oatmeal in the morning."

Her chest aching, her throat so tight she could hardly speak, she told Claire she loved her and clicked off the phone. Then she closed her eyes, sagged back against the cushions and tried to think.

All right. So she might have inherited her mother's illness. The thought terrified her, but it was a possibility she had to face. She'd have to see a doctor for an evaluation, make contingency plans for Claire. But not yet. She still had time before her behavior got too erratic—assuming she really was ill. She'd take this day by day.

And she wouldn't just sit around pitying herself in the meantime. She was stronger than that.

Agitated, needing to do something, anything to take her mind off the fear, she grabbed her crutches and rose. She hobbled into the spotless kitchen and cleared away the remnants of the five-star dinner room service had brought.

Then, her emotions still all over the map, she dimmed the lights and started toward the guest suite to crash. Things always looked better in the morning, her mother had said. But nothing had improved for her mother. And somehow, she didn't see how a few more hours would remedy this mess.

Partway down the hall, she remembered Luke. She paused, wondering if she should check on him before she turned in. He might be having second thoughts about that pain medication he'd refused. Not that she blamed him for being leery given his mother's addiction. But at least she could ask.

She returned to the kitchen and grabbed the pills, then worked her way down his hall. Seconds later, she tapped on his bedroom door. "Luke?" He didn't answer, so she inched the door open and called again. "Luke?"

Still no answer. She went inside and scanned the enormous room. The overhead light was still on, and her gaze zeroed in on the bed. Luke lay face down on the oversized mattress, his arms stretched out, his face turned to the side. His upper body was naked, his lower half covered by sheets. Despite his claim that he'd had work to do, he'd apparently fallen asleep.

She put the pain pills on the bedside table with the antibiotics, poured water from a nearby carafe. Then she hesitated, debating whether to wake him. He needed another antibiotic soon.

Her pulse quickening, she set down her crutches and perched on the edge of the mattress. For a long moment, she indulged herself, letting her eyes travel over his back. His skin was tanned, smooth, the muscles of his broad back clearly defined. Her gaze lingered on his massive shoulders, the strong, rugged lines of his neck. His upper arm was bandaged where the bullet had grazed him, and the cloth gleamed white against his skin.

She touched his arm to check for infection, relieved that his skin wasn't hot. She knew she should wake him, then leave. She couldn't just sit here forever and stare.

But his face held her riveted—the dark, aggressive brows, the black whiskers coating his jaw. He had a strong, masculine nose, thick, ink-black hair, the most intriguing, sensual mouth. Her mind stalled on the memory of how he'd kissed her, and shivers rippled over her skin.

Even asleep he looked virile and dangerous. She'd never seen anyone so powerfully male.

No wonder women found him compelling. He had enormous wealth, the kind of good looks that drew women of every age. And that intensity in his eyes…

But how many women saw the caring part? How many knew about that land? How many glimpsed his complexity or sensed the pain that drove this man?

She snorted at that wild thought. She hardly knew him, either. Her sister was right about that. She'd only met Luke last week.

And as much as she hated to admit it, Kendall was right about something else. She probably shouldn't trust him. She'd made that mistake with Wayne. Marrying Wayne had been the one time she'd taken a chance, the one time she'd let impulse and wishful thinking override common sense. And that had been a disaster.

But if getting close to Luke was wrong, then why did he feel so right?

His eyes opened. He turned his head, and those golden eyes fastened on hers.

And suddenly the air turned too thick to breathe.

"I was dreaming about you," he said, his voice deep, husky.

Her throat went dry. She couldn't move. And she was suddenly, intensely aware of how close he lay, how naked she was beneath her robe.

And a torrent of erotic memories whipped through her—the heat of his mouth, the musk of his skin, the exciting caress of his hands.

His eyes darkened, holding her captive. Warmth pooled between her thighs. He'd dreamed of her, wanted her.

She hungered for him just as badly. She ached to re-live that sensual pleasure, find out where it could lead. She wanted to abandon herself to this delirious attraction—forget the danger, forget her worries, forget the horrific time bomb ticking in her head.

He reached up, snagged the back of her neck with his hand and drew her close.

"Luke," she whispered, her voice raw. "Make me forget."

His eyes turned hotter yet. He tugged her closer until her mouth was inches from his.

He lowered his gaze to her lips, brushed the bottom curve with his thumb, making shivers dance over her skin.

"That's the hell of it." His voice came out rough, almost angry.

"What?" she whispered, too muddled with desire to think.

"I don't want you to forget. I want you to remember. *Remember me.*"

His mouth took hers. She would remember him, all right. How could she help it?

This was the man she was starting to love.

Chapter 9

She was heaven, absolute, erotic bliss.

Luke pulled Amanda against him, his mouth capturing hers in a hot, deep kiss that demolished his self-control. His tongue dueled with hers. Raw heat thickened his blood. He plunged his hand through her silky hair, felt her soft, full breasts pillow his chest, and the perfect, sensual feel of her shut down his mind.

He'd been fantasizing about her for days now—how she'd look naked, her moist heat pulsing around him, those endlessly riveting legs hooked over his back. Kissing her hadn't been nearly enough, had only fired his imagination more.

But even the most vivid dream couldn't match the reality of Amanda. The scent of her slick, creamy skin, the sweep of her satin hair over his chest drew a ragged groan from his throat. He dragged her further over his body, ran his hands up her legs beneath the robe, stroking the velvety sweep of her thighs.

She was so soft, so lush, so damned arousing. The way she yielded to him, melting around him, those provocative moans she made in the back of her throat.

But suddenly she flinched, gasped against his mouth. He broke the kiss, alarmed. "What's wrong?"

"My ankle." She winced, closed her eyes on a shudder of pain.

He silently swore. He'd forgotten her sprained ankle. "Let's change places." He tipped her gently onto her back, slipped a pillow under her foot so he wouldn't bump it again. Then, ignoring his own throbbing arm, he braced himself on his elbows above her.

Her gaze dropped to his bandaged bicep. "Your arm—"

"Doesn't hurt." Not nearly as much as another, painfully engorged part of him did.

But doubt clouded her eyes. She nibbled her bottom lip, her frown deepening, and he tried to beat back the lust.

"Having second thoughts?"

"No, not exactly, it's just…I have to tell you…" Her face turned pink, and her gaze flitted away. "You might not want… I'm not too good at this."

He would have laughed if she hadn't looked so distressed. Not good at this? He was so hot for her he was ready to explode. "What makes you think that?"

"My ex-husband. He said I wasn't…" Her blush deepened, and she fidgeted with the collar on her robe.

He went still. "He said you weren't what?"

"That I wasn't…exciting enough. That he needed to, you know…" Her face flaming, her eyes stayed on her robe. "Watch videos, or look at magazines to get…" Her voice trailed off.

He closed his eyes on a flash of anger, damning Wheeler for all the damage he'd done. Then he tilted up her delicate chin, let his gaze rove her sultry lips.

Her blue eyes were dark with lust. Her tousled hair cascaded around her face. He ached to fist his hands in that glorious hair, kiss the fragile sweep of her throat, explore every rapturous inch of her skin.

Keeping his eyes locked on hers, he trapped her hand and slowly, relentlessly pushed it over his chest and past his belly until she cupped him, cupped all of him, every rock-hard, throbbing inch.

Her eyes widened. Her lips parted on a soundless gasp. He pulsed against her, heavy, thick, ready to erupt.

"I think," he said gruffly, "we can safely say the problem wasn't you."

"No." Her voice sounded strangled. "Not me."

He nipped her lips, parting them with his tongue. And then he drove his tongue in deeply, letting her feel the violent need rocking his blood.

She whimpered in response, wrapped her arms around his neck, bringing her soft body tighter against his. Hunger rippled through him, the relentless beat bludgeoning him like shock waves from a nuclear blast. But he had to go slowly. He wanted to drive her to ecstasy, shatter every illusion she had about her lack of appeal, obliterate every single memory of Wheeler from her mind.

And make her remember *him*.

He forced himself to ease off, even as his body shuddered with need. He slowed and lengthened the kiss, caressed her with long, languid strokes. He slid his hands down her lush, smooth curves, seducing, teasing, arousing. She arched against him, her excitement growing, and he swallowed her moan with his lips.

Unable to resist, he grazed her jaw, her neck, then worked his way down her body, replacing his hand with his mouth. Her nipples pouted in invitation, then pebbled at his heated response. He smiled when she groaned and tugged his hair.

"You're so damned beautiful," he murmured. And her ex-husband was a fool.

He stroked her belly, her thighs, feathering kisses up her sensitive skin until she was shaking with need. He teased, circled, retreated, beating back his own burgeoning hunger, wanting to make this a night she would never forget.

But the restraint was taking its toll. His heart thundering now, his breath growing ragged and fast, he moved back up her body and took her mouth. He plundered deeply, moving over her, letting her feel his insistent need.

But he wanted to make her feel just as desperate, just as crazed. He raised himself up and looked at her—her parted lips, her sultry eyes, the silky tendrils of hair clinging to her flushed cheeks. She was open to him, her entire body exposed, looking like every dream he'd ever had.

He ran his palms down her breasts to her taut belly, back over her satiny thighs. His muscles bunched, and he struggled to keep his own raw needs in check. But she arched her back, and the movement sent a heavy jolt of hunger through his veins. She was torturing him, and he was fast veering out of control.

He poised his body over hers. "Open your eyes." His throat was thick, his voice hoarse. Her dazed gaze rose to his. He trembled, his control eroding, wanting desperately to plunge into that tempting heat.

"Luke," she whispered. "Do something." Her hands gripped his shoulders, his back, and she tried to tug him against her.

He framed her face with his hands, using every ounce of willpower he had to keep from taking her fast. He entered her as slowly as he could, giving her time to accommodate him, to adjust, but the hot, sensual feel of her incinerated his nerves.

When he'd sheathed himself completely, he closed his eyes and rested his forehead against hers, trying to breathe through the rampaging need. He throbbed insistently inside her, his body clamoring to move. But he had to slow down, make this right for her, erase the pain from her past.

He opened his eyes, ran his finger over her cheek. He looked into her eyes, wanting to reassure her, but those mesmerizing blue eyes held him enthralled.

Emotions poured through him, disturbing emotions. Emotions he didn't dare name.

This was sex. That's all this was—a night of sex, nothing more.

He kissed her again, his urgency soaring, his body lost to the need. She closed around him, warm and wet and tight. And his hunger intensified, riding him like a whip, a mandate he couldn't ignore.

He let his body find the primitive rhythm, fulfilling that most basic need. That's all this was, he assured himself through the blaze of heat. Just biology, a man and woman indulging in natural urges, nothing more.

It couldn't be more.

His heart thudded fast. The slow pace made him

crazed. Nothing had felt this urgent, this right in his entire life.

His desperation built. Desire clawed at him, threatening to pull him under. He slid his hand down her body between them, then stroked her most sensitive flesh.

She shuddered and bucked against him. "Luke," she cried. But she was holding back, fighting her release, her nails biting into his shoulders and arms.

But this was a war he intended to win. He gripped her chin, forcing her dazed eyes to his. Willing her to surrender to the pleasure. Submit. "Let go," he ordered.

Her eyes pleaded with his. "I can't. I—"

"Do it. Let go *now*."

She stiffened, came undone with a keening cry. His satisfaction soared. He felt like a conqueror for giving this woman what Wheeler never had.

He gripped her jaw and kissed her, a deep, wild kiss that showed her exactly how ravenous he was. And then he gave in to the need, let his instincts take charge. The pressure built, his body quickening beyond his control. And he exploded into her, his hoarse cry joining hers.

But as he drifted back to earth long moments later, he wondered what the hell he'd just done.

When Luke lifted his head from the pillow hours later, Amanda was gone. He blinked, his vision blurry from lack of sleep, and pondered the now-empty bed. But it was hard to hold on to a thought with pleasure still hazing his brain. It had been one hell of a night. They'd made love until dawn, then finally succumbed to exhaustion and dozed.

The sex had been phenomenal. Amanda had fascinated him with her surprising demands. She'd blasted past her inhibitions, demolishing her preconceptions, proving that her body was made for hot sex.

Made for him.

His own body was sated, depleted. He inhaled the scent of sex on the rumbled sheets, closed his eyes on a groan. Erotic images of the night flashed past, and his body predictably throbbed.

Maybe not so depleted.

And where was she, anyhow? He sat up, scrubbed his hand over his bristly jaw and rubbed his gritty eyes. And his mind danced around the other memories, the emotions that had surfaced during the night. But he pushed those confusing feelings aside. He'd analyze his reaction to her later.

He got out of bed, ignoring the burn in his injured arm, the insistent arousal her lingering scent caused. He pulled on a pair of loose sweatpants, padded barefoot down the carpeted hallway to the front room.

She stood in front of the floor-to-ceiling windows that comprised one wall, staring out at the early morning sky. Her arms were crossed, her shoulders hunched as if she was cold. The wave of possessiveness he felt caught him off guard.

But her eyes met his in the reflection, and something about her expression made him pause.

"Morning-after regrets?"

"I think you know better than that." Her voice turned soft, and he knew she was remembering exactly how much she'd enjoyed the night. "I just couldn't sleep."

It had been spectacular, all right. He walked to her, slid his arms around her waist from behind, and the feel of her warm, soft bottom stoked his desire. He savored the scent of her hair, slid his hands down her belly and thighs.

Her eyes locked on his in the glass. "Again?"

He grunted. He could spend days, months exploring every facet of this woman. But sex could wait. He didn't like that worried look in her eyes.

"So how come you're not sleeping?"

She sighed, and the soft sound twisted his heart. "I just had a bad dream, that's all."

"About your ex?"

"Wayne...the gunman. Everything that's been happening in the past couple weeks. I came out here to read so I wouldn't bother you."

Her lips wobbled, and even in the reflection he could see the fatigue darkening her skin beneath her eyes. He frowned. He hadn't helped much by keeping her up all night.

But maybe he could ease some of her cares. "I didn't have a chance to tell you, but I put in a phone call to Natalie Rothchild last night when we got back. They did a parole compliance check on your ex. He's still in Maryland."

"That's good." But she didn't look relieved. If anything, the fear in her eyes intensified. And he suspected that something else was bothering her, something more than the obvious danger. She'd had the same scared look back at the house.

And he still intended to discover the cause.

"Do you really think Harold Rothchild is behind all this?" she asked.

"It makes the most sense." He released her, walked to the window, braced his forearm on the glass and peered out. The darkness was fading, giving way to the dawn. It would soon be another scorching day under the desert sun.

"His business has been in trouble for years," he added. "He's taken out some high-interest loans that are coming due, and he won't make the payments." Loans from the mob-connected Schaffers. "I've timed it so the Phoenix will take away business at a critical time. He'll have to start selling assets soon. Once that happens, his entire empire will collapse." He couldn't keep the satisfaction from his voice.

"You're saying you planned this? You're doing this on purpose to make him fail?" She sounded appalled.

He swung back to her and met her gaze. "Don't pity him, Amanda. He's ruined enough lives in his time. He deserves far worse than this." The man's indifference had killed his mother, causing her addiction and early demise.

"I see." She let out a short laugh. "And you really think he'd try to kill us to stop this project?"

"He'll do anything to hold on to his power. This is a high-stakes game. No one plays nice, not even me."

Her voice turned low. "But you'd never kill anyone."

"No." But he'd done other things he wasn't proud of, things he'd had to do to win.

She hobbled to the window and looked out. For a long moment she didn't speak, just stared out at the pink sky streaking the horizon beyond the black peaks. "So where is Naked City?" she asked at last.

"Over there." He pointed out a darkened area just past the lighted Strip.

"So you can see your old neighborhood from here."

"Yeah. I can see it from here." It served as a reminder of where he'd come from, kept him focused on his goals. And before long he'd stand right here and watch bulldozers raze that slum.

She gave him a worried glance. "I hope canceling the meeting yesterday didn't cause any problems."

He shrugged. In truth, it had ticked off the investors. He'd spent hours the other night making phone calls, trying to make amends, which had been harder than he'd thought. Canceling that meeting had been a stupid move, foolhardy. This project was too damned important—everything he'd worked toward for twenty years. He couldn't afford to take risks now.

"Do you have a picture of it?" she asked.

"The project? Yeah, on the desk." He strode back to the sofa, got her crutches and handed them to her. Then he crossed the room to the desk.

He flicked on the desk lamp, spread out the rolled-up plans, and secured the corners with weights. She joined him a moment later.

She stood close enough beside him that their shoulders touched, and he inhaled her sensual scent. His eyes roamed her tousled hair, the tempting cleavage exposed by the gaping robe.

He wondered why he wasn't tired of her by now. Usually one night with a woman stifled his curiosity, leaving him bored. Hell, half the time he couldn't wait for the woman to leave.

But Amanda was different. Instead of wanting her out of his penthouse so he could get back to work, he couldn't draw his gaze from her lips.

"So what do you think?" he asked, oddly anxious to hear her opinion.

She pursed her lips, ran her finger over the architectural drawing, slanted her head to see the painted images

along the sides. "It's fabulous." She shook her head, and
her hair slid over her shoulders, glimmering as it caught
the light. "It's a magnificent project, huge, like the
ancient pyramids."

His mouth quirked up. "It's not that great." But her
words sent warmth flowing through him. He was glad
she liked it, that she approved.

He shifted his gaze to the painting of the mythical
bird at the top of the plans. The Phoenix, the mighty,
fabled bird, able to regenerate and recover from death.
Crimson and gold, it would perch atop the casino—
proud, regal, triumphant.

Just like him. Harold Rothchild had treated his
mother like trash, like someone disposable, someone
whose life didn't matter to him. He'd crushed her, assuming that an impoverished nobody could never battle
his power and wealth. He'd been right.

But he hadn't reckoned on Luke.

Amanda's eyes returned to his. "I read an article
about the project in the paper while you were sleeping."
She hesitated, and another small line furrowed her brow.
"It said people have been protesting this project, that
they want affordable housing built there instead."

He shrugged, rolled up the plans and set them aside.
"That's normal. There are always protests with a project
this size."

Her troubled gaze stayed on his. "But what about the
people who live in those apartments? Where are they
going to go?"

"They'll find another place."

"Are you sure?"

"Yeah, I'm sure. It's not a problem." But his growing
desire for her was. And suddenly, he didn't want to

think about the project anymore, not with this warm, willing woman standing there naked beneath that robe.

He moved close, crowding her against the desk. The scent of her skin filled his nostrils and fired his blood. He slid his hand around her neck, studied the pale freckles sprinkling the bridge of her nose. "You worry too much."

Her mouth tightened. "I can't help it. There's a lot to worry about right now."

He couldn't deny that. She'd been shot at, held up at gunpoint, possibly drugged. Someone had even tried to steal her child. And she didn't deserve any of this. She was just an innocent victim, caught in the crossfire of his revenge.

"I'm going to keep you safe," he promised. From whatever threatened her. "I won't let anything happen to you."

"I know." She gave him a tremulous smile.

Her confidence floored him. And those emotions bubbled to the surface again, the desire to protect her, defend her, to claim her as his.

"I meant what I said yesterday," she whispered. "You're a good man, Luke."

"Not that good." Not much better than Rothchild in some respects. "Don't make me into something I'm not."

She slowly shook her head. "You're better than you think."

The hell he was. His anger flared—anger at himself for his ruthless past, anger at her for her misguided trust. He didn't want her looking at him as if he were a hero. He wanted her to see him, see who he really was.

He took the crutches from her hands and tossed them to the carpet, his gaze never wavering from hers. Then he lifted her onto the desk and stepped between her legs.

Right where he wanted to stay.

His hands went to the belt on her robe, and he made short work of the tie. He jerked the robe open and ripped it off. And then he let his gaze slowly rake every provocative, naked inch of her, from her sweetly curving breasts to the heaven at the juncture of her thighs.

His gaze lingered, traveled back up and her already-dazed eyes locked on his. Her lush lips parted. Her breath came in reedy gasps.

And that now-familiar hunger blazed through his blood.

"This isn't going to be nice or slow," he warned her. "I'm going to take you fast and hard."

Shock and excitement flared in her eyes. "I don't want nice or slow. I want you." She raised her hands to his shoulders. Her eyes stayed riveted on his.

Her trust made him even angrier. He slipped himself free of his sweatpants, lifted her bottom and in one, swift motion drove himself home.

They both groaned. But he'd told her the truth. And this time, he didn't play the cultured billionaire, didn't pretend to be nice. He took her hard and rough, treating her with brutal honesty, letting her feel the man he was.

A man raised in the gutter. The illegitimate son of a drifter. In a few hard thrusts, she convulsed.

He joined her barely a second later. Delirium deluged his blood. He was still pulsing inside her when a soft ring sounded across the room.

"That's my cell phone," she said, sounding distracted. "I'd better get it."

"Yeah." And suddenly, since the first time he'd touched her the night before, he needed distance. He didn't know what had just happened, but it scared the hell out of him.

Glad for the interruption, he quickly retreated. He adjusted his sweatpants, stalked across the room to get the phone. By the time he returned to the desk, she stood holding her crutches, safely enveloped in the robe.

Still shaken by what had just happened, he handed her the phone. She looked at the display and frowned, then clicked it on. "Hi. What's up?"

Her face paled. "Oh, God." She swayed, put out a hand to grasp the desk.

He tensed, kept his gaze on hers.

"I'll be right there." She snapped the phone closed, and her panic-stricken eyes met his. "It's Claire. I need to get to the hospital fast."

Chapter 10

Amanda despised hospitals. She hated the squeaky linoleum floors, the ubiquitous blue chairs, the too-soothing voices the nurses always used. And she especially hated that antiseptic smell that permeated the halls—as if it could somehow sanitize the truth and erase the harsh reality of illness, insanity, death.

And now Claire was here, in this despicable place—and it was all her fault. While she'd been indulging the most exhilarating time of her life, lost in the pleasure of Luke's arms, her child was suffering from anaphylactic shock, being rushed to the emergency room where she could die.

No. Claire couldn't die. She refused to even think it. She stuffed down the fear, passed a nurse in her flowered scrubs and sneakers and hobbled even faster toward the emergency-room desk.

"My daughter's here," she breathlessly told the woman in charge. "Claire Patterson. She's in the emergency room."

"Through the double doors." The woman shifted her gaze to a spot behind her.

Amanda turned, relieved to see Luke heading toward her. They'd raced here from his penthouse, only pausing to throw on clothes—and he looked it. His T-shirt was wrinkled, his hair unruly. Morning whiskers coated his jaw. And despite the guarded look in his eyes, she was glad that he'd come in with her, that she didn't have to be here alone.

She didn't know why he'd suddenly withdrawn back at the penthouse. He'd shut down just before she'd received Kendall's phone call. But she couldn't deal with that now. Her emotions were bouncing all over the place, from guilt and dread, to remorse and fear. She'd think about the incredible night and Luke's odd reaction later on.

Desperate to see Claire, she limped through the double doors, past strangers waiting in wheelchairs, people groaning and crying on cots. By the time they found Claire in a curtained-off section, she was so worked up she wanted to wretch.

"Mommy," Claire wheezed, and Amanda's heart plummeted, the dread blasting back full force. Claire looked like a burn victim. Her face was puffed, her lips huge and distorted. Splotchy red welts covered her skin. She clung to Brownie, her eyes nearly swollen shut, looking so small and lost against the starched white sheets that it was all Amanda could do not to cry.

She rushed to Claire's side, set aside her crutches, and perched on the edge of the cot. "Oh, honey. What happened?" She pulled her into her arms, rested her cheek on her head, inhaled her little-girl scent.

Kendall rose from the plastic chair on the opposite side of the bed. "She had a reaction to the oatmeal."

"The oatmeal?" She frowned. How could that be?

"She was fine until then. I used the EpiPen, then brought her here."

Amanda rocked, dabbed the tears from Claire's blotchy face, then shot Kendall a questioning look. "You gave her the stuff from the plastic container, right?"

"Absolutely." Kendall's worried eyes stayed on Claire. "I gave her exactly what you told me. But it happened right after she ate the oatmeal, so that had to be it."

"I believe you." She pulled her gaze back to Claire. Kendall knew all about Claire's allergy to peanuts and understood how serious it was. She wouldn't have made a mistake.

But then how could this have happened? She screened every morsel Claire ate, refusing to even take a chance on commercial cereals. She was so scrupulous, in fact, that she hand mixed a special breakfast blend for Claire using oatmeal, walnuts and flax.

"The doctor will be back in a minute," Kendall added. "She gave her a shot of epinephrine. She said Claire's going to be fine."

"Thank you," she whispered. She cradled Claire closer, grateful that her sister had been there. But it should have been her. She never should have neglected her child—especially for a night of sex.

Guilt tightened her throat, and she glanced at Luke. He stood at the open curtain with his strong arms crossed, his rugged face set in grim lines.

She flashed back to the first time she'd seen him in the casino. Her impression of him had been exactly right—he was ruthless, powerful…predatory.

But he was far more complex than that. He had a tender side, a good side, no matter what he might think. He'd sheltered her. He'd saved her life on that hill. And she could never repay him for last night, for all that he'd taught her about herself. He'd given her an amazing gift, freeing her from the doubts and insecurities Wayne had instilled.

Still, he'd retreated after the shattering intimacy they'd shared. But maybe it was just as well. Claire's accident was a sobering reminder that nothing had really changed since she'd met him. They lived in different worlds.

Maybe he'd punched holes in her protective walls. Maybe he'd made her dream for a while about a man she could never have. But that's all it was, a dream. She had Claire to think about, possibly an illness to confront. No matter how much Luke compelled her, she couldn't turn a brief sexual interlude into a fairy-tale romance. And she certainly couldn't go off the deep end and let herself fall in love with the man.

But as she pulled her gaze from those carnal eyes, she feared that her heart had already taken the plunge.

Three hours later, Amanda settled her exhausted, drowsy daughter down for a nap. The doctor had pumped Claire full of antihistamines and adrenaline, making the welts fade, the dangerous swelling in her throat subside.

Amanda smoothed back Claire's wispy hair, rubbed her back, smiling at the sight of the bear peeking over the sheet. They'd been lucky today. They'd had a bad scare, nothing more. It could have been far worse.

And she had to make sure it didn't happen again. Determined to root out the source of the problem, she pushed aside her own exhaustion and rose.

She limped through the quiet house into the kitchen. Her sister had gone home. Luke had closeted himself in his office to make some calls. Only the tick of the grandfather clock in the hallway and the muted buzzing of gardeners trimming hedges by the pool broke the hush.

She propped her crutches against the counter and opened the pantry, then pulled out the cereal she'd mixed. She popped the top off the plastic container, sniffed and peered inside. No sign of peanuts that she could tell.

Frowning, she closed the container and put it back, then grabbed the can of walnuts from the shelf. She turned the can, looked at the label. *Peanuts.*

She stared at the can in disbelief. *Impossible.* She couldn't have used peanuts by mistake. She never bought them, never even allowed them in the house.

Stunned, she pried off the plastic lid, but there were peanuts inside. And the can was still nearly full, recently opened, just like the one she had used.

Still unwilling to believe it, she frantically searched the shelf. But there wasn't another can. These had to be the nuts she'd used.

Her mind reeling, she stumbled to the table and sank into a chair. How could she have done this? She couldn't have bought the wrong nuts and added them to Claire's food—could she? Because if she had... This was so much worse than misplacing a comb or forgetting where she'd parked the car. *She could have killed Claire.*

Horrified, she dropped her face into her hands. She dragged in a breath, tried to wrap her mind around what she had done. If she'd made this mistake, it proved she had her mother's illness, and it was progressing faster than she'd thought. She would need to tell Kendall, make preparations for Claire's future before she endangered her even more.

But she still couldn't believe it. How could she have done anything so careless? She searched for a different conclusion, desperate for something—anything—that would explain it away. But who else could have done it? Wayne was in Maryland. The police had even said so. And she refused to believe Kendall or Luke could have done anything this vicious to Claire.

Which put the blame back on her.

She pressed her hand to her lips and closed her eyes. She didn't want to face it, but neither could she keep ignoring the proof. She really was losing her mind.

She inhaled, trying to calm herself down, to ease the panic surging inside. Somehow she had to get through this and cope.

But then the muscles along the back of her neck tensed. The fine hairs on her forearms rose.

And she felt it again—that creeping, crawling sensation slithering over her skin. It wormed through her nerves, beat into her skull—that whisper of menace, danger. The feeling that he was back again, watching her.

She gasped air to her strangled lungs, tried to shove the paranoia away. Wayne wasn't here. She couldn't overreact. She had to get a grip on her nerves.

But the fright only mounted, mingled with dread. And she could feel him now, getting closer, closer....

She leaped up and whipped around. The kitchen was empty. Nothing moved. Only the grandfather clock ticked down the hallway, its beats sounding out the relentless chant: He's here. He's here. He's here.

"Who's there?" she croaked.

Silence echoed back.

"Who's there?" she cried again, and her voice rose to a shriek. Her knees began to shake. Terror poured through her cells. She pressed her hand to her throat, struggling not to come undone, but the fear mushroomed inside her, threatening to explode.

This had to be Wayne. He had to be here. She couldn't be losing her mind.

Could she?

She hugged her arms and rocked, let out an anguished moan.

She'd never felt more terrified or alone in her life.

Luke had never felt more out of control. He entered the kitchen a short time later, his gut in turmoil, a headache beating at the base of his skull. His entire life was unraveling before his eyes.

Sex with Amanda had shaken him, affected him in ways he didn't want to examine. The sight of her poor daughter swollen and blistered from that allergic reaction had bothered him even more.

He didn't want to care about them. He didn't want to get involved with Amanda or her child. He needed to focus on his project, on getting revenge on Harold Rothchild and attaining his goal.

Especially now that he'd gotten more bad news. Now even his project was slipping from his grasp—and to save it, he needed Amanda's help.

He spotted her slumped at the kitchen table, her hands covering her face. He hated telling her this latest development and adding to her stress when she was worried about Claire. But he didn't have much choice.

She was as caught up in this mess as he was. The police might even call her in for questioning now.

He slid into the chair across from her, and she lifted her head. His heart skidded at the torment in her eyes. "What happened? Is it Claire?"

She pushed her hair back from her face with trembling hands. "No. She's better. She's napping, but she's going to be fine."

"Then what's wrong?" Her face had paled. Fatigue puffed the skin around her eyes.

"Nothing." Her gaze flitted away. "I'm just tired."

"And I'm Santa Claus."

Her brows snapped together, and he scowled back. "Come on, Amanda. Don't give me that crap. You look like hell. You've been jumping at noises for days. Something's wrong, and I want to know what it is."

Her lips tightened. "It has nothing to do with you. It's just…something I have to deal with alone."

Her answer should have relieved him. He wanted to back away. He'd been trying to distance himself from this woman since the moment they'd met. But he'd be damned if he could do it. The thought of her suffering some private torment tore his insides to shreds.

He reached out and trapped her hand, caressing the fragile bones with his thumb. "Tell me, Amanda. Whatever it is, I'll help."

"You can't help," she whispered. "There's nothing anyone can do."

"Try me."

Her stricken eyes searched his. And he saw her hope, her doubt. The fear.

"Trust me," he said, and after an endless moment, she sighed.

"All right." She squeezed his hand, then tugged her own away. "But there's really nothing you can do. I told you I've been misplacing things."

"Yeah."

"Well, this time I put peanuts in Claire's oatmeal instead of walnuts. I could have killed her."

"So you made a mistake."

She rubbed her arms, looking even more distraught. "It's worse than that. I told you my mother was ill. But I didn't tell you…she was mentally ill, schizophrenic. She suffered from hallucinations, blackouts. She forgot things, did bizarre things—like putting the wrong ingredients in food."

Oh, hell. He sat back and folded his arms. No wonder she was upset. "You think you have the same thing."

She clasped her hands, gnawed at her bottom lip. "It can be genetic. And sometimes it doesn't show up until later in life, until your twenties and thirties."

"You're not mentally ill," he said flatly.

"But—"

"But nothing." He didn't believe it for a minute. "You told me this started after you moved here."

"Right. The night of Rothchilds' party. But—"

"Did anything happen last night at my penthouse?"

"No." A blush rose up her cheeks. "At least nothing like that."

Their gazes locked. Hunger rose and vibrated the air. His blood pulsed hard, and he battled back the urge to haul her across the table into his arms. This wasn't the time for sex.

He cleared his throat. "Look at it logically. All these events have happened in the house."

"Not the time I forgot where I parked."

"But you were here right before that. Someone could have followed you there."

"Maybe." Misery deadened her voice. "But I didn't black out here. That happened at the Rothchilds' casino."

She was right. He shoved his hand through his hair. "So there are inconsistencies. Let's not worry about that right now. Let's just assume someone is doing this to you."

"But—"

"Just assume for a minute."

"All right." She watched him, her forehead creased. And he wanted to hold her, comfort her, erase that anxiety from her face. He got to his feet, paced a safe distance away so he could think. "So who knows about your mother's illness?"

"Kendall, of course. And you do now."

"How about your ex?"

"Yes, but Wayne's in Maryland. He made his parole check. You told me that yourself."

Another detail they'd worry about later. "Tell me more about him."

"Like what?"

"How he acted. Things he did."

She leaned back in her chair, blew out her breath. "Well, he was a pretty classic abuser. When we were dating, he was charming. Extremely attentive. He sent flowers, gifts, made me feel special…desired."

She gave him an embarrassed smile. "I was actually flattered when he started acting possessive. I had no idea… And once I married him, it got worse. He alienated me from my friends, pressured me to quit my job. Then the criticisms started, the violent mood swings…"

"How did you get away?"

She shuddered. "It wasn't easy. He controlled everything, the car, the money. I started substitute teaching when he was out of town and put the money in a special escape fund."

He locked his jaw against the sudden rush of anger. Some day, he was going to confront that brute. He was going to make him pay for hurting her.

And if Wheeler was behind these problems now, that day would come soon.

"It got worse after I left," she said, and her voice wobbled. "The stalking, the phone calls. When I got those hang-up calls at Kendall's, I thought at first it was him. But it couldn't have been him. He wasn't the one in the casino. It wasn't his voice. And he had nothing to do with that ring."

Luke paced to the patio window, mulling that over. He stuffed his hands in his pockets, stared out at the sprinklers forming rainbows in the sun. This situation was complicated. There were too many threads, and none of them seemed to connect.

He turned back to Amanda. "I take it Wheeler knew you were worried about inheriting your mother's illness?" She nodded, confirming his suspicions. "Does Wheeler get custody of Claire if you're ill?"

"No, I don't think so. Not with his criminal record and the abuse. Kendall would take her." She grabbed her crutches and rose. "Even if he could, I can't see that as a motive. He never cared about her. The last thing he'd want holding him down is a child."

"But losing Claire would hurt you." A fact that Wheeler would know. Anyone could see how much she loved and protected her child. "And he knows about Claire's allergy?"

She stopped beside him, and her wide blue eyes searched his. "Yes. He knows everything about us, even that I mix that oatmeal."

"So what's your gut feeling? Is this something Wheeler would do?"

"This is exactly like him. When I had him arrested, he vowed to come after me, to make me pay. And I wish it were him. I'd much rather deal with Wayne than lose my mind. But it can't be him. He's in Maryland."

"So it would seem." He frowned out the window at the golf course beyond the patio. A couple of carts glided past.

"We know he didn't hold me up in the casino," she added. "And he wasn't on that hilltop, either. Unless there really is more than one person involved…" Her face paled, and she looked so spooked suddenly that he dreaded telling her the rest.

But she needed to know the truth. "I just got a phone call from my security chief, Matt Schaffer. He told me the notes definitely matched. The one you got was written by the same person who wrote to Harold Roth-child."

Her face went whiter yet. "So the killer was the one who took photos of Claire."

"It looks that way. It gets worse," he added as she pressed her fingers to her lips. "They've reopened the investigation. They originally arrested Matt's aunt, but she just turned out to be a nutcase."

She frowned, and he knew she still didn't under-stand. "This isn't public knowledge, but in the note Harold got, the killer vowed to get revenge on the family. That means I'm their prime suspect again."

"I don't see how. We told them about the man who

attacked us yesterday. You even described him. And we showed them the note I got and the surveillance tape."

"But I have a motive. And I've been involved in this from the start. You even got attacked in my casino."

"What a mess."

"Yeah." He exhaled. "It's a mess. But let's solve your problem first. I'll get Matt Schaffer on it. He can set up surveillance, find out if someone's entering the house and bypassing the security system."

Her eyes stayed on his. "And if no one is?"

"Then we'll deal with it." Unable to resist, he fitted his hands to her waist, stroked the gentle sweep of her spine. No matter what else was wrong in his life, no matter how much she distracted him from his goals, holding her still felt right. "Don't worry. We'll get through this."

"Thank you," she whispered. "I thought…I thought you'd be so disgusted if you knew. Wayne—"

"Do me a favor." He tilted her chin up. "Don't confuse me with that bastard again."

Her eyes turned dark, her lips soft. "I could never, ever confuse you with him."

He pulled her close, slanted his mouth over hers, making sure to drive that point home. He didn't know what the future held. His life and emotions were in upheaval. But like it or not, last night had changed things. And for this moment at least, she was his.

He ended the kiss before it got out of hand, and pressed her head to his neck. And for a long moment he just stood there with her in his arms. Her warm, supple body curved against his. Her soft breath caressed his skin. He breathed in her womanly scent, feeling the inevitable lust build in his veins.

But then a thought intruded—the reason he'd sought her out. He had a party to attend that night. He needed to put on a good face, subdue the rumors Matt's crazy aunt's release would cause. And he needed Amanda by his side.

But Claire was sick, and he knew Amanda wouldn't leave her yet. He didn't have to ask. He'd seen the dismay in her eyes at the hospital, knew that she blamed herself.

And he couldn't leave them here alone. Candace's killer was on the loose. Wheeler could be lurking around, bypassing his security system and getting into the house. That thought made his blood run cold.

He could move her into his penthouse, but then Wheeler wouldn't show up. And they needed proof he was toying with her so they could trap him and end this mess.

He exhaled, knowing he didn't have a choice. He had to risk fueling the rumors and miss the event. He had to stay here and protect Amanda and Claire.

It could jeopardize his project, he knew that. The investors might see his absence as guilt.

But as his mouth devoured hers again, and he surrendered to the passion clouding his mind, his only concern was pleasuring her.

Chapter 11

Luke believed her. He didn't think she was losing her mind.

Amanda sank into the steamy kiss, her mind reeling, her heart flooded with gratitude to this man. He hadn't recoiled at the mention of her mother's illness, hadn't turned from her in disgust. If ever she'd needed proof that Luke was a thousand times better than Wayne, he'd just provided it in spades.

And she knew at that moment, that she was hopelessly, irrevocably in love with him.

His mouth covered hers, his tongue making deep, bold sweeps of her mouth, and she tightened her grip on his neck. She loved everything about him—his strength and self-assurance, his gruff tenderness. And the thrilling, arousing feel of him drove her wild.

She kissed him back, her heart overloaded with emotions, showing him how much his confidence meant. She ached for him, hungered for him, wanting to get closer yet. Feeling brazen, she rubbed her hips against his, and the long, rigid length of him made her moan. He laughed softly against her mouth.

He gentled the kiss, slid his lips to her jaw, her neck, sending pleasure streaming over her skin. "I'm addicted to you," he rasped.

"I can't stop, either," she confessed. She slid her hands over his hard, muscled shoulders to the short, silky hairs on the back of his neck. His whiskered jaw brushed her cheek, and excitement rushed through her veins.

He bent down slightly, wrapped his arms around her waist, then lifted her into his arms. She gasped at his strength, clutched his shoulders for balance as he turned with her and strode down the hall.

He carried her into her bedroom, kicked the door closed, then lowered her onto the bed. "Claire—" she began.

"I'll check on her. Don't move." He crossed the room and opened the adjoining door. He peeked into Claire's bedroom, then eased the door shut again. "She's asleep." He threw the bolt to lock them in.

Then he returned to the bed, looking predatory suddenly. He planted his feet wide, braced his hands low on his hips. The hungry look in his eyes made her tremble with need.

He stood there, watching her for a long, tense moment, as if debating how to proceed. "Since you can't stop," he said slowly. "Why don't you show me what you need?"

Her breath caught. Awareness rippled through her, and she realized what he wanted her to do. She nibbled her lip, suddenly uncertain, not sure if she had the courage. A week ago, she never would have dared.

But a week ago she'd been insecure about her sexuality, cowed by Wayne's cruel criticism, trapped in a cage of self-doubt.

Luke had unlocked that cage, set her free. And she refused to let her fears imprison her again.

She eyed the heat smoldering in his eyes, the hard set to his jaw, the definite bulge in his slacks. A delicious sense of abandon overtook her. The old Amanda was gone. Now she was going to shock him—shock herself—and take a risk. For once, she wasn't going to define herself by her doubts.

She scooted back on the bed, careful not to bump her injured ankle, then defiantly lifted her chin. And then she slowly dragged off her T-shirt and tossed it aside. She made much shorter work of her bra.

Luke didn't move. His gaze dropped to her breasts, the burn in them scalding her skin. Encouraged, she closed her eyes, let her head fall back, and cupped her breasts with her hands. And then she imagined Luke's hands instead of her own, how he'd touch and fondle and stroke, the feel of his rough, masculine palms, the scorching heat of his mouth. Her breathing grew fast, shivers sparked over her skin as her hands mimicked what she saw in her mind.

She arched back, opened her eyes. He stood frozen at the foot of the bed, his gaze riveted on her breasts. His body had gone rigid. A muscle flexed his jaw. His eyes were hot, dangerous, dark.

Good.

She sank back against the pillows. Keeping her eyes glued on his face, she inched off her shorts. Her underpants dropped to the floor next. His eyes tracked every move.

She paused, naked now, and battled a sudden flurry of nerves. She felt embarrassed, uncertain. But this was Luke, the man who believed in her.

"You're not stopping now." The rough tone of his voice made her shiver with need.

"No," she whispered back. "I'm not stopping now. I want you too much."

"Show me," he said.

She parted her thighs, showed him exactly what she wanted, responding to the slow sliding strokes of her hand. A heavy fullness rippled through her. The need grew into an ache, stripping away the last of her inhibitions.

He stood rooted in place, his hands clenched into fists, following every motion she made. Her skin grew tight. Her entire body tensed. She shuddered, lost in his eyes, willing him closer, needing his hands…his mouth.

"Luke," she whispered, the need unbearable now. And she couldn't stop. The hunger built and swelled, the need for him beyond her control. She breathed faster, harder, wanting him with a wildness she couldn't contain.

"Luke," she cried out again, and then she bucked hard, exploding with pleasure while he still stood immobile and watched.

Suddenly, he erupted into a flurry of action. He ripped off his shirt, kicked off his pants, tossing them to the floor. And then he knelt above her, plunging into her in one hard stroke, bringing her back to the brink. She gasped at the delicious invasion, thrilled to his hard, pulsating feel. He buried himself to the hilt, filling her, claiming her.

"That was the sexiest thing I've ever seen," he said, his voice hoarse.

He kissed her, plundering deeply with his tongue,

searing her with his blatant need. His muscles rippled under her palms. His wide shoulders bunched and strained. The kiss was fierce, provoking, and she kissed him back with everything she had.

Then her body grew taut, the ache unbearable. She moaned against his mouth. He thrust hard, and she combusted in an explosion of bliss. His deeper groans mingled with hers.

For several, long moments, neither moved. Breathing erratically, she trailed her fingertips over the stubble shadowing his jaw and traced the hollows of his cheeks.

He braced himself on his forearms, and she inhaled deeply, relishing his masculine scent. His gaze roamed her lips, her breasts. And then his eyes trapped hers, kicking off a riot of emotions in her chest.

"Do you have any idea how erotic that was?" he asked.

She trembled, shocked that she already wanted him again. She didn't think she could get enough. But it wasn't just the sex, she realized suddenly. His masculine virility compelled her, but it was his essence that captivated her heart.

Her throat closed on a sudden pang of longing, her love for him brimming in her chest. Not wanting him to see how vulnerable she felt, she averted her gaze, stroked the wide line of his shoulders, the firm muscles bulging beneath his sleek skin.

"You've done so much for me," she managed to say around the thickness in her throat. "I can never begin to repay you."

He tipped up her chin, but she kept her gaze lowered afraid to expose the feelings she knew would show in her eyes. She traced the edge of his beard stubble loving how sexy he looked with those straight, dark brows, those masculine lips.

"I know some ways you could try."

The seductive tone of his voice caught her attention, and she braved a glance at his face. His golden eyes gleamed with humor, and her heart warmed even more.

"Is that a promise?" she asked.

"Count on it."

She loved this playful side of him, a side he rarely revealed. But she understood why he kept it hidden. She'd grown up just as he had, shouldering the weight of responsibility, facing the harsh realities of life at a too-young age.

She'd felt the same hopelessness, bitterness, the consuming need to survive. But she'd accepted her life, let go of the pain. She couldn't fight her mother's mental illness. There wasn't a concrete enemy to blame.

But Luke had a target—Harold Rothchild. That fury had sustained him, along with his all-consuming ambition and drive. And she understood his need for vengeance, for respect. She even understood why he feared letting people close.

She frowned, trailed her hand over the tendons running down his shoulder and arm. But waging a constant war took its toll. It hurt his enemies, and it hurt him. Even innocent people got trapped in the fight.

Like the people living in the slums he was going to destroy.

She nibbled her lip, knowing she would do anything this man asked. She just had. And she'd help him get that project approved if that's what he needed most. But maybe she could convince him not to go through with it, to let go of his need for revenge.

To let the pain heal.

He pulsed inside her, and her breath caught. His mouth went to her breast and ignited her hunger again. She closed her eyes, plunged her hands in his thick, silky hair, felt him move his body down hers. And then she didn't think at all.

Luke sprawled on the sofa the next morning, every inch of his body relaxed. He'd never felt so content in his life. Sex with Amanda just kept getting better. She continually surprised him, making him want to hole up with her somewhere and not emerge for months.

He passed a hand over his gritty eyes, pulled out his BlackBerry and yawned. She'd kept him so enthralled he hadn't thought about work for hours—the first time that had happened in years. He checked the phone log, saw that he'd missed a call from his security chief. He punched in Matt's number and waited for him to pick up.

He glanced at Claire playing on the carpet near his feet. The kid had made a full recovery and was busy chattering at her bear. It was just as well that she demanded attention. Without Claire to distract Amanda, he'd never get anything done.

"Schaffer here," Matt said.

Luke got right to the point. "Did you get anything?"

"Yeah. We struck pay dirt. One of the gardeners entered your house early this morning."

Luke went still. His eyes swerved to the window overlooking the pool. The thought of someone skulking around the hallways while he and Amanda slept made everything inside him cold. It was a good thing she'd been with him all night.

He lowered his voice so Amanda and Claire wouldn't hear. "Where is he now?"

"I don't know. He didn't stay inside long."

"How's he getting in?"

"He used the patio entrance this time. He bypassed the system, but he obviously didn't know about the new cameras we installed."

Luke went from the couch to the patio, examined the door. "There's no sign of forced entry."

"He's using the codes. We're checking on how he got them now. And he fits the description you provided— stocky, blond hair."

Wheeler. Satisfaction curled through him, merging with the deep, scorching rage. It was past time to confront that creep.

"Don't notify the police," he told Matt. He needed to think this through, set a trap. "And don't change the codes—we don't want to tip him off."

"All right."

"I'll talk to Amanda and clear it with her, but I want to catch him today." He scowled at a sudden thought. He had another meeting with the investors that afternoon. But he'd just have to postpone it again.

"Got it," Matt said. "By the way, Natalie decided to put me out of my misery and agreed to a wedding date. Mark your calendar for June fourteenth, here in Vegas."

Luke grinned. "I'll be there."

He disconnected the line and slipped his Black-Berry into the pocket of his slacks. So Matt and Natalie were going to tie the knot soon. He'd suspected as much. Their whirlwind romance had made the tabloids, lending credence to the rumors about that missing diamond ring's weird curse—that in the right hands, it brought true love. In the wrong hands, chaos ensued.

His gaze bee-lined to Amanda where she sat at the kitchen table. Her soft, shiny hair tumbled over her arms. Her snug T-shirt cupped her breasts. His gaze lingered, memories of how her skin had tasted stirring his blood. Just watching her filled him with a sense of rightness.

He'd never thought about getting married, never wanted to. But he suddenly understood Matt. The idea of having Amanda around for a while appealed to him—sleeping in her arms every night, waking up with her every day.

He frowned and angled his head, rolling that idea over in his mind. Maybe she wouldn't be in a hurry to leave when this was done. Maybe he could convince her to stay, at least for a while. This woman had a lot of facets he still wanted to explore.

His body stirring, he kept his gaze on her breasts. He had plans for her, all right.

But first they had to catch her ex-husband.

Amanda dragged her attention away from Luke at the patio door to the teaching application in her hands. She stared at the paper blindly, her brain still fried, unable to stop thinking about the rapturous night. She had to pull herself together, though. She was acting like a lovestruck teenager, mooning over him, reliving those delirious sensations he'd evoked.

She exhaled, blowing her loose hair back from her face. She loved Luke, but she had to be practical. He'd never mentioned any feelings for her, especially not love. All she knew for sure right now was that he wanted her sexually.

My, had he driven *that* point home. She closed her eyes, shivering at the erotic memories—his muscles flexing under her palms, his eyes blazing with need. The thrill of having all that power and intensity focused only on her. And the things he'd asked her to do. Her face warmed. She'd never known she had such a wanton streak.

But desiring her sexually didn't mean he loved her. He'd never proposed marriage, never mentioned a future together. Which meant she had to get herself back on track.

She looked at the front room, where Luke squatted down, talking to Claire. And Amanda knew she had to tread carefully. She'd made a big mistake with Wayne. Thanks to her faulty judgment, her daughter's life was at stake.

Luke wasn't Wayne. He wasn't even close. She would never believe the rumors about his supposed role in Candace's murder.

But he was definitely out of her league. And it wasn't just her own feelings she had to protect. Claire could end up attached to him, hurt when they had to leave.

Which meant she couldn't draw this out. She had to make plans, quickly find a job.

Luke rose in a fluid motion, then came toward her. Her gaze stalled on his powerful thighs, the way his shirt clung to his muscled abs. Her throat went dry at the sight.

She frowned at the application again. She had it bad, all right. She understood why that murdered woman had stalked him—especially now that she'd spent two nights in his bed. He was addictive, the perfect man. How could she settle for anyone else again?

"What are you doing?" he asked, sliding into the seat next to hers.

"Filling out a job application. There's an opening for a middle school history teacher."

"That doesn't sound exciting."

She shrugged, trying to keep her mind on the conversation instead of him. "It's a good job, and the school's not far from Kendall's house."

He leaned closer, and his nearness made it hard to breathe. "I thought you wanted to be an archaeologist."

She straightened the papers into a stack. "So?"

"So why don't you go for it?"

She shifted her gaze to Claire, watched her balance Brownie on the back of the couch. "It's not practical. I'd have to go back to school, do research. It would take years. And I have Claire to think about."

Besides, some dreams just weren't meant to be…like staying with him.

He looked as if he intended to argue, but then he shrugged. "I just spoke to Matt Schaffer."

Her pulse sped up. "What did he say?"

"The surveillance tape shows a gardener entering the house earlier today. He matches Wheeler's description."

She closed her eyes, clamped her hand over her lips. And the dread squeezing her chest began to ease.

"So it wasn't me," she whispered. "I really wasn't imagining things."

"No." He caught her hand in his, and gently squeezed. "You're as sane as I am, for what it's worth."

Tears misted her eyes, and her voice broke. "Luke… This is… I can't begin to thank you."

She inhaled, trying to hold back the emotions ricocheting inside. She didn't have her mother's illness. She wouldn't lose Claire. She was free.

And Luke had done this for her. He'd believed in her, helped her get proof.

She sniffed, grappling to stay in control, and wiped a tear from her eye. "How did he get by his parole officer?"

"I don't know. We'll find that out later. But you need to make a decision."

"What do you mean?"

"You have a couple of choices. We can contact the police right now and have him arrested."

He'd go to jail. But eventually he'd get released. And she'd be watching over her shoulder again, always waiting. The terror would never end. "What's the other choice?"

"We set a trap and confront him first, and then call the police."

Confront him. She'd have to see Wayne face-to-face? She tried not to panic at the thought. "What good would that do?"

He leaned back in his chair and folded his arms. "I'm going to put this baldly. He thinks he owns you. In his mind, you're his." His gaze held hers. "He's never going to stop trying to control you—especially since you defied him by getting away."

She shivered, his words chilling her. But Luke was right. Wayne had vowed to make her pay. "But then—"

"That's where I come in. I'll make it clear to him that you're mine now. That's how he thinks, Amanda. It's the only way he's going to let you go. You don't have to do anything," he added. "Just be the bait. You get him here, and then I'll make sure he understands."

She saw the anger simmering in Luke's eyes, the rage. He could do it. He could finally put an end to this perpetual fear.

But only if she had the courage to reel Wayne in.

She glanced at Claire. Her daughter stood clutching her bear now, watching her with anxious eyes.

Her anger flared. Claire didn't deserve this, and neither did she—the constant fear, the years of abuse. He'd even followed her here.

And he'd gone way too far when he'd poisoned Claire. That had been the final straw. It was time to bring this reign of terror to an end.

She locked eyes with Luke. "Let's set the trap."

Chapter 12

The waiting was killing her.

Amanda lay on one of the lounge chairs by the pool, feeling defenseless and exposed in her modest swimsuit, her stomach threatening to revolt. On the surface, the afternoon seemed perfectly peaceful. Insects droned from the nearby hedge. The soft breeze brushed her skin. Beyond the golf course, heat shimmered up from the desert floor, forming a wavering, watery mirage. But Wayne could show up any time now, and it was tearing her insides to shreds.

She focused her gaze on the distant mountains, forced herself to calm down. Nothing would go wrong. They'd gone over this a dozen times. She was not to provoke Wayne into an argument, was not to go anywhere with him—not even into the house. She'd just speed dial the cell phone the second she saw him and let Luke take it from there.

She patted the corner of the towel where she'd tucked the cell phone, squinted at the sparkling pool. Kendall had spirited Claire to the safety of Luke's penthouse. Luke waited just outside the compound, expecting her call. She glanced at her watch, her anxiety mounting as the minutes wore on. What if Wayne didn't show up?

He'd better come. She needed to end this today. She refused to spend day after endless day waiting, not knowing what he would do.

Her skin clammy despite the heat. She sipped her glass of lemonade, trying to soothe her parched throat. Then she flipped the page on the magazine she had in her lap in an attempt to look relaxed.

And then she smelled it—Wayne's scent. It wisped through the air and crept into her nostrils like smoke from a smoldering fire. She kept her eyes glued to the magazine, her heart accelerating into overdrive, her senses hyperalert.

Was that him? Was he behind her? Or had she imagined that scent? She inhaled but only smelled the chlorine from the pool. She didn't dare turn around to check.

Instead she reached for the lemonade again, brought the glass to her lips with a trembling hand. *Stop shaking,* she ordered herself fiercely. *Don't let him see your fear.*

The smell grew stronger. He was definitely behind her. Her breath wheezed out.

She had to call Luke fast.

She set the glass carefully on the table, reached for the phone under the towel. But a gun barrel was pressed against her temple, and she went dead still.

"That's right," Wayne said from behind her, and the sound of his voice made her nausea rise. "Now stand up, nice and slow, or you'll be dead."

She heard the rage in his voice the awful excitement. He actually wanted to kill her. He thought he had the right.

And she only had a second to act. She flicked her gaze to the towel, trying not to move her head. Then she stretched her fingers toward the cell phone, reaching... reaching.

The gun bit into her skin. "Pick up that phone and I shoot. Now get up."

Panic mingling with disbelief, she rose on quivering legs. This couldn't be happening. She couldn't let it. She had to follow the plan...

The gun eased away, and her hopes spiked. But Wayne circled into view, his weapon still aimed at her head. The stench of aftershave assaulted her senses, and she went rigid with fear.

Think, she urged herself fiercely. *Think.* She couldn't let him do this to her.

His face leered close and she forced herself to look. His skin was flushed. A bead of sweat crawled down his jaw. Hatred gleamed in his mean blue eyes.

How had she ever thought him handsome? How had she ever believed she could care for this man?

"I told you I'd make you pay," he said, and the violence in his voice congealed her blood. He moved closer, and his hot breath sickened her gut.

Without warning, he slammed the gun against her head. She cried out, slumped to her knees.

Stunned, blinded by pain, she gasped for air. Oh, God. This was worse than she'd expected. He was vicious, out of control. And she knew with a bone deep certainty that he wasn't going to let her live.

She staggered back to her feet. She battled the spasms in her injured ankle, the violent ache in her head. Blood trickled into her eye. Wayne circled her again, preparing to strike.

And suddenly, anger sparked inside her, outrage that this creep thought he could terrorize her. So what if she got hurt when she defied him? She refused to feed his ego again.

She stepped back, pretending to cower, moving close to the lemonade glass. "Don't," she whimpered, knowing it was what he expected from her.

He flashed that sadistic grin. She took another step back, pressed her too-slick palms to her thighs. "Please don't hurt me," she whispered again. He stepped toward her, and she knew that she'd run out of time.

She switched her gaze to a spot behind him. He fell for the trick and glanced back. She grabbed the glass of lemonade, flung the stinging liquid into his eyes.

He blinked, growled with anger. She hurled the heavy tumbler at his head. The glass bounced off his skull, but it momentarily stunned him, then shattered on the tiles at his feet. Her pulse frantic, she lunged for the phone on the chair.

It didn't matter. Luke vaulted the hedge, slammed into Wayne. The two men crashed to the ground.

Wayne didn't have a chance. Luke rammed Wayne's head against the tiles, punched his face and gut in a flurry of fists. Wayne groaned, cried out. The sickening thuds made her cringe.

But Luke was relentless, fighting with a fury she'd never seen. Within seconds, Wayne lay motionless and was bleeding on the ground, the gun a safe distance away.

Luke rammed his knee into Wayne's throat. "Leave her alone," he ordered. He shoved down harder, and

Wayne let out a helpless wheeze. "She's mine now. Amanda and Claire are mine. Do you hear me?" Wayne's face turned purple, and he gasped for air. "You come near them again and you're dead."

Wayne croaked out his agreement. Luke pressed down for a few more seconds, then finally released him and stood.

Her heart still thundering, Amanda dragged in a shaky breath. Then she walked to where her ex-husband lay. And for a long moment she just stared at him, this man who'd caused her such terror, such pain. He'd seemed so powerful once, so cunning and brutally strong. Now he was just bloody, pathetic, cowed.

And she realized it was over. It was finally over. She was free of Wayne at last.

Luke stood in his casino's ballroom that evening, his words still echoing in his head. *She's mine,* he'd told Wheeler. *Amanda and Claire are mine.* He'd meant the words only for show, to keep Wheeler from bothering them again. But the hell of it was, those words sounded right. Amanda did feel like his.

He glanced at her across the crowded ballroom, watched her fill her small plate with hors d'oeuvres. She wore a thigh-high black dress that molded her curves, showcasing those killer legs. The front was modest, but tight, the fabric cupping her breasts like a lover's hands. But in the back… The dress plunged dramatically to her hips, riveting every man's gaze to her tempting, naked skin.

His throat suddenly dry, he took a swallow of whiskey. He'd touched that skin, made love to every inch of that sensual body. He knew her scent, her taste.

He knew what made her moan, what made her sigh, how her flesh felt hot and moist. He'd made her swollen and aching with need.

She was beautiful, erotic.

And she was his.

She could have died today. Every time he closed his eyes, he flashed back to the image of her bloody scalp, the deranged look in Wheeler's eyes, and the frantic need to protect her consumed him all over again.

"Is the meeting still on for tomorrow?" a man standing beside him asked.

Luke tossed back his last swallow of whiskey, pulled his attention to Fletcher Coddington. The elderly investor's wife was with him tonight, and the voluptuous young woman smiled up at Luke, the invitation clear in her eyes. Luke scanned her collagen-plumped lips, her silicone breasts, the fake, come-hither smile. Maybe the giant rock on her finger was phony, too. It would serve her right.

He looked back at Amanda. She turned his way, smiling at something someone said, and his heart made a swerve in his chest. She was the exact opposite of Coddington's gold-digging wife—authentic, interesting, sincere.

"Montgomery?" Coddington said, sounding annoyed.

He jerked his eyes back to the investor, scrambling to remember what he'd said. The meeting. Right. "It's all set. Ten o'clock tomorrow." It was their final meeting, the day they'd sign the contracts on the Phoenix project and decide if it was a go. The day he'd toll the death knell for Harold Rothchild.

At last.

And he had Amanda to thank for it. Once again, she'd

soothed the investors with her warm smile and gentle voice. She'd diffused questions about the murder, showed everyone her confidence in him. And he knew damn well she'd kept several worried men from backing out.

She looked up then, and her eyes met his from across the room. That familiar heat jolted through him, that feeling of rightness.

"Excuse me," he said and headed toward her, leaving Coddington sputtering behind.

He worked his way through the chattering crowd, ignoring bids for his attention, anxious to get to her side. And that deep sense of possessiveness settled inside him again. He didn't know when it had started, only that it was there—and was growing stronger each day.

The scare today had clinched it. He realized he didn't want Amanda to leave, didn't want her moving back to her sister's house, even when the danger was gone. She belonged with him now.

And it was time to make that clear.

Amanda's pulse quickened as Luke strode toward her across the glittering ballroom, those bourbon-colored eyes locked on hers. Lord, he looked sexy. His broad shoulders filled out his tuxedo. Light from the enormous chandeliers glinted off his ebony hair. His stark-white shirt set off his tanned skin, and he looked so unapologetically masculine, so utterly sensual that thrills of excitement skipped through her nerves.

Breathless, she dropped her gaze to her plate. She had to get a grip. It was bad enough that she was in love with him. She couldn't embarrass them both by ogling him in a public place.

Not that every other woman in the room wasn't doing the same.

A waiter materialized at her side. "Wine?" he asked.

Startled, she studied the waiter's face. But he was too short, too dark to be the man who'd drugged her the other night.

"No, thanks," she said, and he moved on. She doubted anyone would try to attack her tonight, but she wasn't drinking, just to be safe—especially with Candace's killer still on the loose.

At least Wayne was no longer a problem. She nibbled on a crab-stuffed mushroom, relieved that he was locked up. He'd been arrested and charged with a litany of crimes—breaking and entering, stalking, committing numerous parole violations, including possessing a firearm and crossing state lines. He'd stay in prison for years. And when he did get out, he would leave her alone…thanks to Luke.

Luke joined her just then. Adrenaline raced through her veins. She wondered if she'd ever feel normal around him. Every time she looked at him, her pulse went amok.

"Join me on the balcony?" he asked.

"Sure." Her appetite gone, she set down the plate and took his arm. They strolled from the noisy ballroom, moving slowly because of her still-tender ankle.

And suddenly, a thought came out of nowhere, catching her off guard. Maybe he was going to end their arrangement now. Wayne had been arrested. Tomorrow his project would be approved and he no longer needed her help. Candace's killer was still at large, but surely the police would catch him soon.

Which meant Luke might want their masquerade to end.

Her breath fled in a surge of panic. It was too soon for her. Way too soon and not only because of the danger. She needed time to show Luke how much she loved him. Time to heal him from his past pain. Time to convince him to change his mind about the project, to let go of the bitterness and his need for revenge.

"Down here." He led her across the spacious balcony, away from prying ears. And with every step, her anxiety mounted. If he wanted to end it now, what could she say?

They reached the far corner of the balcony, and he stopped. She braced her hands on the railing to collect herself, looking out at the dazzling array of lights. Neon signs glittered and flashed. Honking horns and the muted roar of traffic drifted up.

And a terrible emptiness lodged inside her, threatening to destroy what little composure she had left. But she had only herself to blame for this mess. She'd known better than to fall in love with Luke. He'd been a fantasy from the start, completely unattainable. She'd known that it would end.

Which was poor comfort to her breaking heart.

"I've been thinking," he began, and she closed her eyes, determined to accept her fate with dignity.

"Now that Wheeler's out of the picture, you could stay with me. Move in for real."

Shock rippled through her. She opened her eyes and searched his face, not sure that she'd heard him right. She'd expected him to end their affair, not invite her to stay. "You want me to live with you?"

"There's no reason you have to go back to your sister's house, is there?"

Her lips parted. Confusion still muddled her mind.

"No, but…" This didn't sound very romantic. It was hardly the declaration of love she yearned for. "I…I don't know."

"What don't you know? It makes sense for you to stay. You need a place to live. And we're good together, Amanda." He crowded against her, tugged up her chin. The heat from his body seeped through her skin. "Very good."

He smoothed her hair away from her neck, lowered his mouth to the sensitive skin. She shivered at the sensual touch and closed her eyes, the familiar desire whipping through her like a blast of sand in a desert storm. They were more than good together. They burned.

Her head fell back. Her knees turned weak. He leaned into her, and she shuddered at the hard bulge pressing the juncture of her thighs.

She longed to obey her body's mandate. She ached to take him inside her and tell him yes. She wanted to feel that shocking pleasure every night, the exhilaration of his kiss every day. And she loved him madly. Staying with him was the answer to her dreams.

Almost. He hadn't mentioned marriage or love.

Trying to think through the hunger muddling her brain, she wrenched herself away. She pressed her fingers to her forehead, gazed out at the colorful display of lights.

His offer was tempting. Too tempting. She loved him and owed him so much. He'd awakened her sexually, freed her from Wayne. He'd even risked his life to save hers.

But he didn't love her.

Maybe with time she could make him love her, though. Maybe she could heal him and pay him back.

Maybe if she lived with him, she could convince him to let go of the bitterness, move on from the painful past.

Or maybe she was deluding herself again.

She drew in a breath of air, tried to think this through. She'd made a terrible mistake with Wayne. When she'd found herself pregnant, she'd taken a risk. Even though she hadn't known him well, she'd decided that love and compassion would come with time.

She'd been wrong. Horribly wrong.

She couldn't afford to make another mistake. She didn't only have her own heart at risk this time but Claire's. Her daughter already adored Luke. And before she would let Claire become even more attached, she needed a sign he was willing to change. She couldn't act only on faith, no matter how tempted she was.

"Luke…" She turned to face him again. He watched her with narrowed eyes. "Do you think your project will be approved?"

He planted his hands on his hips and frowned, the abrupt change of subject obviously taking him aback. "We're signing the contracts tomorrow. The investors are all on board."

She hugged her arms, looked out at the area just past the Strip where Naked City was. Not many lights twinkled there.

"Thanks for your help, by the way."

She nodded, then glanced at him again. "The thing is…I'm not sure I did the right thing by helping you. With your project, I mean."

His brow furrowed. "What are you talking about?"

"It's just… It bothers me that those people are going to lose their homes."

"They'll find another place to live."

"But where? What place? Prices are sky high here in Vegas. You know that. They'll end up on the streets."

He crossed his arms, falling into stony silence, and she tried again. "We got kicked out of our apartment when I was growing up. You said you did, too. Don't you remember what it was like? That awful fear?"

"I remember." His eyes turned cold. "Harold Rothchild was our landlord. He took away my mother's job, her house. He killed her with his indifference. And now he's going to pay."

Her heart chilled at the vengeance in his voice. He didn't understand. "But you're doing the same thing he did. There are children in those slums, Luke. Innocent children."

"Forget it," he warned her.

"But—"

"Stay out of this, Amanda." His tone turned hard. "I'm not shelving this project. Not for you, not anyone."

"But that's just it," she whispered. "This revenge… It's not good for you. Not healthy. It's eating you up inside. You have to let go of it, move on from the past."

"Right." He made a sound of disgust. "You mean like you have?"

She flinched at the sarcasm in his voice. "Yes, I—"

"You what? You think you've moved on?" His eyes turned so angry that her throat closed up. "Hell, you're so stuck in the past you're afraid to live your life. Why don't you forget that damn teaching job? Go back to school and become what you want. Start living for yourself for a change."

"But it's not the same thing. I can't just do what I

want. I have responsibilities—Claire. She needs stability, security. I don't have a choice."

He slowly shook his head. "There's always a choice. And you're choosing to stay in the past. You're too scared to take a chance."

The accusation stung. A dull ache pounded her skull. This wasn't about her. It was about him. How had this conversation gone so wrong? "Won't you at least think about it? Delay the project a bit?"

"No. It's all set. I'm not changing my mind."

Her heart plummeted. "Then I…I can't live with you, Luke."

"Because of the project." His voice sounded dead.

"No, it's not just that." Oh, God. She'd made a total hash of this thing. And she couldn't let it end like this. She had to take a risk, make sure he understood.

She dredged up her courage, laid her soul bare. "I don't want to just live together, Luke. I want it all— marriage, a ring, love. I want to have your children someday. And I want you to forget revenge."

His eyes turned even colder. "I'm not proposing marriage."

And she couldn't delude herself into thinking he would change. "Then there's nothing more to say."

He stared at her for a long moment. She thought she was going to be sick. What on earth had just happened? How could he not understand?

"You can stay in the house until the end of the week," he said. "I'll hire you a bodyguard and get a security system installed in Kendall's house to keep you safe."

He turned from her, strode back toward the balcony door. And then he stopped and glanced back. His glacial expression shattered her heart. "I'll call you a cab."

She swayed, clung to the balcony railing, desolation clutching her throat.

And watched the man she loved walk away.

Chapter 13

At one o'clock on a Saturday morning, Las Vegas Boulevard throbbed with life. Flashing lights lured gamblers into casinos. Thrill rides shot riders a hundred stories above the ground. Inebriated tourists milled in and out of strip clubs, spending their hard-earned dollars on shows.

Naked City teemed, too, but the action here was edgier, seedier, far more deadly.

Luke pulled his Jaguar up to the curb in front of his old apartment and cut the engine, then pushed open the door and climbed out. He paused, inhaled the stench of rotting garbage, stepped over the broken glass and trash. Chain link fences locked off the aging, one-story buildings. Graffiti covered the peeling stucco walls. In front of a motel sign missing half its letters stood an overflowing Dumpster, gang tags spray painted on its side.

Not sure what the hell he was doing here, Luke

scowled at the rundown apartments, the ripped-up sofa someone had dumped on the curb. He'd tried to bury himself in work after he'd left the party, tried to fine tune the contracts for the meeting later that day, but Amanda's rejection ate at him, destroying his focus. He'd finally given up and gone for a drive.

He'd ended up here.

And it ticked him off. He didn't want to look at his old neighborhood, didn't want to keep remembering what Amanda had said. She'd been out of line. The Phoenix project had nothing to do with the two of them. She had no idea what this meant to him, how many years he'd worked for this revenge.

He leaned back against the Jaguar and folded his arms, studied the trio of teens strolling toward him from down the street. The faces had changed over time, but Naked City still reeked of the same poverty and violence, the same desperate need to survive.

The teens stopped several yards away and eyed him. Their leader, a kid in pants with its crotch hanging down to his knees, swaggered over. He looked young, maybe all of thirteen with his baseball cap on backward and that peach fuzz gracing his lip.

But the kid sized him up with a worldly expression Luke knew well. He'd been just like that kid once—scared, hungry, too street savvy at an early age. And that's when he'd decided to leave this place. He'd stood right here, gazing at the high-rise casinos glittering on the nearby Strip, vowing to be someone, to never be hungry or powerless again.

And he'd worked his butt off to do it. He'd studied hard, landed a scholarship to a private high school, walked miles every morning to get himself there. He'd made connections at that school, learned how to work the system, taught himself to fit in with a better crowd. And then he'd started making money—lots of it—until he was wealthier than he'd ever dreamed.

But he'd never lost sight of his plan to take down Harold Rothchild.

And in a few more hours, he would succeed.

The kid stuffed his hands in his back pockets, glanced around. "You looking to score?"

Luke eyed the kid's scrawny frame, his hollowed-out cheeks, the desperation in his eyes. "No."

The kid moved closer, his gaze flitting to the Jaguar and back. "I can get good stuff."

"I'm not here for drugs."

The kid nodded. "You want some action. Gina's real hot. I'll go find her for twenty bucks."

The edge of Luke's mouth kicked up. The kid hadn't missed a beat. But then, kids learned early how to wheel and deal on the streets. They bartered for everything—drugs, sex, food, even their lives.

And suddenly, it struck him that he hadn't changed much. He was still cutting deals like this kid was, only with more money and higher stakes.

That thought knocked him off balance. Maybe he hadn't left this life behind. Maybe he was the same punk he'd been back then, just with a more sophisticated veneer.

A low-riding car rumbled up the street then, its shiny chrome flashing, its booming stereo vibrating the soles of his feet.

"Later," the kid said. He hurried back to his friends, and the teens melted into the night.

So the neighborhood's top dog had arrived. Probably the local pusher, the man with power.

And Luke suffered another jolt. He wasn't much different from that pusher, either. All his life he'd been consumed by a need for power, respect.

And Amanda had understood that. She'd seen what drove him, and had challenged him to stop—to stop being that punk from Naked City, to stop trying to prove himself and let the past go.

To give up his plan for revenge.

Scowling at that thought, he climbed back into his car and started the engine. Harold Rothchild deserved to be taken down. He didn't have to question that goal. Rothchild had plenty of sins to account for in his life, including his mother's death.

But if Luke went through with his plan, if he evicted those people from their apartments, he'd be no better than Rothchild was. Or Amanda's ex-husband, for that matter—a man bent on revenge.

He'd lose Amanda's respect.

He'd lose her.

He was going to have to choose.

He gunned the Jaguar's engine, burning rubber as he screamed past the drug dealer's car. He sped to the corner, leaving Naked City behind in a cloud of exhaust.

But as he downshifted for an upcoming stop light, another insight jarred him. And he finally realized what had been plaguing him all night, the real source of his discontent. If he did what Amanda wanted and let go of the need for revenge, what would he have left?

It unnerved him that he didn't know.

"So you want to tell me what really happened the other night?" Kendall asked.

Amanda sat beside her sister on the steps in the

shallow end of the pool, water lapping over her hips. Sunshine sparkled off the rippling water. Birds chirped from the nearby hedge. Claire played on the tiles behind them, giggling and talking to her dolls.

And the last thing Amanda wanted to do was rehash her argument with Luke. She'd spent the past two days struggling to forget about it, trying to erase his words from her mind. But her thoughts kept veering back to that argument like a missile zeroing in on a target, replaying every word, every gesture, analyzing every awful second of that fight.

"Mandy?" Kendall pressed.

She sighed, knowing the futility of trying to elude her sister's questions. Kendall always wormed the truth out of her eventually, so she might as well confess all now. She pulled her knees to her chest, exhaled again. "Luke asked me to live with him, to stay here for a while."

Kendall's mouth dropped open. "Are you serious? Luke Montgomery asked you to move in with him?"

"Yes." She propped her chin on her knees. "I turned him down."

"He asked you to live here and you turned him down." Incredulity laced Kendall's voice.

"I didn't want to just live together. I wanted more." Her mouth twisted. "I wanted marriage, love, the whole deal."

"Oh, God. You're in love with him."

"Dumb, huh?" She managed a wobbly smile.

"No, you're not dumb. He's totally hot. But Luke Montgomery…" She shook her head.

"I know. Completely out of my league." And she only had herself to blame. Kendall had warned her. She'd known a billionaire would never fall in love with her. She'd known straight off that she wasn't his type.

"But he's not like you think he is," she added. "He's a good man, Kendall. Really good." Gentle, caring, protective. Lethal in a fight. Dominant in an extremely exciting way.

She shivered, remembering the hours of unending pleasure, the ecstasy she'd found in his arms. "I've never met anyone like him." And she knew she wouldn't again. Luke was unique. The man she loved. It had been the real deal for her.

Her chest aching, her eyes heavy with unshed tears, she watched a hawk soar silently overhead. And she struggled not to wonder what Luke was doing, what he was wearing, if he was thinking about her at all.

She scoffed at that thought. No doubt he was busy with his project—meeting with the investors, reviewing the plans, attending another glitzy party. He wasn't obsessing over their argument like she was. If he was, he would have called. She had to move on, forget it, stop torturing herself this way.

"Okay, let's break this down," Kendall said, pulling Amanda's attention back to her. "First off, he's obviously attracted to you. Even I could see that much."

"But that's not love."

Kendall pursed her lips, splashed water over her arms. "No, but he watches you. He's always aware of where you are. It's pretty intense, actually. Sexy."

Intense was right. She kept reliving those delirious sensations, his kiss, his touch, the way he'd driven her wild with desire. She'd spent hour after sleepless hour aching to be back in his arms.

"Sex isn't love, though. Not for a guy." She lowered her voice so Claire wouldn't hear. "And he wasn't proposing marriage. He was clear about that."

"That's still a pretty big thing, though, asking you to move in with him."

"Not big enough."

Her brow knitted, Kendall leaned back, propped herself on her elbows and stretched out her sculpted legs. "Are you sure it wasn't more? I mean, I know he's a billionaire and off the charts, but the way he looked at you…"

"I'm sure." The pressure on her chest increased. "And anyway, it's over now. We argued. He was furious."

"You argued about moving in?"

"Sort of." She blew out a heavy breath, turned her gaze to the palm fronds swishing overhead, the cloudless expanse of blue sky. "Mostly about our goals, though. He said I should go back to school, become an archaeologist like I wanted. He claimed I was too afraid to take a risk."

"He's right about that."

Amanda glared at her.

"Well, you are." Kendall's tone gentled. "Listen, you know I love you. And I'll take your side no matter what. But he's right. You've always been too cautious."

"And that's bad? If I hadn't been cautious and practical we would have starved."

"I know. And I owe you big-time for that. If you hadn't taken care of everything, held it all together… You even stayed with Mom after high school so I could dance. But that's the point. You need to do something fun for once. Something you want, just for yourself. You deserve it."

"But I can't just run off to school. Claire—"

"Claire will be fine. You know she will. And I'll help out. I'll do anything you want. I owe you that much after the way you took care of Mom."

"I don't know."

"Life's short, Mandy. You need to go for it before it's too late."

Amanda sighed, watched the sparkling water swirl past. Kendall made it sound easy. But she'd have to take courses, do fieldwork, get an advanced degree. It would take years. But she'd love to examine ancient artifacts, to explore caves like the one Luke owned. Excitement surged through her at the thought.

"Well, think about it." Kendall glanced at her watch. "Listen, I need to go. I don't want to miss rehearsal. But call me if you need me tonight."

Amanda rose with her and grabbed her towel. "No, I'm fine. I don't have anywhere to go now." Not since Luke's project had been approved. "If you could watch her tomorrow, though, that would be great. I need to move our stuff back to your house."

She didn't want to think about moving. It was the final step, the end of her hopes with Luke. But she couldn't put it off. "I'll drop her off early," she added. "Don't forget Luke's security people are coming by to install that system." And a bodyguard would arrive after that. Luke had made good on his promise to protect her, even if he didn't want her around.

She was still trying not to dwell on the thought of moving as she settled Claire down for a nap. She hadn't brought many things to Luke's house—some clothes, Claire's favorite toys, a few books—so she could move out in a couple of trips. At least she wouldn't prolong the agony. Still, just thinking of leaving made her want to weep.

"Mommy, nap with me," Claire pleaded as she tucked her in.

She perched on the edge of the bed, smoothed the hair from Claire's face. "I can't, honey. I need to finish filling out some papers and pack up our things."

Claire clutched her bear, whispered something against the fur.

"What?" Amanda bent down to hear.

"Bad man's coming. Brownie's scared."

Her heart tripped. Her daughter was afraid. "No one's going to hurt us. We're safe now. The bad man's in jail." At least, Wayne was. Candace Rothchild's killer still hadn't been caught.

She gnawed her lip, not wanting to think about that. But the bodyguard and security system would keep them safe.

"But I'll sit here with you for a while, okay?"

She rubbed Claire's back, tucked the blankets tighter around her, waiting for her to drift off. But Claire's anxiety bothered her—bothered her badly.

Ever since Claire had been born, she'd tried to keep her daughter safe, to give her the stable life she'd never had. She'd wanted Claire's childhood to be the opposite of hers—comforting, secure, with a mother she could depend on.

But she'd failed. First Wayne had threatened them, and then the danger had followed them here—terrible danger. And despite her precautions, Claire had sensed it. She'd picked up on the fear. And now she was turning into an anxious, insecure child, exactly what Amanda had hoped to avoid.

Claire's breathing deepened into sleep, and Amanda stood. Still nursing her injured ankle, she left the bedroom door ajar and walked back into the kitchen, her mind a jumble of thoughts. She couldn't blame herself for all their problems. The casino gunman had singled her out for some unknown reason. That certainly wasn't her fault.

She'd made a mistake with Wayne, though. She never should have married him.

She sank into the chair at the kitchen table, stared at the teaching application she still had to complete. She picked up her pen, then set it back down. She didn't feel like teaching again. But she did need a job.

She picked up the pen again, tapped it on the table, tried to drum up some enthusiasm. But it occurred to her that she'd been teaching Claire the wrong lesson. Maybe she shouldn't have emphasized safety all these years. Maybe she shouldn't have tried so hard to avoid risks.

Maybe she should have been teaching Claire to stop being afraid, to go after what she wanted in life and pursue her dreams.

She stared at the application, unable to avoid the truth. Luke was right. She was afraid to change. Change was scary, painful. It took courage and nerve. It was easier to cling to the known, to not risk failure, to find excuses not to try.

She'd asked him to change, though. She'd asked him to give up his lifelong goal, to abandon his need to avenge his mother's death.

And yet she wouldn't even change her career.

She'd been unfair.

Her forehead pounded; her stomach swirled with guilt. That argument *had* been about her. She was more mired in the past than he was.

She shoved the job application aside, pulled her laptop over and booted it up. She clicked on the University of Nevada Web site, searched their listing o graduate programs until she found the right one. Anthropology. She could study right here in Las Vegas. She could do everything she'd always dreamed.

If she was strong enough to try.

She sat back, her mind spinning with all she would have to do. She'd have to retake the Graduate Record Exam, submit an application. Money would be tight. She'd have to live with Kendall longer, find a babysitter for Claire.

But she could do this. She was stronger than she'd once thought. If she could face down Wayne, surely she could make this change. She reached for the teaching application and ripped it up.

She stood, headed for the wastepaper basket, her chest lighter now. Maybe this wouldn't solve all her problems, but it was a start.

But then the telephone rang. She stopped, swiveled to face it, her senses suddenly alert. The only person who had her number here was Luke.

Her pulse pounding, she crossed the room and answered the phone. "Hello?"

"Amanda." Luke's voice rumbled across the line, and she closed her eyes. And suddenly, all the emotion she'd been trying to hold at bay for the past two days broke loose, like a flash flood ravaging a desert gorge.

"Luke…" Her voice broke. Oh, God. Was he calling for another chance? Was he going to admit he was wrong?

"Can you stop by here tomorrow at noon to drop off the keys?" he asked.

"What?" She blinked, her emotions in turmoil, trying to recoup.

"The house keys. I'd like them back."

"Oh, right." She pressed her hand to her chest, struggled to breathe. He only wanted to finish this business, make sure she left on time and returned the keys. Their relationship was over. *Over.* She beat back the rising despair. "I'll be there."

"Good. My penthouse at noon." He cut the connection.

She sagged against the counter and closed her eyes. Tears clogged her throat. Anguish welled up inside, and she shuddered, consumed with regret. He didn't love her. He *really* didn't love her.

And she had to face the stark truth. She couldn't fantasize anymore, couldn't delude herself with false hopes. Her life would go on. She'd move back in with Kendall. She'd raise Claire and pursue her dreams.

But those dreams wouldn't include the man she loved.

Chapter 14

Her stomach jittering, Amanda clutched the handrail in Luke's private elevator as it rocketed to the forty-fifth floor. She trembled at the thought of seeing Luke again—for what could be the last time.

She'd barely slept all night, could hardly hold a thought in her mind. Her emotions careened from hope to dread, joy to despair like a dried leaf buffeted by a storm.

But she knew one thing. She had to maintain her dignity. She couldn't break down, couldn't embarrass Luke by making a scene. She'd simply drop off the keys, thank him for his help and then leave.

The elevator dinged and came to a stop, and the agitation in her belly grew. The door slid open, and she stepped out, her throat suddenly parched. Struggling for composure, she wiped her sweaty palms on her jeans, hoisted her battered purse over her shoulder, forced her feet to walk to his door.

She stopped, glanced back at the elevator, fought down the urge to bolt. This was ridiculous. She wasn't a coward. She could certainly hand him his keys. She inhaled and rapped on the door.

A second later he pulled it open, and her gaze shot to his. And for an eternity she couldn't breathe. She drank in his amber eyes, his somber brows, the sexy grooves framing his mouth. He'd shaved recently, and only the barest hint of whiskers darkened his jaw. Her gaze traveled over the wide ledge of his muscled shoulders, back to his sensual mouth.

And he stared back at her, his eyes roaming her face, her breasts. The hall turned stuffy and hot. Her lungs barely squeezed in air. She wanted desperately to hurl herself into his arms.

But he stepped back. "Come on in."

She nodded, pressed her lips together to suppress the words she shouldn't say. He led the way through the marbled entrance, past the elegant living room, to the windows at the opposite wall.

He turned then, and she abruptly stopped. She tightened her grip on her purse, suddenly tongue-tied, all thoughts wiped from her mind.

And he didn't make it easy for her. He just watched her, his expression unreadable, as if expecting her to speak.

The keys. Her face burned. "Oh, I, um…" She reached into her purse, fished around for the keys and pulled them out. "Here."

"Just set them on the table."

"Right." She placed them on the end table. Her gaze boomeranged back to his.

Seconds passed. She couldn't move. She could only stare at him, soaking in the sight of his face while emotions tumbled inside her—there was so much she wanted to say.

But he didn't want to hear her explanations. If he'd changed his mind about their relationship, he would have told her by now. Instead, he'd only phoned once in the past two days to tell her to drop off the keys.

"You want something to drink?" he asked.

She should refuse. He was being polite. He had work to do, people to see. He might even have a date.

That thought made her want to wretch. She pressed her hand to her belly to quiet her nerves. "No thanks, I—"

"A glass of wine." He strode to the mahogany sideboard, and she struggled to compose herself.

"All right." One glass. She could handle that.

His back muscles flexed as he pulled out a bottle. He worked the corkscrew, extracted the cork with a muffled pop. Her gaze traced the riveting bulge of his biceps, the tendons that ran down his strong arms.

And she wondered how many women had pined for him, how many hearts he'd broken over the years. Wasn't that what they'd said about Candace Rothchild—that she'd been obsessed with Luke? He'd even had a restraining order issued in an attempt to keep her away.

Amanda could hardly blame her. She'd certainly never forget this man. Too choked up to speak, she dragged her gaze to the window and stared unseeing at the city below.

"Here you go." His breath brushed her ear, and she jumped. She hadn't even seen him approach. She inhaled his arousing scent, took the wine glass with quivering hands. She wanted to touch him so badly that she had to take a step back.

She sipped her wine. The silence stretched. He stared at her, his dark brows knitted together, and she had no idea what to say.

And she realized she'd made a mistake. She never should have come here and tortured herself this way. Kendall could have dropped off the keys.

"How's Claire?" he suddenly asked.

"Good. Great." She gulped her wine, and he fell silent again.

"Thank you for letting us stay at your house," she added. "And for what you did with Wayne… For everything."

Oh, God. She was dying here. Why didn't he say anything? She needed to end this ordeal before she completely broke down.

He frowned, looking uncertain suddenly, and a fierce pang of longing lanced her heart. What she wouldn't give to run her hands down his back, feel his muscles flex under her palms. Feel his raw urgency fueling hers.

"More wine?" he asked. She jerked her gaze to her glass, realized with a start that she'd drained it without even being aware.

"No. No, thanks." Breathless, she set the glass on the table next to the keys. How pathetic could she get? She was standing here fantasizing about him, ogling him, her desire clear in her eyes, while he waited for her to leave.

"Well, I'd better go." Before she broke down and begged.

"Amanda." His eyes met hers. He shoved his hand through his hair. "About the project—"

"It was none of my business, really." She twisted her hands, and the words broke loose. "I'm sorry. I shouldn't have said anything. It wasn't my place. Just forget it, okay? And you were right. About me, I mean. I—"

"Amanda—"

"I'm not going to teach. I threw the application away. I'm going to go back to school."

"You are?"

She nodded, her face flaming. So much for dignity and restraint.

The doorbell buzzed. Luke glanced at the door, then back at her.

"Anyhow," she added. "There's your key…and I need to go now. You're busy, and I—"

"No. Wait." He held up a hand. "Stay there. I have something to say."

He strode to the door, and she crossed her arms, wishing again that she'd never come. Luke didn't want to hear her news.

She glanced around the penthouse knowing it would be for the final time. Her gaze landed on the desk where they'd made love, and the images came tumbling back before she could stop them—Luke's eyes glittering with hunger, his mouth hot against hers. That electrifying way he'd watched her, his stark need driving him hard.

She swallowed, her breathing suddenly ragged. She looked at Luke at the door. This wasn't going to work. She had to get out of here now.

She headed toward him just as he shut the door and turned back. He glanced at the envelope in his hand, tore it open, pulled out the letter inside. His frown deepened, and he grew suddenly still.

Something was wrong. "What is it?"

His gaze rose to hers. The fierce intensity of his expression made her breath halt.

"It's another note, like the one you got."

Shock billowed through her. She pressed her hand to her throat. "You mean from the killer?"

"Yeah. He says to meet him in the blackjack pit."

"Now? He's here? In the casino?"

"So it seems." He crossed to the phone, picked up the receiver, then swore. "The line's dead."

"Dead?" Her blood drained from her face. How had he cut the phone lines? Any why? What did that killer have planned?

Luke tossed the note onto the table, tugged his cell phone from the pocket of his slacks. He punched in a number, waited, and his eyes turned even grimmer. "The lines must all be down. No one's picking up in security."

He tapped in another number, waited, then shook his head. "Voice mail. Something big must be happening if Matt's not answering his phone."

She bit her lip. "What are you going to do?"

"Alert security." He snapped his phone closed, slipped it into his pocket again. "Stay here. I'll be right back. You have your cell phone?"

"Yes, but—"

"Good. Call me if anything happens. And whatever you do, don't leave."

"I won't." She watched him head for the door. But that killer would be armed. "Luke," she said, her fear for him making her voice shake. "Be careful."

He paused, turned back, and his eyes held hers. " will." And for several heartbeats, he just gazed at her and beyond the urgency, beyond the determination, lay something deeper, something more intimate. Something that looked a lot like love.

"When I get back, we're going to talk," he promised, his voice gruff. "Now lock the door and stay put." He pivoted and strode out the door.

The door clicked shut. She raced to lock it, then sagged against the wall. Had that really been love she'd seen in his eyes? Was it possible that they'd have another chance?

She couldn't get up her hopes. She could be imagining things. Because if he loved her, then why hadn't he called? And why make her return the house keys? He was even having a security system installed in Kendall's house—a clear sign he wanted her gone.

But she couldn't think about that now, not with the killer so close. She had to stay calm, stay alert. Luke might call for her help.

She dug in her purse for her cell phone, then saw that the battery was dead. She hissed out her breath. Now what was she going to do?

Calm down, she decided. Becoming hysterical wouldn't do Luke any good. She'd just sit tight and wait for him to return.

The doorbell buzzed. Her heart jerked into her throat. She whipped around and faced the door.

Was that security? The killer? Luke couldn't be returning so soon.

She pressed her hand to her rioting chest, willing her pulse to slow. She was acting paranoid. It was probably just Luke. She couldn't let her imagination run wild.

"Who is it?" she called.

No one answered.

Her heart raced even more.

She eyed the phone—no help there. Her gaze landed on the hutch nearby and she saw the room key. He must have forgotten it. And now he'd come back to get it.

But then why didn't he answer? And returning for his room key hardly seemed like a priority with a killer running loose.

Unless he needed it to gain access to private areas of the hotel.

"Luke?" Her nerves twisting even tighter, she pressed her ear to the door. Silence. "Who's there?" she called again.

Nothing. Maybe he couldn't hear her through the door.

Her hands trembling, she scooped up the room key. But then she hesitated again. She couldn't open the door without knowing who was there. What if it wasn't Luke?

The door lock clicked. She watched in horror as the handle began to dip. Someone was coming inside.

And Luke didn't have his key.

Her heart raced wildly. She had to run, escape. *Move.*

She whipped around, searching frantically for a place to hide. She raced down Luke's hallway, ducked behind his bedroom door. She heard the door to the penthouse open and bang against the wall.

She stayed as still as she could and hugged her arms, struggling not to make any noise. It could be the killer. She couldn't let him know she was back here. But he already knew that. Like an idiot, she'd called out, giving herself away.

She listened hard, but her blood pressure roared in her ears. Terrified, needing to find out where he was, she inched back to the edge of the door.

She peeked out. A waiter stood in the entrance next to a room service cart.

Room service. She frowned, suddenly confused.

Maybe she'd overreacted. Maybe Luke had ordered lunch before she'd arrived. But then the waiter turned toward her, and she spotted the gun.

For a second, she stood petrified. The intruder's cold gaze slammed into hers. Then she gasped, jerked back behind the door.

It was the man from the Rothchild's casino, the same man who'd drugged her. And he'd just seen her. She had to run.

But where?

Frantic, she tried to think. The balcony was out. She was forty-five floors up. And all the phone lines were dead.

She dithered, then rushed through Luke's bedroom, raw terror fueling her steps. She should have gone into the kitchen. Back here there was only the bathroom— no way out.

A bullet whined past, splintering the wall beside her head, and the sharp bang deafened her ears. She shrieked, dove into the bathroom, searching for a way to defend herself.

But there was nothing. Not even a can of shaving cream. Her entire body shook.

And then she smelled it. That aftershave. The stench slithered through the air and assaulted her nose.

Her knees quivered hard. She turned and met the killer's eyes.

"All right," he said, and the sound of his voice made her heart quake. "I want that ring. And I want it now."

What the hell was happening? Why hadn't the gunman shown up?

Scowling, Luke hurried back through the hallway

from the security office, his apprehension mounting with each long stride. No one had reported any problems. The phones were still out, but the telephone company had it in hand. He'd alerted the police, posted guards throughout the casino, sent another to check on Amanda while he waited in the blackjack pit for the killer to show.

No one had come.

But why send a note and not show up?

Unless the killer had lost his nerve. Or the extra security guards had scared him off.

But then why did this fear keep gnawing at him, the feeling that something was wrong? The feeling that he'd missed something—something urgent. That danger lurked close.

And why didn't Matt Schaffer answer his cell phone? No one knew where he'd gone—which was too damned strange. His security chief never took time off on the job.

He reached the service elevators, spotted the housekeeping manager checking a maid's cleaning cart. "Has anyone gone up to my suite?" he asked.

She shook her head. "No, sir. Would you like something sent up?"

"No. So no one's used the elevator?"

She frowned. "No one from housekeeping."

"Room service just went up," the young maid beside her said. "He said he had your lunch."

Room service? He hadn't ordered food.

Dread slithered into his gut.

Amanda was there. He'd left her in his penthouse. *Alone.* Swearing, he ran to the elevator, swiped his spare key card in, then punched in the access code.

What had he been thinking? What if the security

guard had arrived too late? The gunman had been after her from the start.

And that note had been nothing but a decoy, a ploy to get her alone.

The elevator started up.

And Luke began to sweat.

Amanda stared down the barrel of the pistol. She was trapped in her worst nightmare, facing a killer. And now she was going to die.

This man had murdered Candace Rothchild. He'd bludgeoned the woman to death. And now he was going to kill her, too. She could see it in his cold, dead eyes.

Terror fought its way up her throat, building, swelling, threatening to explode in a primal shriek. She choked it back, wheezed a breath past her paralyzed lungs. She had to stay in control.

"Give me the ring," he repeated, his fury clear in his voice.

"I don't have it," she said, hating how badly her voice shook. "I told you that the other night."

His eyes hardened. The stench of his aftershave reeked in the air. "You have it. It's in your purse. Hand it over now."

In her purse? Her lips quivered, and she shook her head. "You're wrong. You have me confused with someone else. I don't have it. Really I don't."

"Like hell you don't. I put it there. In the lobby," he added at her blank look. "When your purse spilled on the floor."

She gaped at him. That had been planned? He'd bumped her, planted the ring in her purse. But then he'd changed clothes, accosted her with the gun. But why? It didn't make any sense.

She jerked her purse off her shoulder, held it out. "Here. Take it. Look for yourself." And as soon as he was distracted, she'd bolt past him out the door.

But he was too smart. He shook his head. "Dump it out. Right there."

Her throat convulsed. She wasn't going to get away. Her hands trembling, she pulled open the purse's drawstring, then inverted the contents onto the floor. Tissues tumbled out, then her nail clippers, her car keys, a couple of pens. She shook the bag, and her wallet followed, along with a comb and a travel-sized mirror.

"That's it," she whispered, her eyes on his. She flapped the bag again, but nothing else came out. "I told you, it isn't here."

"It has to be." His face turned red, his voice vibrating with rage.

And images flashed before her eyes—Claire holding her bear...her tiny arms reaching for a hug...Claire's sweet, flushed face as she slept. Luke risking his life to protect her...the hunger burning in his sexy eyes...the incredible bliss he brought to her life.

And suddenly she snapped. She didn't deserve this fear. She didn't deserve to die. And she was fed up with being the victim, fed up with being pushed around and attacked.

Wayne had been bad enough. She'd made a mistake, suffered a lapse in judgment and had paid the price.

But this creep—who the hell was he to threaten her?

"I don't have your ring," she gritted out, walking toward him. She gripped the straps of her empty purse. "I told you that from the start. Now leave me alone."

Furious, she whipped the purse forward, slapping the leather across his face.

The gun fired.

Heat tore through her shoulder, and she screamed.

Chapter 15

Amanda had been shot. *Shot.*

Her scream still echoing in his skull, Luke glanced around the hallway outside his penthouse, took in the dead guard slumped by the door. He slammed his key card into the lock, kicked the door open, and it crashed back against the wall.

He burst inside, desperate to find her, then frantically scanned the room. Empty. *Damn.* Where had that bastard taken her?

A soft cry drifted from down the hall.

Adrenaline stormed through his veins, but he fought to contain it, knowing he'd endanger her if he rushed. Forcing himself to walk softly—to not alert the gunman—he inched his way down the hall.

He'd never forgive himself if Amanda died. He'd been a fool to leave her alone. He pushed the panic to the back of his mind, refusing to think about that now. He had to focus, concentrate to keep her alive.

When he reached his bedroom door, he paused. He listened intently, but silence thundered back. Where the hell had they gone?

He flattened himself against the wall, then peeked inside. Nothing. The bedroom was empty. Only the bathroom was left.

He raced across the bedroom, pressed himself to the wall by the bathroom door, and listened again. And then suddenly he heard Amanda. She let out an agonized moan.

She was injured. She had to be bleeding. He felt wild at the thought. He clenched his hands into fists, trying not to let his mind go there...trying not to think about her suffering, dying.

He loved her.

The realization bolted out of nowhere, but he instantly knew it was true. He loved her. Amanda was his destiny. And he wasn't going to let her die.

His mind shut down. His vision hazed. The primitive need to avenge her raged.

And he couldn't control it anymore. He burst through the doorway into the bathroom. In a glance, he took in Amanda lying in a pool of blood, the gunman kneeling a short distance away.

Crazed now, insane with the need to protect her, Luke flew at the killer with a guttural cry. He slammed into his side, flattened him to the marble floor. And then he rammed his fist into his face, grunting, pounding, hitting him again and again, punching his jaw, his gut, his head.

The gunman stopped struggling and went slack.

"Luke," Amanda called. "Luke, stop." Her weak voice penetrated the haze.

He sat back on his heels, hauled in air to his heaving lungs, studied the unconscious man sprawled on the floor—the same man who'd attacked them in the hills. He confiscated the gun, whipped out his cell phone and called 911, then rushed to Amanda's side.

Oh, hell. Her face was too white. Blood seeped from her shoulder onto the tiles. Alarmed, he leaped up and grabbed a towel, then pressed it to her shoulder to staunch the flow. "Hold on," he urged her.

She peered up at him. Her pale lips tightened with pain. "Luke," she whispered.

"I love you," he told her, and pressed the wadded towel down hard.

She whimpered. Her eyes rolled back, and she went slack.

Frantic, terrified that she would die, he felt her wrist and checked her pulse. It was weak, but she was alive. He sagged back on his heels in relief.

But then he leaned toward her again, cradling her as best he could, keeping the towel pressed over her wound. She was so pale, so blasted weak. His throat wedged tight with dread. And he just held her, soothing her—this amazing woman he loved.

An eternity later, voices shouted down the hall. And then people swirled around him, police, paramedics. Radios squawked. Gurneys rolled in. People barked out orders and unloaded supplies. In his peripheral vision, he saw the police handcuff the gunman and haul him away.

"Mr. Montgomery," someone said. Luke ignored him, his entire attention focused on Amanda's face, willing her to survive. Her lips were tinged blue, her face so pale that her freckles stood out on her nose.

"Mr. Montgomery, you'll have to let go so we can help her. Please let go, sir. She needs our help."

The paramedics. "Right." He had to let her go.

The hell he did. He pried his hand from the towel, forced himself to rise and step back. The paramedics swarmed her, checking her vital signs, giving her oxygen, strapping her pale, fragile body into a gurney and rushing away.

And he knew right then that he couldn't do it. No matter what else happened in his life, no matter what anyone wanted, he could never let this woman go.

He loved her. And she was forever his.

Amanda surfaced from a deep, dark haze hours later. She blinked her eyes open, then zeroed in on Luke. He sat slumped in an armchair across the hospital room, his gaze trained on her.

He instantly leaped to his feet. "You're awake."

He rushed to her side, perched on the edge of her cot, and she couldn't take her eyes from his face. His hair wasn't combed. Black bristles coated his jaw. And he looked so dear, so much like everything she'd ever wanted, that tears sprang to her eyes.

He grabbed a glass from the metal table beside the cot. "Your throat's raw from the surgery. You've been out for a couple of hours."

He adjusted the straw, brought the glass to her face and she took a cooling sip. Her right hand was hooked to an IV. Heavy bandages encased her left shoulder, making it impossible to move. She thought back, tried to sort through the morass of memories—the gunman's chilling eyes, his rage when he didn't find the ring, the huge satisfaction she'd felt at whipping his face with her purse. Then excruciating pain. Luke bursting in.

Had he really told her he loved her?

Or had she hallucinated that part?

"They removed the bullet from your shoulder," he told her, not budging from the bed. She closed her eyes, enjoying the warm, solid feel of him, the way his thigh wedged securely against her hip.

"The doctor said it all went well," he added. He picked up her left hand and stroked it, and she sighed at how comforting that felt. "No complications. The bullet missed the critical parts. He's stopping by later to explain the operation and rehab."

"Gunman," she said around the dryness in her throat.

Luke helped her take another sip of water and made a sound of disgust. "The guy's a Houdini. He escaped. It was the damnedest thing. They had him handcuffed and were waiting downstairs for another ambulance to arrive. Somehow he got out of the cuffs, overpowered another guard and used his clothes as a disguise. No one knows how he did it. But he's smart. He even knocked out Matt Schaffer earlier to steal his key."

Her heart dove. So the killer was on the loose again. The danger wasn't gone.

"Don't worry," he added, as if reading her mind. "I've hired more bodyguards for you and Claire. And I've added even more security to my house. Claire's coming by later, by the way. Kendall thought it was better to wait."

Amanda frowned, wondering if the painkillers had muddled her mind. Why was he talking about his house?

He leaned closer, and his face was inches from hers.

She traced the crinkles at the corner of his eyes with her gaze, the faint lines creasing his brow. But his somber expression made her heart lurch.

"I'm sorry, Amanda. I never should have left you alone."

"Not your fault," she rasped out.

"Yeah, it was. It was my fault you were even there. If it hadn't been for the plans I wanted to show you... And then when I heard you scream..."

"It almost killed me," he confessed, his voice so anguished it brought a lump to her throat. "Seeing you bleeding on the floor..."

He shook his head, and his voice turned fierce. "I won't make that mistake again. I'm keeping you safe for the rest of your life."

Her heart beat fast. She stared at him, not sure she understood.

"I know this isn't romantic," he said. "You deserve better. And I'll ask you again later, somewhere with flowers, music..." He shoved his hand through his hair. "Hell, I don't even have the ring. I left it in my safe. But I can't wait. I need to know."

His eyes pleaded with hers. "I love you, Amanda. Marry me."

Her lips parted in shock. He loved her? She hadn't imagined that part? "You bought me a ring?"

"I was miserable without you. You were right about the project, about the revenge. I didn't call you because I was having the plans redrawn. That's what I've been doing for the past two days, overseeing the drawings. I wanted to wait until they were done."

Her breath hitched. "You changed the project?"

"You'll like it." He traced the veins on her hand with

his thumb, sending shivers racing over her skin. "The investors are happy. It's still basically the same, but we modified it so it's more like a village. There's a training center attached, a place for career counseling, some affordable housing, too."

She squeezed his hand, her heart filled with love for this man. "It sounds perfect. You're perfect. I love you, Luke."

He reached out and touched her cheek. He gazed at her with so much love in his eyes that her own eyes flooded with tears. "Then you'll marry me?" he asked.

"I'll marry you. As long as you don't mind being married to a student. I'm going to be in school for the next few years."

His lips curved up. A sexy gleam lit his eyes. "I've got a cave you could survey—for the right price."

She smiled back. "A price, hmm? And just how much will this cave cost?"

His eyes heated. "You. Every day for the rest of my life."

"It's a deal," she whispered. And then his mouth captured hers, and she didn't speak again for a long, long while.

Two weeks later, Amanda put on her final touch of lipstick, then appraised herself in the bathroom mirror. Her skin color had rebounded since the shooting. Her dark circles had faded, thanks to Luke's constant pampering and insistence that she rest.

This was her first night out without the shoulder harness, and she was making the most of it with her slinky red dress—the same one she'd worn the night she met Luke.

Of course, she wore a few new accessories with the

outfit now—a brilliant gold choker necklace and matching earrings. A fabulous antique diamond engagement ring. She stretched out her fingers and smiled at the gorgeous stone.

"Ring, Mommy," Claire called from the other room.

"Just give me a minute." Her lips curved in amusement. Claire loved to look at her ring and admire how the diamond caught the light. Luke joked that they had a future gemologist in their midst.

"My ring," Claire said again.

Amanda misted herself with a bold new scent, then dragged in her breath. That was the best she could do. She just hoped it was good enough to catch Luke's attention tonight. Now that her shoulder was mending, she had a list of very sensual demands she was going to insist he fulfill.

She turned off the bathroom light, walked into her bedroom. Claire sat in the middle of the bed, surrounded by the contents of her purse.

"Oh, Claire. I have to leave soon, and I need my purse." She slipped on her high heels, then crossed to the bed. "Let's put everything back, okay?"

"My ring, Mommy." Claire held up her fist, and Amanda frowned.

"What have you got there?"

"My ring." Claire opened her small hand, and Amanda's jaw dropped. An enormous diamond ring sat in her palm.

She propped her hip on the bed, so stunned she could hardly breathe. "Let me see." Claire handed it over, and she held it up to the light.

"Oh, my God." It was incredible. Six or seven carats minimum, the diamond unlike anything she'd ever seen.

At least she thought it was a diamond. Colors sparkled and swirled in the center of the stone, changing from blue to violet to green.

"What are you doing?" Luke asked from the doorway.

She couldn't take her eyes off the stone. "Luke, look at this. You won't believe it." She held up the ring, and he frowned.

He strode to the bed and she rose, handing it to him. He studied it for a second, then let out a long, admiring whistle. "Well, I'll be damned. It's the missing ring. The Tears of the Quetzal. The one Candace Rothchild had."

"But where did it come from?" She jerked her gaze to Claire. "Where on earth did you find this?"

"Your purse," Claire said, and her bottom lip trembled. "My ring."

Amanda picked up her purse, staring at it in disbelief. "But it wasn't in here. I know it wasn't. I dumped everything out."

"In the hole, Mommy."

"The hole?"

She opened the empty bag and checked inside. She pulled the lining up, and sure enough, a hole had ripped along the seam, fraying the silky fabric. Her gaze flew to Luke's. "She's right. There is a hole. The ring must have worked its way through. It's been there all along."

His forehead furrowed. "We'd better get it to the police right away. We can drop it off on our way out."

"Good idea."

"We can't keep this ring," Luke said to Claire, his voice gentle. "Someone lost it, and we need to take it back. But how about if we buy you a special ring tomorrow? Will that be all right?"

"You could ask Aunt Kendall if she'd like to shop with us," Amanda added, and Claire consulted her bear.

"Okay. Aunt Kendall," Claire called, and scrambled off the bed. She raced from the bedroom, and Amanda smiled.

"I still can't believe we found the ring. It's gorgeous."

"Yeah, gorgeous." His gaze burned into hers, then dipped lazily over her lips, her throat…her breasts.

"They say it has a legend," she said, suddenly breathless. "That whoever has it falls instantly in love."

He moved closer, and his eyes turned hotter yet. "You think the legend came true?" His voice came out graveled and deep.

Her heart pounded fast. And she remembered the first time she'd seen him, right after her purse had spilled, just seconds after that gunman had slipped the ring inside. She'd definitely found true love at first sight.

"So what do you think?" he repeated, moving closer. And then his hands were on her back, her hips, pulling her firmly against him. Her body softened, anticipating his touch, and she dropped her head back with a sigh.

"Is the legend true?" he asked again.

"I think," she whispered back, "that at the rate we're going, we're worthy of a legend of our own."

He grunted in agreement. And then his mouth took hers, and she showed him her deep abiding love.

Epilogue

The man hunched behind the wheel of his car under the cover of darkness. He waited, his gut seething, his gaze trained on the police station door.

Damn them all. Damn the woman for hiding the ring. Damn Luke Montgomery for holing her up in his house. And damn the Las Vegas traffic that had kept him from overtaking Montgomery's car tonight. He'd been watching their house for the past two weeks, waiting for a chance at that ring.

But Montgomery had foiled him—again. He fingered the bruise discoloring his jaw, the ribs still aching from Montgomery's fists. He'd underestimated that billionaire.

His mistake.

The police station doors swung open just then. Montgomery and his woman strolled out, then paused in a circle of light. Montgomery pulled her close, and they started kissing, getting so hot and heavy he nearly blew the horn to force them apart. But they finally stopped and strolled away.

So the police had the ring now. It didn't matter. This was a blip, just a minor bump in the road. He'd lost the ring, but he would recoup. He would change his strategy, turn this to his advantage, let this lull them into thinking the matter was done.

And then he would strike.

One by one, he'd vowed. He let out a high-pitched laugh. If anyone thought this was over, they were dead wrong.

* * * * *

⊚ INTRIGUE

Coming next month

2-IN-1 ANTHOLOGY

BRANDED BY THE SHERIFF by Delores Fossen

Gorgeous Sheriff Beck is determined to protect single mother Faith and her baby from a killer. Even if saving their lives means facing off with his own family...

THE 9-MONTH BODYGUARD by Cindy Dees

Tasked with protecting pop star Silver, Austin must also guard the baby she's secretly carrying. Is he ready to go from fearless bodyguard to brand-new daddy?

2-IN-1 ANTHOLOGY

SNOWBOUND WITH THE BODYGUARD by Carla Cassidy

Janette knows bodyguard Dalton is the only man who can help her and her tiny daughter. Could braving a snowstorm together turn the three into a family?

LADY KILLER by Kathleen Creighton

Photographer Tony has been commissioned to track accused murderer Brooke. Convinced of her innocence, Tony is ready to fight for her freedom – and her love!

SINGLE TITLE

WILD HUNT by Lori Devoti
Nocturne™

Hellhound Venge travels the nine worlds looking for ways to grow stronger. Yet only Valkyrie Geysa, his natural enemy, has the power to make him a better man.

On sale 15th January 2010

INTRIGUE

Coming next month

2-IN-1 ANTHOLOGY

THE SHARPSHOOTER'S SECRET SON by Mallory Kane

Years ago bad-boy Deke broke Mandy's heart. Now he's back
from the air force and ready to make amends. Can Mandy
let him back in – and let him know he has a child?

FURY CALLS by Caridad Piñeiro

When Blake turned Meghan into a vampire, he hadn't realised
she would be angry. To win back her love, he must now show
her he's no longer the devilish rogue she once knew...

SINGLE TITLE

SMALL-TOWN SECRETS
by Debra Webb

Dana was relying on sexy Colby agent Spence to help her
uncover the dark secrets that haunted her troubled past. But
she wasn't expecting him to sweep her off her feet!

SINGLE TITLE

PROTECTING HIS WITNESS
by Marie Ferrarella

Undercover cop Zack is Krystle's sworn protector. He is an
expert in safeguarding her from mob hits. Yet no one can
defend her from the powerful passion he inspires!

On sale 5th February 2010

Available at WHSmith, Tesco, ASDA, Eason and all good bookshops.
For full Mills & Boon range including eBooks visit
www.millsandboon.co.uk

A DARK MOON IS ON THE RISE...

These five sizzling paranormal romance stories take you deep into a stormy world of power and passion where wonderfully wicked pleasures are impossible to deny.

It's time for the night to awaken!

Available 15th January 2010

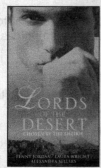 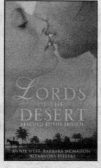 

millsandboon.co.uk Community

Join Us!

The Community is the perfect place to meet and chat to kindred spirits who love books and reading as much as you do, but it's also the place to:

- ■ Get the inside scoop from authors about their latest books
- ■ Learn how to write a romance book with advice from our edito
- ■ Help us to continue publishing the best in women's fiction
- ■ Share your thoughts on the books we publish
- ■ Befriend other users

Forums: Interact with each other as well as authors, editors and a whole host of other users worldwide.

Blogs: Every registered community member has their own blog to tell the world what they're up to and what's on their mind.

Book Challenge: We're aiming to read 5,000 books and have joined forces with The Reading Agency in our inaugural Book Challenge.

Profile Page: Showcase yourself and keep a record of your recent community activity.

Social Networking: We've added buttons at the end o every post to share via digg, Facebook, Google, Yahoo technorati and de.licio.us.

www.millsandboon.co.uk

2 FREE BOOKS
AND A SURPRISE GIFT

We would like to take this opportunity to thank you for reading this Mills & Boon® book by offering you the chance to take TWO more specially selected books from the Intrigue series absolutely FREE! We're also making this offer to introduce you to the benefits of the Mills & Boon® Book Club™—

- **FREE home delivery**
- **FREE gifts and competitions**
- **FREE monthly Newsletter**
- **Exclusive Mills & Boon Book Club offers**
- **Books available before they're in the shops**

Accepting these FREE books and gift places you under no obligation to buy, you may cancel at any time, even after receiving your free books. Simply complete your details below and return the entire page to the address below. You don't even need a stamp!

YES Please send me 2 free Intrigue books and a surprise gift. I understand that unless you hear from me, I will receive 5 superb new stories every month, including two 2-in-1 books priced at £4.99 each and a single book priced at £3.19, postage and packing free. I am under no obligation to purchase any books and may cancel my subscription at any time. The free books and gift will be mine to keep in any case.

Ms/Mrs/Miss/Mr _____ Initials _____

Surname _____
Address _____
_____
_____ Postcode _____

Send this whole page to: Mills & Boon Book Club, Free Book Offer, FREEPOST NAT 10298, Richmond, TW9 1BR